DEMONFIRE

Newspaper reporter Eddy Marks thinks she knows everything about her quiet hometown. She couldn't be more wrong. Turns out Evergreen, California, is the site of a vortex that allows demons to cross over to Earth, and the only one who can stop them is an unbelievably sexy fallen demon named Dax . . . who has just crashed into Eddy's life.

Since he was cast out of Abyss, Dax has been a lost spirit with no hope of redemption. Now the Edenites have promised him eternity in Paradise—if he can destroy the forces wreaking havoc on Earth. Losing Earth to chaos is unthinkable. But succeeding—and leaving behind this headstrong, sensual woman who tempts and intrigues him beyond measure—will test him to the core.

Also by Kate Douglas

Wolf Tales

"Chanku Rising" in *Sexy Beast*

Wolf Tales II

"Camille's Dawn" in *Wild Nights*

Wolf Tales III

"Chanku Fallen" in *Sexy Beast II*

Wolf Tales IV

"Chanku Journey" in *Sexy Beast III*

Wolf Tales V

"Chanku Destiny" in *Sexy Beast IV*

Wolf Tales VI

"Chanku Wild" in *Sexy Beast V*

Wolf Tales VII

"Chanku Honor" in *Sexy Beast VI*

Wolf Tales VIII

"Chanku Challenge" in *Sexy Beast VII*

Wolf Tales 9

"Chanku Spirit" in *Sexy Beast VIII*

Published by Kensington Publishing Corporation

DEMONFIRE

THE DEMONSLAYERS

KATE DOUGLAS

ZEBRA BOOKS
Kensington Publishing Corp.
http://www.kensingtonbooks.com

ZEBRA BOOKS are published by

Kensington Publishing Corp.
119 West 40th Street
New York, NY 10018

All Kensington titles, imprints and distributed lines are available at special quantity discounts for bulk purchases for sales promotion, premiums, fund-raising, educational or institutional use.

Special book excerpts or customized printings can also be created to fit specific needs. For details, write or phone the office of the Kensington Special Sales Manager: Attn.: Special Sales Department. Kensington Publishing Corp., 119 West 40th Street, New York, NY 10018. Phone: 1-800-221-2647.

ISBN-13: 978-1-4201-0999-3
ISBN-10: 1-4201-0999-5

First Printing: March 2010

10 9 8 7 6 5 4 3 2 1

Printed in the United States of America

Dedicated with love
to the amazingly talented author
who taught me so long ago
what paying it forward really means.
Pat, this one's for you.

Patricia Lucas White died
after a long and courageous battle
with pancreatic cancer
on July 13, 2009.
I will miss her wonderful wit
and wicked sense of humor.

ACKNOWLEDGMENTS

When I first realized, over twenty years ago, that I wanted to write books, I had no idea what was in store for me. First of all, I learned it's not nearly as easy as I expected, but more important, I've learned it's a lot more fun than I ever imagined. My thanks to every one of you who have helped me reach my goal—but especially my agent, Jessica Faust of BookEnds LLC, for believing I had the talent; and my editor, Audrey LaFehr, who has given me every possible opportunity to succeed in this amazing business. Also my sincere thanks to Kensington editorial assistant Martin Biro, who hit the ground running and probably hasn't had time to take a breath since he joined the company.

As always, my gratitude and appreciation go to my amazing beta readers—on this project Jan Takane, Rose Toubbeh, Amanda Haffery, Sandi Potterton, Camille Anthony, Karen Woods, Margaret Riley and Ann Jacobs. And, to the talented authors willing to take time from their hectic careers to read the first book of my new series and offer a quote—Stella Cameron, Alyssa Day, Virginia Kantra, Angela Knight and Jayne Ann Krentz (a/k/a Amanda Quick and Jayne Castle). Thank you so much—now, if there was just a way for me to absorb some of your amazing talent. . . .

Last but not least, to my husband—there really are no words. Thank you doesn't even come close.

The Legend of Lemuria

Thousands of years ago,
the continent of Lemuria
disappeared beneath the sea,
much in the manner of Atlantis.
However, unlike the Atlanteans,
Lemurians are not considered lost—
legend says they relocated their entire
technologically advanced society to a safe location deep
within the dormant volcano known as Mount Shasta,
in the Cascades range of northern California.

Much has been written about these tall and graceful
beings, of their great intelligence and beauty, their
advanced technology and supernatural abilities; but no
actual proof of their existence has ever been discovered.

That doesn't mean, of course, that they're not really there,
living in quiet splendor in their cities of gold,
deep within the mountain.

Remaining hidden, after all,
is just one of their many talents.

Chapter One

Sunday night

He struggled out of the darkness, confused, disoriented . . . recalling fire and pain and the soothing voices of men he couldn't see. Voices promising everlasting life, a chance to move beyond hell, beyond all he'd ever known. He remembered his final, fateful decision to take a chance, to search for something else.

For life beyond the hell that was Abyss.

A search that brought him full circle, back to a world of pain—to this world, wherever it might be. He frowned and tried to focus. This body was unfamiliar, the skin unprotected by scales or bone. He'd never been so helpless, so vulnerable.

His chest burned. The demon's fireshot, while not immediately fatal, would have deadly consequences. Hot blood flowed sluggishly from wounds across his ribs and spread over the filthy stone floor beneath his naked hip. The burn on his chest felt as if it were filled with acid. Struggling for each breath, he raised his head and stared into the glaring yellow eyes of an impossible creature holding him at bay.

Four sharp spears affixed to a long pole were aimed directly at his chest. The thing had already stabbed him once, and the bleeding holes in his side hurt like the blazes. With a heartfelt groan, Dax tried to rise, but he had no strength left.

He fell back against the cold stones, and his world faded once more to black.

"You're effing kidding me! I leave for one frickin' weekend, and all hell breaks loose. You're positive? Old Mrs. Abernathy really thinks it ate her cat?" Eddy Marks took another sip of her iced caffé mocha whip and stared at Ginny. "Lord, I hope my father hasn't heard about it. He'll blame it on the Lemurians."

Ginny laughed so hard she almost snorted her latte. "Your dad's not still hung up on that silly legend, is he? Like there's really an advanced society of humanoids living inside Mount Shasta? I don't think so."

"Don't try and tell Dad they don't exist. He's convinced he actually saw one of their golden castles in the moonlight. Of course, it was gone by morning." Eddy frowned at Ginny and changed the subject. She was admittedly touchy about her dad's gullible nature. "Mrs. Abernathy's not serious, is she?"

"I dunno." Ginny shook her head. "She was really upset. Enough that she called nine-one-one. I was on dispatch at Shasta Communications that shift and took the call. Shascom sent an officer out because she was hysterical, not because they actually believed Mr. Pollard's ceramic garden gnome ate Twinkles." Ginny ran her finger around the inside of her cup, chasing the last drops of her iced latte. "I heard there was an awful lot of blood on her back deck, along with tufts of suspiciously Twinkles-colored hair."

"Probably a coyote or a fox." Eddy finished the last of her drink and wished she'd had a shot of brandy to add to it. It would have been the perfect finish to the first vacation she'd had in months—two glorious days hiking and camping on Mount Shasta with only her dog for company . . . and not a single killer garden gnome in sight. She grinned at Ginny. "Killer garden gnomes aren't usually a major threat around here."

Ginny laughed. "Generally, no. Lemurians either, in spite of what your dad and half the tourists think, but for once, Eddy, don't be such a stick in the mud. Let your imagination go a little."

"What? And start spouting off about Lemurians? I don't think so. Someone has to be the grown-up! So what else happened while I was out communing with nature?"

"Well . . . it might have been the full moon, but there was a report that the one remaining stone gargoyle launched itself off the northwest corner of the old library building, circled the downtown area, and flew away into the night. And . . ." Ginny paused dramatically, ". . . another that the bronze statue of General Humphreys and his horse trotted out of the park. I didn't check on the gargoyle, but I went down to see the statue. It's not there. Looks like it walked right off the pedestal. That thing weighs over two tons." She set her empty cup down, folded her arms, and, with one dark eyebrow raised, stared at Eddy.

"A big bronze statue like that would bring in a pretty penny at the recyclers. Somebody probably hauled it off with a truck, but it's a great visual, isn't it?" Eddy leaned back in her chair. "I can just see that big horse with the general, sword held high and covered in pigeon poop, trotting along Front Street. Maybe a little detour through the cemetery."

"Is it worth a story by ace reporter Edwina Marks?"

Eddy glared at her. "Do not call me Edwina." She ran her finger through the condensation on the scarred wooden table top before looking up at Ginny and grinning. "Maybe a column about weird rumors and how they get started. I'll cite you as Ground Zero, but I doubt it's cutting edge enough for the front page of the *Record*."

Ginny grabbed her purse and pulled out a lipstick. "Yeah, like that rag's going to cover real news."

"Hey, we do our best, and we stay away from the tabloid stuff—you know, the garbage you like to read?" Laughing, Eddy stood up. "Well, I'm always complaining that nothing exciting ever happens around here. I guess flying gargoyles, runaway statues, and killer garden gnomes are better than nothing." She tossed some change on the table for a tip and waved at the girl working behind the counter. "Gotta go, Gin. I need to get home. Have to let Bumper out."

"Bumper? Who's that? Don't tell me you brought home another homeless mutt from the shelter."

"And if I did?"

Ginny waved the lipstick at her like a pointer. "Eddy, the last time you had to give up a fostered pup, you bawled for a week. Why do you do this to yourself?"

She'd be lucky if she only bawled for a week when it was time for Bumper to leave. They'd bonded almost immediately, but she really didn't want a dog. Not for keeps. "They were gonna put her down if no one took her," she mumbled.

Ginny shook her head. "Don't say I didn't warn you. One of these days you're going to take in a stray that'll really break your heart."

Eddy heard Bumper when she was still half a block from home. She'd only left the dog inside the house while she went to town for coffee, but it appeared the walls weren't thick enough to mute her deep-throated growling and barking.

Thank goodness it wasn't nine yet. Any later and she'd probably have one of the neighbors filing a complaint. Eddy picked up her pace and ran the last hundred yards home, digging for her house keys as she raced up the front walk. "Bumper, you idiot. I only left you for an hour. I hope you haven't been going on like this the whole time I've been gone."

She got the key in the lock and swung the front door open. Bumper didn't even pause to greet her. Instead, she practically knocked Eddy on her butt as she raced out the front door, skidded through the open gate to the side yard, and disappeared around the back of the house.

"Shit. Stupid dog." Eddy threw her keys in her bag, slung her purse over her shoulder, and took off after the dog. It was almost completely dark away from the street light, and Eddy stumbled on one of the uneven paving stones by the gate. Bumper's deep bark turned absolutely frantic, accompanied by the added racket from her clawing and scratching at the wooden door to Eddy's potting shed.

"If you've got a skunk cornered in there, you stupid dog, I swear I'm taking you back to the shelter."

Bumper stopped barking, now that she knew she had Eddy's attention. She whined and sniffed at the door, still scratching at the rough wood. Eddy fumbled in her bag for her keychain and the miniature flashlight hanging from the ring. The beam was next to worthless, but better than nothing.

She scooted Bumper out of the way with her leg and unlatched the door just enough to peer in through a crack. Bumper whapped her nose against Eddy's leg. Shoving frantically with her broad head, she tried to force her way inside.

"Get back." Eddy glared at the dog. Bumper flattened her ears against her curly head and immediately backed off, looking as pathetic as she had last week at the shelter when Eddy'd realized she couldn't leave a blond pit bull crossed with a standard poodle to the whims of fate.

She aimed her tiny flashlight through the narrow opening. Blinked. Told herself she was really glad she'd been drinking coffee and not that brandy she'd wanted tonight, because otherwise she wouldn't believe what she saw.

Maybe Mrs. Abernathy wasn't nuts after all. Eddy grabbed a shovel leaning against the outside wall of the shed and threw the door open wide.

The garden gnome that should have been stationed in the rose garden out in front held a pitchfork in its stubby little hands like a weapon, ready to stab what appeared to be a person lying in the shadows. When the door creaked open, the gnome turned its head, glared at Eddy through yellow eyes, bared unbelievably sharp teeth, and screamed at her like an avenging banshee.

Bumper's claws scrabbled against the stone pathway. Eddy swung the shovel. The crunch of metal connecting with ceramic seemed unnaturally loud. The scream stopped as the garden gnome shattered into a thousand pieces. The pitchfork clattered to the ground, and a dark, evil-smelling mist gathered in the air above the pile of dust. It swirled a moment and then suddenly whooshed over Eddy's shoulder and out the open door.

A tiny blue light pulsed and flickered, followed the mist as far as the doorway, and then returned to hover over the figure in the shadows. Bumper paused long enough to sniff the remnants of the garden gnome and growl, before turning her attention to whatever lay on the stone floor. Eddy stared at the shovel in her hands and took one deep breath after another. This was not happening. She *had not seen* a garden gnome in attack mode.

One with glowing yellow eyes and razor-sharp teeth.

Impossible.

Heart pounding, arms and legs shaking, she slowly pivoted in place and focused on whoever it was that Bumper seemed so pleased to see.

The mutt whined, but her curly tail was wagging a million miles a minute. She'd been right about the gnome. Eddy figured she'd have to trust the dog's instincts about whoever or whatever had found such dubious sanctuary in her potting shed.

Eddy squinted and tried to focus on the flickering light that flitted in the air over Bumper's head, but it was jerking around so quickly she couldn't tell what it was. She still had her key ring clutched in her fingers. She wasn't quite ready to put the shovel down, but she managed to shine the narrow beam of light toward the lump on the floor.

Green light reflected back from Bumper's eyes. Eddy swung wider with the flashlight. She saw a muscular arm, a thick shoulder, and the broad expanse of a masculine chest. Blood trickled from four perfectly spaced pitchfork-sized holes across the man's ribs and pooled beneath his body. There appeared to be a deep wound on his chest, though it wasn't bleeding.

In fact, it looked almost as if it had been cauterized. A burn? Eddy swept the light his full length. Her eyes grew wider with each inch of skin she exposed. He was marked with a colorful tattoo that ran from his thigh, across his groin to his chest, but other than the art, he was naked. Very naked, all the way from his long, narrow feet, up those perfectly formed, hairy legs to . . . Eddy quickly jerked the light back toward his head.

When she reached his face, the narrow beam glinted off dark eyes looking directly into hers. Beautiful, soul-searching dark brown eyes shrouded in thick, black lashes. He was gorgeous. Even with a smear of dirt across one cheek and several days' growth of dark beard, he looked as if he should be on the cover of *People* as the sexiest man alive.

Breathing hard, her body still shaking from the adrenaline coursing through her system, Eddy dragged herself back to the situation at hand. Whatever it was. He hadn't said a word. She'd thought he was unconscious. He wasn't. He was injured . . . not necessarily helpless. She squatted down beside him, and, reassured by Bumper's acceptance and the fact the man didn't look strong enough to sit up, much less harm her, Eddy set the shovel aside.

She touched his shoulder and grimaced at the deep wound on his chest, the bloody stab wounds in his side. Made a point not to look below his waist. "What happened? Are you okay? Well, obviously not with all those injuries." Rattled, she took a deep breath. "Who are you?"

He blinked and turned his head. She quickly tilted the light away from his eyes. "I'm sorry. I . . ."

He shook his head. His voice was deep and sort of raspy. "No. It's all right." He glanced up at the flickering light dancing overhead, frowned, and then nodded.

She could tell he was in pain, but he took a deep breath and turned his focus back to Eddy.

"I am Dax. Thank you."

"I'm Eddy. Eddy Marks." Why she'd felt compelled to give her full name made no sense. None of this did. She couldn't place his accent, and he wasn't from around here. She would have recognized any of the locals. She started to rise. "I'll call nine-one-one. You're injured."

His arm snaked out, and he grabbed her forearm, trapping her with surprising strength. "No. No one. Don't call anyone."

Eddy looked down at the broad hand, the powerful fingers wrapped entirely around her arm, just below her elbow. She should have been terrified. Should have been screaming in fear, but something in those eyes, in the expression on his face . . .

Immediately, he loosened his grasp. "I'm sorry. Please forgive me, but no one must know I'm here. If you can't help me, please let me leave. I have so little time. . . ." He tried to prop himself up on one arm, but his body trembled with the effort.

Eddy rubbed her arm. It tingled where he'd touched her. "What's going on? How'd you get here? Where are your clothes?"

The flickering light came closer, hovered just in front of his chest, pulsed with a brilliant blue glow that spread out in a pale arc until it touched him, appeared to soak into his flesh, and then dimmed. Before Eddy could figure out what she was seeing, Dax took a deep breath. He seemed to gather strength—from the blue light?

He shoved himself upright, glanced at the light, and nodded. "Thank you, Willow."

Then he stood up, as if his injuries didn't affect him at all. Obviously, neither did the fact he wasn't wearing a stitch of clothes. Towering over Eddy, he held out his hand to help her to her feet. "I will go now. I'm sorry to have . . ."

Eddy swallowed. She looked up at him as he fumbled for words, realized she was almost eye level with his . . . *oh crap!* She jerked her head to one side and stared at his hand for a moment. Shifted her eyes and blinked at the blue light, now hovering in the air not six inches from her face. What in the hell was going on?

Slowly, she looked back at Dax, placed her hand in his, and, with a slight tug from him, rose to her feet. The light followed her. "What is that thing?" Tilting her head, she focused on the bit of fluff glowing in the air between them, and let out a whoosh of breath.

"Holy Moses." It was a woman. A tiny, flickering fairy-like woman with gossamer wings and long blond hair. "It's frickin' Tinkerbelle!" Eddy turned and stared at Dax. "That's impossible."

He shrugged. "So are garden gnomes armed with pitchforks. At least in your world. So am I, for that matter."

Eddy snapped her gaze away from the flickering fairy and stared at Dax. "What do you mean, you're impossible? Why? Who are you? What are you?"

Again, he shrugged. "I'm a mercenary, now. A hired soldier, if you will. However, before the Edenites found me, before they gave me this body, I was a demon. Cast out of Abyss, but a demon nonetheless."

He knew she was bursting with questions, but she'd taken him inside her home, given him a pair of soft gray pants with a drawstring at the waist, and brewed some sort of hot, dark liquid that smelled much better than it tasted. She'd handed him a cup; then as she left the room, she'd told him to sit.

He sat, despite the sense of urgency and the pain. The snake tattoo seemed to ripple against his skin, crawling across his thigh, over his groin and belly to the spot where the head rested above his human heart. He felt the heat from the demon's fireshot beside the serpent's head burning deeper with each breath he took. Exhaustion warred with the need to move, to begin the hunt. In spite of Willow's gift of healing energy, he felt as if he could sleep for at least a month. Instead, he waited for the woman, for Eddy Marks. He sipped from the steaming cup while she opened and closed drawers in an adjoining room and mumbled unintelligible words to herself.

The four-legged creature stayed with him. Eddy called it "damned dog," but she'd also said its name was Bumper and it was female. The animal appeared to be intelligent, though Dax hadn't figured out how to communicate with her yet. She was certainly odd-looking with her bullet-shaped head, powerful jaws, and curly blond coat.

"Sorry to take so long. I had to hunt for the first aid kit."

The woman carried a box filled with rolls of bandages

and jars and tubes of what must be medicine. He wished his mind were clearer, but he was still growing used to this body, to the way the brain worked. It was so unlike his own. This mind had memories of things like bandages and dogs and the names for the various pieces of furniture he saw, but too much in his head felt foggy. Too much was still trapped in the thinking process of demonkind, of kill or be killed. Eat or be eaten.

The only thing that was absolutely clear was the mission, and he was woefully behind on that.

Of course, he hadn't expected to encounter a demon-powered gargoyle armed with fire just seconds after his arrival through the portal. Nor had he expected the power of the demons already here. Eddy had no idea she had truly saved more than his life.

So much more was at stake. So many lives.

Her soft voice was laced with steel when it burst into his meandering thoughts. "First things first," she said. "And don't lie to me. I'm trusting you for some weird reason, when I know damned well I should call the authorities. So tell me, who are you, really? Who did this to you? How'd you get this burn?"

Blinking, he raised his head. She knelt in front of him. Her short dark hair was tousled, and her chocolaty brown eyes stared at him with concern and some other emotion he couldn't quite identify. Thank goodness there was no sign of fear. He didn't want her to fear him, though she'd be better off if she did.

He shook his head. He still couldn't believe that blasted demon had gotten the drop on him. "I really am demonkind. From Abyss. The wound on my chest? It was the gargoyle. He surprised me. I wasn't expecting him, especially armed with fire."

She blinked and gave him a long, narrow-eyed stare.

"Hookay. If you say so." She took a damp cloth and wiped around the burn on his chest. The cool water felt good.

Her soft hands felt even better. Her touch seemed to spark what could only be genetic, instinctive memories to this body he inhabited. He felt as if his mind were clearing. Maybe this world would finally start to make sense.

She tilted her head and studied the burned and bloody wound. "That's the second reference to a gargoyle I've heard tonight," she said, looking at his chest, not his face. "They're not generally part of the typical conversation around here."

Shocked, he grabbed her wrist. She jerked her head around and stared at his fingers. He let go. "I'm sorry. I didn't mean to startle you. Have you seen it? The gargoyle? Do you know where it is?"

She stared at him a moment, and then sprayed something on the wound that took away the pain. She covered it with a soft, flesh-colored bandage before she answered him. "No," she said, shaking her head, concentrating on the bandage. "Not recently."

Her short dark hair floated against the sharp line of her jaw. He fought a surprisingly powerful need to touch the shimmering strands. He'd never once run his fingers through a woman's hair. Of course, he couldn't remember having fingers. He'd never had any form beyond his demon self of mist and scales, sharp claws, and sharper fangs.

She flattened all four corners of the bandage and looked up at him. He wished he were better at reading human expressions. Hers was a mystery to him.

"Last time I saw it," she said, "it was perched on the corner of the library building where it belonged, but I heard it flew away. It's made of stone and most definitely not alive, which means it shouldn't be flying anywhere. What's going on? And what are you, really? You can't be serious about . . ." She glanced away, shook her head again, and then touched the left side of his chest, just above the first puncture wound. "Turn around so I can take care of these cuts over your ribs."

He turned and stared at the fireplace across the room. After a moment he focused on a beautiful carved stone owl, sitting on the brick hearth. The owl's eyes seemed to watch him, but he sensed no life in the creature. It was better to concentrate on the bird than the woman.

Her gentle touch was almost worse than the pain from the injuries. It reminded him of things he wanted, things he'd never have.

He was, after all, still a demon. A fallen demon, but nonetheless, not even close to human. Not at all the man he appeared to be. This form was his for one short week.

His avatar.

Seven days he'd been given. Seven days to save the town of Evergreen and all its inhabitants. If he failed, if demonkind succeeded in this, their first major foray into Earth's dimension, other towns could fall. Other worlds. All of Earth, all of Eden.

Seven days.

Impossible . . . and he'd already wasted one of them.

He would have laughed if he didn't feel like turning around and heading back to Abyss—except Abyss was closed to him. With only the most preposterous of luck, he might end up in Eden, though he doubted that would happen, no matter how he did on his mission. The promises had been vague, after all.

So why, he wondered, had he agreed to this stupid plan?

"I asked you, what's going on? I'm assuming you know how my cheesy little Walmart garden gnome suddenly grew teeth and turned killer. Try the truth this time. With details that make sense."

He jerked his head around and stared at her, understanding more of his new reality as each moment passed, as the memories and life of this body's prior owner integrated with his demon soul.

Eddy sat back on her heels, and her dark eyes flashed with as much frustrated anger as curiosity.

He glanced down at his side. There were clean, white bandages over each of the wounds from the demon's weapon. The big burn on his chest was cleaned and covered. The entire length of his tattoo pulsed with evil energy, but if he ignored that, he really did feel better.

Stronger.

He sensed Willow's presence and finally spotted her sitting in amongst a collection of glass figurines on a small bookcase. Could demons enter glass? He wasn't sure, but at least Willow would warn him in time. He caught the woman's unwavering stare with his own. She waited more patiently than he deserved for his answer. "I always tell the truth," he said. "The problem is, will you believe me?"

She nodded and stood up. "I'll try." She stalked out of the room. He heard water running. A moment later she returned, grabbed his cup and her own, and left again. This time, when she handed him the warm mug of coffee, he knew what to expect.

He savored the aroma while she settled herself on the end of the couch, as far from him as she could get while still having room to sit.

She was close enough for him to pick up the perfume from the soap she'd used to wash her hands, the warm essence of her skin, the scent that was all hers.

He shrugged off the unusual sensations her nearness gave him. Then he took a sip of his coffee, replacing Eddy's scent with the rich aroma of the drink. He couldn't seem to do anything about his powerful awareness of her. Of this body's reaction to her presence, her scent, to every move she made.

He could try to ignore her, but he didn't want to. No, not at all. It probably wouldn't work anyway.

She curled her bare feet under herself and leaned against the back of the couch, facing him. He turned and sat much the same way, facing her.

Bumper looked from one of them to the other, barked once, and jumped up on the couch, filling the gap between them. She turned around a couple of times and lay down with a loud, contented sigh. Her fuzzy butt rested on Dax's bare foot; her chin was on the woman's ankle.

"Bumper likes you." She stroked the silly-looking beast's head with her long, slim fingers. "If she didn't approve, you wouldn't be sitting here."

Dax smiled, vaguely aware that it was an entirely new facial expression for him. Of course, everything he did now, everything he felt and said, was new. "Then I guess I'm very glad Bumper approves. Thank you for battling the demon, for taking care of my injuries. You saved my life."

She stared at him for a long, steady moment, as if digesting his statement. There was still no fear in her.

She would be safer if she were afraid.

"You're welcome," she said. "Now please explain. Tell me about the garden gnome. What was it, really?"

He arranged his fingers in a steeple in front of his face and rested his chin on the forefingers. Had the one who first owned this body found comfort in such a position? No matter. It was his body now, for however long he could keep it alive, and resting his chin this way pleased him. "The small statue was inhabited by a demon from the world of Abyss. They've broken through into Earth's dimension, but the only form they have here is spirit—that dark, stinking mist you saw after you shattered the creature was the demon's essence. They need an avatar, something made of the earth . . .

ceramic, stone, metal. Nothing alive. The avatar gives form and shape; the demon provides the life."

She nodded her head, slowly, as if digesting his words. "If I hadn't seen it . . . Good Lord . . . I still can't believe I saw what I saw out there." She glanced around the room. "Where's that little fairy? The one you called Willow?"

"She's actually a will-o'-the-wisp, not a fairy. She's a protector of sorts. She gathers energy out of the air and shares it with me. Helps me understand this unfamiliar world, this body. Right now, she's sitting on your bookcase. I think she likes being surrounded by all the little figurines on the top shelf." He looked over his shoulder at Willow. Her light pulsed bright blue for a second. Then, once again, she disappeared among the tiny glass statuettes.

Eddy shook her head. She laughed, but it sounded forced, like she was strangling. Mostly, her voice was low, sort of soft and mellow. It fit her.

"I'm generally pretty pragmatic, unlike my father, who believes every wild story he hears. I can tell it's going to be really hard for me to deal with all this. Just point to Willow as a reminder that the impossible is sometimes possible. . . . You know, when I look at you like I think you're lying."

"I promise to do that." He smiled over the edge of his cup and took a sip of the dark brew. She'd said it would perk him up, whatever that meant. He did feel more alert. He hoped it wasn't because danger was lurking nearby. He still didn't understand all this body's instincts.

"You said you were a demon, but you look perfectly human. What exactly do you mean?"

"Exactly that. I'm a demon from the world of Abyss. It exists in a dimension apart from yours, but I was sent here by people from another world, one called Eden that's in yet another dimension. The two worlds never touch, never interact.

Complete yet separate, they are entirely dependent on the balance that holds them apart as much as it connects them."

"So what does that make Earth?"

He stared at his cup of coffee a moment, picturing the three worlds as he imagined them. "Earth is the fulcrum," he said, raising his eyes to study her reaction. "Eden on the one side is a world of light filled with people who are inherently good. Abyss, on the other, is a world of darkness, a land of fire and ice populated by creatures who personify evil. Earth is in the center, holding them apart, keeping them in perpetual balance. . . . Or, at least, that's the way it's supposed to work. The way it's always worked in the past."

Her brows knotted over her dark eyes, and she looked confused, but at least she was still listening. Dax ran his fingers through Bumper's curly coat. The dog was a hard-muscled, frilly contradiction—she had a powerful body with strong jaws, yet she was covered in a curly blond coat that made her look utterly ridiculous. Dax couldn't imagine anyone creating an animal like Bumper on purpose, yet somehow the combination worked.

Sort of like Earth. "Your world is mostly populated by a mixture of different kinds of humans—some who will always try to do the right thing, as well as those who are set on doing something evil. The best of you and the worst of you are balanced by the vast majority who are sort of like this dog of yours, a blend of both good and bad, beautiful and ugly." He laughed. "Smart and stupid. Somehow, it all works, and, on the whole, humans get along and live their lives."

She snorted. He grinned at her. "Well, most of the time, anyway."

Shaking her head, she set her cup down. "I beg to differ with you—people don't get along that well. There are wars going on all over the world, people are starving and dying, we have to worry about terrorists blowing things up, and . . ."

"I know. That's why I'm here. Evil has grown too powerful on your world. It's giving demonkind a foothold. Balance has reached a tipping point. It's slipping over to the side of darkness. The people of Eden recognized the danger, but they're incapable of fighting. Their nature doesn't allow it. They can, however, hire fallen demons to fight their battles."

She ignored his reference to himself and instead asked the one question Dax didn't want to answer.

"What happens if the balance slips too far?"

He didn't want to think about that. Couldn't allow himself to consider failure. Bumper raised her head, stared beyond Dax, and growled. Dax looked down at the dog, but he spoke to Eddy. "Then the demons of Abyss take over. If Evergreen falls to the demons, they gain a powerful foothold in your world. If this town falls, others may follow. The fear is that all of Earth will fall to darkness and demons will rule. There's a risk that eventually, even Eden will be overrun."

"Dax? I think you need to turn around."

He snapped his head up at the quaver in her voice and caught Eddy's terrified gaze. He spun around on the couch, and his feet hit the floor just as the stone owl by the fireplace stretched its gray wings and clicked its sharp beak, as if testing to make sure things worked.

Willow shot up from the bookcase so fast she left a trail of blue sparkles in the air behind her. Dax leapt to his feet, pulled in the energy Willow sent him, and pointed both hands at the owl, with his fingertips spread wide.

Fire burst from his fingers in long, twin spikes of pure power. He caught the owl as it prepared to take flight, trapped the creature in a blazing sphere of heat and light, and blew it right through the wire screen and into the fireplace.

Eddy screamed. The creature screamed louder, sounding

eerily like the garden gnome Eddy had flattened. The cry cut off the moment the flaming owl hit the back of the firebox and shattered. A dark wisp, stinking of sulfur, coalesced in front of the broken pieces, but before it could race up the flue to freedom, Dax called on Willow's power once again.

This time a blast of icy air caught the amorphous mass of darkness, freezing it before it could make its escape. It hovered a moment, quivering in midair, then fell to the hearth and shattered into a thousand tiny pieces of black ice.

Dax hit the ice with a burst of flame. The pieces sizzled and disappeared in puffs of steam.

He took a deep breath and turned away from the mess. Eddy sat on the end of the couch, with Bumper caught in her shaking arms. Both of them gaped, wide-eyed, at the fireplace. Before Dax could assure Eddy that everything was all right, at least for now, she raised her head and stared at him.

"Okay." Her voice cracked, and she took a deep breath. "I take back what I said. You won't need to point to Willow for proof. I promise to believe anything you tell me. Explain, please, what the hell just happened."

Chapter Two

Dax wiped his hands on her dad's old sweats and sat down on his end of the couch as if nothing had happened.

Bumper struggled in Eddy's tight grasp, raking Eddy's thighs with her sharp nails. Luckily Bumper couldn't tear through Eddy's heavy jeans, but before the dog freaked entirely, Eddy set her free. The stupid mutt jumped off the couch and raced to the fireplace. She sniffed the small pile of rubble that had once been Eddy's beautifully carved stone owl, sneezed, and then trotted back to the couch as cocky as if she'd been the one to defeat the demon.

Bumper jumped on the couch between Eddy and Dax, but this time she rested her head on Dax's thigh and gazed at him with pure adoration.

Eddy couldn't blame the dog one bit. Even though she was still trembling and her heart pounded like a whole set of drums, she knew she stared at Dax the same way.

It was impossible not to.

Dark tendrils of thick, black hair clung to his forehead and jaw. His bare chest, bisected with the colorful snake tattoo, gleamed with a light sheen of perspiration from his efforts. The gray sweats hung low on his lean hips. He epitomized sex appeal and good looks, and to top it off, he'd just saved her from a completely impossible attack by a demon right here in her very own living room.

If she could believe what she'd just seen.

"Before we were so rudely interrupted . . ." He actually grinned at her.

She had to swallow twice before she found her voice. "Go on. Please. Don't let me stop you." She clasped her hands in her lap to keep them from shaking. There had to be a logical reason for all this. Either that, or she was every bit as loony as old Mrs. Abernathy.

"You asked what would happen if things got out of balance." He nodded toward the fireplace. "That's a good example. It's happening now. Demons are slipping into this dimension through a pathway that's normally closed to them, a portal in the energy vortex that is your mountain."

Not exactly what Eddy wanted to hear. "You're kidding, right?" He didn't look like he was kidding. In fact, he looked awfully serious for someone making a joke. "The vortex is all New Age folklore. No one around here really believes it exists, unless you count my father, who is the king of otherworldly theories, or the stores and companies catering to the tourists. The vortex is no more real than the Lemurians."

"The what?" Dax frowned and stopped rubbing Bumper's ears. Bumper growled and wagged her tail. Dax went back to rubbing.

Eddy couldn't sit still any longer. She bounced to her feet and began pacing around the small living room. "Lemurians. They're not real, unless you ask Dad." She spun around and laughed. "He's going to be thrilled when he finds out about you. Proof that some of his crazy theories are actually true." *Dax and the demons.* It didn't get any better.

"According to local lore, they're a race of mystical beings—tall, beautiful people with strange powers who supposedly live inside Mount Shasta in rooms made of gold. Legend says they're descendents of people from the lost continent of Lemuria that sank beneath the sea, that they had advanced science and technology thousands of years ago. They were even supposed to have flying machines, sort of like the old Atlantis myth."

Dax shook his head. He twisted around in his seat so he could follow her erratic pacing. "Atlantis is no myth. It really existed, and its descendents are still around. I've never heard of Lemuria. I'll need to look into it. The vortex, though, is definitely real. How do you think I got here?"

Eddy stopped in her tracks and stared at him, looking for a twitch, a smile, anything to tell her he was teasing.

He wasn't.

She glanced at Willow. As if the sprite knew she was being watched, she flashed bright blue and just as quickly faded.

Okay. Point made. Eddy took a deep breath. "Why don't you tell me exactly how you did get here. Just promise to ignore me if I look incredulous."

Dax stared at her for a long, slow moment. Then he shook his head, and his gorgeous lips turned up in an unbelievably sexy grin. "Eddy Marks, I doubt I could ever ignore you . . . not for any reason."

She felt it right between her thighs. A hot lick of heat that had no business firing her senses and making her muscles clench, especially after a hokey come-on like that. It took a tremendous amount of will to continue gazing directly into those smoldering eyes of his. *Demon's eyes.* She had to remind herself that, for all his appeal, Dax not only was a stranger, but he'd also already admitted to being one of the bad guys.

"I'm waiting," she said, planting her hands on her hips, ignoring his innuendo and her body's traitorous response.

He still had that cocky grin plastered on his gorgeous face, but at least he had settled back against the couch. "I was a demon. An immortal in a world of evil. It suited me for a long time, and then it didn't." He shrugged. "For some reason, I began to question the life, the constant desire to cause pain, to kill." He shook his head, shrugged. Gave her a self-deprecating grin. "I guess I learned the hard way. One does not question evil. I got tossed out of Abyss."

The snake tattoo crawling out of his waistband slowly writhed across his belly and chest. Mesmerized, Eddy blinked. She must be more exhausted than she'd realized.

The subtle motion stopped. The tattoo stayed put. She swallowed and raised her eyes. It was too unsettling to steal even the quickest glance at his body, when things like that happened. "Where does a demon go that's worse than Hell?"

Dax ran his fingers lightly over his tattoo. Had he felt it move? He stared at her for a moment before he answered.

"Earth."

Eddy blinked. "What? Life on Earth is worse than Abyss?"

"For a demon, yes. I might have been reborn here as a petty criminal, some kind of crook leading a useless life, causing other people grief, or worse. I could have become a dictator, a hired killer, a terrorist. Part of the balance of good and evil that keeps this world in line. Not a pleasant way to spend one's time, especially when you're beginning to question everything about the demon's way."

"So what happened?"

"I was still in the void, the space without substance that exists where the dimensions of Earth, Abyss, and Eden aren't. I was unsure whether or not I even rated a rebirth after being cast out. It's still not clear to me how, but a contingent from Eden managed to snag my soul out of the void.

"I vaguely recall a very one-sided discussion. Somehow they convinced me to take on the job of ridding Evergreen of the excess demons finding their way through the portal in your vortex before the balance could tip too far on the side of evil. Since I'd given up my demon body as well as the ability to manipulate inanimate objects when I was cast out of Abyss, the Edenites gave me a living avatar, this body. The snake tattoo holds my demonic powers of fire and ice for fighting demons. And they gave me Willow, of course, to feed me the energy I need to use my weapons. She's actually a creature of Eden, and she draws her power from the air around her."

"What exactly are you supposed to do?"

"My charge is to shut down the portal in the vortex between Earth and Abyss, and destroy any of the demons who've made it across the dimensions. Evergreen may be just one small town, but all of its citizens are at risk. If I fail, demonkind will continue to gain strength in this dimension. Other towns, other humans will be in danger. At the very worst, all three worlds could eventually fail with me. Of course, that's not what Abyss wants. Their goal is to rule Earth, and maybe even Eden."

"But why Evergreen? Like you said, it's just a tiny little town."

"Mount Shasta." He shrugged as if it was entirely obvious.

Eddy frowned. "I still don't . . ."

"The mountain is the vortex," Dax said. "The source of power for the portal between Earth and Abyss. Evergreen is the closest community to the mountain and the portal that allows demonkind entrance to this dimension. Demons aren't strong enough yet to move very far from the mountain—their link to Abyss—but with each day that passes, they gain strength in this dimension."

He glanced away, and took a deep breath. When he turned back, Eddy could have sworn she saw a glint of green fire in his eyes. "If they prevail," he said, "you will fully understand the meaning of Hell on Earth."

She really, really couldn't believe she was standing here in her own front room having this conversation. Her reporter's instincts were screaming at her to grab her tape recorder, her feminine instincts were all aflutter, and her brain didn't seem to want to function on any familiar level at all.

If it did, she wouldn't be accepting this outlandish tale as truth. Shouldn't she be questioning everything Dax said? *Yeah,* said a tiny voice in her head. *Except that there's this little blue fairy flying around and a garden gnome armed with a pitchfork, and the stone owl tried to fly and . . .*

She paused at the back side of the couch, planted her hands on the curved top, and leaned closer to Dax. "How come I've never heard of Eden or Abyss? How come you guys know about us and each other, but we don't know about you?"

He wound his fingers in Bumper's curly coat, almost as if anchoring himself with the dog. "Absolute evil is always aware of absolute good, and vice versa. In a way, Eden and Abyss are two sides of the whole. Those of you Earthbound are too busy fearing both, so you make us the stuff of legend and religion. Christians have Heaven and Hell, Muslims have Jannah and Jahannam, Buddhists . . . well, you get the point. Every religion has its own name for Paradise balanced by some form of evil underworld."

Damn. He had a plausible answer for everything. "So what did they offer you? What would make a demon agree to fight against his own kind?"

He smiled. His eyes sort of unfocused as he gazed off into the distance. "Remember, I'd already been kicked out of Abyss. The Edenites offered me my own shot at Paradise, at life on Eden. The odds are against me, of course. I wasn't a perfect demon, so it's hard to imagine myself as a perfect human. You must prove to be pure, without any stain of evil on your soul, but it's a greater chance than I had before."

"What's the alternative if you fail?"

"Besides the end of life as the three worlds know it?" He laughed softly, but Eddy had a feeling he wasn't really joking. "Remember, this body of mine is borrowed. I was given the form of a man who died somewhere on Earth at some point in time—there's little meaning to time in the void—when I accepted the Edenites' proposal. This body will disappear at the end of my seven days. I, once again a demon, face eternity in the void, but this time without chance of rebirth of any kind. Nothing beyond memories forever of the pain and misery I knew on Abyss. Knowing I'd come just this close . . ." He held his thumb and forefinger a hairsbreadth apart. "This close to eternity in Paradise. I can't imagine a more painful hell, knowing I'd come so close and yet failed. Worse than my life on Abyss, for all its agony."

He raised his head and gazed directly into her eyes. Eddy felt his need, his desperate hope for that one slim chance at Paradise, and her heart sort of tumbled in her chest. If there was any way to help . . .

Bumper suddenly sat up and growled. Her curly hackles rose along her spine, and she stared over the top of the couch at the sliding glass door leading to the backyard.

Eddy and Dax both glanced from Bumper to Willow. The tiny creature pulsed in shades of blue, flitted away from her perch on the bookcase, and buzzed around the room. Each lamp she passed went out.

"What is it?"

Dax held a finger to his lips. "Grab Bumper. Don't let go of her."

Eddy nodded, though she doubted Dax saw her. The room

was pitch dark without the lights. She wrapped her fingers around Bumper's collar and fumbled for the leash on the table beside the couch. It took her a moment to find it in the dark, longer still to snap it to the dog's collar for added insurance. Bumper might only weigh fifty pounds, but she was all muscle and sinew under that curly blond coat.

Eddy's eyes slowly adjusted to the darkness. She felt the shift of air currents as Dax slipped away and padded on bare feet toward the sliding glass door. He didn't seem to have any problem seeing in the dark

She heard a strange sound in the garden, a clattering noise she couldn't quite place. Bumper growled, but instead of lunging, she pressed tightly against Eddy's leg. Eddy hunkered down with the couch between her and the door, and peeked over the top to see what was going on. Willow hovered beside Dax. Her faint glow was barely visible, reflecting off the glass door.

Dax shouted, "Eddy! Out of the way!"

He dove to one side as the plate glass shattered into a million pieces. A huge, bronze horse galloped into her front room. Its rider waved a deadly sword.

General Humphreys? No way!

Eddy screamed and grabbed Bumper. She lifted the dog's fifty-pound body as if she didn't weigh an ounce, hauled her across the room and around the corner, where they hid in the hallway that led to her bedroom.

Lights flashed. Dax shouted what had to be a curse in some language Eddy'd never heard. Her little house shook, and the smell of sulfur almost choked her. Banshee howls came from more than one direction, and she couldn't stand it a minute longer.

Hanging on to Bumper, Eddy peeked around the corner. Dax stood in the far corner of the room next to the fireplace with his back to the wall. His arms were stretched out in front of his powerful body as he lit up the room, shooting blast after blast of fire at the bronze horse and rider.

The horse reared, and Eddy's ceiling fan turned to toothpicks when the general's sword caught the spinning blades. Dax fired another blast, and the top half of the general separated from the horse and tumbled to the floor.

It rose up, wobbling on its bronze torso, then pivoted on both arms and moved around beside the rearing horse, caging Dax in the corner.

The general's legs remained in the saddle, raking the bronze flanks of the horse with sharp spurs. Half a dozen small stone statues—three cats, two squirrels, and one little deer with spreading antlers—scurried across the floor. Some carried garden tools and sticks; all of them headed for Dax and his bare feet.

Willow flitted from one side of the room to the other, gathering energy out of the air to throw to Dax.

Bumper tugged at the short leash, her snarls and barks adding to the din. Her powerful jaws dripped saliva; her razor sharp teeth clicked with each snap. In one brief flight of hysterical fancy, Eddy realized she looked like a killing machine in a Shirley Temple wig. With a quick prayer, she unhooked the dog's leash, and Bumper launched herself into the melee.

The small statues scattered, though one squirrel wasn't quite fast enough. Bumper caught it between her jaws, shook her head, and snapped the thing in two. The dark mist inside floated toward the ceiling.

Dax hit it with a burst of fire, and the mist disappeared in a sizzle of white steam. Then he quickly fired on two of the stone cats, destroying them along with their demons. Bumper had gotten the last squirrel and was chasing down the stone deer, barking nonstop. She dodged the deer's antlers and the slashing bronze hooves of the horse, but her frenetic attack effectively took everyone's concentration off Dax.

No one seemed aware of Eddy at all.

She grabbed a wooden chair and raced into the front room, raised it over her head, and clobbered the top half of the general across the back. The chair shattered on contact, but the demon-powered statue toppled to the ground, where Dax hit him with a burst of icy wind.

The bronze froze and splintered. As black mist poured out of the cracks, the icy blast caught it, and frozen drops clattered to the ground where Dax steamed them out of existence with a shot of fire.

Empowered by her success and Bumper's effective attack, Eddy grabbed another chair and swung at the rearing horse's back legs. This chair shattered as well, but the horse dropped to all four feet and turned toward Eddy.

Its jaws opened wide, and she saw row upon row of sharp, silvery teeth where teeth shouldn't be. The horse's eyes glowed an eerie yellow, and she realized the broken chair legs she held were no defense at all.

Bumper must have sensed her danger. She snapped the spine of the stone deer she'd attacked and charged the horse. Instead of going for the throat, Bumper sank her teeth into the right rear leg, up high, just beside the horse's belly.

Animated by the demon inside, the bronze seemed to have the texture of plastic, and there was nothing Bumper liked more than her plastic chew toys. Hanging by her powerful jaws, hind legs scrabbling for purchase on the tattered carpet beneath her feet, Bumper finally threw the bronze beast off balance.

Dax zapped the last of the stone cats and its resident demon with fire, then spun in place and hit the fallen horse with a shot of freezing air. This time, when the bronze cracked, two misty creatures escaped. He caught each of them in a flaming arc, burning them until the black mist turned to steam and evaporated in the suddenly quiet room.

Still growling, Bumper backed away from the fallen statue, and leaned against Eddy's shaking knees. Eddy's lungs ached with each tortured breath.

Dax reached out and caught Willow out of the air before she could tumble to the ground. Eddy sensed the tiny sprite's utter and complete exhaustion.

She'd given everything she had to Dax.

Eddy'd given everything she had, period. Including her home. She flipped on the only lamp still standing.

The small living room was littered with crumbled stone and large chunks of metal. Black scorch marks disfigured the walls, and Dax's fire had burned holes in the carpet. The ceiling fan still spun, but only one blade remained. The air reeked of sulfur. Broken glass was everywhere, destruction complete.

Explaining this one to the insurance company was going to be a bitch. Eddy leaned over, rested her hands on her knees, and struggled to get her ragged breathing under control.

Then she heard the wail of sirens in the distance. "Dax. You need to get out of here," she gasped. "The police are on their way. Where can you go?"

"Wherever you go, Eddy Marks."

She jerked her head up and gaped at him.

He held his big hands out, palms up. Willow sat in his left palm with her wings drooping and her head hanging low, but she was safe. Eddy stared at the hands protecting the tiny sprite—the same hands that shot fire and ice at marauding demons. The same hands that had stroked Bumper's curly head with such gentleness.

"I could not have done this without you and Bumper," he said simply. "I need both of you." Dax glanced at the tiny figure in the palm of his hand. "And Willow, of course. I will always need Willow. You have to come with me, Eddy. It's too important. I can't do this by myself. I need you."

He held his right hand out to her. "Besides, the demons know where you live. They'll return. You're not safe here. I will not leave you unprotected."

Eddy stared at his hand. Glanced at the snake tattoo that had come back to life and seemed to ripple across his entire torso. Then she looked down at Bumper. She was parked on her butt between the two of them, but with her doggy gaze fixed firmly on Dax and her curly tail going like a high-speed metronome. Eddy laughed. None of this made sense. The sirens were coming closer. Her house was ruined. Dax had a huge grin on his face, like he was having the time of his life.

And so am I.

Hadn't she just complained to Ginny that nothing exciting ever happened? Eddy gazed at the destruction that had once been her perfect little living room. Then she raised her head and grinned at Dax. "And you're saying I'll be safe with you, a guy who's admitted he's a demon?"

"A fallen demon, Eddy. Too good for Hell."

"Well, in that case, what can I possibly be worried about?"

Still laughing for God knew what reason, she grabbed her purse off the floor, checked to make sure her cell phone was inside, and snapped the leash back on Bumper. "I sure hope you know where we're going."

Dax grabbed her hand, pulled her close, and shocked her to her toes with a quick kiss. "I do now. We're headed straight up the mountain. I'm going to need more help than one skinny girl and a curly-headed dog. We're going to find the Lemurians."

Oh, crap. She felt laughter burbling up again and bit it off before she gave in to complete hysterics.

Eddy's brain slipped into overdrive. She put on clean

socks and laced up her hiking boots. Her jeans and tank top would have to do—the police cars were pulling up across the street and she didn't want to get caught in the house. They went out the back through the broken glass door. She worried about Dax's bare feet and the glass all over the carpet, but he and Bumper both got out of the house without cutting themselves.

A block away, she grabbed Dax's hand. "Before we head up the mountain, you need boots and a shirt. We're going to my father's house first. It's not far."

"He knows of the Lemurians?"

"He thinks he does." She tugged Bumper's leash, and they slipped down an alley. Exhausted from the battle, Willow rode along perched on Eddy's shoulder. Carrying the sprite with her felt absolutely perfect. Eddy loved seeing the pale blue glow that was barely visible in her peripheral vision.

Somehow, knowing Willow was there was reassuring. She wasn't losing her mind at all. Dax was real. The demons were real, and this really was happening.

Not that it was good. No, if what Dax said could happen actually did, it was going to be awful, but just knowing that these creatures existed, that she wasn't absolutely crazy, was somehow life affirming.

Dad was going to love it.

Her childhood home was dark, but she spotted lights on in her father's workshop out back. Since her mother's death, her dad spent most of his time in the shop, puttering with his model trains or building birdhouses.

It had become a neighborhood joke how Ed Marks had singlehandedly turned this part of town into the bird high-rent district with his fancy designs. There wasn't a tree without at least one of his birdhouses for blocks around, but tonight, from the noise coming out of the shop, it sounded as if he was busy with his model trains. He'd spent years on the layout, a perfect miniature scale model of Mount Shasta and the surrounding towns.

McCloud, Edgewood, Weed, the town of Mt. Shasta. Their own little community of Evergreen. All to scale, all perfect. "Dad? Are you in there?" Eddy stood just outside the door and tapped lightly.

She remembered years ago, when her mom was still alive and her dad much younger, that he'd been as big and powerful-looking as Dax. The mature man who opened the door wasn't at all frail, despite a slight limp from his bad hip, but the physical bulk of hard-worked muscle and youthful strength was gone. He was still tall, but leaner now, with deep grooves in his cheeks from years of smiles, and his once dark hair was shot with gray.

"Eddy! Sweetheart, what are you doing out so late? Come on in. And . . . ?" He stared sharply at Dax, standing beside Eddy with bare feet and bare chest. After a quick appraisal, including a second glance at the sweats Eddy had borrowed from him a few days before, he opened the door wide.

Bumper wriggled all over until Ed leaned down and ruffled her curly head. "Brought home another stray I see." He paused a moment and picked some glass splinters out of the dog's thick fur and then shot another sharp look at Dax. Then he glanced at Eddy and led them over to a group of tall stools beside the model-train layout.

"Okay. What's up?"

The look he gave Eddy reminded her of the first time she'd brought a date home in high school. "Dad, this is Dax." She reached up to her shoulder and cupped Willow in her palm. Then she held the glowing ball of light in front of her. Willow stood up and spread her tiny wings.

Ed sat down—hard—on the closest stool.

"This is Willow. . . . And Dad? I have a whole lot of really weird and wild stuff I have to tell you."

* * *

Dax liked Eddy's father immediately. The man remained calm in spite of the story his daughter told. He asked intelligent questions, seemed relieved that no one had been hurt during the attack on her home, and offered to go over and repair the damage.

Then he took them inside Eddy's childhood home, opened a large cabinet, dug around for a thick file, and dropped it into Dax's hands. "Can you read English?"

Dax stared at the papers in his hands. "I don't know if I can read at all." He flipped open the first page and stared at the black marks running in straight rows from side to side. Willow made a quick buzz across the pages, and the printed symbols suddenly made perfect sense. He raised his head and grinned at Eddy's father. "Yes, it appears I can."

He flipped through page after page, reading stories about the ancient continent of Lemuria, how it had sunk beneath the waves, but not before the inhabitants were able to reach safety on Mount Shasta. According to Ed Marks' research, the Lemurians now inhabited the inner caves and secret valleys of the mountain. They had once been known as demon fighters, powerful warriors able to best the demon hordes of ancient times in epic battles that had changed the course of history through many dimensions. Supposedly they had powers mere humans barely understood.

Powers that just might tip the balance between success and failure. All Dax had to do was find people who, according to Eddy, didn't exist.

But, if he believed her father, they did. . . . And hadn't Ed believed in demons and will-o'-the-wisps?

Dax raised his head as Eddy and her father walked back into the room.

"We made some sandwiches." Eddy sat down beside him and stuck a plate in his hands. "What about Willow?"

Dax shook his head. "She exists on energy, as I once did. As a demon, I only ate my enemies to keep them from coming back to fight again." He took a bite, chewed a few times, and paused. "This is my first meal as a human. It's good."

Eddy and her father exchanged an unfathomable look and then burst out laughing. Eddy leaned over and kissed Ed on the cheek. "You win, Dad."

Ed slapped his knee and laughed again. "Dax, my boy, you have managed to give me the creditability I've always lacked in my poor, pragmatic daughter's eyes. Thank you."

Dax merely smiled around a huge bite of his sandwich.

"Dax, the police stopped by here a little bit ago while you were going through the file. They wanted to let Dad know what had happened to my house and make sure I was okay. I didn't tell them anything about the demons or you, and we let them think the mess was from vandals."

Dax nodded. "Probably for the best." He glanced down at Bumper, who stared back at him with soulful eyes. Without a second thought, he tore off a bite of his sandwich and gave it to the dog.

Bumper's curly tail thumped the floor.

Dax glanced at Eddy, but she was talking with her father. He looked back at the dog, grinned and slipped her another bite.

Then Dax turned and watched Willow as she perched on Ed Marks' shoulder. Her blue glow looked strong and healthy, and he could tell she was loving every minute of attention Eddy's father gave her. Dax turned away from the tiny sprite and looked at Eddy. He studied the long, narrow line of her slim back beneath the cotton tee she wore, and his body tightened. His heart seemed to flip in his chest before settling back into a strong, steady beat. He relished the warm glow of contentment he felt merely from being near her.

Energy surged through his body. He felt strong. Whole. The pain from his demon tattoo faded into the background.

Right now, at this moment, he experienced a sense of peace he'd never once imagined.

The invasion of Evergreen was well under way, and he had less than a week to help put things back into balance. Failure was not an option, and with the demon's tattoo burning across his torso, he would be fighting a constant battle against pain as well as the one against the clock.

But he had Eddy by his side, a powerful ally in Willow, and a loyal companion in Bumper. He had purpose, a destination, even the beginnings of a plan that might actually work.

For the first time in his immortal existence, Dax truly understood what goodness felt like.

Understood it, and loved it. If, when this mission ended, he still missed his shot at Eden and must be cast into the void, these were the memories he would take with him. Memories of Eddy and her father, of Willow and Bumper . . . memories strong enough and good enough to last forever.

For now, though his borrowed body was fed, it desperately needed rest. Dax glanced at Eddy just as she yawned and knew she was exhausted as well. Sunrise was only a few hours away. Time to rest and then begin their journey up the mountain.

He needed to remind himself to think like a human. Demonkind were more active in the darkest hours. They'd be safer traveling out in the open in the light of day. Once inside the mountain, until they contacted the Lemurians, there would be no place that was safe, not as long as they followed the pathway to the portal where the demons were slipping into this dimension.

He would think no more of demons tonight.

Ed showed Dax to the guest room a few moments later. It was next to the room where Eddy would sleep. Close, but not quite close enough.

The thought brought a smile to his lips. Eddy Marks was a surprise he'd not expected during his week on Earth. This body's reaction to her presence was a gift, one he ached to explore.

Tomorrow. After he'd recharged with sleep.

With that thought in mind, Dax stretched out at a cross-wise angle to fit his full length on the double bed, and closed his eyes. He drifted off with thoughts of Eddy in his mind, and Willow curled up on the pillow beside his head.

Chapter Three

Monday morning—day two

Waking up in her childhood bedroom was disorienting, to say the least, especially in the gunmetal gray predawn light after only four hours' sleep. Eddy dragged herself out of bed and took a quick shower, found some clean bikini panties in her old dresser, and put on the same jeans and T-shirt she'd worn the night before.

She skipped a bra, opting for comfort over style. Then she dug around in the closet, found a soft sweatshirt from high school, fluffed her wet hair with her fingers, and wandered out to the kitchen, drawn by the rich scent of freshly brewed coffee.

Her father and Dax were already up, sipping coffee and studying a large topographic map of Mount Shasta that covered most of the kitchen table. Eddy got a cup for herself and leaned over Dax's shoulder to look at the familiar map.

"Good morning, Eddy." Dax slipped an arm around her waist. He glanced up at her as if they were a couple that had been together for ages, not merely accidental acquaintances that had known each other less than a day, brought together by a bizarre set of unbelievable events.

He'd shaved, and his hair was still wet from the shower. He wore what appeared to be an old pair of her dad's Levi's, though they'd certainly never looked this good on her father. Dax's chest was still bare. The snake tattoo shimmered, as if alive.

Dax's dark eyes, veiled behind thick lashes, seemed to look right inside her. "Did you sleep well?"

"Yeah." She shivered, almost preternaturally aware of the light touch of his fingers spanning her hip, the weight of his muscular arm around her waist. "You?"

Dax nodded. "I've never slept in a bed before. I think I could grow used to such luxury."

"Really?" Ed peered over his reading glasses. "Where do demons sleep?"

Dax shrugged. "Wherever they are when they grow too exhausted to stay awake: the ground, in a tree, a cave. . . . Sleep is a rarity on Abyss. One can't afford such vulnerability."

His offhand comment slammed Eddy back to Earth. He wasn't just the most gorgeous guy she'd ever seen, who, for some unfathomable reason appeared to find her attractive. No, he was a demon, a mythical creature that, for all intents and purposes, didn't really exist.

At least not as Eddy saw him.

Mist, scales, and claws. That's how he'd described himself. Not tall, dark, and handsome.

More like scary, scaled, and dangerous.

She'd have to keep reminding herself that the man she saw wasn't real. He was merely a sexy avatar.

A demon in human form.

One with a very short life span. In less than a week, he would be gone.

He shifted the weight of his arm around her waist and tightened his fingers against her hip. The heat from his warm body, so close against hers, seeped into her skin. A shiver of pure desire raced up her spine, spread low between her legs.

It settled with a delicious pulse of damp need, deep in her core.

With a sinking feeling, Eddy knew it was already too late. Gazing into Dax's dark eyes, she felt her heart give a funny little flip, felt the rhythmic tightening in her womb, the damp flush to her skin.

Damn. She was in a whole shitload of trouble. Merely one morning after she'd whapped a killer garden gnome over the head, and here she'd gone and fallen in lust with a demon.

Of all the idiotic, lame-brained, stupid . . .

With a quick jerk, she pulled out of Dax's grasp and stalked across the kitchen to gaze out the window above the sink. This was not good. Not good at all. She glanced back over her shoulder. Dax watched her with a small frown between his thick, dark eyebrows.

Quickly, Eddy turned away and stared at the shimmering, snow-capped peak of Mount Shasta, rising up out of the morning mist. An early snowstorm had left a blanket of white on the upper reaches of the fourteen-thousand-foot peak. Now, sunlight caught the southern shoulder of the mountain and turned the ice to fire. If she used her imagination, she could almost see the spires of temples and the mythical city of a forgotten race.

Almost. Except it wasn't true. It couldn't be. None of this. Not the demons, not the Lemurians, not the feelings that made her heart pound and her womb ache.

Not the gorgeous man sitting at her father's table, watching her so intently and probably wondering why she was acting like such a bitch. Eddy's shoulders slumped. She blinked back the tears of self-pity that threatened to blind her, and slowly turned around.

At least it was lust, not love, that had her all twisted up inside. She wasn't in love. Love took longer. It needed to build and grow.

It most assuredly did not smack one upside the head. Not in real life.

Of course, there weren't demons and deadly garden gnomes in real life, either. She managed a smile and then quickly hid behind another sip of coffee. Her father, oblivious to the currents swirling around him, was pointing at the map, talking away about fire trails and road access. With a final look, Dax turned around in his chair to follow Ed's pointing finger.

Willow buzzed across the room and hovered in front of Eddy's nose, so close Eddy saw two of her.

He needs you.

What? Eddy blinked.

The tiny sprite moved back a bit, just far enough that Eddy could actually see her face, read her expressions. It was the first time she'd gotten a really close look at Willow. She was absolutely beautiful. Her tiny ears were pointed like an elf's, and her body was dressed in a fitted tunic the brilliant blue of sapphires. Her eyes were the same bright blue, her tiny lips red, her long hair like spun gold. Her wings, fluttering as rapidly as a hummingbird's, might have been made of crystal the way they shimmered and glowed with a reflected rainbow of light.

Don't forsake him. We all need you.

She really had heard Willow! The sprite's voice echoed in Eddy's mind, each word as clear as the note of a flute.

Eddy straightened up and grinned at the sprite. Somehow she didn't see herself arguing with a person no bigger than her pinky finger. *I'm not quitting*, she thought, wondering, at the same time, if this was the right way to converse with an honest to goodness will-o'-the-wisp.

Good.

Must be.

Willow turned and buzzed back to her place on the table beside Ed's coffee cup. Even at this distance, Eddy was almost certain she saw the sprite smirk.

Before she could say a word, a shiver ran along her spine, that someone-walking-on-her-grave feeling. She jerked around to the window as a banshee cry overhead brought Dax and Ed to their feet. Bumper growled, Willow zipped across the room, and they all stared out the window.

The gargoyle, a black silhouette against the pale dawn sky, flew not twenty feet overhead, winging its way toward town. It didn't look down, didn't pay any attention to them.

A sense of pure evil followed in its wake.

"He's probably returning to the building where the gargoyle belongs," Dax said. "Demons are stronger at night. It takes less energy to bring the avatar to life. Once the sun is up and the demons are at rest, we need to leave."

Eddy nodded. No matter her misgivings, this wasn't the time for second thoughts. She had to believe the threat was real. Real, and terrifying beyond anything she'd ever known.

She plastered a smile on her face. "Got anything in the fridge, Dad? I'll make us some breakfast."

"I shopped yesterday. Help yourself." Ed looked Dax up and down and then touched his shoulder. "Come with me, son. The jeans fit fine, so we know you're about my size. You'll need stout boots and a warm shirt. It can be cold on the mountain, even in September. After we get you outfitted, I want you to take a look at the model railroad layout in my shop. I've built a miniature of Mount Shasta, entirely to scale. It might help."

Dax nodded. With one long, questioning look at Eddy, he

followed her father out of the kitchen. Bumper trotted gleefully behind, with Willow perched in the curls between her ears.

Dax was totally aware of Eddy sitting behind him with Bumper while her father drove a fascinating little vehicle with huge tires, no top, and very little room in the backseat. Ed called it a Jeep. Eddy called it a piece of junk, but she smiled when she said it, so Dax figured she didn't really mean what she said.

He was learning. There was so much about this world he found fascinating. He couldn't imagine Eden being anywhere near as beautiful, or as filled with wonders. It certainly couldn't have anyone as captivating as Eddy Marks. Knowing she sat behind him, close enough to touch should he so choose, gave him an unbelievable feeling of contentment.

She seemed more relaxed, now that they were actually on the road. He still hadn't figured out what had upset her earlier. Of course, there was a lot he hadn't figured out, but as knowledge seemed to be filling his brain quickly, he wasn't going to worry about it. He'd understand her soon enough—or not at all.

Smiling, Dax settled back in his seat and watched the scenery fly by. Willow perched on the dashboard and stared out the windshield. She was as fascinated as Dax by how far and fast they were able to travel, by the tall trees and rugged terrain and the huge, snow-covered peak ahead.

She'd only known Eden. He'd never seen anyplace other than Abyss. Both of them were overwhelmed by the immense beauty around them.

Dax had no idea how he'd gotten to town the night before. He barely recalled the demon gargoyle's attack near the portal. He still wasn't sure how he'd ended up in

Eddy's potting shed, but thank goodness she'd been the one to find him.

She was such an amazing woman. Strong and unafraid, and she could cook too. He'd eaten so much at breakfast he figured he'd never have to feed this body again, but when he'd said as much to Eddy, she'd laughed and stuck four thick sandwiches in his backpack.

He guessed she knew what she was talking about.

They followed a narrow dirt road that wound up the northwestern flank of the mountain, and it was exactly as Ed had shown him on the model in his workshop. At one point, Ed got out and used a heavy tool to cut a thick chain blocking the road, but now even that track had grown impassable.

Ed parked the Jeep and turned off the motor. "I think this is as far as I can take you. I'd go with you if I could, but with my bad hip I'd just slow you down."

Ed took Dax's hand in his. His grip was firm, and somehow comforting, but Dax sensed a challenge in the older man's grasp as well.

"Good luck, Dax. Take care of my baby girl. She's all I have left, and I want her home in one piece."

Dax nodded. "I would give my life to save her." He squeezed Ed's hand before turning loose, aware he'd made a powerful pact with Eddy's father. One he could not fail.

"I know. That's the only reason I'm going along with this harebrained scheme." Ed's eyes seemed to burn right through him before he turned around and looked at his daughter in the cramped backseat. Dax heard him sigh when he smiled at Eddy. "I love you, sweetie. Be careful."

She threw her arms around her father's neck and hugged him. "I will, Dad. I love you too." She kissed his cheek and climbed out of the back with Bumper bouncing along behind her.

Dax grabbed his pack. Willow buzzed two circles around Ed and landed on Dax's shoulder.

Ed turned the key, and the motor roared to life. "Follow that draw, and it should take you close enough to the area you described. This entire mountain is the vortex, and your portal shouldn't be far. You said Willow can sense their presence, so I imagine she'll find it before too long. Eddy? Have you got a signal on your cell?"

Cell phones. Another amazing thing on this world. They didn't even need telepathy. They could call each other and actually speak. Eddy held up her cell phone. "I do, Dad. We'll call you when we can. Hopefully we'll be ready for you to come get us by tomorrow. Figure noon, okay?"

"If I don't hear from you before noon, I'll be right here waiting tomorrow night. Got that?"

"Yep. Now don't forget to call Harlan. Tell him I won't be in to work, at least for a couple days."

"You know, you might lose your job, sweetie. He's not going to like it."

Eddy glanced at Dax and back at her father. "I can't believe I'm saying this, but if we're not successful, we all stand to lose a lot more."

Ed nodded, but his smile was strained. "There is that. I'll call him when I get home. I'll let him know you might just have one hell of a story for him." Ed backed up, turned the little Jeep around, and headed down the narrow dirt road.

Dax and Eddy stood there, staring, until Ed's departure was nothing more than a wisp of red dust settling to earth. The magnitude of the mission ahead of them hit Dax hard and fast. He felt the snake tattoo shift under his flannel shirt, and he shuddered against the painful burn as his body fought the curse of the demon's fire.

Only six more days. It was time to get moving. He caught Eddy staring at him. "Are you ready?"

"I hope so." She grinned, slung her pack over her shoulder, and started up the draw her father had pointed out.

Dax followed with Bumper at his heels and Willow flitting alongside. The enormity of their task almost brought him to his knees. He wondered if he would have had the courage to make this journey alone, if not for the tall, slim girl leading the way.

Eddy glanced over her shoulder at him and smiled without breaking stride. "I've always loved any excuse to hike this mountain, but I have to admit, this is a first."

Definitely a first. Everything he did on this world was a first, but Dax merely nodded. He hoped it wasn't a *last.* His heart was full. He was thankful to whatever gods ruled Earth that he'd been granted Eddy Marks as a soldier to march beside him . . . or in front of him.

He watched the slight sway of her perfectly shaped behind encased in snug denim pants, and, for at least a short while, put the pain and worry out of his mind.

Eddy adjusted the pack on her shoulders and shoved sweaty strands of hair out of her eyes. They'd been hiking for a couple of hours, and before too long they'd be hitting the loose scree and volcanic rubble above the tree line that was totally impossible to walk on. This late in the season, even with the light snowfall they'd had, there wasn't enough to cover the loose rock on the upper flanks of the mountain. It wasn't just difficult—it was downright dangerous.

Like fighting demons wasn't?

What in the hell have I gotten myself into?

Eddy stopped and took a drink from her water bottle. Dax did the same. Then he cupped his hand and poured water into his palm for Bumper.

The dog lapped it up and sat at Dax's feet with a stupid

grin on her face. "I think Bumper's in love." Eddy flashed a smile at Dax, but quickly turned away. No way did she want her mind—or his—shifting along those lines.

She'd tried love a time or two. It wasn't at all what it was cracked up to be. If she'd learned anything in her twenty-nine years in this world, it was the fact she didn't need another person to complete the woman she wanted to be.

That didn't mean she couldn't enjoy the occasional relationship—as long as it came without strings. Eddy Marks was all about lust, not love, but what red-blooded girl wouldn't fall in lust with a sexy guy like Dax?

He's a demon, you idiot.

Yeah, but he's still one of the good guys.

Right. Like you know this for certain?

Well, her libido could argue with her common sense all it wanted. They still needed to find the Lemurians and the portal in the vortex . . . if either actually existed.

Willow buzzed by her face, and Bumper growled. Even Eddy sensed a shift in the currents, a feeling of something not quite right.

"Shhh." Dax tugged Eddy's hand and slowly knelt behind a fallen tree alongside the trail. He held a finger to his lips and motioned toward a large tumble of dark rock. "Look closely, on the downhill side of the biggest boulder."

Eddy held Bumper close to her side and crouched next to Dax. She stared over the top of the splintered trunk at the pile of rock. It was like every other pile of rock on the side of this ancient volcano, most likely left over from some monstrous cataclysm eons ago. She opened her senses, searching for whatever it was that had caught Dax's attention.

Birds chirped, cicadas buzzed, and the sound of Bumper's panting added a steady rhythm to the soft symphony of sound. As she stared, the rock seemed to shudder and swell.

Eddy shot a quick glance at Dax, but his focus on the

boulder was absolute. She looked back just as a shadow along the downhill edge of one of the boulders seemed to detach itself and float away on the soft breeze.

Dax rose to his feet and held his hands out. A burst of icy air caught the shadow. Like the demons he'd stopped in Eddy's living room, this one dropped to the ground in a pile of frozen shards. Dax leapt over the log, raced across the rocky ground with Bumper on his heels, and hit the icy bits with fire.

A burst of steam quickly dissipated until nothing remained beyond a scorch mark on the ground. Dax raised his head. The bloodthirsty look of feral satisfaction on his face set her back a step. Then he grinned as if nothing had happened. "I think we've found the portal," he said. "Are you ready?"

"No. Of course not," she muttered. But she adjusted her pack, climbed over the fallen tree, and carefully crossed the rock-strewn ground.

Dax walked slowly around the pile of boulders. Willow buzzed alongside, dipping down occasionally to check the ground, then flying up over the higher reaches, above their heads. The stink of sulfur, a smell Eddy had learned to associate with the demons, lingered.

It gave her goose bumps to realize they'd been so close to one as it made the crossover from Abyss to Earth. Dax paused near the downhill side of the largest boulder.

"It's here," he said. "I don't recognize it, so I'm not even sure it's the same one I came through, but this is definitely one of the portals."

Eddy looked at the solid wall of rock. The boulder was the size of a small car. "I don't see anything there." She shrugged. "How do you get through it?"

Dax ran his hand over the rough surface. As Eddy watched, he pressed against the boulder. His hand disappeared up to his wrist. He pulled his hand out and continued to study the surface.

Wide-eyed, Eddy touched the hard surface. She pressed. Nothing happened. She pushed harder and then, frustrated, slapped the rock. Nothing. "I don't get it."

Dax put his hand next to hers. "You're not actually trying to go through the rock. You're moving from one dimension to another. Think of the journey. You have to see the pathway beyond the wall of rock. Picture a long tunnel and then push your hand into it."

"What if it's not really a tunnel. What if there's a big lake or a small room on the other side? What if there's fire?"

"That can't happen, so it doesn't matter. You can only pass through where a portal exists, and portals only go where they should. What matters is what you're expecting. If you see this as a doorway instead of a solid wall of rock, you will find the opening. Try it."

Eddy stared at the lichen-covered boulder. Patches of yellow, orange, and green grew across the rough surface. The rock was warm to the touch from the noonday sun. She made herself look beyond the colored surface, beyond the solid reality of the stone.

She pictured a tunnel. Cool and dark, it beckoned. She pressed her hand against the warm rock. Instead, she felt a cool draft of air from the tunnel as her hand disappeared all the way to her elbow.

She shrieked and tugged. Her hand slipped easily out of the stone. "Oh. My." She stared at Dax. "That is just too weird." She took a couple of deep breaths and shook off the shivers coursing down her spine. "Is it going to be dark in there? How do we know where we're going? I really don't want to end up in Abyss."

Dax laughed and grabbed her hand. He felt so warm and solid, she immediately calmed down. "Neither do I. We need to think of the Lemurians. When we step through, I want you to hang on to Bumper's leash and hold my hand so we're not separated. I'll recognize the dimension for Abyss and should be able to pick out the one for Eden. If there's a third, we'll know it's the Lemurians."

Eddy nodded. "What if there's a fourth?"

Dax sighed. "Then I guess we'll go to Plan B."

"What's that?"

He shook his head. "Haven't got a clue, but we'll figure something out."

"Why doesn't that give me a sense of confidence?"

"Probably because you're hungry." He walked a few steps down the hill and found a shady spot beneath a stunted pine with a few large rocks beside it. "I thought breakfast would last forever, but now I'm glad you made me bring sandwiches. I'm starving. This body needs a lot of fuel. Would you like to eat?"

"Sure. Why not?" *Kill demons, find the portal, take a lunch break. Sheesh.* Eddy found a spot on a smooth rock and sat. She noticed Dax kept his attention focused on the portal, even while he worked his way through two of the sandwiches. The last thing they needed was a demon joining them for lunch.

Except that's exactly what I'm sitting beside. She took a deep breath and a bite of her sandwich, and put that thought out of her mind. Denial was easier. Not necessarily safer, but definitely easier.

The sun reflected off the dark scree, and it was warm here, even this high up on the mountain. Dax slipped his flannel shirt off and draped it over the rock. Eddy almost choked. She'd been trying so hard not to think about him, about the attraction she felt, but there was no denying her body's response.

Demon or not, the man was gorgeous. He'd replaced the

bandages on his chest and side after his shower, but they didn't detract from the powerful muscles or the lean strength of him. Even the snake seemed to fit, glistening across his flat belly and winding up his chest. The head rested just above his nipple with jaws gaping wide, as if to swallow that perfect copper-colored disk whole.

Suddenly the snake writhed across his skin. Dax shuddered. His body curved forward, and he gasped, as if in terrible pain. Eddy reached out and grabbed his arm as he sat down, heavily, on the rock next to hers.

"Dax? What's wrong? Are you okay?"

"A minute . . ." He closed his eyes and took a series of deep breaths. His face was chalky. Perspiration beaded his forehead. The snake tattoo glowed hotly against his skin. After a moment, he opened his eyes and slowly ran his fingers over the inked scales.

"What is that thing?" Eddy knelt in front of him with her hands resting on his knees. His body trembled; his breathing was ragged. Willow zipped between her and Dax, glowing like a tiny spotlight.

Her blue glow bathed his chest. Dax slowly straightened, took another deep breath, and let it out. "Thank you, Willow." He placed his hands over Eddy's. "I'm sorry if I frightened you."

"What happened? I swear I saw that tattoo move across your skin, almost like it was trying to coil to strike. What is it?"

He looked down at his chest and ran his fingers along the colorful tattoo. "As I told you before, this holds my demon powers. The part of me that controls fire and ice, that keeps this body alive. When the Edenites gave me this avatar, they placed the tattoo on my body as a repository of all that made me demonkind. Locked away like this, the powers are mine to control.

"When I passed through the portal, the gargoyle caught me before I had full use of my avatar, this body. He hit me with cursed demonfire. The burn on my chest? It was charged with a curse that seems to be turning my powers against me. I've been fighting it, but it grows stronger by the hour."

"What can we do?" Eddy pressed the flat of her palm against the tattoo. It rippled beneath her hand. She bit back a small scream and managed to hold her hand in place, but she hoped like hell the curse couldn't harm her.

After a moment, Dax frowned and touched the back of her hand. "Your touch calms the pain. Thank you. Maybe you draw some of the power." He shook his head. "I don't know. This is new to me." He stood up. "I should be able to keep it at bay for a couple more days, at the very least. Long enough to finish my mission. After that, it won't matter anymore."

Eddy folded her hands on her thighs and looked up at Dax, standing so tall in front of her. "It matters to me," she said. "I don't want to think of you hurting."

Dax looked away without acknowledging her comment. Then he held his hand out. She grabbed it. He tugged her lightly to her feet and smiled as if he'd not been close to collapsing in agony only moments ago. "Are you ready to find the Lemurians?"

"I guess so." She watched him out of the corner of her eye as she snapped the leash on Bumper. Dax cleared up the left-overs from their lunch, saved the extra sandwich, and tucked it and the trash into his pack. Then he slipped his shirt on and buttoned it, hiding the snake away behind soft flannel.

She wondered if he'd looked anything like the tattoo in his own world. He'd said he was a creature of scales and claws and sharp fangs. Snakes didn't have claws.

Dax was no longer a demon. But, what made a creature a demon? Wasn't it the powers he called upon? Dax had those powers. They were inked into his skin, crawling across his thigh, his belly . . . his groin. She thought of the way the colorful snake crossed from his upper thigh and passed just above the thick root of his penis. She hadn't meant to look quite so closely, but she'd never forget what she saw.

He was beautiful everywhere. Absolutely beautiful.

With that thought in mind, she grabbed Bumper's leash and followed Dax back uphill to the pile of dark boulders. It was time to go through the portal, into the vortex.

"Hold tightly to Bumper's leash. She obeys you well and should be able to follow you through the portal. Don't let go of my hand. I'll need to choose the correct path as soon as we enter so we don't end up in either Eden or Abyss."

Eddy gulped. "What happens if we take the one to Abyss?"

"You would not survive the world's atmosphere. I doubt I could either, not in this body. And if we go to Eden, we would be destroyed before we could set foot on their world."

"I thought they were the good guys." She slanted a glance at Dax and caught him frowning.

"That's what they tell me. However, they protect their goodness by obliterating anyone foolish enough to try to enter without invitation."

"I thought they couldn't kill."

"They don't. The entrance to their world is warded with spells based on demon magic."

Eddy shook her head. "Ya know, at least the demons are honest about their killing. The Edenites are hypocrites. They let demons do all their dirty work so they can stay pure."

"It does seem that way, doesn't it? C'mon. Let's do it."

Eddy laughed. "You're even starting to sound human. What's going on?"

He studied his hands a moment and then gazed solemnly at her. "The longer I'm in this body, the more I understand it and the more I seem to become like the person who once inhabited it." He shrugged.

Eddy stared. Even that simple gesture was something she'd bet he'd never done as a demon.

He flashed a grin at Eddy. "I think my avatar belonged to a soldier, though I imagine his soul has gone on to its final rest. Whatever remains is impatient. It wants action. Let's go."

He slipped Willow into his shirt pocket. She poked her head out. Gently he shoved her back down again, caught Eddy's hand in his, and stepped through the dark wall of stone.

Eddy wrapped Bumper's leash a couple of turns around her hand, and the dog followed as they passed from Earth's dimension into an area of shimmering light. She felt a low hum of power that seemed to come from all around them.

"Wow." Eddy felt dizzy from the colors and glimmering light. Dax stood perfectly still, as if studying a subway map, but she spun around, gawking. "There's definitely more than three choices," she said. "Have you got Plan B figured out?"

Dax shook his head. "Not really." Then he pointed to an area of dark red light that pulsed with a terrifying energy. "Abyss," he said, and then turned and showed Eddy another area glowing in shades of gold and silver. "That's the way to Eden."

"Where's that one go?" Eddy stared at a green and turquoise area of light that throbbed with the tempo of the sea.

"I'm not sure, but I'd guess it leads to Atlantis. Can't you smell the brine in the air?"

Eddy sniffed and caught a faint whiff of ocean. "Oh." *Atlantis? Good Lord.*

Bumper whined and tugged at the leash.

"Is that it?" Eddy looked in the direction Bumper seemed intent to lead. A steady golden glow ebbed and flowed with the same rhythm as the beat of her heart. She felt drawn to it, just as Bumper seemed drawn.

Dax nodded. "It is. I'm almost positive. Willow, what do you think? Does that one feel right?"

The sprite poked her head up out of his shirt pocket. Her light glowed brightly before she settled back down. Only a slight shimmer escaped.

"Willow agrees. Let's go."

He led the way, stepping into the glowing, rippling shimmer of color. Eddy felt a tug, as if something pulled her forward, as well as a sense of fear that tried to push her back. The walls of light seemed to close in about them; the air grew thick and hard to breathe. Bumper growled. Then she whined and wagged her curly tail. She pulled Eddy and Dax forward while golden light shimmered all around them.

Eddy was aware of sound growing louder and louder, a steady roar that pulsed and ebbed with the beat of her heart and filled her head, her ears, her entire body with noise. Dax kept moving forward, but his grip on her hand tightened.

They were stopped by a solid, flowing wave of gold that could have been molten metal. It fell like a waterfall from somewhere overhead. Dax reached forward. Eddy bit off a scream, expecting to see the flesh burned from his bones, but he parted the wave. It separated and flowed over and around his hand like golden quicksilver, without leaving a mark, though it didn't part enough to let them see through to the other side.

Dax turned to look over his shoulder, gazing steadily at Eddy. "Can you do this?"

She nodded. She'd never felt so terrified, nor so sure of herself, in her life. They had no idea what lay on the other side. She glanced down at Bumper. The mutt tugged at her leash, anxious to race through the golden wall.

Dax leaned over and surprised Eddy with a kiss. He

wrapped one arm around her waist and dragged her body close against his. His lips moved over hers; his tongue tested the seam between them.

She hesitated, but for only a moment. Then she opened for him. His breath was sweet and hot; his tongue licked at her lips and the soft recesses inside her mouth.

She whimpered, a small sound deep in her throat that seemed to vibrate against his soft groan of need. Her body trembled, and hot licks of sensation swept over her shivering skin. She pressed her hips against him, against the hard ridge of his erection, oblivious to their frightening, fascinating surroundings, to danger, to anything beyond the scent and touch and pure eroticism of Dax, of this moment, of the man who touched her so sweetly.

It was Dax who finally broke the kiss, licking her lips, nibbling along the line of her jaw, and then planting a tiny kiss on the tip of her nose before setting her back on her feet. He cupped her face in his big hands and looked into her eyes.

"Thank you, Eddy Marks. No matter what happens, you have shown me a world I never expected. One I didn't dream existed. You've already given me my taste of Paradise."

She bit her lips between her teeth, but there were no words. Everything she felt was in her eyes: excitement, fear, confusion, arousal. When Dax smiled, she knew he understood.

She only wished she did. He wasn't real. He wasn't even human.

He was everything she wanted, and more. And he couldn't have been more wrong for her. More impossible. She tasted him on her lips, and all her feminine muscles clenched in need.

Desire trumped fear.

If he thought this was Paradise, what would he think if she showed him where that kiss of his might lead? She wasn't willing to let it go—not the kiss, not Dax, not the feelings coursing through her body, flowing like the golden curtain guarding their way. She wanted more of it, more of Dax.

More of Paradise.

He said he had less than a week. She wanted more!

Much, much more.

Dax took her hand. Eddy grabbed Bumper's leash and set aside everything but their mission. *Lemurians*. She had to focus on finding the Lemurians.

Dax squeezed her fingers. His smile was confident. Bold. Willow ducked down into his pocket. Eddy tightened her grip on Bumper's leash, and together they stepped through the flowing veil of gold.

Chapter Four

Monday night—day two

Alton, first son of Chancellor Artigos of the Ruling Council of Nine and heir apparent to the throne of Lemuria, leaned against one of the golden columns in the Inner Sanctum of the Lost City and cursed.

Quietly, of course. It wouldn't do to upset the status quo.

Even though he was bored to tears with the status quo.

It didn't help his disposition any that he was heir to the throne of an immortal king. Not that he wanted anything to happen to his father, but there wasn't much hope for job advancement.

Since he was also immortal—though he could be killed, old-age and illness weren't issues—he'd been heir apparent for what felt like forever. Dear old Dad was just as healthy and hard-headed now as he'd been back before the citizens of Lemuria had packed up their doomed kingdom and moved to a separate dimension within the mountain known as Shasta so many thousands of years ago.

Of course, the sanctuary the elders had chosen was deep inside a dormant volcano, one that tended to erupt every six hundred years or so, which meant packing everything up and evacuating until the mountain settled into dormancy once more. During the last eruption they'd moved through a portal in the vortex to Sedona in the American Southwest. Fascinating country, rich with ancient spirits and unique connections through a different set of dimensional portals and vortexes.

At least it had engendered a bit of excitement.

Anything was better than the endless philosophical discussions that now occupied the ruling class of Lemuria. Arguing dogma got old after a few thousand years, especially when no conclusions were ever reached. Alton had only needed a couple of clandestine journeys to the world outside Mount Shasta to be reminded once again that there was more to life than philosophical discourse and unending debate.

Earth was amazing, its humans even more so. They seethed with emotion. Humans seemed to act without thought or concern for the common good.

No . . . they felt, and then they reacted, generally without thinking, but damn, they certainly seemed to enjoy the ride. Alton envied humans their emotions. What would it be like to feel, to experience joy, passion, excitement, even fear again?

Not since his long-ago childhood had he been free to feel. It wasn't proper, now that he was grown. It was unseemly to allow the baser passions their freedom.

To hell with unseemly. What would it be like, to feel passionate enough about something to be willing to take risks for it? His thoughts drifted to a night many years before when he'd left this hallowed place and walked with his bare feet through rain-washed dirt.

A storm had recently passed, and the ground was muddy and slick. It stuck to his bare soles and stained the pristine hem of his white robe, but he'd buried his feet in the soft, wet muck and watched it ooze up between his curled toes. Cold and slimy and so very real . . . he'd felt a connection to the earth unlike anything he'd known before.

He'd even stepped on a sticker. Hurt like blazes until he'd found it and pulled it out of his heel, but he'd actually relished the pain, the small dot of blood that was a persuasive reminder that yes, he was alive.

It was so easy to forget, down here amongst the elders of his world, men who could spend months arguing a simple point merely for the sake of the argument.

What would it be like to fight over something that actually mattered? To believe strongly enough to risk everything for a cause bigger than himself?

"Alton? What are you doing here?"

Jerked out of his musings, Alton glanced up as Taron, his one true friend, approached. Tall, lean, with his single vermillion braid hanging as neatly bound as always down his back, Taron looked the part of the brilliant mathematician he'd grown to be.

It was easy to forget they'd once been boys together in old Lemuria, racing through sand dunes and swimming in the pristine sea without a care or worry to their names. They'd known passion then. The joy of being children in a world surrounded by azure seas beneath cerulean skies.

Alton glanced up at the intricate design in the gold leaf overhead and sighed. "Just wondering how to fill my days without going crazy."

Taron frowned. "Crazy? You? Shouldn't you be preparing to one day lead the citizens of Lemuria? As heir apparent . . ."

Alton shrugged. "Apparently you haven't paid attention. When one's father, also the world's ruler for life, is immortal, 'tis foolish to aspire to his position." He raised an eyebrow.

Taron laughed out loud. "I see your point. Actually, I'm pleased to find you here otherwise unencumbered. I need to talk to you." He glanced right and left, as if assuring that no one would hear what he was about to say, and then spoke very softly. "We have a problem. Large numbers of demons are passing through the vortex from Abyss to Earth. I'm concerned. Their numbers appear to be increasing exponentially."

Frowning, Alton gestured to Taron to follow him around the column he'd been leaning against, to the quiet alcove behind it. "How do you know this?"

"I noticed the influx about a week ago." Taron shrugged. "I stepped beyond the golden veil for a change of perspective and happened to notice a new portal in the vortex leading directly to Abyss. I was curious and decided to watch it for a while. Demon stench was impossible to ignore. I counted many demons taking the form of wraiths and disappearing through to Earth. It didn't take long to realize their numbers are increasing."

"Did you report it to the council?"

Taron merely raised one expressive eyebrow. Alton sighed. What was the point? Demons entering Earth's dimension had nothing to do with Lemurian politics—at least as far as his father and the ruling body were concerned.

"Some day my dear father and his eight fellow senators are going to be shocked when they discover their arguments are worth no more than dust on the feet of demons in the overall scheme of things." Alton glanced over Taron's shoulder at the small, mannerly groups of white-robed figures filling the great plaza.

Taron nodded. "How quickly they forget we were once fearsome warriors, that our people fought demonkind to a standstill."

Alton cut loose with a derisive snort. "If they were to

remember those days, they'd be forced to recall the days when our swords still spoke to us as fellow soldiers."

Taron merely shook his head in disgust. "We were once a proud people, Alton. Not anymore. Look at what we've become."

Alton looked, and then he sighed. The debates went on as usual: the level of voices never raised. The arguments remained the same. Century after century of the same discussions, the same gentlemanly disagreements.

Why in the gods' hells couldn't someone just get angry once in a while? He glanced down at the same white robe he wore every day. The one that made him look exactly like every other male in the huge auditorium.

He was going to end up exactly like them. A clone of his father—a man without imagination or passion. Without a ray of hope for anything more from his life.

Hells . . . what would it be like to fight for something important, to earn his sword's respect, to have it actually acknowledge him? Obviously he hadn't proved himself worthy enough to bear it, which was why he'd left the damned thing in his quarters. He'd never actually witnessed a sword that spoke, but history was rife with examples. His, however, was not one of them. When he raised his head, Alton caught Taron staring at him with an odd glint in his bright green eyes. "What?"

"You truly do look bored and dissatisfied."

"I am. Very." Alton huffed out a frustrated breath. "Day after day, the same conversations, the same arguments, the same talk, talk, talk. It goes nowhere. Solves nothing." He glared at Taron. "I can't stand it!"

"Come with me, then. I have something you might find interesting. Something that may be linked to demons."

Without waiting, Taron turned away and headed down a long hallway leading to another level, one where the technicians labored to keep their society on its usual level footing. Alton had often envied them their caste designation. At least they had purpose, a job to do, one that society actually depended upon.

"Slow down," he said, taking longer steps to catch up to Taron. "Where are you taking me?"

"We had a rather unusual incident this morning." Taron grinned at Alton, as if he carried a secret much too good to keep. "I only learned of it by accident, but it appears a couple of humans managed to cross through the golden veil."

"Humans?" Alton caught up to Taron. "How'd they get in?"

Taron shook his head. "I'm not sure, though rumor has it one of them reeks of demon. I was headed down to see them when I spotted you. Thought you might be interested."

"Does my father know?"

Once again Taron raised his eyebrows. He kept going. "Of course. He gave orders they be incarcerated and forgotten."

Alton practically growled. "Typical. So they're locked up?"

"Why do you think we're going to the dungeons, my friend? Pay attention!"

Alton blinked. Taron was right. He really did need to pay closer attention.

"Who passes?"

A guard stepped out of the shadows with his sword raised. Taron and Alton stopped. Alton glanced at the guard's shiny steel sword. At least the man didn't have to worry about his sword refusing to speak—only the ruling caste carried crystal. Alton stepped forward. "Heir Apparent Alton to interrogate the prisoners. Take us to them immediately."

The guard saluted, and, without question, turned and led them through a large gate and then into another long hallway. This one was even darker and narrower than the first. Alton glanced at Taron and flashed him a quick grin. At times like this, being the heir, apparent or otherwise, had its pluses.

The guard stopped in front of a barred door. Inside, behind the bars and a barrier of pure energy, two terribly dejected-looking humans and a rather odd animal covered in curly yellow hair sat huddled together on a single sleeping cot. Alton dismissed the guard. As soon as the man was gone, he glanced at Taron. "Shall we?"

"I'm ready if you are. Between the two of us, I think we can take them should they offer resistance." He grinned after making his dry comment, obviously not all that concerned with any particular threat from the prisoners.

With a wave of his hand, Alton directed the bars to part. The energy field winked out of existence. The sense, but not the scent, of demon wafted from the room. Alton glanced at Taron and frowned. He received a questioning shrug in return.

Totally confused and not just a little uncertain, the two Lemurians entered the cell.

Dad was going to be so disappointed in his much-lauded Lemurians. *Jackasses!* Eddy and Dax had barely stepped through the flowing wall of gold when they'd been nabbed by a couple of big bruisers who looked tough enough to work for the Siskiyou County Sheriff's Department—except the deputies back home were a hell of a lot nicer.

The guys that caught them this morning were sorely lacking in diplomatic skills. Brawny and powerful-looking in spite of the blue robes that reminded her of something you might wear at an expensive spa, the Lemurian guards hadn't said word one to either her or Dax.

No, they'd merely trapped them in some kind of energy beam so they couldn't do anything but follow orders, and marched them down a dark tunnel, straight to this damned little cell. Eddy glanced at Dax, but he wouldn't even meet her eyes. She couldn't imagine how awful he must feel. Sent to save the world with only a week to achieve the impossible, and they'd spent at least the last two hours locked in a stupid cell, Lord knows how far under the ground. A cell with bars across the doorway and, for added assurance, some kind of sizzling, sparking beam that looked like it would fry anyone who tried to go through.

Obviously some of the stories she'd heard about the Lemurians and their advanced technology were true, but the part about them being honorable and brave warriors was a crock. All her dad's talk of Lemurians battling demons throughout history was just that—nothing more than hot air. It looked like none of it was going to help them a bit.

Now how the hell were they going to get out of here?

Bumper whined. Eddy stroked her blond curls. "It's okay, girl. We'll think of something. They can't leave us here forever."

Says who?

Willow's telepathic voice carried the sound of tears. Eddy glanced to her right and saw the sprite's little face barely peeking out of Dax's shirt pocket. Her wings were droopy, and there was no shimmer to her at all.

Not a blue sparkle to be seen.

"We'll get out, Willow," Eddy said. "Don't give up hope."

Dax raised his head and looked at her. "How do you do it?" He shook his head. "You never show fear. You never give up. I wish I were more like you, Eddy Marks."

His sad smile made her heart clench. Then she remembered the taste of his lips on hers and the kiss they'd shared. "You're not giving up, Dax. None of us are." She wrapped her fingers around his hand and squeezed. "I'm not sure how, but we'll get out of here. They have to help us."

She felt the slightest pressure against her fingers as Dax returned her squeeze. Just the warmth of his hand in hers made her feel better. More connected. Stronger.

She looked around the tiny room that seemed to have been carved out of solid rock. It was light, and the air was fresh, even though there were no windows or visible light fixtures.

And no way to contact anyone, anywhere. She thought about the cell phone in her pack and almost laughed. The company said you could get a signal anywhere, but she figured that must mean as long as you were in the same dimension.

Bumper yipped. Eddy's head shot up. She stared at what they'd figured had to be some kind of energy field blocking the door. The bars clanged, though she couldn't see them through the brilliant glare. Then the wall of light between them and freedom suddenly winked out of existence.

It took her eyes a minute to adjust to the lack of glare. She blinked and looked way up into the eyes of two of the tallest, most beautiful men she'd ever seen in her life.

Well, almost the most beautiful. She tightened her grasp on Dax's hand and realized there was no comparison. As beautiful as these two strangers were, they weren't even close to her fallen demon. She shivered, more aware than ever how possessive she was beginning to feel about a guy she hardly knew at all. A guy who'd already explained he was here on borrowed time.

At least he was smiling, and with that smile, Eddy felt as if things looked brighter. Willow poked her head out of Dax's pocket, and her glow was once again brilliant. Sapphire blue sparkles exploded behind the little sprite as Willow leapt into the air. Dax stood and held his hand out to the first of the two men. "I am Dax. I'm glad you've come. I was wondering if anyone would help us."

The guy had to be close to seven feet tall. He had long,

shiny blond hair that fell past his waist, and the greenest eyes Eddy had ever seen on any man. He paused and glanced at Dax's outstretched hand. After a brief hesitation, he reached out and very briefly shook hands.

Then he stepped back, in an obvious move to put more space between them. "You carry the sense of demonkind, though not their stench," he said. His eyes narrowed, and he gave Dax a look of absolute loathing. "Even without their stink you are not welcome here. We do not deal with demons."

"Excuse me." Eddy popped to her feet, but she clasped her fists at her sides to keep from taking a swing at the pompous ass. "How dare you! Damn it all, he's trying to save us all from demons, and you've got us locked in here for Lord knows how long when we don't have any time to . . ."

Eyes wide, the Lemurian took a quick step back, even though he was almost a foot taller than her five foot ten. At least she'd gotten the jerk's attention. Willow flitted through the air and then hovered in front of the second Lemurian. He grinned at her, obviously fascinated by both Eddy's outburst and the little blue flash of Willow's feminine fury.

Dax wrapped his fingers around Eddy's arm and gave her a slight tug. Willow continued to hover, Bumper whined, and Eddy clamped her lips together. Attacking the guy you were here to ask favors of probably wasn't a very smart move on her part.

She took a deep breath. "I'm sorry," she said, well aware she didn't sound sorry at all. She held her hands out, though, to show she meant no harm. "Look, it's been a really, really shitty day." She glanced at Dax, and she was almost certain he was biting back a grin. She wanted to hit him. How the hell could he find anything in this to laugh about?

She turned back to their two visitors. The men stood perfectly still, studying them as if they were monkeys in a zoo, though Eddy had to admit that Willow was getting more than her share of the attention. At least the guy with the red braid was actually grinning at the sprite.

"I'm sorry," she said again, stiffly. "My name is Eddy Marks. This is Bumper, and that's Willow. We came here to request your help. We didn't expect to be thrown into jail."

"I see." The one with long blond hair turned to the other guy with the red braid that went to his butt. It was more than obvious they were somehow talking without any sound, though the one with the braid acted as if he'd rather just watch Willow.

After a moment of silent communication, the blond one nodded at Eddy. "I am Alton. This is Taron. We will speak with you of your reasons for invading our home. Why, human, have you and this creature who is demon in human form, come to ask for our help? And why do you think we would be willing to give it?"

Dax watched the emotions playing across Eddy's expressive face and figured this might be a good time to step in, even though the Lemurian had addressed her, not him. He rested his fingers on Eddy's forearm and stepped forward. "Because if you aren't willing to help us, Lemurian, we all—your world included—risk losing everything."

The tall one with the red braid down his back finally shifted his gaze away from Willow and raised one very expressive eyebrow. "Everything? That's fairly inclusive, isn't it?"

Dax nodded. "Everything," he said. "Demonkind have launched an invasion of the small town of Evergreen, the first step of what is feared might be an assault on all of Earth. I've been charged with the task of halting them before they gain a foothold. The balance of power is tipping, and if it tips too much . . ." He let the sentence hang there in the still air between them.

The Lemurians shared another telling glance. The one with the long red braid folded his arms across his chest and stared at Dax. The blond took a more aggressive stance. "We are aware of the demons' incursion onto Earthen soil." He made a dismissive sound and slashed his hand through the air. "You're saying you are all that stands between our linked civilizations and the chaos of demon rule?" He shook his head. A condescending smile curved his full lips. "I find that hard to believe. One man, a demon in human guise, at that, cannot expect to fight all of demonkind."

Dax glared at the arrogant fool staring down at them and fought a powerful desire to punch him in his long, aristocratic nose. If he'd still been in demon form, he could've dealt with him in a couple of quick bites. "One man who retains his demon powers," he said, squaring his shoulders and tapping himself on the chest. "Accompanied by one loyal beast, a will-o'-the-wisp with her own set of unique powers, and one very brave woman."

He turned and looked at Eddy with pride. "I do not fight alone."

Eddy snapped her head around and stared at him, wide-eyed. Dax squeezed her arm and winked at her. Didn't she realize how much he needed her? He slipped his arm around her waist. "We may be a small band, but we know our enemy. For now, demonkind are contained in one little town where we have a chance at victory. At least we have the courage to fight. Do you?"

The blond one, Alton, blinked. He looked like he wasn't used to anyone disagreeing with him about anything.

Or challenging him, either.

The one with the red braid covered his mouth and coughed, but he looked more like he was hiding a smile.

Alton took a deep breath, as if he seriously pondered Dax's comment. "Why Lemuria? There must be others more capable of fighting. We're philosophers, teachers—no longer warriors. And why is it that, while you appear human, I sense demonkind in you? Explain, please. . . . How is it you possess demon powers?"

Dax took a deep breath. He looked at Eddy. She squeezed his hand, sharing her amazing self-confidence.

"They asked," she said.

Dax nodded . . . and then he explained. Both Lemurians listened with surprising patience while he told them of being cast out of Abyss, of his first strange meeting with the Edenites in the void, and of the trip through the vortex into Earth's dimension while still unaccustomed to his new human body. He described the demon's attack and the curse he constantly battled.

"The curse lives within your own demon powers?" Taron frowned, as if confused by Dax's description. Dax opened his shirt to the snake tattoo, writhing in a slow yet hideous dance across his body. Alton and Taron exchanged horrified glances.

"Dax, wait." Eddy pressed her hands to the snake. The pain lessened. Dax sighed in relief as the writhing tattoo stilled. The Lemurians gazed at Eddy with new respect.

Dax felt stronger when he buttoned his shirt and continued with his tale. The one with the red braid actually smiled when Dax told of his first meeting with Eddy. Both Lemurians laughed aloud as he described the battle held in Eddy's small living room. It hadn't been funny at the time, but . . .

"And when Eddy told me of the mythical Lemurians with their special powers, with their illustrious history of battling demonkind, I knew we had to at least try to find you." He looked directly into Alton's green eyes. "You are right. I know we can't defeat an enemy as powerful as this demon horde by ourselves. That's why we've come here. We're not too proud to admit we need your help. Your people have to recognize the risk to all our worlds. We need your assistance to halt the invasion before it extends to other cities, other countries on Earth. There's very little time before a tipping point is reached. Before it's too late."

"Dax has less than a week," Eddy said. "Then his powers and this body he's been loaned will be gone. We need you."

She gazed at Dax, and her deep brown eyes glistened. Tears? For him? No, he thought, of course not. For her world. She wept for her world. As well she should.

Alton studied Dax for a long, silent moment after he finished speaking. He glanced at his companion, and his full lips quirked up in a smile when he spotted Willow perched on Taron's shoulder. She seemed perfectly at ease with him. Dax found that reassuring—if Willow wasn't concerned, these two must be okay.

Even Bumper had given her approval. She'd sprawled on the floor between the Lemurians with her butt on Taron's sandaled foot and her nose resting on Alton's bare toes. Neither man seemed to mind, though Dax noticed Alton was surreptitiously rubbing Bumper's ear with his big toe.

As tall as Dax was, these two towered over him, though their bodies were leaner, their muscles long and spare. They looked as if they would be strong warriors, though neither man carried arms.

Alton slipped his foot out from under Bumper's head. "I will speak to the Nine immediately," he said. "I would free you if I could, but I am loath to countermand my father's orders. Taron? Will you see that our guests are fed and that they have sufficient bedding for the night?"

"The night?" Eddy almost jerked free of Dax's arm that was lightly draped around her waist. He tightened his hold when she clenched her fists.

"We don't have time to stay here for the night! Don't you understand? We're running out of time. Dax told you—he has less than a week before this body he's in disappears. We've used up an entire day and accomplished nothing."

"Eddy." Dax looped his fingers into the waistband of her jeans and held on tight. "We must eat and rest and replenish our strength. Alton will return." He turned and looked steadily at the tall Lemurian. Alton met his gaze. He nodded.

Dax realized he trusted him, pompous ass or not, to do the right thing. That was all anyone could ask at this point. And he did need rest, if only to gain enough strength to fight the curse feeding off his demon powers. The pain was worse, growing more difficult to control. If not for Eddy's soothing touch . . .

Alton turned toward the barred door and paused. "I'll return at dawn with news of the Ruling Body of Nine's decision. Taron will see to your needs. Rest now."

He raised one hand. The bars slid aside, and he left. Taron stared toward the open door for a long moment. When he held his palm next to his shoulder, Willow stepped to the flat of his hand. He held her out in front of his face and stared at her with an expression of intense joy. Then he handed her to Dax with a regretful smile, as if he truly hated to part with the sprite.

"Amazing. I've heard of the little people before, but never . . ." He seemed to catch himself and nodded to both Dax and Eddy. "I'll return shortly with food and more bedding." He leaned over and patted Bumper's head, glanced at the narrow cot bolted to the wall, and shook his head. "I apologize for the lack of amenities. I'll be back shortly."

He was as good as his word. Within a few minutes he returned with two guards carrying folded blankets and big pillows. He'd also brought bread and cheese and fresh water, and food for Bumper that looked like dry cereal but kept her long, curly tail wagging. He gave them brief instructions on using the facilities that were hidden behind what had looked like a wall but was really a door into a small bathroom.

Eddy was obviously pleased with that bit of information.

Before Taron left, he paused in the doorway to their cell, sighed, and then gave them a helpless look. "I promise to let you know as soon as Alton has word. The Nine can be . . ."

He shook his head without finishing the sentence, and left.

Dax sat on the edge of the narrow cot and chewed slowly on a hunk of bread while Eddy paced the small cell. He forced his frustration under control, though he had a feeling the one who had first lived in this body had not been a patient man. He was anxious to meet the enemy. He wanted to fight, not sit on his ass eating bread and cheese. There wasn't a damned thing he could do, stuck here in this little cell.

Nothing. He glanced at Eddy. She'd stopped pacing and stood in the middle of the small space with her shoulders bowed and her head down. She nibbled on a piece of cheese and stared at the bedding, looking so dejected he was afraid she might cry.

Dax stood up. "Eddy? I . . ." He sighed. How the hell could he bring her spirit back? He had to do something, but what? Caring about another was a completely unfamiliar responsibility. As a demon he'd cared only for himself, had worried about nothing beyond his own survival. Now he had so many others—Willow, Bumper, and Eddy. Even Eddy's father. He was concerned about every one of them.

Something in him had changed. Continued to change.

The Edenites wanted a demon—a killer—for the very traits that made him a demon. His vicious temper, his murderous skills, his willingness to kill without regret. Compassion hadn't been part of the package, until they'd stuck him in this human body. Was its original soul causing this?

He'd not been totally evil as a demon, which was exactly why he'd been booted out of Abyss, but he hadn't been a very nice guy, either. No matter. He was what he was—and what he was becoming. He had to help Eddy. Anything to encourage her. To encourage himself.

Bumper jumped up on the mattress where he'd been sitting, stretched out full length on the narrow bed, and groaned. Willow zipped across the room and snuggled under Bumper's chin, obviously prepared to get some rest.

"What?" Eddy stared at him. Dax realized he must have been talking to himself. "Let me help you," he said, reaching for a thickly folded pad.

Eddy didn't say a word. She merely nodded and grabbed the other end. Together they spread it out on the floor. Working quietly, they built a bed with two pillows at one end and soft blankets covering the thick pad.

A bed that seemed to offer options Dax wasn't certain how to pursue, or even if he should. Part of him ached to take her, to satisfy the churning need that built in this body with every second they spent together. At the same time, he realized he was staring at her again, thinking of giving her comfort, of wrapping his arms around her, feeling the warmth of her body close against his.

Who was he? Demon or human? Saint or sinner? The questions roiling in his head had his tattoo burning in angry turmoil. As much as he wanted the satisfaction of plunging deep inside Eddy, of taking his pleasure with her perfect body, he wanted the woman who'd stood beside him in battle. Wanted her filled with spirit and strength and that amazingly strong sense of purpose. It hurt him to see her like this.

She looked beaten, unfocused.

From the beginning, when she'd found him in that damned

potting shed, Eddy had seemed such a powerful force to him. Sure of herself. Intelligent and forthright.

Her discouragement and frustration made him ache. She was a woman of action. A woman of strength. Now, even though her body needed rest, she fought it.

Even as she fought her attraction to Dax. He knew that instinctively, just as he knew he had to control his growing feelings for her.

Demons have no feelings.

Except he wasn't entirely a demon anymore, and the man he was becoming more like by the hour seemed to be telling him this was neither the time nor the place.

But will it ever be?

He silenced the persuasive voice in his head, sat down on their makeshift bed, and reached for Eddy. She stared at his outstretched hand and frowned. He wasn't sure what she was thinking, so he lowered his hand and patted the mattress beside him. "Rest beside me, Eddy. Bumper and Willow can have the lumpy bed. This will be more comfortable. We both need to rest."

She finally seemed to come to a decision; she folded her long legs and sat on the mattress. A moment later she sighed and lay down, facing away from him. "I'm not sure if this is a very good idea," she said.

"I promise to behave." Now he merely had to hope his demon side was capable of keeping that promise. Dax stretched out behind her and wrapped his arm around her slim waist. She went taut as a bowstring. After a moment she relaxed and let him pull her against his chest.

Her perfect bottom snuggled close against his belly, where it fit into the curve of his hips. At least she fit at first. Then her warmth seemed to raise the temperature of his. He felt his cock stir, swell, and come to life. Fighting his demon-driven needs, he ignored it and silently begged Eddy to do the same.

The scent of her hair was sweet. He nuzzled his nose into the short, silky strands, inhaling as much of her as he could drag into his lungs. Memorizing her scent.

His fingers rested against the waistband on her jeans. He spread them wide across her lower belly and felt her suck in a tight breath, but she didn't say a word.

He wasn't certain what she wanted. He didn't really know what he wanted, either. He had his demon self under control for now, but this human body of his obviously had ideas of its own. His pants grew tight, and the ache in his groin left him wanting to do a lot more, to rub against the full curve of her bottom, to wrap her as close to him as possible.

His demonic side thrummed with sexual desire, with the carnal lusts that had once ruled his body. The feelings he had for Eddy were different. They confused him; they were so hard to define—not based entirely on his instinctive interest in her woman's curves and valleys.

Not limited to the powerful drive to want, to take, to conquer. They were something else. Something impossible to define within the parameters of demon knowledge and what little he'd figured out from his human body.

Eddy shuddered against him. Dax's wandering thoughts flashed out of existence. He raised up on one elbow and gazed at her face. "Tears, Eddy?" He trailed his finger across her damp cheek, beneath her eye. Then he lifted his finger to his lips and tasted salt. "Why?"

"Why?" She rolled over on her back, sniffed, and scrubbed her face with the heels of her palms. "How can you ask me that? We're stuck here. They're never going to let us out, and the days are going to pass, and if all you say is true, the demons will take over and . . ." She sniffed and turned her face away.

"And what, Eddy?" He wasn't sure what drove him, but Dax leaned over and touched his lips to hers. Again he tasted salt, but he pressed harder, mouth to mouth, tongue to lips. It reminded him of the kiss they'd shared only hours earlier, before they passed through the golden veil into the land of the Lemurians.

Then he'd wanted to give her courage. To take courage from her, because she was truly the bravest woman he could possibly imagine. Now, when her lips parted, it was the most natural thing in the world to slip his tongue between and run the tip over her sharp teeth and then across the slick inner surface of her warm mouth.

She moaned and kissed him back. Her lips sealed over his thrusting tongue, and she sucked him into her mouth. The tip of her tongue dueled with his, dragging an unexpected groan from deep in Dax's chest.

Eddy whimpered. She rolled over into his embrace, grinding her hips against him, pressing her soft belly close to the erection trapped behind his taut denim jeans. His body responded even more, reacting to everything Eddy did—every touch, every sound—with purpose. With intent. There were instincts ruling him that were more powerful than anything he'd known as a demon. Instincts tempered by a need to protect, to guard the woman.

When he was still a demon in a demon's body with a demon's will to survive, it had been merely kill or be killed. Fuck or be fucked. Eat to survive. Kill to survive. Killing and eating were often each a part of the same act. If you ate your enemy, he was your enemy no longer.

If you were lucky, you fucked him first.

Dax wasn't going to eat Eddy, though the minute the thought filtered through his mind, he imagined her intimate flavors on his tongue and knew he'd eventually taste her.

He wasn't going to fuck her either. Not now. Not tonight.

Tonight they needed rest. They needed to recharge bodies weary from lack of sleep, from fear, from the stress of so many lives, so many worlds, resting on their very slim chance of success.

He forcefully subdued the demon within, calmed his human needs as well, and rolled away, lay beside her, and pulled her close against him once again. She sighed and silently acquiesced. Rolled to her side, snuggled her bottom in the curve of his hips, and rested her cheek on his biceps. Her short, dark hair felt like silk where it brushed his chin. Once again, he breathed her in, took her scent deep into his lungs.

Absorbed her. Remembered everything about her and stored those memories for the time when he'd not have her close.

He pressed his palm against her belly, slipped lower over the worn denim fabric, trailing one finger along her zipper. He knew that somehow he skirted an edge, a line neither of them was ready to cross. With that knowledge came a surprising sense of control. The pressure on his body eased; his cock lost some of its tumescence and no longer ached. He curled his fingers over the softly rounded mound at the apex of Eddy's thighs and rested his hand against her.

She clasped his fingers between her legs, and her breath shuddered out of her lungs. He held his hand still, caught in the feminine warmth of her strong thighs, held tightly against her woman's mound. Held her there, pressing her close so that her bottom rested against his groin. The soft globes of her buttocks cushioned the length of his cock.

It was good, this closeness. This comfort they took from one another, shared with each other. Her cheek rested on his left arm, his right held her close, and his fingers felt the warmth, the heat, and life of her. It was enough, for now. It would have to be enough.

After what seemed like forever but was probably no more than a couple of minutes, Dax felt Eddy's body relax in sleep.

He'd never known such contentment in his life. Had never imagined anything so sweet as Eddy Marks asleep in his arms. His plans were going to hell. They were trapped in a prison cell somewhere deep inside the mountain in another dimension from the community he'd been sent to help, and he had no idea if they'd already failed, if there was any hope at all for success.

Eddy sighed and snuggled closer. Her body relaxed, and in spite of all that had gone wrong this day, Dax realized he was slipping into sleep with a smile on his face.

Chapter Five

Tuesday morning—day three

Dax came awake with the all-too-familiar pain from the demon's curse pulsing within his tattoo. Bumper growled softly. Then her tail began to thump the bed, and she whimpered. Dax blinked in a vain effort to dispel the dark shadows in the small cell. It had been brightly lit when he and Eddy lay down to sleep. Willow zipped by overhead, and her blue sparkles left a small trail of incandescence.

The energy barrier was gone. The bars were open, and Alton stood in the doorway. He carried a pack over one shoulder and the jeweled hilt of a long, shimmering sword poked out of a tooled leather scabbard strapped to his back.

Taron stood beside him. Eddy struggled awake in Dax's arms. He turned her loose, sat up, stood up, and tugged Eddy to her feet. "What's going on?"

"Shhh." Alton held a finger to his lips. "I spoke with the Nine. I'm sorry. They have no intention of setting you free." He shook his head in disgust. "Fools. All of them, nothing but fools. They want no part of any battle between demon and human. It might upset our *oh, so glorious* way of life."

His soft bark of laughter wasn't the least bit humorous. "The council has decreed that you be held as trespassers and tried on charges of threatening the sanctity of Lemurian society. The crime, my friends, of trying to save our worthless lives, of attempting to warn my people of the threat to all of us, is punishable by death."

There was no ignoring the contemptuous sound in his voice. "The Ruling Council of Nine is not known for speed. I imagine they will be debating your fate for many years to come, if they even have those years left to them. We must hurry. They sleep now, but soon will rise. I believe you, and I believe the threat of demon invasion is real. Gather your things. We have only a few minutes before the guards return from a fool's errand on which I sent them. We must go now."

Taron grabbed Alton's arm with an expression that said this was the continuation of an argument already in motion. "My friend, you risk everything. Your future, your heritage. I can't let you take these risks alone. I beg you, take me with you."

Alton shook his head. "Taron, you're my oldest, my only true friend. Stay. Please, for me? Do your best to convince them that I've made the right move, one that will ultimately save their stubborn necks. You have the records showing the demons' steady increase on Earthen soil. Stay here. Convince them, or I can never return."

"What if they don't listen? What if . . . ?"

"Make them listen. You're my only hope if I ever want to see my home again. You and I both know these travelers bring us a true warning. The demon invasion is not going away." He rested a hand on Taron's shoulder. "Besides, my friend. I'm not traveling alone. I have this man's assurance that his is a courageous band of warriors." He glanced at the four of them. "I'm not making jest of your promises, my new friend. I am trusting in your ability to fight bravely, or I wouldn't be giving up everything I've ever known to come with you. Hurry. I'll get you out of here, but I'm going with you. Once I help you escape, I'll have sealed my fate with my people."

Eddy looked up from tying her boots. "Alton, I'd tell you not to take the risk, but I can't do that. From what Dax has told us, this is too important. If we don't stop them . . ." She huffed out a big breath and looked away. Then she grabbed the leash and attached it to Bumper's collar. Dax checked his laces, nodded to Alton, and straightened up. Willow flitted in front of Taron and left blue sparkles shimmering in a line across his chest as she buzzed the Lemurian. She landed on Dax's shoulder.

Dax turned to Eddy. The tattoo beat a steady cadence of fire across his chest. He ignored it. "Are you ready?"

She nodded. Taron hugged Alton tightly and then stood back.

Dax held out his hand to Taron. The Lemurian took it in a firm shake. Dax looked down at their clasped hands and once more realized he was making a pact. He raised his head and looked steadily into Taron's green eyes. "We will protect your friend. This I swear."

Taron nodded. "I'll hold you to that one, DemonSlayer."

Eddy held on to Bumper's leash, and Dax grabbed her free hand. He looked about the small cell, once more at the tall Lemurian standing in the shadows, and then followed Alton down the dark tunnel with Eddy's hand tucked tightly in his.

When Dax glanced at her, she flashed him a big smile. There was no fear in her now. None. They were on their way. He held tightly to the promise he'd made to Taron, to watch out for the tall Lemurian. Held it close to his heart, both the promise and the name with which Taron had gifted him.

DemonSlayer.

It was a title he would carry with pride. He was no longer

a demon. In spite of the curse, he would become their greatest nemesis. With Eddy, Bumper, Willow, and now Alton beside him, Dax finally had the confidence they might actually prevail.

Alton led them through a series of lava tubes and tunnels within the mountain. He walked with the confidence of one who had, as he'd quietly explained, explored every inch of the dark passages with Taron when they'd come here as children, shortly after the original continent of Lemuria was rocked by volcanic explosions and destroyed.

When she asked him how long ago that had been, Alton merely shook his head and whispered, "Millennia."

That was a little hard to swallow, but so was picturing Alton as a child. It was difficult for Eddy to imagine him as anything but a fearsome warrior as he led them, walking confidently with his crystal sword held aloft. Shining like a brilliant torch, it cast a silvery glow bright enough to light their way.

The passageway seemed to go on forever, and Eddy felt as if she'd been walking for hours. Her stomach rumbled from hunger, and the bottle of water she'd been carrying was almost empty when Alton turned and held a finger to his lips.

"We're passing close by the main plaza. It's just on the other side of this wall. Sounds carry through the stone, so be very quiet. We'll reach the veil shortly. Once we pass through, we should be out of danger, at least from Lemurian guards."

Eddy cast a quick glance at Dax. He'd hardly said a word on the long walk, and his face appeared lined with strain and fatigue. Leaning close to him, she whispered in his ear, "Are you okay?"

He nodded, but she felt a shudder pass through his

body. The demon's curse! How could she have forgotten?

"Hold Bumper." Eddy shoved the leash into Dax's hand and squeezed his fingers around the strap. She practically ripped the top two buttons off his flannel shirt in her haste to get it open. Then she slipped her hand inside and pressed her palms to his chest.

Alton watched them, frowning but not interfering, thank goodness. Eddy glanced up into Dax's eyes. She felt his angry frustration. He hated the fact he had no control, that the damned curse should have the power to slow them down.

Even though Eddy couldn't actually see the tattoo beneath his shirt, she knew exactly where it was the moment she touched it. His skin burned her hands. She felt the snake writhe and ripple beneath her palms as she softly stroked the small portion she could reach.

The Lemurian watched them through narrowed eyes. It was obvious he was as intrigued as he'd been when she'd done this earlier, when Dax was explaining their quest. Now, as then, Eddy paid him little heed. Dax needed her. She felt it. Welcomed it.

Willow sat quietly on her shoulder. Bumper had planted her butt on the stony floor and leaned against Eddy's leg. She could have sworn she felt their energy, their strength pouring into her as she tried to ease Dax's pain. If only she had a clue what it was that she was doing!

Whatever it was, her touch seemed to work. After a few minutes, she realized they were actually breathing in sync. As her heart rate slowed and her breathing calmed down, the same thing seemed to happen to Dax. She felt the tension flow from his body. The tattoo was still, his skin cooler beneath her palms.

"Thank you."

She barely heard his soft whisper as he stroked the back

of her wrists with his fingers. "I don't know how or why, but when you touch me, the pain melts away."

Eddy grinned and pressed her fingertips against his cheek. "I guess it doesn't matter, as long as it works." She slipped her other hand free of his shirt and fastened the buttons she'd undone. Her palms actually felt burned, as if she'd touched a hot stove.

Alton stood by, impatient now that Dax seemed better. Eddy nodded to him. Without a word, he turned away, and they quietly hiked down the long tunnel. Voices, faint echoes, could be heard through the rock. Then the only sound was the steady roar of falling water.

Only it wasn't water. It was the same wall of what appeared to be molten gold. Alton paused near the base, where the shimmering liquid disappeared into the ground without a puddle or splash to mark its passing.

"It's energy," Alton explained in a low voice. "Much like the energy barrier in your cell, except this is a three-dimensional representation of melted gold. There's no substance, only an image disguising the portal between the Lemurian dimension and Earth's. Follow me."

He stepped through the golden veil. Eddy held tightly to Dax's hand as they followed Alton. She recognized the tunnel they'd followed on their way in, even the spot where they'd paused, where Dax had kissed her.

His fingers tightened around hers, and she glanced up at him. When he smiled, she knew exactly what he was thinking.

If only she could be so certain of her own thoughts. Heat spread over her chest and face, and she looked away. Alton was already moving on. Walking through the glowing, swirling light of the portal with a purposeful step, he passed through without pausing.

Walking away from his home, away from everything

familiar to him. It struck her then, what a huge thing this was for the Lemurian. By choosing Eddy and Dax over his own people, Alton had exiled himself from the only life he'd ever known. She let go of Dax's hand and rushed to catch up to the tall Lemurian.

Without hesitation, Eddy raced through the portal, into the main cavern that was peppered with passageways to other worlds. Alton stood in the middle, staring at the many shimmering gateways.

"Alton? Wait, please."

He stopped and turned around. The expression on his face gave nothing away. "We must hurry, Eddy. We need to put more distance between ourselves and Lemuria. What do you want?"

She grabbed his hands in both of hers. "To thank you. Taron was right. You're risking everything for us. Thank you."

He flashed a quirky smile, and she realized again how handsome he was. When he sighed, he looked entirely human. "Only yesterday I was complaining that my life was boring, that there was nothing exciting in my world. Nothing to look forward to. It appears my complaints were too much temptation for my gods."

Dax caught up and placed a hand on Eddy's shoulder. "It does appear that way, doesn't it?" His eyes narrowed. He jerked his hand away from Eddy and whipped around. "Look!"

Eddy spun about as Bumper let out a low, threatening growl. The wall across the cavern from them shimmered an angry red and the surface began to waver. A thick, black smudge of oily mist reeking of sulfur seeped through the glowing rock. Dax shoved Bumper's leash into Eddy's hands, stepped around Alton, and ran ahead of the small group.

He stopped directly in front of the portal, raised his hands, and spread his fingers wide. An icy blast shot from his fingertips and encompassed the mist. It froze in midair and shattered into hundreds of small shards of black ice. Dax quickly hit them with bolts of blazing fire from his fingertips.

Hissing, the steam dissipated and disappeared.

All of them stood silent, waiting to see if any more demons would appear. After a moment, Dax's shoulders relaxed, and he took a deep breath. Eddy ran shaking fingers over Bumper's curly head, and Willow popped out from behind Alton's shoulder, where she'd taken refuge beneath his thick fall of blond hair.

"Effective." Alton shook his head, but he was staring at Dax's hands. "Very, very effective. Ugly things, aren't they?" He nodded toward the spot where the demon had died. "I had no idea you were so well armed." He cast a curious glance at Dax's perfectly normal-looking fingers, and frowned. "Why didn't you merely overwhelm our guards when they captured you?"

Dax merely shrugged. "That would have been foolish."

Alton tilted his head, obviously considering Dax's answer. "Well, you might not have ended up in a cell."

This time Dax shook his head. "It would have been counterproductive. We came to ask for your help, not to fight you. Attacking men who were merely doing their duty wouldn't have helped our cause, nor would it have been honorable."

Alton stared mutely at Dax for a long moment. Then he turned away, held his crystal sword high for the light it cast, and strode forward, toward the dark red portal where the demon had emerged.

Eddy heard him muttering quietly as he passed her.

"Demonkind with more honor than the council. Amazing."

Alton paused in front of the section of wall that pulsed like a thing alive. The colors shimmered in a loathsome, nauseous swirl of reds that perfectly fit his mood. It took a few deep breaths to calm his anger, the disgust he felt for his people. How could they ignore such a horrendous threat?

He glanced over his shoulder to make certain no guards followed them. Then he turned, took a deep breath, and faced the portal within the vortex. Taron hadn't exaggerated. It reeked with the filthy stench of demon, and displayed all the signs of an active route from Abyss to Earth.

The demon in human form stepped up beside him. *Dax.* Alton reminded himself that despite the sense of demon clinging to him, Dax was one of the good guys. Unfortunately, Alton's sword didn't seem to care. He tightened his grasp on the hilt to keep it from attacking the man.

Dax appeared puzzled by the gateway to his home world.

"Is this the one you came through?" Alton nodded toward the wall. Power surged through his blade once again. He pointed it off to his side, away from Dax. The thing jerked in his hand as it tried to strike out, to kill the demon beside him. Alton held the sword still.

Dax shook his head. "I'm not sure. The whole night is just a blur to me. I remember thinking the demon that attacked me was expecting me. He was lying in wait, but not here. It was somewhere else that he hit me with his cursed fire." He glanced about the cavern and shook his head. "Damn. I'm not even certain if it was inside the cavern, or after I'd stepped out of the mountain. Nor am I sure if I came through from Abyss or possibly straight from Eden."

Willow buzzed close to Dax as he stared at the ground a moment. Was he organizing confused thoughts, or twisting the truth? Alton wished he could trust him more, but as much as he wanted to believe, it was hard to ignore the sense of evil still clinging to Dax's human body.

Hard to ignore his sword's obvious desire to kill. A sword

that had never drawn blood, that still hadn't given Alton its name. Obviously, it wanted demon blood.

The power of the demon pulsed beneath fragile human skin or, as Dax maintained, in the tattoo hidden now beneath his shirt. Alton's intuition struggled with the powerful sense of demonkind, the feeling that had all his instinctive responses on high alert whenever Dax stood this close to him. Maybe it was worse here because of the strong scent of the others that had passed through this particular portal.

Sulfuric stench filled the air near this passage to Abyss, and the sense of evil surrounded them. Surprisingly, though, the dog didn't seem to mind, and the will-o'-the-wisp certainly appeared loyal.

As for the woman? She was loyal too, but that was to be expected. A woman always stuck by her man, though the women Alton knew were not meant to fight. They lacked the killer instinct, the physical strength, and mental prowess to do battle.

Women of Lemuria knew their place in society. They brought comfort to the men, raised the rare child born to a very few, made a home where a man could find peace.

Eddy Marks didn't appear to understand those rules a bit. When she caught him watching her, she didn't glance away as a maiden should. No, she practically dared him to disagree with her. As lovely as she was, he knew a woman like her would be an exhausting mate for any man. The demon was welcome to her.

Alton held tightly to his sword and turned his attention to Dax once again. "Concentrate. Did it wait for you here or outside of the mountain?"

Dax closed his eyes a moment. Willow sparkled in the air and then settled on his shoulder. He jerked his head up, and his eyes flashed. "Thank you, Willow. Outside," he said, grinning broadly at Alton. "I was outside the mountain when

I emerged through the portal. Willow reminded me that it happened as I stepped out into the half light of early dawn. Neither Willow nor I recall how we got here—inside the cavern—or what portal we came through, but I remember now how we got out."

He took a few steps, as if reliving the memory. "I stepped out of the dark cavern, passed through the portal to the gray light of morning in Earth's dimension. Willow was behind me. The gargoyle waited, perched among rocks. It struck the moment I stood up. I was unsteady, still not used to this body."

He turned toward Eddy. "I remember standing up, stretching one leg and then the other, facing down the mountain away from the sun. Knowing that was the way I needed to go, because Willow had told me. The gargoyle rose up into the air, shouted something in a language I didn't understand. Then it cast demonfire at my chest. Demonfire powered by a curse."

Dax shuddered and wrapped his arms around his waist. "I remember pain. Horrible pain and the gargoyle hovering over my body. Then it was gone. The sky was light and then dark. I must have been unconscious throughout the day." He shook his head and turned to the woman. Frustration was in every word he spoke. "My next clear memory was waking up in that little shed outside your house, Eddy. When the demon's avatar stabbed me with the pitchfork. I have no idea how I got there from here."

Blue sparkles lit up the air. Dax nodded. "I should have guessed. Thank you, Willow, for guiding me to Eddy."

Eddy reached for Dax's arm. "You know what that means, don't you? We have even less time than we thought. I've been counting days since Sunday night. If you actually arrived early Sunday morning, we have less time than we'd hoped."

"Then we've no time to waste," Alton said. "Stand back.

My sword dislikes demons. I don't want it tempted by your proximity." Dax and Eddy backed away.

Alton held his sword out and touched the roiling red surface of the portal. He concentrated his power through the crystal blade, felt the link between himself and the energy in the portal. The blade glowed in colors all across the spectrum until it finally shimmered a brilliant green. The rock appeared to congeal, and all sense of movement slowed. Within minutes, a solid wall of twisted, melted stone covered the area where the doorway into Abyss had been.

"Good! That one's sealed." He held his sword pointed toward the earth. The glow had dimmed now, but it still shimmered brighter than mere crystal as Alton glanced about the cavern. "The other gateways belong here. I recognize Atlantis, Eden, and Earth. The one we just passed through goes to my world."

Dax frowned. "That's it? You've just closed the portal so they can't get in?"

Alton smiled and sheathed his sword. There was enough light from the remaining portals to see without the glow from the crystal blade. "That one is closed and sealed. I imagine there are others. The mountain is a huge vortex, and this is but one small cavern. Most likely some of the demons are capable of creating more gateways to Abyss, though it will take them time. The trick now is to find and kill all of the demons who have crossed over. Taron has evidence of a massive influx over the past few days. I'm afraid we have our work cut out for us."

"Great. Just what I wanted to hear." Eddy tightened her hold on Bumper's leash. "We need to hurry. I want to see what's going on in town. I'm worried about Dad." She reached into her pack and pulled out a small contraption, flipped a lid, and gazed at a blank screen. "No signal here. What was I thinking?"

Laughing, she grabbed Dax's hand and grinned at Alton. "Okay, Lemurian. We need to get out of this mountain. Then I'll call my father and have him come pick us up."

Unused as he was to taking orders from a woman, Alton realized he was already headed toward the portal that would lead them outside. He must think about that. She definitely carried the aura of command about her. He held his hands up and felt for the shift in dimensions, the point where they could safely pass through.

He'd hate to end up somewhere besides their destination, but it had been known to happen. "This way," he said. He took Eddy's hand and stepped into the darkness. He sensed the others following close behind and wondered if Eddy held as tightly to Dax as she did to his hand. Seconds later they stepped out into the starlit sky just below the snow line on the scree-strewn flank of Mount Shasta.

Alton turned Eddy's small hand loose and gazed up at the mountain's peak, glistening with snow in the first glimmer of early dawn. He felt a huge lump in his throat and realized he was near tears. He'd not felt such a wealth of emotion even on the night he'd slipped outside and walked across rain-washed ground. Stars still filled the night sky to the west, chased by the imminent rise of the sun. The eastern horizon shimmered with the advent of dawn.

Time in this dimension must be linked to that of Lemuria. He'd have to ask Taron what he knew. His friend was the one who always had the answers.

Taron. Already he missed him. His humor, his wise countenance, his ability to find laughter wherever he went. He wished Taron were here with him now, sharing this beautiful morning—a morning like none he'd experienced since he was but a child. Other than a few clandestine visits outside of Lemuria, neither of them had left their underground world. The risk of discovery had kept them as prisoners within their own dimension.

He'd forgotten how much he missed the smells of clean earth and rocks still carrying the heat of yesterday's sun, of growing grass and melting snow. The cool sweep of fresh, clean air blowing over his skin almost made him forget why he was here.

The decision he'd made, one that would forever change his life. He'd chosen to throw his lot in with absolute strangers. Their story was more outlandish than anything he'd heard before, but it was one he couldn't help but believe.

His choice had not been made lightly, though he knew there would be times in the coming days when he might regret it.

Probably would regret it.

But he knew, without any doubt at all, he'd rather regret leaving the life of ease he'd lived for so long, than know he'd done nothing to preserve the world that had given him so much. He thought of his sword, still nameless, strapped across his back. Maybe now he would prove his worth to the sentience within the crystal blade. Maybe it would finally speak to him.

He glanced up at the sound of Eddy's soft voice.

"Thanks, Dad. We're fine. We'll meet you there in about an hour or so. I'm okay, and I'm really sorry we had to wake you so early. Okay. I love you, too . . . and Dad? I've got a great surprise for you. G'bye."

Alton stared at the woman as she folded up the thing she'd called a phone and stuck it back in her pack. A communication device. It struck him as odd that of this entire band, only the will-o'-the-wisp actually used telepathy. He'd had no idea humans were so primitive, though that thing Dax did with his hands was pretty impressive.

Of course, that was all tied to Dax's demon powers and

the odd tattoo he claimed was now cursed—a curse Eddy somehow seemed able to control. Such a beautiful woman, yet so fierce. She didn't look like a fighter with her big, brown eyes and wispy dark hair. She had the look of a sprite about her, much like their companion, Willow.

A warrior woman of Earth, a tiny will-o'-the-wisp from Eden, and a demon with a borrowed human body, united against a demon invasion. How in all the hells did the pieces fit together?

Alton sensed that Eddy watched him watch her. Unwilling to voice his real concerns, he asked, "Who were you talking to?"

"My father." She smiled and nodded toward the valley. "It's a long hike to town. He's driving up the mountain to get us. We'll meet him at the end of the road in about an hour."

She touched his forearm and smiled up at him. "I can't wait for my father to meet you, Alton. He's going to be absolutely beside himself."

With that confusing statement, she hoisted her pack and slung it over her shoulder. Dax grabbed the dog's leash, and the will-o'-the-wisp, much to Alton's surprise, elected to perch on his shoulder.

The sun was barely peeking over the mountains when they started down the mountainside. Thoughtfully, with his eyes wide open, Alton walked away from all he'd ever known.

Dax sat in the same chair he'd been in just yesterday morning, only this time the Lemurian Alton sat across the table from him while Eddy's father cooked breakfast—and he was all too aware that another day of the seven allotted to him had passed.

Gone, as if they'd never been. Dax rubbed his hand over

his chest in a vain attempt to ease the constant pain pulsing through his tattoo. The demon's curse grew stronger by the hour, the pain more intense, while his ability to draw on his demon powers seemed to fade with each passing moment.

Would the demons win, after all? Two days down, and so far all they'd managed to do was close one portal, while he knew at least one of the demons must have the ability to create more. How else would that gateway between Earth and Abyss have opened?

At least they'd gained another soldier in Alton, but would he be enough? According to Ed, the demons were everywhere. He'd heard reports of odd happenings in town, and he'd destroyed two ceramic garden figurines just last night when he caught them walking across his back lawn.

He'd destroyed the figurines, but without a weapon that would actually kill a demon, he'd allowed the stinking mist to escape. That meant those demons had probably gone on to animate yet another set of avatars.

"Dax?" Ed stopped midway between the refrigerator and the stove. "As serious as the situation appears, have you thought of contacting the authorities? Could the police or military help? They've got some pretty big weapons."

Dax shuddered at the mere thought of the government getting involved. "That's the worst thing that could happen, Ed. Demons thrive on chaos. They gain strength from death and destruction. The minute the military steps in, you've got all three of those things."

Alton agreed. "Military means soldiers with guns, which have no effect on demons. Flamethrowers, maybe, but can you imagine the panic? The loss of innocent lives? It would give the demons who've already crossed over a huge reservoir of power."

"We need to keep this as quiet as we can," Dax said. He

rubbed his hand across his chest. The pain was constant now. He sensed the tattoo taking on a life of its own.

"It's not going to be easy." Ed poured eggs into the frying pan as he spoke. "I'm hearing reports from all over town of strange occurrences that have to be demonic, but no one seems to have connected the dots. In fact, Eddy, Harlan called, wondering when you were going to get a story to him about all the weird goings-on. He didn't sound very happy."

"That's probably an understatement, knowing Harlan." Eddy drummed her fingers on the table. "I'm going to have to come up with some kind of excuse for not working. There's just no way I can show up at the paper until this is settled."

"So how do we keep things quiet?" Dax threw the question out, not really expecting an answer.

Alton leaned back in his chair. "I can help."

Dax turned and stared at the Lemurian. "How?"

"Hypnosis. Mass compulsion. Lemurians are fairly adept. How do you think we've kept our presence hidden for so long?"

Ed laughed. "You haven't hidden it entirely. I knew you existed."

Alton nodded. "Agreed, but everyone, including your daughter, thought you were nuts." He laughed along with Ed. "I can discourage memories through compulsion, though I can't entirely erase them. I can target one person or the entire community, but I can only do it a few times before the subjects begin to build up an immunity."

"Then we save it for when we really need it." Dax took a sip of his coffee. He stared at the dark brew in the thick mug. He was really going to miss coffee when . . .

Eddy interrupted his musings. "The last thing we need is Channel Three news showing up with their remote broadcast truck and beaming our demon invasion into every living room in the country." She shook her head and stared at her father.

Then she grinned and looked directly at Dax. "Is it just me, or does it feel really weird that we're back here in Dad's kitchen getting ready for breakfast? It makes the past two days feel sort of dreamlike." She paused to pour herself another cup of coffee. "Except, of course, we didn't have Alton before."

She flashed a bright smile at the Lemurian. Dax felt an entirely new kind of pain that had nothing to do with the demon's curse. Then Eddy walked back to the table and brushed her hand lightly over Dax's shoulder as she passed by him. He raised his head and caught the bright promise in her eyes.

A promise for him, not Alton. Suddenly Dax had a name for the pain he'd felt. *Jealousy.* Nothing more than jealousy, and there was no time for that. Not now, when time was so short and every second counted. When every fighter counted.

Ed carried two huge platters to the table and set them down. "Dig in, guys." He grinned at Alton and then at Dax "I still can't believe I'm sitting down to breakfast with you two."

Willow buzzed by and flittered in front of his nose. Ed laughed. "Excuse me, I didn't meant to exclude you, Willow."

Eddy took a seat, but she glanced at her father. "I'm waiting for you to say, 'I told you so.'"

Ed just shook his head. "No need. Having Dax, Alton, and Willow at our table gives me all the satisfaction I need."

Their conversation made no sense. Food, however, made perfect sense. Dax turned to the heavily laden table. Steam rose from piles of bacon and a mound of scrambled eggs. Fried potatoes, sliced strawberries, bananas, oranges, and a plate of toast—and all of it smelled wonderful. He grabbed a strip of bacon. Eddy began loading up her plate.

Alton merely stared at the bounty. "Amazing. We have similar foods in Lemuria, but they're all manufactured. Created to be wholesome and appetizing for us. I can't recall ever seeing, much less eating, the actual foods themselves."

Dax grinned at him through a mouthful of bacon. "I've never had food like this in my life. It doesn't try to bite back."

"Euuwwww . . ." Eddy made a face at him. "Not an image I want while stuffing eggs in my mouth. Killer chickens? Yuck."

Dax scooped some of everything on his plate while Alton did the same. "Not chickens, no, but demons come in all shapes and sizes on Abyss. Here they might be nothing more than stinking clouds of black mist, but on Abyss they're often multi-limbed, some with wings, others with bodies covered in scales like razors, some with claws almost as long as Alton's sword."

"What about you, Dax? What's your demon body like?" Ed paused with a forkful of potatoes in front of his mouth. "I can't picture you as anyone other than what you are."

Dax slathered honey on a piece of toast and practically moaned when the sweet, gooey stuff hit his taste buds. He swallowed and tapped his chest, ignoring the pain. "I looked a lot like my tattoo. Brightly colored scales and long, sharp fangs, except the art's more snakelike than I was. I had four multi-jointed arms." He wiggled his fingers. "I have a feeling I'm gonna miss those extra arms in battle. I had claws on all the joints as well as on my hands. I only had two legs but . . ."

He raised his head, suddenly aware of the silence at the table. Eddy stared at him with a look of absolute horror on her face. Ed and Alton didn't look at him at all.

They watched Eddy.

Dax felt as if someone had punched him in the gut. He set his fork down and carefully wiped his mouth with the napkin. All very civilized. *Human.* He thought of delaying even longer, of taking a swallow of his coffee, but it wouldn't change a thing.

He reached across the table for Eddy's hand. She quickly slipped it into her lap. Her rejection made him feel physically ill. "Eddy? What did you think I looked like? I've never lied to you. From the beginning I said I was a demon with scales and claws. Sharp teeth . . . the whole bit."

"I know." Her voice was so quiet he barely heard her. "It's nothing." She waved her hand, as if shooing all of them away. Maybe she was trying to erase the graphic visual he'd just given her. "Eat your breakfast. Please. Don't mind me."

Alton nodded and took another forkful of eggs. Ed munched slowly on a piece of bacon. Dax stared at his plate and realized his appetite was gone.

He might look like a human. He was even beginning to think like one, but as far as Eddy was concerned, he was still a demon. Still the creature of her nightmares.

Carefully, he folded his napkin and excused himself from the table.

Chapter Six

Eddy watched Dax as he carefully folded his napkin and set it on the table. She should have said something, anything, as he stood and quietly left the room, but she didn't. She couldn't. She wanted to slap herself, but she'd completely forgotten he wasn't human.

She'd been so busy fighting her attraction to a man she hardly knew, she'd not even considered who or what he really was.

So what . . . like it matters?

He'd put his life on the line, just as Alton had. Just as Willow or her dad had.

The same as me.

They were all on the same team. Her reaction had been totally inexcusable. No matter what he once was or who he was now, she'd been rude and dead wrong to act like there was anything at all awry with him. She owed him an apology, whether he'd accept it or not.

"Excuse me." Mortified, Eddy kept her head down as she left the table, unwilling to meet either her father's eyes or Alton's.

Dax had quietly slipped out the back door.

Eddy followed him. She found him, finally, out in her dad's workshop staring at the train layout with the scale model of Mount Shasta in the middle.

"Dax? I'm sorry. I . . ." She paused in midstep as he turned around and smiled sadly at her.

"It's okay, Eddy. I forget, too." He looked down at his long, lean body, comfortably dressed in worn Levi's, boots, and a plaid flannel shirt. Then he raised his head. His gaze was direct, without shame or subterfuge. He was what he was.

"I've already grown so used to this body, I don't think of myself as a demon. Not anymore."

He hissed out a sharp breath and flattened his hand to his chest. Eddy bridged the gap between them.

"The tat?"

He nodded. She quickly reached for the top button on his shirt, but he covered her hand with his and gazed directly into her eyes. "Maybe it's better if I just deal with it."

No need to slap herself. Dax could do it for her. She lowered her head and stared at her toes. "Maybe it's not. I can help you. The pain exhausts you, and we need you healthy."

She felt his chest rise and fall with his sigh, but he moved his hand away from hers. She unbuttoned his shirt, this time opening it all the way to the waistband of his jeans.

The tattoo looked angry and inflamed, writhing over his muscular abdomen and crawling up his powerful chest in a slow, rhythmic pulse. The burn appeared to be healing, but the tattoo was a thing alive. She could have sworn the beady eyes on the snake watched her.

Every time she saw it, the tattoo seemed more alive, more aware, almost as if it gained life with the passage of time. She covered its head with her palm. Used her other hand to cover the scaled belly on the tattoo. It pulsed and writhed beneath her fingers. She shuddered and concentrated on not jerking her hands away from the damned thing.

Closing her eyes, she projected good, healing thoughts, on taking the pain from Dax and sending it away . . . far, far away where it couldn't hurt him. She had no idea what she did, or if it really worked, but if Dax thought her touch helped ease the pain, she was willing to do anything for him.

Demon or not.

The heat from the tattoo surged beneath her palms, burning her skin until she shivered with the intense pain. Even so, she kept her hands pressed close against it and thought of Dax without pain. Imagined the curse healed and his powers intact.

She didn't have a clue what she was doing. Absorbing his pain, somehow? She had no idea. She felt like a fraud, but after a couple of very long minutes, Dax's skin grew cooler and the sense of movement beneath her hand stopped. All she felt now was naturally warm skin and the slow, steady beat of his heart.

She didn't want to take her hands away. At some point, Dax's arms had slipped around her waist. Now he rested his chin on the top of her head, and his hands gently rubbed her lower back. Held in his comforting embrace, she could so easily forget what he was and why he was here.

And how soon he would be gone.

Held close, comforted by his strength and the goodness in him she couldn't deny, all Eddy could think of was the way his body felt this close to hers, and how he'd held her against him and comforted her last night when she'd been so frustrated—and more than a little afraid.

He might have been a demon at one time, but she sensed nothing evil about Dax now. Without even considering the consequences, Eddy leaned closer and pressed her lips to his chest, right over the cursed tattoo.

She felt Dax's sigh and slipped even closer as he tightened his arms around her. She turned her face and rested her cheek against the muscular curve of his pectoral muscles where the snake's fearsome mouth gaped wide, fully aware of the creature's scales and fangs, of its brilliant colors and deadly threat.

Of the fact it appeared to have a life of its own, a sentience separate from Dax.

Dax said it carried his demon powers, easily accessible so that he could use them while in human form, but since the demon's curse, it was fighting every minute of every day to turn those same powers against him.

Except that somehow, for whatever reason, Eddy seemed to exert her own power over the curse. She couldn't deny what she'd just experienced, no matter how impossible it seemed. Her touch soothed the snake and contained the demon powers. She only hoped it was enough.

It had to be. Worlds depended on Dax. And, for what it was worth, Dax depended on her.

Dax rested his cheek against the top of Eddy's head and held her close. His heart actually ached more than the damned tattoo when he held her like this. His throat seemed to swell with all the things he wanted to say, words he hardly understood. All these feelings pouring through him were so unexpected, so hard to deal with.

He hadn't expected anything like Eddy when he took the Edenites' offer. He'd expected nothing but one bloody fight after another, and maybe, just maybe, a shot at Paradise. No one had said anything about the humans he might meet.

About Eddy Marks.

It was all about the demons and the battle he must not, could not, lose. Was that why he'd found Eddy? Had she been put in his path on purpose? If so, he knew exactly why, and damn, but it was so unfair.

She was the one he was fighting for. Not for a chance at Paradise, or to prove himself as a warrior. It wasn't for Alton or Ed or even Taron and the promise Dax had made to him. Not even to save the world.

It was all for Eddy. Everything. He knew that now. If he lost the battle, he would be condemning Eddy Marks to death, or a life under demon rule even worse than death.

He felt the tattoo move across his flesh. Felt the power in it surge across his upper thigh, over his groin, and up his belly to the point above his heart, power running through his veins like liquid fire. Not the demon's curse. Not this time. Now it was the strength of Dax's own convictions bringing the thing to life, overpowering the curse, at least for now.

He lifted his head and cupped Eddy's face in his palms. She gazed up at him, her dark brown eyes brimming with tears, her lips slightly parted. Dax felt drawn to her mouth, felt the purity of her love, a love he doubted even Eddy understood.

He knew he'd never figure it out, but he would protect it. Protect her. He lowered his face and captured her lips with his. She whimpered, making a low cry deep in her throat. Her arms slipped around his waist; her hips thrust forward until she and he connected in a solid line of heat and life and hope.

Dax kissed her, well aware he made yet another promise. The most important promise of all. "Once a demon, but a demon no more," he whispered between the small, quick kisses he left on her lips, her chin, the line of her jaw. "For all the days left to me, I will keep you safe, and when I am gone, I swear I will still watch over you."

She raised her head, smiled at him, and touched her fingertips to the side of his mouth. "I refuse to talk about you leaving. We have work to do." She leaned away so she could reach his shirt, and slowly, one by one, closed the buttons over his belly and chest. "Way too much to do to spend time out here like this. No matter how much I want to."

He took a deep breath and forced his fears back inside where they belonged. "You're right." He took her hand and turned toward the house. "That doesn't mean I have to like it."

She laughed and leaned against him, hugging her arms around his biceps. "Let's see if they left us some breakfast."

They stepped out of Ed's workshop and started back toward the house. A harsh scream ripped through the mid-morning quiet. Bumper barked. Ed and Alton raced through the front door. Ed called out, "Dax! Eddy! Across the street!"

Eddy and Dax ran through the yard toward the sound of yet another horrifying scream.

Under other circumstances, Eddy thought, this might have been humorous, but it wasn't funny at all. Not even considering that Mr. Puccini had been the grumpiest neighbor on the block for as long as she could remember, and he probably deserved a good scare. When she was little, she used to wish even worse things would happen to him, but not this, not now.

Backed up against the corner post on the front porch of his little Craftsman-style house, the old man was wide-eyed and trembling and obviously terrified. He clasped one hand over his heart and clutched the porch railing with the other. Blood dripped from a small gash on his left hand.

A ceramic turkey with a razor-sharp beak full of even sharper teeth advanced in an awkward, uncoordinated gait. Blood spotted its beak, and a few small spatters marked the porch. The air reeked of sulfur.

It was enough to make Eddy's blood run cold.

Especially since it was at least ten o'clock in the morning and the sun was high in the sky. She grabbed Dax's wrist as the four of them circled the animated creature. "You said demons lost their power in daylight."

He shot her a frustrated glance. "They do. Usually."

"What is that thing? Get it away from me!" Mr. Puccini's voice quavered. His breath shot out in short gasps.

"We will, Dom. It'll be okay." Ed moved around to stand beside his neighbor. The ceramic turkey let out a squawk that was somewhere between a gobble and the strangled cry of a banshee. It slowly pivoted its head from its primary target to stare at Ed, and then on around in a full circle to take in Alton, Eddy, and Dax.

When it saw Dax, it screeched again. The body spun to match the direction the beak was pointing, until the entire creature faced him. Ed grabbed his elderly neighbor by the arm, tugged him past the brightly painted turkey and down the steps.

"Move him out of harm's way, Ed. Around the side of the house." Dax's voice was calm, his demeanor that of a man in charge.

Eddy glanced at him and realized he didn't want their neighbor to see what he was about to do. "C'mon, Dad. Let's get out of Dax's way." She slipped around behind Dax and helped her father walk their dazed neighbor around the corner of his house.

Alton stayed beside Dax. His crystal sword glowed through the scabbard across his back. His white robe flowed about his ankles.

Eddy and her dad got Mr. Puccini to the side yard, where there was a small garden bench. As she helped him sit, Eddy heard a loud whoosh and a prolonged sizzle. A banshee screech with a strange stereo effect cut off in mid howl. The stink of sulfur dissipated within seconds.

Mr. Puccini stared at Ed and then turned to Eddy. "What in God's name . . . ?" He shook his head, wide-eyed and still confused.

Dax touched Eddy's shoulder. "They're gone," he said. "Here. I think Alton can help."

Alton squatted down so that he was at eye level with their elderly neighbor. "Are you okay?"

"Who the hell are you?" Dom Puccini gaped at Alton and then glared at Ed. "What kind of crazies you got hanging out at your place, Ed?"

"Friends of Eddy's, Dom. They're good kids."

Eddy leaned close to Dax. "I guess he's feeling better."

Alton slowly passed his palm in front of Mr. Puccini's eyes. The man shut his mouth, and his head turned to follow the movement of Alton's long fingers.

Alton moved his hand away, and Mr. Puccini blinked. "What'd you say your name was, young man?"

Ed quickly interrupted. "They're my daughter's old college friends, Dom. I want you to meet Al and Dax. Boys, this is Mr. Puccini. He's been our neighbor since Eddy was just a tiny thing."

The old man shook his head. "What happened? I can't remember what happened." He tried to stand. Alton held out a hand and gently helped him to his feet.

Mr. Puccini's gaze went up, and up higher, as Alton stood. He shook his head again, still obviously disoriented. His white hair stood up in tangles and tufts about his florid face.

Dax took Mr. Puccini's other arm, and he and Alton slowly walked him back to the front porch. Dax looked over the man's head at Eddy and shrugged.

She smiled and waved her hand toward the shattered pile of what was left of the ceramic turkey. "I think you must have tripped over old Tom, Mr. Puccini. We heard you yell. . . ."

"And there was a loud crash," Dax added.

"You might have bumped your head. Looks like you cut your hand on one of the shards." Ed helped Mr. Puccini sit on the porch steps. "Eddy? Can you get a broom and maybe find a bandage?"

"Right away, Dad." She grabbed Dax's hand and dragged him inside the house. Alton followed close behind. "Check the place," she whispered. "See if there're more demons around."

Willow poked her head up out of Dax's pocket and took off on a quick search of her own. Dax followed her. Eddy wet a clean washcloth and found a box of bandages. Alton grabbed the broom, dustpan, and a small wastebasket after she pointed out the broom closet, and followed Eddy back to the porch.

Dax and Willow were right behind them. "It's all clear," Dax said. Willow poked her head out of his pocket. He carefully shoved her back down. "Stay put."

Frantic barking echoed from across the street. Eddy glanced toward her dad's house. "I don't think Bumper likes being left behind," she said, kneeling in front of Mr. Puccini. Carefully she wiped the blood off the long scratch on the back of his hand and covered it with a clean bandage. "You might want to get that checked, Mr. Puccini. Give your doctor a call."

Still looking dazed, he nodded his head. "Good idea. I can't believe I don't remember what happened."

Alton cleaned up the remnants of the shattered turkey while Dax held the wastebasket. He dumped the broken shards of ceramic and handed the broom and dustpan to Ed.

Eddy stood up and patted the old man's shoulder. "We're going to head back home and let Bumper out, Mr. Puccini. I'm glad you're okay."

"Thank you, Eddy. You're a good girl." He stared at the broken shards of ceramic Alton had dumped into the wastebasket and shuddered. "Evil thing. Absolutely evil." He looked at Ed, and frowned. "I never thought of Muriel's ceramic turkey as evil before. Now why . . . ?"

"Falls can be dangerous, Dom. Eddy's right. You better have your doctor take a look. If you need a ride over to the clinic, I'll be glad to take you." Ed glanced at Eddy.

"We're going home now, Dad." She grabbed Dax's hand, and Alton followed them across the street. As soon as they were out of hearing, she let out a deep breath. "Okay, what now? And Alton, thank you. That hypnosis thing really is a cool trick. I was wondering how we were going to explain Muriel's turkey turning killer."

Alton nodded. "You realize this is only the beginning. Those demons were merely a fraction of the many that must be infesting this area."

"Those demons? There was more than one?" Eddy paused with her hand on the front door.

"There were two controlling the ceramic bird. Possibly the ones your dad saw last night. He merely broke their avatars, but he didn't kill them. There were two demons, working together in broad daylight." Dax's glance shifted from Eddy to Alton. Back to Eddy. "Not only are they going against their nature by being out in daylight, they appear to be learning to cooperate. When they do, they're obviously stronger."

"What if they're spreading out? Going past Evergreen? They could be in the town of Mount Shasta or McCloud or up in Edgewood, or . . ." Eddy opened the door. Bumper launched herself through the doorway, wiggling and whining as if she'd been abandoned for days, not minutes.

Ignoring the dog, Eddy gazed at both men. "What are we going to do if they're in other towns, if they move to the bigger cities? We're not that far from Redding or Sacramento."

Dax shook his head. "I don't think they'll travel far from

the mountain. At least not yet. It's their link to Abyss. They don't belong in this dimension, so they have no corporeal form without an avatar. They can't remain mist for long without getting sucked back to Abyss. I imagine they're finding avatars as soon as they reach town."

Eddy rubbed her hands over her arms, as if she'd felt a sudden chill. The sun was high in the sky, and the day was warm, but she shivered anyway. "What's to keep them here?"

Dax flashed her a lopsided grin. "Ceramic creatures can't travel far. The only one I've seen with much mobility is the gargoyle, since it's a creature that can fly." He paused a moment. "That one confuses me. Flying a stone creature would take a lot of power. It took two demons to animate the turkey. More to make the bronze horse and soldier come to life. How does the gargoyle find enough power to travel through the air, to strike me with a curse? I want another look at that one."

"Now?" Alton asked.

Dax nodded. "Now would be a good time, during daylight." He studied Alton for a moment. "However, Ed's clothes won't fit you, and there's no way you can go out like that."

Alton held his arms out. "What? You don't like the robe?" Then he laughed. "I'll stay with Ed. Unlike you two, he thinks I'm wonderful." He shook his head and sighed. "Do you realize that's the first time the heir apparent to the Ruling Council of Nine has ever used a broom and swept trash?" Eddy punched his arm, and he laughed. "I'll stay with Ed. See if we can come up with a plan. You and Dax find me something to wear. I have a feeling tonight's going to be busy."

* * *

Eddy measured Alton for sizes, fastened the leash to Bumper, and led Dax out the door. "We can walk. It's just a couple of blocks to downtown. I want to hear what people are saying."

Dax took her hand as they walked along the sidewalk. The moment his fingers wrapped around hers, she turned her head and caught him watching her. "What?"

He shrugged and glanced away. "I have fewer than five days left with you. I don't want to waste them. I really like the way your hand feels in mine." He slanted her a quick glance and then looked straight ahead.

She had to moisten her lips to speak. "I don't want to waste any time, either." The thought of Dax leaving sat like a lead weight in her chest. Stupid, really, to fall for a guy who'd be gone forever by the end of the week. Absolutely stupid.

They walked in silence, but Eddy felt as if every nerve in her body were located in the palm of her hand, the sensitive tips of her fingers. As tall as she was, she'd always felt awkward and oversized walking hand in hand with a guy, but Dax was so much taller, so much broader, she felt feminine beside him, even in her jeans and hiking boots.

The sun was warm on her shoulders. The scent of pine and cedar tickled her nostrils. Birds chattering in the gardens they passed and the constant jingle of Bumper's leash and collar played a symphony punctuated by their footsteps and the distant rush of traffic passing by on the interstate.

They reached the main street in town, Lassen Boulevard. Once the old highway, it was now a busy thoroughfare lined with small stores selling everything from crystals with dubious magical properties to hardware and baked goods. They passed a tiny café tucked in between two other shops. The smells wafting through the open door stopped both Eddy and Dax.

"We didn't eat much breakfast," she said, leaning toward the doorway.

"I agree."

"C'mon, girl." Eddy tied Bumper's leash to a bike rack in front of the store. The dog stretched out in a sunbeam and groaned blissfully.

Eddy rubbed her belly. "I think she'll be okay here."

Dax patted Bumper's head and got a couple of thumps of her tail in response. Then he took Eddy's hand and hauled her through the door. The place was almost empty, so they grabbed a booth near the front window, where they could keep an eye on the dog. Dax stared at the walls, at pictures of huge logs lashed to railroad cars and men of another age standing atop tree stumps with crosscut saws longer than they were tall. He was obviously fascinated by all the old photos of the surrounding area, as much as by the concept of food.

The waitress poured coffee for both of them and left menus. Eddy glanced down at hers. "It's almost lunch. How about a hamburger?"

Dax frowned. "I don't know what a . . ."

"I'll order. You'll love it."

Dax nodded and went back to studying the photos. Eddy studied Dax. Everything was new to him. Walking down a small-town street, sitting in a café, the taste of coffee. Hamburgers and fries, sunshine overhead, and the sound of birds.

What was that like, to be faced with something new every time you went anywhere, saw anything? Touched anyone?

She thought of the warmth of his hand in hers, the sound of his beating heart when they'd slept so close together, and realized that everything about Dax was just as new to her. His touch, his bravery, his quirky sense of humor. How much of it was the demon, and how much the man who'd once inhabited the perfect body that now belonged to Dax?

No . . . it doesn't belong. It's on loan . . . a short-term loan. She couldn't let herself think of that. Five more days. Just her luck. Finally meet a guy who fit every need she'd ever had, including a few she hadn't known about, and he turns out to have the life span of a moth.

The waitress set their plates in front of them. Grabbed a bottle of catsup off the next table and stuck it in front of Dax. Eddy noticed the woman gave him a thorough once-over before she spun around and headed back to the kitchen.

Dax stared at his plate. "What are these?" He picked up a crisp French fry.

"Ambrosia. Here." Eddy dumped a blob of catsup on his plate, swirled a fry through the sauce, and held it up to his mouth. Dax smiled and parted those perfect lips, and she placed the fry on his tongue.

He closed his mouth, chewed for a moment, and closed his eyes with a look of pure bliss. "I had no idea . . ." He picked up another fry, dipped it, and popped it in his mouth. "Absolutely no idea."

Grinning, Eddy took a bite of her burger. They ate in silence, but she couldn't help but wonder if they'd have a chance like this again. It felt like a date . . . a perfectly normal date with a really good-looking, but perfectly normal, guy.

She watched him eat, noticed how he concentrated on each bite, chewing with his eyes closed, savoring the flavors. What would it be like to have that attention paid to her, to have that concentration, that focus from a man like Dax?

She shifted in the vinyl booth. Tried to ignore the hot clench of feminine muscles, the deep sense of yearning that built between her legs and seemed to settle in her womb. Damn, she was asking for trouble.

Like you haven't already got it? She wasn't sure if the stupid voice in her head was going to make her laugh or cry first. She forced her attention away from the man sitting across the table, away from the need pulsing through her body, and thought about the job they had to do.

Dax finished his burger and fries and was swirling one of Eddy's fries through a puddle of catsup left on her plate when the door to the restaurant burst open. He spun around, prepared to fight, as a tall, slim woman with skin the color of dark caramel barged through the door.

"Eddy Marks! Where the hell have you been?"

"Ginny! Hi." Eddy waved the woman over. "You're wearing your uniform. When did you start working day shift?"

"When all hell broke loose, that's when." Ginny grinned at Dax and stuck out her hand. "Hi! I'm Ginny Jones, Eddy's only friend in the world. Who're you?"

Eddy laughed and winked at Dax. "This is Dax. He's my other friend."

Other friend? Dax glanced at Ginny, then at Eddy, and back at Ginny. "Hello, Ginny." He shook her hand and frowned at Eddy. "What about Alton? Willow and Bumper? Aren't they your friends, too?"

Eddy shot him a big grin. "I'm teasing. Just teasing." She scooted over, and Ginny plopped down next to her on the bench seat. "What do you mean, all hell broke loose?"

"Your house for one thing. It's trashed. Don't lie to me, sweetie. I've seen it, and I've been worried sick since I heard about it. I called Ed, and your dad just said it was vandals. What happened?" Ginny grabbed one of Eddy's fries and popped it in her mouth.

"Vandals, just like Dad said. I'm staying at his place until we get it fixed. What else is going on?" She shoved her plate, still half covered with those absolutely delicious fries Dax had been munching on, in front of Ginny.

Ginny managed to eat French fries and still talk a mile a minute. "Remember what I told you about Mrs. Abernathy's cat? That she said Mr. Pollard's garden gnome ate Twinkles?" Ginny shook her head. "We've had at least a dozen reports like that. Cats, dogs, even a gerbil, all disappearing, and people calling in to blame it on garden gnomes and statues and all kinds of shit. It's like everyone in town is doing drugs."

Eddy shot a serious look in Dax's direction. "Ginny's a nine-one-one dispatcher, so she hears all the emergency calls."

He nodded, not entirely certain what 911 was, but if people were making reports, it wouldn't be long before someone started putting all the stories together.

Ginny plopped another French fry in her mouth. "I heard they found the missing statue in your front room, all in pieces."

Eddy nodded. "They did. The place was trashed when I got home the other night after we had coffee. A neighbor must have called it in. I just went straight to Dad's—I was afraid they might still be around."

"What about that dog you said you got? How come it didn't protect your place?"

"She hid in the bedroom. I think they scared her." Eddy glanced out the window, and Dax knew she was probably sending a silent apology to Bumper. So many lies they were telling . . . he hoped they could keep the stories straight.

Eddy pointed to Bumper. "That's my brave watchdog right there."

Laughing, Ginny nodded. "Ah . . . the one I tripped over. That is one silly-looking mutt. Reminds me of pit bull in a Marilyn Monroe wig."

"Really? I think it's more the Shirley Temple look." Eddy

waved at Bumper. The dog wagged her tail and lay back against the sun-warmed sidewalk.

"No matter." Ginny's dark eyes narrowed. "Eddy, you know what I told you about picking up strays . . ." She turned a focused eye on Dax. "Where'd you guys meet? I don't remember hearing about you before, Dax."

"I ran into Dax on my weekend hike." Eddy sent him a quick smile. He smiled back as if all the lies made perfect sense. "We actually knew each other in college, but we haven't seen each other in years. He surprised me when he looked me up at Dad's yesterday. I didn't expect to see him again so soon."

Dax reached across the table and took her hand in his. "How could you expect any man who met you not to want to see you again as soon as he could manage?"

Ginny's eyes went wide. "Oh. Wow . . . uhm, is it warm in here?" She laughed. "Anyway, like I was saying, stuff's really gone crazy around here, and I didn't know where you were. I thought you might be working—you know, covering all the stories—but there hasn't been a thing in the paper."

Eddy slammed her hand over her mouth. "Oh, crap. I forgot to call Harlan! Ginny, we need to leave. I haven't even checked in at the paper since I got back. I had Dad call, but it's been one thing after another and . . ." She grabbed her wallet out of her pocket, left money on the table for their lunch, and bumped Ginny with her hip.

Ginny scooted out of her way, but not before she grabbed the last of the fries. "I can tell you've got other things on your mind." She turned and looked directly at Dax, but he wasn't sure what she was thinking. "Call me, or I will never speak to you again."

Eddy grabbed Dax's hand. "I promise, sweetie. Honest. Or you can catch me at Dad's, okay? See you later."

"Nice to meet you, Gin—"

Eddy pulled Dax out of the café before he could finish his sentence. "C'mon. The newspaper office is just a couple of blocks away." She untied Bumper, and then they headed north along the main street.

"Eddy, look." Dax pointed to shattered pottery in front of a small gift shop.

There were more piles of dust and pottery shards along the way. Remnants of broken figurines.

"Those were stone squirrels," Eddy said, pointing to the front of one store. "Those were ceramic birds. I think they used to hang on chains in front of a store across the street." She took a deep breath and stared at Dax.

"I smell it too," he said, studying the carnage. The stink of sulfur was faint, but still lingered. "It almost appears as if the avatars fought one another, which wouldn't be unusual for demonkind." He shook his head.

"Where are they now?" Eddy clung tightly to his hand.

"They've found new avatars or returned to Abyss. I know of no one here with the ability to actually send them into the void."

"No one but you. What about Alton?"

"Alton carries the crystal sword," Dax said. "It's supposed to kill demonkind, but only Alton can wield it. If another tries to hold it, they risk almost certain death."

"I'll remember that," Eddy said. "How come he didn't use it at Mr. Puccini's house? You killed the demons there, didn't you?"

"I did." Dax paused and looked steadily into Eddy's eyes. "Just as Alton senses demon about me, so will his sword. He can't use it near me, or the sword will try and kill me. He told me a Lemurian's sword is sentient. It can speak. His has not, but it has the potential. Until then, there's no way for Alton to tell it that I'm not the enemy."

"Then how can you fight demons together?"

"Very carefully, Eddy. Very, very carefully."

"Clean out your desk, Marks. You're fired."

Dax clutched Eddy's hand tightly in his and fought a powerful desire to punch the overbearing slob who was Eddy's boss right in his beefy red nose. Eddy didn't say a word. She merely nodded and turned away from the man.

Dax let go of her hand and took Bumper's leash, while Eddy silently walked into a small cubicle near the front door. Her boss stared at Dax, doing his best to intimidate him. The tattoo pulsed in white-hot pain across his torso. Dax figured if he could tolerate the pain of a demon's curse, there was nothing this idiot could do to hurt him.

Except when he hurt Eddy. Standing here, unable to come to Eddy's defense made his heart actually ache. There was nothing he wanted more than to wipe up the ground with this buffoon, but he'd promised Eddy.

This was a promise he'd happily break, if only he could.

Harlan, she'd said his name was. He owned the newspaper Eddy worked for, and he hadn't given her so much as a minute to explain why she needed time off this week.

Not that she could tell him what was going on, but he'd started cursing at her the minute she walked in the office. He was still cursing. Only now, Dax realized, the words were directed at him.

"Are you deaf?" The man planted his hands on top of his desk and leaned forward, as if he wanted to come after him.

Dax sort of wished he would. He felt a surge of anger pulsing through his chest. Demon anger.

"I said, what the fuck are you staring at?"

Dax took a deep breath and glanced at Eddy. She was filling a small box with items from her desk. There were tears on her cheeks. The anger inside Dax pulsed hot and heavy. He turned around and glared at Harlan again. "I was merely wondering if you were as stupid as you look. I guess you are."

He felt Willow stir within his pocket, reminding him there were more important things than dealing with Eddy's jerk of an ex-boss. Tamping down the sense of demon fury, Dax tuned out Harlan's cursing and turned his back on the man. "C'mon, sweetheart. Anything I can carry?"

She shook her head, a short, sharp jerk that told him how close to the edge she was. He knew she loved her job. He also knew he needed her more than this newspaper did. Evergreen needed her.

Dax opened the door and followed Eddy into the sunshine. She walked out with her back straight and her head held proudly, even though Dax knew she was hurting. He was so proud of her he wanted to cheer.

As soon as they were outside, he stopped and took the box out of her arms. Then he leaned close and kissed her, right there in front of the people on the street and the cars going by. Her lips were soft, wet from her tears, salty. He licked his tongue across her lower lip and then backed away. She gazed at him, looking bewildered and lost.

"I need you more than Harlan does," he said. He rested his forehead against hers. "The man's an ass. Are you okay?"

Eddy nodded. "I just never got fired before." She sniffed.

"You've never been recruited to save an entire town before either. It's been a pretty busy week."

She laughed, though it sounded more like a sob. "I'll try and remember that. It puts things in perspective."

Dax tucked Eddy's box under his arm, raised his head, looked up the street, and then down. "We need to buy clothes for Alton. Where?"

She sniffed and straightened her shoulders. Dax

recognized the moment when she found her control, put Harlan and his foul temper behind her, and looked forward. His own anger, demon anger, slipped away and disappeared.

"C'mon. The feed store is this way." She smiled at him, looped her arm through his elbow, and tugged him along with her. Bumper trotted beside them with her tail curled in a perfect blond arc over her back.

"Feed store? I thought we were shopping for pants."

Chapter Seven

Tuesday afternoon—day three

"Remind me never to try and explain a feed store to a demon." Eddy fixed herself a glass of ice water. Dax took it out of her hand before she got a single swallow.

He took a sip and glanced at Alton. "What would you assume one would buy at a feed store?"

Alton shrugged. "Feed?"

Eddy took her glass from Dax. He smiled and said, "I rest my case."

Eddy sighed. "Do the clothes fit, Alton?"

"Yes, they do." He held his arms wide, showing off the dark blue plaid flannel shirt with the sleeves rolled up to his elbows, the crisp new blue jeans Eddy'd been absolutely shocked to find with a size thirty-four waist and a forty-inch inseam, and the sturdy work boots and heavy socks that added at least an inch and a half to his already impressive height.

With his blond hair tied back and a Sacramento Kings cap on his head, Eddy thought he resembled a very tall, very lanky cowboy, which meant he shouldn't stand out all that much in her small town.

Except for the sword, which he wore strapped to his back. "Any way to disguise the sword?" She walked around behind him and stared at the crystal glimmer shining through the leather scabbard on his back.

"I can use a glamour to fade its presence, but I can't actually hide it. Not until we can communicate."

Eddy crossed her arms over her chest. "Dax mentioned that. Does your sword actually have a mind of its own?"

"It does." Alton reached over his shoulder and stroked the silver hilt. "I have to keep it sheathed because it really wants to kill Dax, and there's no way for me to explain, at least not yet, that he's one of the good guys. At some point, if it ever feels I'm worthy, it will give me its name, and we'll be able to converse."

"You're not worthy yet?" Eddy laughed when she asked him, but it wasn't all that hard to imagine the sword as more than a mere weapon. The blade was crystal, as clear as glass, but faceted like a diamond. The hilt looked like sterling silver, but there were jewels set into the pommel. Sapphires? It was much too beautiful to look all that functional, though the blade looked razor sharp. "How long have you had it?"

"Many thousands of years, but I've never drawn blood with it. Closing the portal to Abyss was the most I've ever asked of my sword, and it performed perfectly. However, it was obviously not all that impressed with me, or it would have spoken." He shook his head. "Though I've kept it close at all times, I've never had reason to show it my worth."

"That's just weird, that you have to prove yourself to your sword." Eddy planted her hands on her hips as she studied the thing. "How will you know?"

Alton shrugged. "It will speak to me."

"Hi there, this is your crystal sword talking? Like that?"

"Just like that." He smiled, and then he stretched his long arms overhead and yawned. "I'm going to need some sleep before we get into any serious demon hunting. I was up all night arguing your case before the Ruling Council of Nine. Even Lemurians need their rest, and I've not slept since yesterday."

"We all need rest." Dax folded his arms over his broad chest and leaned against the kitchen counter. "I've come to realize this body needs to be replenished on a regular basis. Sleep, food—things I could do without for long periods when I was a demon."

Eddy noticed the lines of strain on his face seemed deeper than they'd been earlier, and she knew the pain from the curse must be growing stronger. Willow buzzed across the room and hovered in front of Dax before settling on his shoulder.

A trail of blue sparkles covered the front of his shirt and then slowly faded, almost as if Dax absorbed their energy.

Eddy flashed the little sprite a smile. *Thanks, Willow.*

Willow sent a burst of sparkles toward Eddy. *I wish there were more I could do*, she said. *He suffers so.*

I know. Eddy tried to catch Dax's eye, to see if he needed her, but he seemed to be staring at something outside the kitchen window.

"Dax?" she asked. "What are you looking at?"

He jerked his head around, blinking. "Sorry. I was thinking. Trying to figure out how much the curse has affected my abilities."

"You zapped Mr. Puccini's turkey without any trouble."

"That I did, but the fire and ice are only a fraction of the demon powers I should have." Absently, he rubbed his hand across the front of his chest. "I'm wondering if I can still disincorporate and take on an avatar."

Ed glanced up from the paper he was reading at the

kitchen table. "You can do that? Even with a human body, you can still turn to mist and slip into statues and stuff?"

Dax shook his head. "I don't really know. I could as a demon, but I don't know for sure if I can anymore. Since I've been given this human body of flesh and blood, I wonder if I can animate living things. I haven't tried it yet, though I think I know how to do it." He laughed. "At least in theory."

Bumper snored and rolled over on her back. All eyes in the kitchen focused on the dog. Eddy raised her head. "Could you enter Bumper?"

Dax shot her a pleased glance. "Quite possibly. I imagine I'd need Willow's help. It will take more energy to reduce this corporeal body to demon mist, but it should work." He knelt down beside the dog. Bumper opened one eye and stared at him.

"Whatdaya think, girl? You willing to give it a try?" Willow buzzed by and hovered just over Bumper. Blue sprinkles glittered against the dog's curly blond coat. Bumper groaned and closed her eyes again.

Dax raised his head and grinned at Eddy. "I guess that's an affirmative. Maybe tonight, after I've rested. I'm afraid to try it now, when I'm too tired to think clearly."

"Probably a good idea." Eddy glanced away from the dog and caught Dax studying her. She wished she knew what he was thinking, what he felt. She smiled and then looked away, unwilling to let him see everything in her eyes. She had the feeling that he read her like an open book, while she was completely clueless about what was in his thoughts.

It was disconcerting, to say the least.

"What's the plan for tonight?" Ed looked up from his stack of newspapers. He'd spread them out across the kitchen table between Alton and himself. They'd picked up dailies from a couple of neighboring communities and were looking for articles mentioning strange current events—like demons roaming through other towns. "At least it still looks like the only demons are right here in Evergreen," he said. "There's no mention of any strange activities in any of the papers."

"What about the *Record*?" Eddy glanced over his shoulder.

"A brief mention of the missing statue turning up in your house after vandals destroyed the place, and another report of damage at the nursery when someone must have gotten in and destroyed a number of stone garden decorations. Pigs, deer, birds . . . that sort of thing. Stuff Harlan probably took directly off the police reports." He raised his head. "Just in Evergreen, though. So far it looks as if we're the only ones with a demon infestation."

"Let's hope so," Alton said. "We really need to see how bad it is. Taron said many demons had come through the portal, but he never gave me a number. That was my mistake, not to pin him down, though with some demons getting sent back to Abyss when their avatars are destroyed, and others teaming up, it may be impossible to ever get an exact count."

"Will we ever know if we get all of them?" Eddy glanced toward Dax. He merely shrugged. Not the answer she wanted.

Alton said, "We need to patrol the town. Thing is, we'll have to split up. Dax and I can't work together. Though I've not killed with it before, I know my sword has a strong affinity for demonkind." He grinned at Dax. "I'd hate like the nine hells to behead the wrong demon."

"Thank you." Dax dipped his head toward Alton. "I'd hate it even more if you beheaded the wrong demon. I've grown quite fond of this head, which means you're going to work with Ed while I stick with Eddy. I suggest we wait until dark before we go out. Demonkind should be active then, so we're more likely to find them."

He shoved himself away from the counter, pulled a folded

map out of his rear pocket, and spread it open on the kitchen table. It was one of the maps the local visitor's center handed out to tourists.

Dax pointed to two areas circled in red. "Let's split this up. Eddy and I'll take this area here, west of the freeway, as well as the north end of town. Alton, you and Ed take the southern and eastern sections, here. Look for evidence of demon activity—check any stores that carry ceramic or stone creatures that could become avatars."

Eddy pointed to a large green section. "That's the memorial park. There are a lot of stone statues at the cemetery. Can the demons use those? Some of them are pretty big."

Dax rubbed the back of his neck. "They handled that bronze statue without any trouble."

"What about angels?" Eddy realized she was rubbing her neck exactly like Dax. They were all feeling the stress. She stopped and crossed both arms over her chest. "Can demons use angel statues for avatars? That just seems wrong."

"As far as I know, Eddy, they can animate anything of the earth, no matter what form it's in, as long as it represents a creature, real or fantasy, that can walk, fly, slither . . . whatever. We know there's a pretty good-sized stone gargoyle flying around."

"Crap. You're right. Then we really need to check out the cemetery. Which reminds me." Eddy took a deep breath. "Dad, when Dax and I were out today, the gargoyle was right where it belonged on the parapet of the old library. There was no way to get close enough to see if the demon was still in it or not, but we both could sense its malevolence. It feels evil. If you see that thing anywhere, take cover."

"That's why I want to go out after dark," Dax said. "I realize it's going to be more dangerous then, but if the demon's still using the gargoyle as an avatar, we'll have a better chance of seeing it fly. I want to know where it goes when it's out and about, and what it's doing. If possible, I want to destroy it."

Alton frowned. "Why the interest in the gargoyle?"

"Besides the fact it's the one that hit me with the curse?" Dax rubbed his hand across his chest. "It seems to be smarter than demons in general. So far, most of the ones we've come across have been pretty stupid . . . mindless, actually. Merely acting on instinct. The majority of demons are like that, even on Abyss. The ones that think, the smart ones, are the troublemakers. I think the demons in the statue that attacked us at Eddy's house were functioning on a higher level. That wasn't an arbitrary attack. They were looking for me—I'm certain of it—but they didn't fight very intelligently. I'm wondering if they might have been directed by another demon."

Alton asked, "The gargoyle?"

Dax nodded. "It was waiting for me at the portal. Somehow it either knew I was coming, or sensed my presence. However it knew, it was prepared with the one thing that might actually stop me." He took a deep breath and closed his eyes.

Without asking, Eddy unbuttoned the top buttons of his shirt and pressed her hand to the writhing tattoo. The heat was almost more than she could tolerate, but the thought that Dax lived with this horrible pain was worse. She'd do whatever it took to help.

The tattoo felt like as if it were trying to crawl off his chest. She pressed one palm against the snake's body and held the other right over the fanged head, forcefully holding the damned thing still. Within a few minutes, the heat had cooled to a healthy body temperature, and the tattoo no longer moved.

She swept her palms over the snake's now quiescent body and let out a deep breath. "It's getting worse, isn't it?"

Dax nodded. "It is, but I can do this. With your help, Eddy . . ." He wrapped his fingers around her hand and gently squeezed. "We only need a few more days. . . ."

He didn't need to say more. He only *had* a few more days, and they were flying by much too quickly. Then he would be gone, whether they'd beaten the demons or not. Eddy slowly fastened the buttons on his shirt and raised her head. She caught her dad looking at her.

She didn't meet his eyes. Instead she glanced at the Lemurian. "Alton, why don't you take the guest room and get some sleep? Dax can stay in my room with me. I want to be able to control the pain so he can rest."

"Eddy? Honey, are you sure?"

She glanced at her father and smiled. "Yeah, Dad. I'm sure."

He nodded slowly. "Okay." He sighed and gave Eddy a small smile. "I just wanted to be certain."

She held his gaze for a long, very grateful moment. "Thanks, Dad. I appreciate it. C'mon, Dax. I'm beat." She caught his fingers and tugged lightly.

Willow buzzed around the two of them and then landed on Alton's shoulder. Eddy snapped her fingers for Bumper. The dog raised her curly head, yawned, blinked slowly, and then put her chin back down on Alton's booted foot.

Alton continued to study the map. Ed made a show of looking over his shoulder. Dax seemed totally unaware of the undercurrents in the room, or the fact that, for the first time since they'd met, he and Eddy were going to be totally alone.

Eddy hadn't really appreciated her king-sized bed or the fact her room had its own bathroom until now. She paused beside her big bed and touched Dax's arm. "Go and get a shower. You'll sleep better."

He looked at her as if sleep was the last thing on his mind.

She felt a little curl of heat in her belly and shoved him toward the bathroom. Sometimes it was necessary to remove temptation.

Still, Eddy followed Dax and grabbed a couple of clean towels out of the linen closet. She left them on the counter, along with a toothbrush still in the wrapper and a new razor.

Did Dax even know what everything was for? She raised her head and caught him watching her with a bemused smile on his face. Once again, she wished she had an idea what he was thinking. He was still so hard for her to read. She slapped a tube of toothpaste next to the toothbrush. "Here," she said. "If you need anything else, just yell."

Then she scooted past him before he said anything, and made a point of closing the door behind her as she left. She heard the water go on, the sound of the shower door sliding open and then closed. She paused beside the bed. Pictured his big body sprawled out across the rumpled covers and immediately turned to stare instead at the closed bathroom door.

Now she imagined him in there under the warm spray, with his hair slicked back behind his ears, brown eyes closed, face lifted to the pulsing jets of water. His thick, dark eyelashes would be all clumped together from the spray. Water would glisten like tiny beads across his broad, broad shoulders.

The muscles in her belly clenched. A spike of need so strong it felt like a physical touch raced from her suddenly taut nipples to pool in her lower abdomen. Her vaginal muscles tightened in reflexive reaction. She sighed.

Damn. Just like his curse, her response to Dax was growing stronger by the moment. Her need for him seemed to have taken on a life of its own, but there'd be no cooling touch from Dax to control her beast. No. If Dax touched her, things were just going to get a whole lot hotter.

"Get a grip, girl." She couldn't stand here watching the bathroom door like an idiot! She had to do something, anything, to take her mind off Dax naked.

By the time she heard the taps shut off, Eddy had the bedding changed and the blinds drawn. The room was comfortably dark, even though it was only a little after one in the afternoon. They had at least six or seven hours before they had to go out on patrol.

Dax stepped out of the bathroom followed by a cloud of steam, and all her good intentions to think of anything but him flew out the window. His dark hair clung to his cheeks and neck. He hadn't shaved, and the day-old stubble on his chin and cheeks made him look even sexier, if that was at all possible.

Water beaded his chest, and the tattoo glistened, crawling up his belly from the lower right, crossing the left side of his chest, and curling around his well-defined pectoral. He'd wrapped a short towel around his hips, but the tail of the snake peeked out beneath the towel on his right leg, just above his knee. The jaws still gaped over his nipple—right over his heart.

All Eddy could think of was where the snake traveled between those points. How it crossed the soft skin where his thigh met his groin, passed over the thick root of his penis through the dark thatch of pubic hair, and curled up the left side of his belly.

The visual was crystal clear, the way she remembered what he'd looked like naked when she found him in her potting shed. . . . Was it only the night before last? Hours ago, actually. How could she feel as if she'd known him forever? Already her relationship with Dax had an intimacy she'd never experienced with another man, even if they'd been lovers.

Would she and Dax ever . . . ? She wasn't ready to go

there. Not yet. Eddy cleared her throat and ducked past Dax, into the steamy bathroom. She dug into her stash of disposable razors and showered, quickly shaved her pits and legs, washed and conditioned her hair . . . all without allowing herself to think about the man in the next room.

Whether it was from denying her mind the directions it wanted to take, or the schedule they'd been on the past couple of days, when Eddy finally shut off the shower she realized she was completely exhausted.

And confused. Really, really confused. She stared at her image in the foggy mirror and admitted she didn't have a clue what she wanted with Dax. Pregnancy wasn't a fear—she was on the pill—but was she ready for that level of intimacy?

Was she ready for sex with a guy who wasn't even human? Did Dax even want her? He'd kissed her, touched her as if he cared, but he was the first to admit he wasn't human.

Except he was more human, more of a man, more than any man she'd known. She rubbed her short hair dry, slipped quietly out of the bathroom . . . and realized all her worry was for nothing.

Dax slept soundly on the far side of the bed. The blankets were pulled up to his waist, but he lay on his back with his left arm stretched above his head. The other draped across the blanket covering his belly.

His lips were slightly parted, and his face, relaxed in sleep, looked angelic in spite of the shadow of a day's growth of beard. Without any self-consciousness at all, Eddy dropped the towel on the floor and crawled into bed to lie naked beside him. She snuggled close and wrapped her right arm over his, across his chest. Her palm rested on the snake's head.

She could have sworn she felt the smooth, hard surface of

fangs, but that was impossible. She felt heat, though, and the slightest movement, as the curse tried to fight her cooling touch. She thought of healing, of goodness and love, and within a few moments the skin beneath her hand was cool and blessedly still. Dax sighed. The tension left his body with his warm exhalation, and he relaxed into deeper sleep.

He was such a big, powerful man that holding him like this, watching him sleep, hit her like a punch to the heart. She'd never been needed by anyone before, not like this. She actually had the power to help him, to ease his excruciating pain and help him get some much-needed rest.

His skin still felt damp from his shower. His dark lashes were so long and thick they looked almost fake lying against his face in dark half moons. So beautiful. So absolutely perfect.

Except, he was a demon. Silently, she spoke the word, wrapping her lips around the shape of the sound. *Demon.*

Impossible. All of this, utterly impossible. Smiling, her hand still covering the snake's head, Eddy slipped into sleep, surrounded by the feel, the scent, the very essence of the most amazing man—the most human man—she'd ever known.

He'd never felt so refreshed, so completely rested. Dax lay there for a moment in that blissful period between sleep and full wakefulness, and silently categorized the many sensations he wanted to take with him if he ended up back in the void.

Eddy's amazing scent was a seductive lure all by itself. Her touch that both excited and soothed him, the soft puff of her breath as it left her lips. The warmth and life of her, the soft swell of her bare breast against his chest, the slow, even cadence of her breathing. Even the weight of the one leg she'd somehow wrapped across him.

Paradise was a dream, but he couldn't imagine any paradise even remotely as wonderful as waking up in a clean, warm bed with a beautiful woman sleeping beside him.

One particular beautiful woman.

His eyes remained closed, but he smiled. Paradise had to be waking up with Eddy Marks curled against his body with one shapely leg stretched across his thighs. Her hand rested on the tattoo, her fingers gently caging the vicious-looking mouth with its four sharp fangs. She must have held her hand there even as they slept, soothing the pain, cooling the fire.

No wonder he'd slept so soundly.

The house was quiet. Alton and Ed must still be sleeping. Regretfully, Dax opened his eyes. He had no business lying here in such comfort when demons prowled the earth. He had work to do, and it was growing late. The room was almost dark—a glimmer of light leaked in around the blinds—but it had to be close to dusk. He should be thinking of waking himself fully, of getting out of bed and preparing for the night ahead.

For the battles to come.

But all he could think now was how good this felt, how perfect. Eddy sighed and snuggled closer. She was warm, and her skin was as smooth as silk. Her hair smelled like flowers, and he wanted to bury his face in the short, sweet tangle. Her fingers curled against his chest, and her lips touched the sensitive skin stretched across his ribs. When she exhaled, he felt the little puffs of air against his side. It sort of tickled—in a good way—and it was a feeling unlike anything he'd ever experienced.

His cock was hard as a post. That was sort of familiar—he'd been hard most of the time in his demon form, though it hadn't felt anything remotely similar to this. For a demon, an erection wasn't a thing of pleasure—it was merely a way of life when on Abyss. You had to be ready to kill or eat or fuck, or else you were the one who ended up dead, eaten, or screwed.

Now though, he was hard, and his cock was trapped beneath the smooth muscles of her thigh. Close, but not close enough to another taste of Paradise. Dax lay there for a few minutes, imagining how it would feel to part Eddy's soft nether lips and slide the thick head of his cock between them. She'd be tight.

He'd been huge as a demon—he was almost as large in his human form. Her feminine muscles would have to stretch to give him entry. Once he was deep inside, she'd clasp him with those muscles, and he'd be able to feel the soft, rhythmic ripples all along the length of his shaft.

He lay there a moment longer, imagining the tightness, the moist heat, the sense of belonging she would grant him, should he ever find himself buried deep inside Eddy Marks.

Imagination was about the only way he was going to know.

Now certainly wasn't the time for sex. For making love. He'd never made love before, and it would definitely be lovemaking if he took Eddy. This body knew how. As each hour passed, Dax felt the symbiosis with his borrowed body grow more powerful, his understanding of the things it had done and what it knew becoming clearer, easier to understand.

He knew this had been a soldier's body, one plucked from the morass of swirling time accessible through the void. Nameless to him, the soldier whose face Dax wore, whose body was now a strong and healthy receptacle for the demon's consciousness, had fallen in a fierce battle at a place called Normandy during the prior century. He'd died a hero, and his badly damaged body had been buried as one of many unknown soldiers at a place called Colleville-sur-Mer in France.

The names meant nothing to Dax now, though the brain within this body retained the memory of its final resting place. Most of the memories of the man would be with the body's original spirit, resting now, he assumed, in Paradise.

Dax was glad he'd been given the body of a hero, a man in his prime who had been in his midthirties when he fell in battle. Repaired and strong, now, it gave him hope that his demon spirit might somehow learn whatever the body could teach.

From the beginning, he'd known to touch softly, to proceed with caution. Things like shaking hands, brushing teeth, combing hair. Shaving and dressing and putting on pants and shoes and the cadence of speech, of reading expressions. In the beginning, he'd needed Willow's help to understand, but now he seemed to manage quite well on his own.

He still needed her for drawing energy, both to access the demon powers within his tattoo, and to fight the curse inhabiting the damned thing. When Eddy wasn't there with her healing touch, it was Willow he turned to for help.

Eddy snuggled closer against him. He thought of waking her. They needed to get moving. Then he thought of waking her and making love to her. He knew she wanted him. Knew they would both be swept up in the intimacy, the act of love, but dare he risk it? Lovemaking with Eddy could be highly dangerous to her.

If they were fully intimate, their dynamics would surely change. How would he control the curse if he was buried deep inside her feminine heat? It took all his strength to hold the growing power of the cursed tattoo under some semblance of control, yet he knew, without any doubt at all, that sex with Eddy would take away every bit of his control.

And what of the demon? What if his demon self surfaced?

What if that creature decided to make Eddy his own? It wouldn't be lovemaking then. No, it would be fucking, pure and simple.

Eddy deserved more than that. She deserved better than Dax.

She moved again and wriggled closer, and then he heard a soft little gasp of surprise and knew she was awake.

Awake and fully aware of how close she lay beside him, how intimately their bodies touched. She knew how his body responded to the weight of that one delicious thigh—knew by the way his erect cock pulsed between her warm, muscular leg, and his belly.

"Did you sleep okay?" he asked.

All heavy-lidded and warm, she blinked and rubbed the side of her face against his chest. "I did," she said. And then she yawned. "How about you?"

"I slept well, thanks to you."

"What'd I do?" She blinked and then slowly closed her eyes, as if it was too much effort to keep them open.

"You kept your fingers over my tattoo. You drew the pain through all the hours. I slept entirely without pain, without any action from the curse at all. Your touch is magic."

She arched her back and pressed herself against his hip. He felt the brush of that small thatch of hair between her legs, the way it tickled his flank. Her thigh moved over the length of his cock, a slow, seductive slide that effectively destroyed all his good intentions when he swelled even more against her.

There was no sense of his demon self, but he couldn't relax. Not while she kept up the slow slide of her thigh over his shaft, moving just enough to drive him wild. Her body writhed and undulated against him. He thought of the snake tattoo, the way it moved in a painful dance over his torso.

This was almost the same, and yet so amazingly different,

this rhythmic dance of Eddy's. There was no pain, but the pleasure was so extreme it was torture to lie here and accept it without responding.

"Eddy?" He groaned, leaned close, and kissed her soft lips. "Do you have any idea what you're doing?"

Eddy's eyes stayed shut, but she nodded, smiling broadly. She kept up the slow thrust and retreat of her hips against his flank, of her thigh over his erection.

Dax slipped away from her clasping legs, wrapped his legs around hers, and rolled over on top of her. He trapped her wrists in his hands above her head and held her legs close together. His cock pressed against her pubic mound . . . close, but not close enough.

"We have to get moving," he said, leaning down and kissing her. She grinned at him, totally unrepentant.

"You're not moving nearly enough." She pouted. He leaned close and nipped her full lower lip.

"We don't have time. Not now," he said, though there was nothing he wanted more than to lift his hips, allow her to spread her legs the way she would if he didn't have them trapped between his, and sink into her heat.

Just thinking about it made him groan. He leaned his head down and rested his forehead on Eddy's. "I will make love to you, Eddy Marks, but it's going to be when we have the time to do it right. Not when your father is waiting outside the bedroom door."

"Oh shit!" She twisted away, stared at the door, and whispered, "Dad's out there?"

Dax nodded, grinning, and whispered just as softly. "He is. I'm getting up now. You can let him in when you're decent."

Dax slipped out of bed, but not so fast that Eddy didn't get a good glimpse of what she'd been holding trapped beneath her leg. She'd never seen him erect. If she had, she might not have let him escape so easily.

Damn, but he was absolutely gorgeous with his muscular butt and flat belly, the ripple of muscles across his chest and shoulders. The smooth line of his back and the way it curved into the most perfect manflank she'd ever seen in her life.

She swallowed back the first thought that popped into her head, how she'd just love to take a big bite of that beautiful sweep of muscle and warm male.

Even the tattoo was beautiful in a terrible way. The curve and color emphasized Dax's powerful physique, the natural strength in his long, ropey muscles. When he paused beside the bed and stretched his long arms up over his head, she heard the sound of his spine popping and joints cracking.

The snake's mouth gaped open. She was almost certain she saw a gleam on one of the long fangs and a spark of intelligence in the creature's eyes, but then Dax turned away and grabbed his clothes off the chair beside the bed. While he pulled on his pants, Eddy snatched up her clothes and raced into the bathroom.

She glanced over her shoulder as she clutched the door and realized Dax had turned and watched her bare-assed run across the room with typical male appreciation. He winked at her. Then he reached for the bedroom door.

Giggling, Eddy slammed the door to the bathroom shut before Dax opened the bedroom door to her father. She heard her dad's voice but couldn't tell what he said, or if the men even stayed in the room. She used the bathroom, washed her face, and brushed her teeth. Then she carefully opened the door.

The bed was straightened up, though not made. The room was empty, and Dax and her father were gone. Eddy wrapped a towel around herself and dug through her old dresser in search of clean socks and fresh underwear.

In just a couple of hours, they'd be going into battle. For some stupid reason, her mother's warning about always wearing clean undies in case you have an accident was planted firmly in her head.

It was easier than thinking of what lay ahead.

Chapter Eight

Tuesday night—day three

Dax and Alton sat at the table, poring over the city map with a plate of sandwiches and a bowl of chips in front of them. Dax heard Eddy come into the kitchen, but he didn't turn around. When she stood behind Dax and reached for half a roast beef sandwich, he tilted back, leaned the top of his head against her belly, and grinned up at her. "Ed makes good sandwiches. I could get used to these."

She shook her head, and the damp strands of her short hair slapped the sides of her face. "Then you'd better learn to make them. I only cook when I have to." She took a bite and pointed to a spot on the map. He glanced down and followed where her finger led.

"There's a big nursery here. I thought of it while I was in the shower—it's got a whole section devoted to ceramic garden creatures. Deer, mice, birds—all sorts of things. There's a huge statue of a grizzly bear just outside the front. I can't remember if it's stone or plastic or maybe concrete. I guess it's okay if it's plastic, right?"

Dax nodded. "Stone and ceramic seem to be the avatars

of choice. I'm not sure about plastic. Its basic component is petroleum, but that might be a stretch."

"Well, we haven't seen any plastic flamingoes flapping around, and all the garden gnomes I've seen have been made of cheap ceramic." She chewed and swallowed a big bite. "Alton, the nursery is here on the southeastern end of town, so you and Dad need to check it out."

Alton nodded and made a note on a small tablet. His list was already long. Willow buzzed across the room and hovered in between the Lemurian and Dax, but her focus was entirely on Dax. Her tiny wings beat so fast they practically disappeared.

You must see if you can achieve the transfer, she said, speaking telepathically to him.

Damn. He'd completely forgotten. Dax nodded, and Willow zipped across the room again to hover beside Bumper.

Dax turned to Eddy and shrugged. "Maybe I need to make lists the way Alton does. Willow just reminded me I have to see if I can disincorporate and transfer into Bumper." He grabbed a sandwich and pushed his chair back. When Eddy started to follow, he stopped her. "Watch from here if you like, but don't come close. Not until I've done the transfer a few times. There's a risk that I could take over the body of the wrong living entity. I only want to do this with Bumper. It might be too confusing if I end up sharing your body."

Eddy stared at him a minute. Then she burst out laughing and leaned close. He caught a whiff of her fresh scent and the flowery essence of her shampoo. His delight in her scent was so great he had to close his eyes. Would he ever grow used to such pleasure?

Whispering in his ear, so close that her breath tickled him, she said, "Dax, you can share my body any time you want."

Dax took a long, slow breath, giving himself time to grasp whatever control he could. Then, as calmly as he was able, he cast her a sidelong glance. "How come you didn't tell me that before I fell asleep?" Before she could move away, he planted a quick kiss on her full lips.

She blinked in surprise. He liked that he'd gotten her back after her tease. Then he stood up, grabbed another half of a sandwich off the plate, and went out in the backyard with Bumper and Willow on his heels.

He left Eddy sitting in the kitchen with a big smile on her face. One almost as broad as the smile on his.

Dax found a quiet corner out in the backyard near Ed's workshop. Someone nearby had recently mowed their lawn, and the rich scent of freshly cut grass tickled his nostrils. The air was still, the early evening quiet. It was as good a time as any to practice something he wasn't really certain he could do.

Bumper sniffed around the bushes, peed on a tuft of grass, and then planted her butt at his feet. Willow flitted around, checking the area as he'd asked her to, making sure there were no demons in hiding. He knew he'd be vulnerable until he got the hang of this.

"Okay, Willow. Have you explained to Bumper what we're planning?"

Willow hovered in front of Dax's face. Bumper yipped. It appeared they were ready. He wished he felt better prepared. Wished he had a better understanding of what he could and couldn't do.

"You'll need to show me what to do first."

She continued to hover in front of his face. Instead of speaking in his head, Willow let him see visually how to transfer his consciousness from his human body into a living creature. It was a three-part process—moving his consciousness, the part that made him Dax, out of the human body;

reducing the human body to all its separate molecular components so that he wouldn't be leaving a mindless shell behind that could be captured or destroyed by his enemies; and transferring his consciousness into a living avatar.

It was essentially what the Edenites had done to him after they found him in the void. He'd existed there as consciousness only. His demon form had stayed in Abyss, probably as a meal for one of his many enemies. The group from Eden must have reached into the maelstrom of time and found this soldier's body after its spirit had already flown.

Of course, they had refurbished it, added the tattoo and a few upgrades, and Dax had been sent through the portal as a human. Yet in essence, he was still the demon. The very soul of this body was demonkind. The powers that coursed through the tattoo, bound though they were by the curse, were still those of a once-powerful demon.

He vaguely recalled he'd been quite powerful on Abyss. So many of the memories of his life before the void were faded, the recollections twisted and confused by the memories still a part of this body.

He hoped the power he'd once wielded as a demon would help him now. He stared at Willow, studying the process she showed him, imagining each step that would disassemble the molecules of the human body and yet leave his conscious mind intact.

It all made such perfect sense. He had to be certain to separate his consciousness first, or even his thoughts would dissipate with the evening breeze, never to recombine again.

Still, what sounded complicated and confusing was really a very simple process—as long as he didn't screw anything up. The idea of floating free of his body without an anchor scared the crap out of him, but he had Bumper standing by, ready and willing to play host, and Willow for advice. He should be fine.

He glanced once toward the house and saw Eddy's face in the kitchen window. Her hands were clasped in front of her lips, as if in prayer. Knowing she was so close, so worried about him, gave Dax the courage he needed to take the next step.

He gazed once again at Willow. She glowed brightly, drawing energy out of the air and sending it to him. Dax absorbed it, inhaling as if he filled his lungs with oxygen, but taking all the energy Willow had to give.

He paused a moment and allowed his mind to absorb the energy. Felt the pressure build inside until power literally pulsed in his veins. Then he began the process that should separate him from his human body. The sensation was unlike anything he'd felt before—a sudden twisting of reality, as if he'd been sucked down a long, narrow tube.

Then nothing. He blinked. Looked down at his human hands, his large human feet. Ran his fingers over his arms and stared at Bumper.

She wagged her tail and yipped.

He tried it again, drawing power, taking each step that should free his consciousness and disassemble his body.

He should have been looking at the world from less than two feet off the ground. He wasn't. He was still Dax, still human, still staring down at the dog and wondering what had gone wrong.

"Willow? What the hell happened?"

There was no sign of the sprite. "Willow? Willow, where are you?"

I am here.

He stared down at the dog. Bumper's tail swished in rapid delight. There was a suspicious blue sparkle in her big, brown eyes.

"You're in Bumper? I'm supposed to be in Bumper. What happened?"

Obviously your human body is unable to disassemble. Mine, however, does it beautifully.

"I can see that." He planted his hands on his hips and realized he felt mildly ridiculous talking to the dog. "How come you can do it and I can't?"

Bumper yipped.

Willow answered. *I imagine it has something to do with your powers, the tattoo, and the curse. If you disincorporated your body, what happens to the tattoo? If it dissipates, do your powers disappear?*

Dax let out a big sigh. "I hadn't even thought of that. So, you can take on an avatar but I can't."

That's how it appears.

"Will you be able to get your body back?"

He heard Willow's laughter. Feminine, almost sultry, she said, *I certainly hope so!*

"Great." He wasn't used to being bested by a sprite. Dax folded his arms across his chest and tried once more to draw the power, to make the switch.

And again, nothing happened.

He glared down at the dog from his usual height.

She stared at him out of intelligent eyes.

"Willow? Are you still there?"

Yes. I like this body. I can't fly, but I'm stronger and I feel more sensations. Watch! She took off and ran around the yard a few times. Dax watched, frustrated, as Willow discovered what it was like to run like a dog, to smell the different scents and hear the sounds through Bumper's ultrasensitive ears.

Obviously, this was one demon power he'd lost. At least he still had his fire and ice. "Willow?"

I'm here.

"I want you to come out so I can see how long it takes you to get your body back."

Do I have to?

"Please, Willow. This isn't a game. Even though I can't switch, we may have need for you to be able to do it. I need to know how fast you are."

I know. Okay.

Willow took a bit longer than Dax expected, but within a few seconds she buzzed by him, leaving a trail of blue sparkles in her wake.

I want to do it again!

Should he really feel jealous of a sprite? "As often as you like, Willow. As long as Bumper doesn't mind."

Willow buzzed around him, then disappeared into the dog. Bumper didn't seem the least bit concerned when Willow popped in and out of her consciousness.

Disappointed in his own lack of ability, Dax watched as the sprite improved the speed of her shift with each attempt. The tattoo throbbed across his torso, energized most likely by his failed attempts and frustration. It seemed that the thing was more painful whenever he used his demon skills. The pain appeared to be worse, if that was at all possible, when he attempted something and failed.

How long before it was too much? How long before he couldn't handle it, couldn't keep the damned thing from gaining sentience? That's what was happening. He knew it, sensed the snake growing stronger, more self-aware each time it began to move across his body.

"Dax? Are you okay?" Eddy walked across the lawn. He could barely see her. Hadn't realized it had grown dark while he'd been out here. "Alton and Dad are ready to leave. I thought we should probably get going too. Are you okay? Are you ready?"

He nodded. "I am." He studied his shoes. "I failed to make the transfer."

"I know. We watched." She grabbed his hands in hers. "I'm sorry. Did Willow? We couldn't tell for sure."

He nodded. "Yes. With ease." His failure left a sour taste in his mouth. He couldn't believe he was jealous of a will-o'-the-wisp, but Willow had managed something he'd been so sure he could do, and she'd done it perfectly.

Eddy gazed into his eyes with more awareness than he wished she had. "It's not really an ability you'll need, is it? I know you thought for sure you'd be able to make the switch, but it shouldn't affect how you fight, should it?"

He shook his head. "I can still fight. Willow thinks it's because my powers are in the tattoo. Maybe I can't disassemble the tattoo and retain my demon powers. I wish I had a better understanding of what I can and can't do."

Bumper shoved her nose against his leg. He rubbed her curly head. "At least Bumper didn't seem to mind a bit when Willow moved in."

Eddy reached down and rubbed Bumper's ears. "Bumper doesn't mind anything as long as someone's paying her attention, do you, girl?"

Bumper leaned against Eddy's leg and groaned.

"See? What'd I tell you? C'mon. The guys wanted to talk to you before they leave."

Dax grabbed her hand. "First, I need . . ."

"I wondered if all that stuff would make this worse." She sighed, shook her head, and quickly unbuttoned his shirt. When her cool hands covered the snake, he almost wept. The moment she touched him, the pain seemed more manageable. Even his frustration faded away. The longer she pressed her palms to the tattoo, the better he felt.

When Eddy leaned close and pressed her lips against the snake's vicious head, the pain disappeared entirely. His body felt strong again. Whole. He leaned forward and rested his forehead against Eddy's. "I could not do this without you. Thank you."

She flashed him a bright smile, though he still sensed

the worry she hid from him. Then she buttoned his shirt closed for him, touched his cheek with her fingertips, and turned toward the house. "C'mon. They're waiting."

He heard the tremor in her voice. She was definitely worried. What could he do, to take the worry away?

The only thing he knew. Kill the demons. Make the world safe before he either returned to the void or took his place in Paradise.

For some reason, he didn't find the same sense of satisfaction those options had given him in the past. Wondering about his changing frame of mind, Dax followed Eddy back into the house with Bumper and Willow right behind.

Alton stood in the kitchen with his sword out, checking the blade in the bright overhead light. He glanced up, saw Dax, and quickly sheathed his sword, but it was obvious the weapon fought him. It looked as if it took all of Alton's considerable strength to force the thing back into the scabbard.

Dax stood back, waiting in the doorway until it was safely encased in leather.

"It doesn't understand why I won't let it kill you, Dax." Alton laughed. "Don't ever try and sneak up on me. The sword will know the moment you get within striking distance."

"I'll remember that." He eyed the thing respectfully. The blade was at least five feet long and appeared to be made of pure diamond, sharp as a razor. Not something he wanted to go up against in battle.

Dax put the evening's failure out of his mind. Tonight they faced their first true test. "Alton, you and Ed are going to take the southern part of town and cover the area around to the east. Eddy and I will go north and west. Be careful on the eastern side since that's closest to the mountain. If you discover heavy demon infestation anywhere, I want you to contact us. Ed's got a cell phone, and so does Eddy. I can't count on my telepathy in this body. It's not consistent."

"No problem." Alton strapped the scabbard across his back and checked to make sure the grip was perfectly placed for quick retrieval. "Maybe we'll get a little action tonight and my sword will finally tell me its name, eh?" He flashed a grin at Dax and took a step toward the door. "Ed? You ready to go?"

"I am." Ed wrapped his arms around Eddy and gave her a tight hug and a kiss on top of her head. "Be careful, sweetheart. Don't take any chances. Be sure and listen to Dax."

She hugged him back. "I will, Dad. You be careful too. Do you and Alton want Bumper?"

"You keep her. We'll be okay." Ed glanced at Dax. "Take care of my little girl, Dax. Keep her safe."

"Yes, sir." Dax held a hand out. Ed took it in a firm grasp. "You have my promise."

Ed nodded. "Remember to lock the house up, Eddy. I've got a key." He looked around the kitchen as if he couldn't quite believe where he was going. Then he flashed Eddy a huge grin, turned away, and followed Alton out the back door.

Eddy stared at the door for a moment after it closed. Then she shook her head, laughing. "All the years my dad's believed in flying saucers and ghosts and demons and I've teased him about it. Now I find out he was right and I was wrong."

Dax shrugged. "I can't say much about flying saucers, though I understand Atlanteans have a form of transportation that might appear . . ."

"No!" Eddy laughed and held both her hands over her ears. "Let me hold on to at least a few of my delusions. Please?"

"If you say so." Dax waited while she grabbed a jacket for the cool night air and locked the back door behind her dad and Alton. Then she led him out the front door.

Dax followed close behind and stood at her side while

she locked the door. Eddy left the porch light on, as if they were just going out for a regular evening.

As if you could call hunting demons a regular anything. He wondered how they'd fare this night, if all of them would still be alive come morning. It was so beautiful out, but when Dax glanced up at the night sky, he felt as if time were spinning by at Mach speed.

The tattoo shivered across his chest, and he felt the heat beginning to build once more. Three days almost gone, and they'd yet to face demonkind in force. Three days since he'd been cursed, and the curse grew in strength by the hour.

Dax gazed along the dark and silent street and wondered, once again, what the night would bring.

"I've made a list of the places with stuff demons can use as avatars, all on the way to the cemetery, but that's not even counting all the little garden statues in everyone's yards and the ceramic stuff in houses." Eddy raised her head and caught Dax looking back at her. She smiled at him, and for a moment she wasn't terrified of what might come. She wasn't afraid for Dax and the pain he suffered from the curse. For just a moment, she was a woman gazing at a man and thinking things a woman in love would feel.

Things she'd better stop thinking right now. *Damn . . . where'd that come from? Double damn. . . .* She'd been avoiding the L word really well until now. Eddy blinked herself back to the job at hand and tore her gaze away from Dax. Took a deep breath and willed her heart to stop racing.

She glanced once more at her list and then much more carefully at Dax. She wasn't about to let herself be caught up in those gorgeous dark eyes of his. Not now. "Okay, how about we set the cemetery as our eventual destination, and just check as many of these places along the way as we can." Eddy took a final look at the list, folded it up, and stuck it in her pocket. Then she grabbed Bumper's leash and zipped her jacket closed. It was cool out, but not cold. She wondered what kind of weather demons preferred.

Willow flitted around for a moment and then settled in the curls between Bumper's ears. Dax clicked on the flashlight he'd borrowed from her dad. Then he turned it off, and on again. There were no streetlights in this part of town, and they'd need the light.

"You lead," Dax said. "I'm not really sure where we're going."

Eddy nodded and took off with Bumper leading the way. They followed the road to the main boulevard and headed north. Shops were closed, but there were still a few restaurants open, and all seemed normal for a Tuesday night. Music filtered out of a small bar. There was a burst of loud laughter, more music, and voices.

"It's a nice town, Eddy. Good people live here."

Eddy nodded. "They do. That's why I hate to think of anything awful happening here. Demons! It's so hard to believe. Like something out of a horror movie."

Dax wrapped his fingers around her hand. He was so big, his hands so much larger than hers that he made her feel almost petite. She looked up at him and smiled. It was such a natural thing, even if highly unusual for her, to be walking down Lassen Boulevard holding hands with a really gorgeous guy.

His fingers suddenly tightened around hers. He pulled Eddy into the shadows beneath a decorative awning. Bumper whined.

So much for natural.

"Shush, Bumper."

Bumper's ears went back, but she didn't make another sound. Dax tapped Eddy's shoulder and pointed to a shadowed area across the street. At first she didn't see what he pointed at.

Then part of a shadow detached itself from a darker area. What looked like a small panther moved clumsily along the sidewalk. Eddy stared a moment longer and realized it was a carved stone cat, one that had sat upright in front of the store for years.

Now, though, it slunk along the sidewalk. Awkward at first, it seemed to gain coordination with each step, sniffing at the ground and then raising its head in the air as if to sniff the wind. It paused with one paw raised, nose in the air, its posture preternaturally alert.

Bumper growled, low in her throat. Eddy pressed her jaws together with her fingers. The dog whined, but she stopped growling.

As Eddy watched, the stone cat turned and stared directly at her. Instead of blank stone eyes, she faced red, glowing coals. The cat opened wide an improbable mouth framed in flashing rows of razor-sharp teeth. It screamed a piercing banshee howl that raised all the hairs along Eddy's spine.

It crouched low, and, without warning, leapt halfway across the street in a single bound.

"Eddy! Get back!" Dax raised his hands. His brow furrowed in concentration. The cat leapt again. This time Dax caught it with a wall of frozen air that knocked it to the ground. Bumper barked and growled, jerking hard at the leash. Eddy wrapped the strap around both her hands and held on. Willow flitted over Dax, gathering energy to fight the demon.

The stone cat sprawled on the ground, stunned. Dax shot it with a burst of flame. The stone cracked open. Black mist oozed through the fissures. Dax caught the mist with his icy blast once more, freezing it into shards of ice. Then he seared the frozen demon with flame. It sizzled and dissipated into the air.

Before the last wisp of steam had vanished, Dax grabbed Eddy's hand and tugged her along the street, around a corner and behind a small crystal shop, with Bumper bouncing joyfully beside them. As soon as they got into the shadows, he wrapped his arms around Eddy and covered her mouth with his in a hard, uncompromising kiss.

She heard footsteps thundering by and laughed against his mouth. "And here I thought you just couldn't stay away from me."

He chuckled and pressed his forehead against hers. "I can't, but I also don't want to have to explain what we're doing to your curious police. Not yet."

She stepped up on her toes and kissed him hard and fast. Then she grabbed his hand. "Let's go. That mess in the street will keep the cops busy for a while."

They slipped out from between the buildings and headed away from the commotion, down the street toward the old library. Bumper trotted alongside as if fighting demon cats were an everyday event, but she slowed her pace when they reached the library. The stone building was empty now, merely a shell of its former glory, and, according to laws regarding earthquake safety, badly in need of restoration.

At one time there had been two gargoyle statues on the roof at either side of the main front door. Years ago, one had been vandalized and destroyed, but the remaining gargoyle had survived. They'd both seen it there, holding court from the corner mount earlier today.

Now the corner was empty. "It's gone." Dax's flat words gave just a hint of the frustration he must be feeling as they stared at the point where the gargoyle had been attached since long before Eddy's father was born. Now the shelf of quarried stone stood empty, mute testimony to the demon that had chosen the statue as its avatar.

"Listen!" Eddy tugged Dax's hand and pointed toward the west, in the direction of the cemetery. The faint sound of screeching and deeply resonant howls barely registered. Bumper growled and tugged the leash.

"We need to see what's going on."

Dax stared at her for a moment, as if trapped by indecision. "Eddy, maybe you should try and find your father and Alton. Go with them."

"You're kidding, right?" She glared at him, silently daring him to give her such a stupid order. He looked as if he'd like nothing better than to send her home. "I'm going with you, Dax. We're a team, remember?"

He sighed, long and loud. "I remember. That doesn't mean I have to like it." He rubbed his chest and took a deep, shuddering breath.

Eddy reached for his top button.

"We don't have time," he said.

"Don't be stupid." She was angrier than she had a right to be. Angry at Dax for wanting to keep her safe, at the demons for creating this mess, at Harlan for firing her. Angry at a life that was currently spinning totally out of control. "We don't have time not to. Hold still." She parted the buttons and gasped. The snake stared directly into her eyes with a malevolence she'd not expected. Eddy took a deep breath and slapped both hands directly over the serpent's head. She was almost certain she felt the texture of his scales, the hard surface of fangs, but the intense heat quickly overwhelmed any other sensations.

Holding her hands against the tattoo, she drew the heat into her own body, aware of a difference this time, as if she dealt with an actual creature, not merely a cursed tattoo. It took longer to cool the heat, and when it was done, her arms felt heavy and her heart thudded in her chest.

The curse was growing stronger. How much longer would she have any effect on it? How long before the thing attacked her when she tried to cover it with her hands?

What the hell would she do if it did attack?

"Thank you," Dax said. He bowed his head. "It's worse, isn't it? I can feel it. It's coming to life. Just now, when I zapped the demon . . . the first time, nothing happened. It was harder to draw my powers. I felt as if they were fighting me, refusing to respond."

"Yeah, but they did respond. You're still in charge. It's okay, Dax. I can handle the pain if you can." She forced a laugh. "Ain't no tattoo gonna get the best of me!"

She wanted to wrap her arms around him and hold him close, just hug him hard until the damned curse was gone, but when he held his hand out, she took it. Then she followed him down the dark lane that would lead them to the cemetery.

In the distance, Eddy heard faint screams and banshee howls, interspersed with the nearby chirp of crickets and the hoot of an owl. She shivered, held tightly to Dax's hand, and kept her senses on high alert.

There was a small hardware store with a nursery along the road to the cemetery. Dax held a finger to his lips as they drew near. "I sense demonkind nearby," he whispered. "Stay alert."

Bumper growled and strained at her leash. Willow zipped around the side of the building, while Eddy and Dax crossed the parking lot. Two large dusk-to-dawn lights illuminated most of the asphalt and the front of the store, but the dark shadows could have hidden an entire army of demon-powered avatars.

They peered through the windows into the store, but

nothing seemed amiss. Dax used the bright beam on the flashlight to illuminate the gardening area, but all seemed quiet.

Willow returned after making a full circle around the building and nursery. She hadn't seen a thing, but the feeling persisted, so strong now that even Eddy felt it.

The distant cries and howls ebbed and flowed with the wind, but the sound was so eerie it made Eddy shudder. "Maybe you sense the demons at the cemetery," she said. "It seems quiet here."

"I know," Dax said, flashing the light across the parking lot once more. "But the quiet feels wrong. Do you hear crickets? That owl that was hooting earlier?"

Eddy stared at him, wide-eyed. He was right. There was no sound other than the occasional roar of a truck going by on the freeway and the distant cries from the direction of the cemetery.

They stood together beneath the light in the parking lot, listening for anything—even the normal sounds of the night that should have created a backdrop for the silence. Eddy's muscles tensed, almost as if she waited for a blow.

An earsplitting shriek shattered the silence. Eddy spun around to face the sound. Dax stepped in front of her, protecting her body with his, as something large and dark flew by just over their heads. The force of its passing threw Willow into a spin. Dax threw his arms high and shot flames into the sky. Eddy looked up just in time to catch the silhouette of the gargoyle circling overhead, getting set up to come back at them once again.

The thing circled high and then dove straight at them, jaws agape, mouth filled with rows of sharp teeth. The eyes glowed red as it zeroed in on Dax. As he raised his hands to fire on the demon, Bumper tore free of Eddy's grasp and leapt into the air. Dax pulled his hands back just in time as Bumper's jaws closed around one wingtip. The gargoyle spun in a tight circle and slashed at the dog's tender nose with a clawed foot.

Bumper yipped and turned loose of the wing, rolling and tumbling across the parking lot. Eddy ducked as the gargoyle dove straight for her. Dax couldn't use his weapons, fighting so close, but he grabbed for the creature's wing and managed to knock it off balance.

It missed Eddy and skidded across the parking lot with Bumper once again hot on its tail. Dax took a quick look at Eddy, then raced after the dog and the gargoyle. Eddy ran right behind him and dove for Bumper's leash. She managed to catch the strap at the end and tugged as hard as she could. She had to get Bumper out of the way so that Dax could hit the demon with fire and ice, but by the time she got control of the frantic dog, the gargoyle had leapt into the air once again. It circled high above and screamed as if it cursed them all.

The thing hovered a moment. Its wings made a loud, grating noise as they slowly flapped, moving much too slowly to actually keep a stone statue airborne. The visual was disconcerting, to say the least.

Then it tucked its wings, bared rows of glistening teeth, and with an earsplitting screech, dove straight for them once again. Willow zipped behind Dax.

"Move, Eddy. Out of the way!"

Eddy rolled to one side. Gravel cut into her elbow and forearm as Dax let loose a barrage of flame. The gargoyle screamed a banshee cry of pure frustration that seemed to echo off the rooftops, but the flames didn't slow it down, nor did the icy wall that Dax threw next.

Bursting through the sheet of ice as if it were only so much mist, the gargoyle totally disregarded Dax's most powerful weapon. Willow shot off to the right. Dax dove to the ground and rolled to the left. The creature slashed at his face as it passed.

Lying on his back on the asphalt parking lot, Dax pointed his fingers at the gargoyle once again. Nothing happened. He looked for Willow and spotted her nearby, sparkles dimmed but still gleaming in the darkness. Again he tried. Nothing!

Thank goodness the demon didn't seem to notice Dax was suddenly powerless. With a vicious snarl, it kept going and disappeared into the darkness, flying toward the cemetery.

"Shit. Shit, shit, shit." Eddy gently rubbed her scratched elbow to dislodge the embedded gravel and broken bits of glass. She glared at the dark sky until she finally spotted Willow. Her sparkles were almost gone. Slowly she dropped down out of the sky to land on the asphalt, obviously exhausted.

Then Bumper whimpered. "Oh! Baby . . ." Eddy knelt down and wrapped her arms around the dog. "Dax, shine the light on her, please? I want to see how badly she got hurt."

Shaking his head, Dax slowly rolled to his feet. Cursing beneath his breath, he scooped Willow up in one hand and held the flashlight close to the dog. There was a long scratch that cut across Bumper's nose and ran under her eye, but it didn't appear too serious. She stretched her tongue out and licked the tiny drops of blood away. Eddy stared at the scratch a moment longer and then turned to Dax. "Could it be poisonous?"

He shook his head. "I doubt it. The demon is still mist, even though it's in an avatar, and the gargoyle is made of stone, not living flesh. If she'd been struck by demon claws, I'd say it was definitely poisoned, but I don't think they have that power with an avatar."

"I need a weapon." Eddy crouched there with her arms around Bumper and thought of what she could have done to the gargoyle. It was the one who'd cursed Dax, and now it had come after them.

"I agree. Eddy, I'm so damned sorry. I never thought of arming you." He sighed. "I didn't think you'd need anything. I thought I was strong enough to protect us both."

Willow's wings fluttered, and she stared up at him, obviously upset. Dax shook his head. "No, Willow. It was not your fault. You sent me plenty of energy, but the snake was stealing it." Sighing, Dax held his hand out. Eddy took it, and he pulled her to her feet. "There was nothing there when I tried to hit the demon a second time. No flame, no ice. If it had turned on either of us then, I couldn't have done anything to stop it."

He glanced down at her torn sleeve and bloodied arm. "Crap. You're bleeding."

"I'm okay." She looked at the scrapes and scratches. Then she gazed into Dax's dark eyes. "I want a baseball bat," she said. "A big, heavy baseball bat. I know how to use one. I could have hit that thing when it flew over me if I'd had something I could swing at it."

"Where would I find such a thing?"

"That's easy," she said, aware once more of the sound of crickets. "My dad's got a couple of them. Good, sturdy northern white ash baseball bats. I played on the boys' Little League team when I was a kid, and I was pretty damned . . ." She glanced up at Dax. He stood perfectly still. His jaw was clenched, his eyes closed.

This time Eddy didn't even ask. She merely stood up, unbuttoned his shirt, and pressed her palms against the snake. It was definitely moving, pulsing like a thing alive beneath her hands. Willow perched on Dax's shoulder and watched.

Eddy realized the snake gained more strength each time Dax battled demons, and tonight he'd lost his powers after taking just a couple of shots at the gargoyle.

Whatever energy Willow sent to him appeared to strengthen the curse as much as, if not more than, it empowered Dax. After only three days, it was almost more than he could handle.

The sounds coming from the cemetery grew louder. With her palms pressed to his chest, Eddy stood on her toes and planted a quick kiss on Dax's mouth. Before he could kiss her back, she pulled away. "I'm calling Dad and Alton," she said. "Personally, I want backup. You can just stay clear of Alton's sword."

Dax didn't say a word, but his gaze was on Eddy's bloodied arm when he nodded in agreement. As soon as his burning flesh had cooled, Eddy dug out her cell phone and called her father.

Chapter Nine

Late Tuesday night

Ed leaned against a thick oak, gasping for air. After a few deep breaths, he cocked a wary eye at Alton. "I've discovered that building model-train layouts and birdhouses doesn't get a guy in shape for hunting demons."

"Neither do esoteric arguments and philosophical discussion, but we're doing well, Ed." Taking a few deep breaths himself, Alton gazed proudly at the sword he clasped in his right hand. It still hadn't spoken to him, but it had definitely drawn blood, if that black demon stink could be considered as such. It felt warmer when he held it now, almost as if it pulsed with life. The grip fit his hand better; the weight seemed more perfectly balanced. "How many is that? I've lost track."

Ed frowned. "I don't know." He began counting off on his fingers. "The first two—the garden gnome and the stone goose we found just down the street from my house. Then there were three more in the church parking lot. I never expected a demon attack by two angels and the Virgin Mary!"

"I guess Dax was right when he told Eddy they could use angels as avatars. I wondered that myself."

"True, but wonder no longer." Ed frowned. "Let's see, there were the three ceramic cats next to the gas station, the ones you got in midair . . . what, maybe four or five of those metal hummingbirds?"

Alton nodded. "At least five." The little metal birds had the potential to be deadly adversaries. Quick and able to maneuver as well as their live counterparts, they'd been armed with sharp beaks and had no hesitation using them. The puncture wound in his left shoulder was proof of that.

"I'm running out of fingers . . . that's thirteen so far, and there were at least half a dozen more between the gas station and the nursery—squirrels, a couple more stone cats, the turtle, a frog . . ."

"Don't forget the one that jumped us near that fast-food restaurant."

Ed shook his head, but he was definitely grinning. At least he appeared to have finally caught his breath. "I'll never see Ronald the clown in the same way," he said. "All those teeth!" Ed gave an exaggerated shudder. "Okay, that's at least twenty before we got here, and I have no idea how many were waiting for us in the parking lot. Eddy was right to send us here."

Alton glanced at the parking lot outside the small nursery. "They did seem to be waiting, if not for us, for something. It was odd, the way they were all massed here."

The asphalt was littered now with piles of scorched ceramic and stone rubble. The stench of sulfur hung thickly in the still night air. They'd been attacked by an entire army of garden gnomes, stone squirrels, turtles, and rabbits—even a concrete bench designed in the shape of a pig.

Alton's sword had quickly proved adept at dispatching demons. If only he knew for certain they were actually dead.

He feared they might merely have been returned to Abyss. At least with the portal closed, sending them back to Abyss was as good as dead—until another portal in the vortex was created.

"I'd guess we destroyed at least another two, maybe three dozen more here." Ed gazed about the littered asphalt as if he couldn't believe what they'd done. He cast a sideways glance at Alton. "Retirement's certainly more exciting than I expected."

Then he shook his head and took another deep breath. "All these years Eddy's looked at me like I had a screw loose whenever I mentioned Lemurians. Not that she doesn't love me, but she's such a pragmatic kid, a 'seeing is believing' sort. More like her mother than me, but I always hoped I'd get a chance to prove I wasn't a complete whack job. I certainly never expected anything like this."

He gazed off in the distance. Then something seemed to catch his attention. He stared at the entrance to the store and scratched his head.

Alton sheathed his sword and flexed his fingers. He liked Ed. The man had a good heart, an accepting nature, and an open mind. While he enjoyed a good discussion, he didn't seem to feel the need to prove his opinion over anyone else's. It was obvious he loved his daughter enough to let her be her own woman.

A love like that was more special than most realized. Alton thought of his father, a man who saw his son as an extension of himself, not as his own man. He had no respect for Alton's beliefs, his needs. No respect for Alton as a man grown.

Ed saw Alton in a different light entirely. As a warrior, a savior come to help protect those Ed loved from the demon threat. Alton realized he felt like a warrior, as much from Ed's belief in him as from the circumstances.

They'd fought their first battle, and they'd done well. Not only did he and Ed enjoy one another's company, they made a good team. The evidence of their skill was scattered all about. Alton realized he'd gained more confidence in this one battle fighting beside Ed Marks than in anything he'd done over his entire life—a life that already stretched for thousands of years.

He'd discovered new strengths in himself, new abilities. A sense of fulfillment for having accomplished something entirely physical. There was an amazingly invigorating quality about armed combat. It was even better with a brave companion standing beside him.

He thought of Taron. His friend would love every moment of this fight against demonkind, but the battle Taron waged on Alton's behalf was an important one, if Alton ever hoped to return to his home.

If I have a home to return to.

What if the bad guys won this one? He hadn't let himself think of anything other than victory, but their odds weren't all that great.

He wondered how Dax and Eddy fared, if they'd met much resistance. Dax suffered greatly from the demon's curse. Alton had the feeling it was a race to see if Dax's short span on Earth would outlast the power of the demonic curse that was slowly strangling him. They were almost at the end of his third day. It had been obvious this evening that Dax was in constant pain. Would Eddy's touch be enough to keep the cursed tattoo under control?

There was more strength in the woman than Alton had thought possible. Women on Earth were nothing like the women of Lemuria. No, here their power and intelligence was equal to that of the men. But would it be enough?

So much weighed against them. There'd been no word from Taron, no sign of Lemuria electing to help. Maybe his people had lost their desire to fight, their need to protect their own. It was difficult to believe they'd once been a race of warriors.

Alton flexed his fingers and thought of how good it felt to grasp the hilt of his crystal sword, to swing that shimmering blade through stone as if he cleaved butter. It was becoming more an extension of his arm than he'd ever believed possible, though he'd carried it all his adult life.

Yet it still had not shared its name. What kind of warrior was he, that his sword refused to acknowledge him? He tried to remember the last time he'd seen a sentient, speaking Lemurian sword. His culture abounded with tales of ancient warriors and their partnered swords, but if he'd ever heard one speak, it had been many long years ago.

Alton squared his shoulders. He knew he fought bravely, but was bravery enough? Did they have the strength they'd need to see this through? It was difficult to imagine their small band overpowering all the demons who'd made it through the portal.

If only he knew how Taron was doing. Was his friend having any luck convincing the Lemurians to take up arms against their age-old enemies?

Would they even remember how?

He knew from his history lessons that his people had once been powerful warriors who'd kept demonkind under control, but once that control was achieved, they'd continued to fight other peoples until their many battles had almost obliterated the more civilized aspects of their society.

The art of negotiation had saved them, and once they'd established secure treaties with their known enemies, their skills had shifted entirely to the art of debate.

Now they'd merely argue a person to death before they'd actually lift a weapon. Unfortunately, you couldn't argue with a demon. They knew only three things: eat, fuck, and kill. Demons weren't known for diplomacy, and a demon never surrendered.

Still, even though their days as warriors were long past, each Lemurian male carried a sword, if only for ceremonial purposes. All males were trained in the art of swordsmanship, though what they learned was more ritual than reality, especially when their swords remained mute.

Would his sword ever awaken?

How many demon deaths did it take to impress a crystal sword of Lemuria? How many more demons would he kill before the creatures were finally gone from this dimension? Would they be able to kill them all? He felt as if his thoughts whirled in ever more convoluted circles. Circles that merely took him back to the beginning of his original argument.

Obviously the Lemurian talent for debate and discussion was more deeply ingrained than he'd suspected, if he could carry on such a discussion with himself, and manage it all in the course of mere seconds. Shrugging off the sense of doom settling over his shoulders, Alton turned his attention back to Ed. The older man had fought valiantly, swinging a six-foot pry bar as if it were an iron mace.

From the beginning, they'd worked well together. Alton's superior strength and size had given him the upper hand, and he'd destroyed almost half of the avatars waiting here at the nursery on his own. He'd whipped his sword in wide arcs, slicing through the creatures as they attacked. The crystal blade had cut through them as if they were made of paper, not stone or ceramic.

Ed had gone for the rest, crushing their brittle bodies with his heavy iron bar. Once Ed destroyed the avatar, Alton had merely swept his sword through the stinking demon mist, and they'd disappeared in a flash of fire and smoke, leaving behind the unmistakable stench of sulfur.

He hoped that meant they were dead. He needed to check

on that with Dax. A demon, reformed or otherwise, should know what it took to kill one of the bastards.

"Alton, I just realized what's bothering me."

Alton looked in the direction Ed pointed, toward the entrance to the store.

"Remember earlier, when Eddy mentioned this place? She said it was the store with the big grizzly bear in front. Notice anything missing?"

Alton shifted his gaze from the noticeably barren store entrance and carefully studied the surrounding area. "No sign of a bear. Any idea where it might have gone?"

"When we first got here, the creatures were all in the parking lot, as if they were waiting. Remember? We thought they were massing to attack us, but I'm wondering if they were merely getting ready to join up with others somewhere else. We were walking east, and they were all facing us. What if they were getting ready to go somewhere west of town when we showed up? They might have been as surprised as we were. They certainly didn't put up an organized fight."

Alton tried to picture the creatures as they'd first seen them. He really did need to pay closer attention, as Taron so often reminded him. "They were definitely facing west. If you're right, that would take them into town."

"Or, it would take them out to the cemetery, where Eddy and Dax were headed." Ed slung his pry bar over his shoulder. "I suggest we follow the same route. I bet we'll find the bear along the way. As big as it is, it's probably got more than one demon running it."

"I don't like that a bit. If you're right . . ." Alton shook his head. "When demonkind begin to cooperate, they get scary."

Ed's dry laugh sounded anything but humorous. "You mean they're not scary like this?" He waved a hand in front of him, encompassing the shattered pieces of stone and ceramic littering the parking lot. "I really wonder where that bear went. . . ."

"Let's find out. Which way will lead us to Dax and Eddy?"

"This way." Ed pointed to a narrow country lane. "This road leads us back to the main street where we can take a jog over the freeway, and from there go directly to the cemetery. Almost due west, which is the direction all these guys were headed."

Alton merely nodded. Everything he saw showed evidence of cooperation among demonkind. Unheard of, but so were a lot of the things he'd witnessed over the past few hours. He followed Ed, worrying even more how this would all turn out.

The closer they got to town, the more demons they found. Ed thought of calling Eddy, but he was too busy ducking overhead attacks from small bronze hummingbirds with deadly beaks or bashing in garden gnomes that raced out of yards and leapt off of porches as they tried to block the way.

"I had no idea how many people put little statues in their yards," he said, swinging his iron bar at a pair of ceramic gnomes. Both shattered. A sulfuric stench filled the air as the demon mist floated free of the avatars.

Alton stepped up with his sword and with one swing of the crystal blade, quickly sent them off in flames. "It's an odd human custom, that's for sure. Why so many with pointy hats and round bellies? Is it some sort of religious icon?" Alton knocked another metal hummingbird out of the sky, sliced it with a flick of his wrist, and destroyed the demon as it escaped.

"I'm beginning to wonder." Ed stepped over a pile of broken gnomes. His cell phone rang. He grabbed it out of his pocket and flipped it open. When he saw the number, his heart gave a lurch. "Thank goodness, it's Eddy." He took the call quickly, relieved to hear her voice. She sounded confident, though concerned enough that she and Dax wanted Ed and Alton's help. He was smiling broadly when he put the phone back in his pocket.

"Just what I thought. They're still working their way to the cemetery. She said they've killed a couple of dozen demons so far, but they can hear sounds that make them think there are a lot more at or near the cemetery, which is just west of their location. They want us to join them before they go in. She and Dax don't want to attempt to enter the place on their own. It's a pretty good hike for us, about twenty minutes or so."

Alton stared toward the west, as if he were trying to hear the banshee howls and growls of demons, but the night was quiet. "Do you think we should go back for your vehicle?"

"No." Ed shook his head. "We'd miss any demons along the way."

"I agree." Alton started forward with what appeared to be a new sense of purpose. Ed had to stretch his legs to keep up with the long-legged Lemurian.

"The whole point of this exercise is a foot patrol to see what we're dealing with. Hopefully we'll find your missing bear between here and there." Alton started to sheath his sword, stared at it a moment, and kept it in his hand.

As many demons as they'd come across, Ed figured that was a pretty good move. He rested his pry bar over his shoulder as if he were carrying a rifle. He and Alton swung to the right and headed north on Lassen Boulevard. "We can cross the tracks at West State Street," he said. "That'll take us to Fir, which'll get us over the freeway to the cemetery."

It was unusually quiet in town. Even the small bar on the corner was dark. They passed a few piles of ceramic and stone pieces. "Looks as if Eddy and Dax have been this way."

Alton merely nodded, and continued scanning the alleyways and side streets they passed, but all was quiet.

They were almost to State Street when a scream cut through the night. Close by, human, not a banshee howl. Ed and Alton both stopped. It was difficult to tell from what direction the sound had come.

She screamed again. Ed was certain it was a woman. "This way!" He held his pry bar like a spear and raced down the street to a small minimart just around a bend in the road.

Alton quickly passed him, running full tilt with those long legs of his. He held his sword out in front of him. The crystal blade shimmered with its own light, but even with such a brilliant beacon, it was all Ed could do to keep him in sight.

Alton rounded a corner and disappeared just as the woman screamed again.

It appeared they'd found their bear. Alton skidded to a halt at a point where the main route they'd been following jogged to the left. Streetlights illuminated the corner. A small group of people had gathered, but most of them were all on the far side of the road, away from the action.

A young woman had wedged herself behind a large garbage Dumpster. Armed only with what looked like a slat from a wood pallet, she was trapped against a wall with the huge demon-powered grizzly shoving at the metal container and taking swipes at her with his paw.

She swung at him with the broken slat, but claws at least six inches long barely missed her as the creature forced its broad shoulders between the Dumpster and the brick wall. She retreated as far as she could, still poking ineffectually with the slat. The massive concrete bear appeared to be moving the Dumpster, widening the gap where the woman was trapped with the force of his powerful shoulders.

A couple of young men were trying to help, but the rocks they threw merely bounced off the concrete hide. From the sound of their curses and the lack of cooperation between them, Alton thought they appeared to be more than a little inebriated.

The grizzly's jaws gaped wide, but there were no grunts or bestial roars. Instead, an eerie, banshee-driven wail echoed off the surrounding buildings and raised the tiny hairs along Alton's spine. The creature swung its huge head in the direction of the two young men.

One of them glanced up and saw Alton as the bear took a swipe in his direction. The kid screamed and ducked. "I'm outta here," he said, scrambling away on all fours. The other young man was right behind him.

Disgusted, Alton worked his way around behind the bear and stabbed at it with his sword. The bear deflected the blade, swatting it away with its huge front paw. Screaming its banshee howl, the huge creature reared up on hind legs as thick as tree trunks and pivoted, towering over Alton's tall frame as if he were but a child.

At least Alton had turned its attention away from the woman. She'd wedged herself between the Dumpster and the wall, as far out of the bear's reach as she could go.

Ed was still trying to catch his breath, but he swung his iron bar at the backs of the bear's concrete legs. The iron rang out like a church bell as one leg shattered. Ed scrambled out of the way. The creature dropped to three legs, barely missing Alton. Alton stabbed again, piercing the creature's chest this time, but for whatever reason, the crystal sword penetrated but didn't shatter the concrete.

The grizzly screamed again. It turned toward Alton with its jaws spread wide. Multiple rows of razor-sharp teeth reminded the Lemurian of pictures he'd seen of ancient sharks, but this was no fish.

Screaming in that eerie, otherworldly wail, the bear whirled once again, pivoting on three legs as easily as it had moved on four. It swung a huge paw at Ed. Alton reared up over it like a matador sticking a bull and drove the sword between the creature's concrete shoulder blades, burying the crystal blade to the hilt.

The bear jerked back and swung in a circle on three legs. Alton tried to hang on, but the hilt of the sword ripped from his hands. The woman screamed when the bear faced her once again. Alton had no time to consider the stupidity of his actions. He leapt to the bear's rough, stonelike back and clung there, scrabbling for a good hold on the sword's hilt.

Enraged, the bear twisted and turned as it tried to shake him loose, tossing Alton about as if he clung to the back of a rodeo bull. Finally it stood on one hind leg, moving with impossible dexterity in spite of the missing limb, roaring and screaming that bloodcurdling banshee wail.

The crowd of spectators was growing. Alton was vaguely aware of shouts and cursing, words of encouragement, the distant wail of sirens. As the bear dropped back to three legs, Alton pulled the blade free of the creature and swung in a mighty arc.

The bear's massive concrete head fell to the ground, and the body crumbled beneath Alton's legs. Four separate demons emerged in a thick, black sulfuric cloud. Once again Alton swung the sword. His blade passed through three of the demons, exploding each in a burst of flame.

The fourth paused in midair. Then it turned, as if consciously considering an attack in this form. Alton slashed the crystal blade through the stinking mist. A brief flash of flames and the mist disintegrated until only the sulfuric stench and a pile of crumbled concrete and stone remained.

Alton sheathed his sword and slipped between the metal Dumpster and the wall. He held out his hand, and the woman ran to him, sobbing now that the danger had passed. Gently Alton lifted her in his arms and held her close, running his hand along her spine.

She was long and lean, and he felt each vertebra as his fingers soothed her. She breathed in short, choppy gasps, obviously terrified but, for the moment, trusting him as she curled close against his chest. It was a unique sensation to hold her close. Women in Lemuria would never allow a man to touch them so, but then a woman in Lemuria would never have been in jeopardy such as this one had been.

Nor would a Lemurian woman have had the courage to try and defend herself against demons with only a scrap of wood as a weapon.

"It's okay," he said, talking softly. "You're safe now. The creature is gone."

Ed stood beside him. "Alton, the police are coming. What do you want to do?" Then he peered closer at the woman in Alton's arms. "Ginny? Is that you, sweetheart? Are you okay?"

She struggled in Alton's grasp. Reluctantly, he set her feet on the ground. She stepped away from him.

"Ed? Where's Eddy? What are you doing here? What happened? Who is . . . ?" She raised her head and looked directly at Alton. For the first time, he got a good look at her face. He could have sworn his heart stopped beating. She was utterly beautiful, with skin much darker than Eddy's and golden eyes that reminded him of the stone called tiger's-eye.

He knew that Roman soldiers wore the stones when they went into battle, and somehow that trivia seemed terribly important to him at this moment. Tiger's-eye for protection, to help focus energy on the fight.

Nine hells! He needed to focus.

What was he doing, staring into those mesmerizing eyes? Ed tugged anxiously at his sleeve.

"Alton? How the hell are we going to explain this? The police are almost here."

"We're not." Alton waved a hand in front of Ginny's eyes. She blinked and turned toward Ed.

Alton held both hands out to the crowd of men and women who had gathered to watch his battle with the demon bear. Without a single word exchanged between them, the two young men who'd fought the grizzly stepped in front of the group and swung roundhouse blows at each other. Within seconds, there was a full-scale brawl on the corner—men fighting men, women rolling on the ground, fighting other women.

Ed shot Alton an inquisitive glance. "Effective," he said. "Ugly, but very effective." Then he took Ginny's arm. "Ginny? You need to go home now. You're just half a block from your place. We'll walk with you."

Ginny jerked her head back and forth in a definite negative and tugged her arm free of Ed's grasp. "Ed, what the hell is going on?" She glared at Ed and then turned her attention on Alton. "Who are you? What was that thing that attacked me?"

She should have forgotten. Alton stared at his fingers and then at Ginny. He'd just wiped away the memory of her attack. At least he thought he had.

Obviously she had a very strong will.

Ed frowned at Alton. Alton shrugged. Once again he concentrated on the young woman. Passed his hands across her eyes. Strengthened the powers of his mind to block everything that had happened.

She turned her head slowly and gazed at Alton. Frowned, as if trying to place him. "What are you doing to me?" She stared at him, her eyes unfocused and confused.

Fighting him. Still strong enough to fight his powers.

Alton felt caught there in time, as if the world around them ceased its spinning, as if the demon threat no longer existed. He was not an immortal, not a Lemurian here on a mission of such otherworldly importance. No, he was merely a man, enthralled by the soft, confused gaze of the most beautiful woman he'd ever beheld. She blinked, her lips parted.

Alton took a step back. What was he thinking? She was human. Not even royalty. He was a Lemurian warrior, the son of Lemuria's leader. The heir apparent.

Ginny blinked, still obviously confused. She shook her head again and looked at Ed.

Ed tugged gently at her elbow. This time she allowed him to lead her as they turned away from Alton. Ed walked down the street with his hand wrapped around her arm, supporting her. Alton followed closely behind.

Two patrol cars raced by as the three of them disappeared into the shadows along the side street leading to a quiet neighborhood.

"She lives here," Ed said. He nodded toward a small duplex set back from the street. "Let me get her inside. Then we need to find Eddy and Dax."

"No. Wait." Ginny stopped and planted her feet. Frowning, she gazed up at Alton. "You never told me what that thing was. That bear wasn't real, was it? What the hell's going on? Ed? Who is this guy? What'd he do, that funny thing with his hand?"

She brushed her hands over her face, scrubbed at her eyes. Planted her hands on her hips and glared at Alton.

Standing behind Ginny, Ed shrugged helplessly and shook his head. They couldn't let her remember what she'd seen.

Alton wasn't sure it would work, but he reached for Ginny, lifted her up to her toes, and leaned over and kissed her. Their mouths connected, hers slightly parted in shock, his firmly covering her soft, full lips, and he poured the strength of his hypnotic powers into her startled mind.

She fought him for but a second, until the strength of his mental touch calmed her, confused her, left her breathless and wondering who she was kissing and why. Alton felt her confusion, sensed her blossoming desire, and realized he could end the kiss at any time.

Slowly, reluctantly, he moved his lips over hers for one, last taste and then set her gently back on her feet. Ginny blinked, touched her fingertips to her mouth, and then turned away.

Ed gently took Ginny's arm and walked with her into her house.

Alton waited impatiently. He refused to think about the kiss, but it had been the only way he knew of to overwhelm her strong will. He couldn't risk her recalling that she'd almost been killed by a concrete statue of a grizzly bear.

One that was powered by not one, but four demons. Four of the evil beings, cooperating . . . demons, working together.

It was worse than he'd thought.

So was his reaction to the woman. *Ginny.* Her name was Ginny, and his kiss had made her forget.

Unfortunately, the taste of her lips, the soft curve of her breasts against his chest, the taste of her sweet mouth were all he could think of. He'd never reacted to any female on such a visceral level, especially not one so inappropriate. He had no time for a human woman. None at all for one with a will as strong as Ginny's.

He grabbed his sword out of its scabbard and focused on the blade. Focused on the fact it hadn't spoken to him even now, after he'd vanquished the bear.

This was important—the battle, the sword, destroying demons. Not the woman.

What was the point? Lemurians were immortal. Humans had a life span that barely registered on his own personal calendar.

So why did he care? Would she wonder what had happened tonight? How she'd gotten home?

Would she remember him?

He hoped not. She had to forget, just as he would.

Ed walked out a few minutes later. "She'll be okay," he said. "Ginny's tough. She and Eddy have been friends for years. She's a nine-one-one dispatcher so she's perfectly aware there's some strange stuff going on, but she doesn't have a clue what it is. Hopefully we can keep this under wraps for a few more days, but with things like that bear . . ." He glanced up at Alton. "What do you make of that? There were four demons inside that thing."

"Nothing good," Alton said. He put thoughts of Ginny behind him and focused on the here and now. "It means our enemies are learning to work as a single unit. They're cooperating, as if there's actual intelligence behind them. That's something demons just don't do—at least they haven't in the past. It makes them a lot harder to fight."

They walked faster now. Both Dax and Eddy could be in danger. Alton didn't like being so far from them. Even so, no matter how he tried, Alton couldn't get the image of Eddy's friend out of his head.

"You're sure she's okay?"

"Who? Ginny?" Ed nodded. "Yeah. Ginny's tough. She's going to be fine."

"Did she seem to remember anything?"

"She remembered a brawl in front of the minimart. I let her think she'd gotten pushed around a little. Told her I recognized her and grabbed her before she could get hurt. I think she bought that." He laughed. "I have to admit, whatever you did when you kissed her left her really scrambled."

Alton laughed, but he didn't answer Ed. He couldn't. He had no idea what he'd done or why he'd done it. Stupid. What a stupid move.

Except his kiss had worked when his usual method hadn't. He'd done what he had to do. No more, no less. He'd always been a man of focus—why must he remind himself of his purpose? He had a battle to fight, not a woman to woo.

Alton paused and listened as a sound came to him on the evening breeze, a fierce whisper on the wind that sent shivers along his spine. He recognized the distant howls and shrieks of demonkind, blending almost innocently with the steady hum of traffic passing by on the freeway beneath the overpass.

"We need to hurry. There's something building—I hear the cries of demons. That way." He pointed to the west, beyond the freeway.

"That's where the cemetery is. Where Eddy and Dax were headed. Lordy, I hope they're okay. C'mon!" Ed took off at a slow, awkward trot down the quiet street. It was well past midnight, and they'd already fought many battles. Ed was older, a human male past his prime. It was obvious his strength was waning, though his love for Eddy, his fear for her safety, kept him going.

It was so easy to forget how fragile humans were. Their passion and their bravery made them seem more powerful, as if nothing could ever slow them down or defeat them.

Yet the power of their passion could carry them just so far. They were hampered, always, by their frail human bodies. Not only a finite life span, but the physical limitations that were part of their humanity.

Limitations they must somehow overcome if they were to win this fight against demonkind. There was no room for defeat. No time for failure. Ed would have to find the strength to fight, just as Alton must. He whipped his sword out once again and held it high. He stared at it a moment, waiting for the voice.

Why wasn't it speaking to him? Where had he failed as a warrior? He was doing exactly what he'd feared all along: going into battle beside Dax before he could converse with the sword.

Until he could order the sword not to attack Dax, it would see the demon in his borrowed human body as the enemy. They'd have to fight far from one another.

Dax had more than enough on his plate. He certainly didn't need to fear Alton and a sword that, so far, denied communication. What in all the nine hells did he need to do to prove himself worthy?

The crystal blade glowed brighter than ever, almost as if it mocked him, even as it lit their path along the dark country road.

Chapter Ten

Dax raised his head from the low berm where he and Eddy waited near the cemetery. There was no wind. The waning moon cast a silver glow across the stone monuments and statues, though much of what he wished he could see lay in darkness. It was difficult to define what was shape and what was shadow, what moved and what merely appeared to shift in and out of the bands of light that stretched between the trees.

Still, the constant screams and howls of demons fighting amongst themselves hinted at the vast numbers gathered here tonight. Demons were not known for cooperation, but it appeared one among them was attempting to organize the ungodly host.

Eddy's heat bled through Dax's jeans and flannel shirt. He felt the soft rise and fall of her body with each breath she took, sensed the curiosity that overpowered her fear. She'd not hesitated tonight to stand beside Dax when they'd run across demons during their patrol of the city streets. She'd found a crowbar alongside the road, something that must have fallen off a workman's truck, and while it wasn't her requested baseball bat, she'd swung it with enough power to crush any number of demon-powered avatars.

His own powers had returned. As long as he used them sparingly, he'd had enough to destroy all the demons Eddy had set free. They'd left a trail of shattered stone and cracked ceramic from the center of town to the cemetery. Eddy had the clawed weapon in her hand right now, ready to use it against their enemies. Dax leaned close and kissed her cheek. He wasn't sure why, only that he knew he had to touch her.

She turned, smiled at him, and whispered, "What was that for?"

He shook his head. "I'm not sure, but I know I want to do it again, when we're someplace a little more private."

"Your timing sucks. You know that, don't you?" She covered her mouth with her hand to muffle her laugh and bumped him with her shoulder. Dax bumped her back; then he raised up on one elbow, turned his head, and looked down the dark road leading to town. A pale glow shimmered in the distance.

Alton's sword. "I see your dad and Alton," he said, lying back down beside Eddy. A stone angel circled nearby, screaming in an unholy voice. Another joined in, circling beside the first. They might have been placed beside graves representing holy messengers, but now they flew with powerful beats of marble wings and their eyes glowed either yellow or red in the night.

Dax and Eddy both ducked their heads. Bumper whimpered and shivered beside him. Even her tail had quit wagging. Willow hadn't left Dax's pocket since they'd nestled down into their hiding place.

"We're awfully close, here," Dax said. "I suggest we go back up the road to meet your dad and Alton. I think I'd rather decide our next move a bit farther from the action."

"Agreed." Eddy slithered backward on her belly until

she was below the top of the berm, out of sight of the demons massing in the cemetery and the hellish angels flying overhead.

Dax was right beside her. He stood first and grabbed her hand, pulling Eddy to her feet. She stumbled when Bumper nudged her leg. Dax held even tighter to her hand and tugged her along beside him.

Willow popped out of Dax's pocket and flew toward Alton and Ed. They all met at a point a few hundred yards from the cemetery, under the protection of a huge cedar. Alton sheathed his sword as they drew close. He and Ed remained clearly visible in the pale moonlight.

Eddy gave her father a quick hug and got a kiss on the cheek, but Dax noticed how quickly she returned to his side. He wrapped an arm over her shoulders.

"What's going on? We could hear the noise all the way from town." Alton held his palm out for Willow. Once she landed, he set her on his shoulder. "Any idea how many there are?"

"It's hard to tell," Dax said. "Have you noticed the demons teaming up? We've destroyed a number of large avatars powered by two demons working together."

Ed nodded. "Alton had quite a fight with the bear statue from the nursery. That big grizzly? It put up one hell of a fight, but when Alton finally beheaded the damned thing, it had four demons inside. It almost got Ginny Jones over near the minimart on North Mount Lassen."

"Is Ginny okay?" Eddy's fingers tightened on Dax's. "What happened?"

Alton shrugged. "We're not sure, but we heard a scream and found her trapped behind a Dumpster, putting up a good fight with a wooden slat. The bear had his shoulders wedged between the Dumpster and the wall, trying to shove the container aside using brute strength. We stopped it before it got to her, so she's okay. Shaken, but I made her forget the attack. As far as she and the people who saw it know, she got too close to some people fighting."

"How'd you manage that?" Dax pulled Eddy close and wrapped his arm around her.

Ed laughed. "Alton used his power of suggestion to start a street brawl. When the police arrived, there were at least twenty men and women fighting in the middle of the street."

Alton shrugged again. He actually looked embarrassed. "I'm sorry. It was the best I could come up with in a hurry."

"As long as it worked . . ." Dax paused. "Get back. Quick" He grabbed Eddy and dragged her and the dog close to the thick tree trunk. Alton and Ed moved with them, until they were all pressed up against the rough bark.

"Listen." Dax held a finger to his lips. "Do you hear that?"

Bumper whined. Eddy wrapped her fingers around Bumper's muzzle and gazed up at Dax. "What's that noise?"

"More demons. It's too dark to see them, but I can hear them. I sense them, too, moving along the road. They're coming this way."

Alton rested his fingers on Dax's shoulder. "Look toward the freeway. Where the glow from the overhead light hits the frontage road. There are hundreds more of them."

"I see them now." Ed wrapped his fingers around his iron pry bar. "Eddy, when they get close, why don't you turn Bumper loose? That way she can get away if she has to."

Eddy glanced at Dax. He nodded. Ed's suggestion was a good one. As far as they knew, no humans had actually been harmed by the demon-powered avatars, but a number of pets had fallen victim. The demons appeared to be gaining strength and mobility within their chosen creatures. Dax hated to think of harm coming to any of his little band, including Bumper. She'd proven to be a loyal beast.

"She's a good fighter with the little ones," he said, running his fingers through Bumper's curly blond topknot.

"That's because she thinks they're chew toys." Eddy smiled when she said it, but she quickly released the snap on the leash and held on to the dog's collar.

Willow zipped off Alton's shoulder, shimmering in a whirlwind of blue sparkles. Dax inhaled the energy she pulled out of the air for him. He felt it pulse along his spine and the length of the snake tattoo, which had remained somewhat quiet for the past hour or so. He wondered if it was merely biding its time, preparing to attack.

It was definitely affecting his powers. The first time, when he'd called on the fire and flame in Eddy's little house, he'd felt as if he could throw bolts of either for as long as he needed to fight. This evening, though, he'd discovered there was a limit to his strength. It appeared the cursed serpent had the ability to siphon off the energy Willow sent him. After killing just a handful of demons, he'd had to stop and allow Eddy to use her healing powers to control the pain.

The last time, he was certain she'd felt the snake's fangs beneath her palm. The thing was growing stronger. He feared it was becoming sentient, that soon it would turn on him. Would he have the strength to fight a battle against a creature that was literally part of his own flesh and blood?

The demons coming up the road drew closer. Alton was right—there must be hundreds of statues. Moonlight illuminated all kinds of garden critters: pot-bellied gnomes and concrete benches that looked like pigs and cows, metallic hummingbirds flittering overhead, and stone cats, squirrels, and antlered deer creeping along the ground. They all moved with obvious intent and purpose, somehow drawn to the cemetery.

The screaming and banshee howls seemed to have settled a bit. Then a loud, familiar wail split the night. Eddy grabbed

Dax's hand. "The gargoyle. Look!" She pointed at the creature flying low over the berm where they'd been lying. It followed the road and swooped over the advancing horde of stone and ceramic creatures.

Dax raised his hands as the gargoyle drew close and shot a bitter-cold blast of icy wind at the creature. It encased the gargoyle in solid ice. The creature dropped to the ground, bounced once, and lay still. Bumper tore loose from Eddy's grasp and raced toward it. The crowd of demons marching closer paused in the middle of the road.

Then they began to mill about in confusion. Dax thought of the way an anthill looked if you disturbed it. The demons seemed to lose their focus, to wander without leadership now that the gargoyle was down.

A banshee wail cut through the clattering and banging of stone creatures in turmoil, and the gargoyle raised its head. It swung one huge, clawed paw at Bumper and sent the dog tumbling and yelping. Dax hit the gargoyle with a blast of freezing air.

The stone should have shattered, but instead the creature rose slowly on awkwardly shaped hind legs and stared directly at the little band of warriors hiding beneath the branches of the cedar. It hissed what sounded like a curse between long, curved teeth and mimicked Dax—holding its clawed hands out toward him as it called out in an unknown language.

An invisible blade slammed into him. Dax felt hot steel pierce his chest. Crying out, he slapped his hand over the snake tattoo and stumbled to his knees. Blinded by pain, he raised his hands and sent another blast of ice in the gargoyle's direction.

The creature hissed, but the sound died in the frozen air, and it toppled over on its back. Dax ran his hand across his chest, searching for the blade that struck him, but there was nothing there. The tattoo burned as if acid had been poured along its length, writhing from his knee, across his groin to his heart. He bit back a cry as agony seared his body. The strength went out of his legs. Shaking uncontrollably, Dax fell, collapsing face-first into the dirt as his world went dark.

Eddy screamed. She leaned over, grabbed Dax's shoulders, and somehow found the strength to roll him over to his back. His eyes were closed, his lips twisted in agony. He gasped for air through slightly parted lips. Her hands shook as she ripped his shirt open. The snake tattoo hissed and undulated across his chest. The eyes sparkled with life, and its long tongue flickered away from Dax's flesh.

Eddy slammed her hands down on the tattoo and sent every good, healing thought she could muster straight from her heart and down through her palms. The tongue flickered between her fingers, a living entity empowered with whatever curse the demon had fired at Dax.

Eddy's arms quivered with the strength it took to hold the snake in place. It shuddered and pulsed beneath her hands, burning her flesh with its hot scales and hotter tongue. Once again the forked tongue flickered between her fingers, and she felt the slick length of curved fangs beneath her palm. When the broad head pushed against her hands, Eddy pushed back.

She refused to think of the fangs, whether they were venomous or not. Refused to consider the fact she might not be strong enough, her questionable abilities not powerful enough to hold the filthy thing at bay. She wondered if the tail of the serpent moved with the same alacrity as the head, but she couldn't worry about that, not now. She had to hold it back. Had to keep it from growing any stronger.

Dax shivered, and his body jerked as convulsions wracked

his powerful frame. Eddy wasn't sure if it was from the pain or her touch or the internal battle he was having with the curse. His breath still huffed in and out in short, sharp bursts, and Eddy felt the pain rising through her hands, up her wrists to her forearms as the snake fought her.

As she fought the curse.

"Go!" she screamed, glancing over her shoulder at Alton and Ed. "Don't let them get away!"

Ed touched her shoulder. "Is he . . . ?"

"Just go. He's alive. There's nothing you can do for Dax, but you have to stop them."

Cursing furiously, Alton took off running, pulling his sword from the scabbard as soon as he was out of striking distance from Dax. Ed ran with him, swinging his metal bar like a long golf club, crushing the stone and ceramic creatures.

Alton's sword flashed, destroying demon after demon in bright bursts of sulfuric flame. Eddy heard Bumper barking with a sense of relief. If she could make that kind of noise, she couldn't be too badly hurt. Eddy glanced up to see where the dog was and realized Bumper had begun working the huge group of avatars like a herd of sheep, circling from the rear and herding them toward Ed and Alton.

Her dad marched through the middle of the throng of avatars, swinging his big iron bar and leaving shattered stone and pottery in his wake.

Alton fought like a berserker. His sword flashed overhead, striking the demons as Ed destroyed their avatars. The snap and pop of demon mist bursting into flame filled the night.

The scent of sulfur drifted their way. It made Eddy's eyes burn, but she took it as a good sign. Alton's sword must be killing the demons, not just sending them back to Abyss. The sparking fires, the stink of burnt demon—it was exactly what happened when Dax struck them with his fire.

Willow stayed close to Eddy, hovering overhead and sending energy through her. Eddy felt it racing along her arms, through her fingertips, and into Dax, dulling the pain in her arms, strengthening her sense of control over the cursed serpent.

The sounds of battle, the acrid stink of sulfur, and the screams and wails of many demons dying faded away as she held her hands to Dax, as she willed him to be strong, for the curse to sleep once more. She didn't turn around, didn't allow her concentration to waver. She was vaguely aware of her father's shouts, of Alton's battle cries.

Bumper's barking was a thing of joy, as if she'd finally found her true calling in life: herding demons.

Dax's eyes opened, clear now, and focused. He reached up and grasped Eddy's wrist. "What happened? The gargoyle . . . ?"

Eddy glanced to her right, to the point where the gargoyle had fallen. It was gone. There was no rubble, no sign it had died. "It got away, I think. That last curse it sent might have weakened it. Are you okay?"

He took a few deep breaths, closed his eyes, and exhaled. "The pain is gone. Unfortunately, so is my strength. Thank you, Eddy. I've never experienced anything like that, even when I was a demon." Dax tried to sit up. Eddy pulled her hands away from his chest. She noticed with relief that the tattoo was once again merely colored art on Dax's chest. The eyes were flat, the tongue no longer flickering. Her hands still burned, though, and she felt the shape of the fangs against her palms.

She rose shakily to her feet and offered Dax her hand. He took it and slowly stood. Willow hovered, flitting about them until Dax finally held out his hand. She landed in his palm and glared at him with her tiny hands fisted against her hips. It was obvious she was reading him the riot act.

Then, when she was done, Willow buzzed away in a flurry of blue sparkles.

Dax raised his head and gazed at Eddy with horror. "Willow says the snake came alive, that you had to hold it with both hands to keep it from crawling off my body." He grabbed her hands with both of his and turned them palms up.

The skin was blistered but not broken. "Did it bite you?"

She shook her head. "No, but I felt the fangs. The serpent's tongue actually slithered between my fingers. It acts as if it's trying to crawl away. Dax, what happens if it does? What if I can't hold it in place?"

He lowered his lips to her hands and kissed one palm, then the other. When he raised his head, Eddy was positive there were tears in his eyes. "I can't let you do that anymore."

"What happens if it crawls away?" She tugged her hands free of his. "Answer me, Dax. I deserve the truth."

"I will die." He gazed toward the sounds of battle, where Ed and Alton, with Bumper's assistance, had destroyed almost all of the avatars and their sulfuric demons. The gargoyle was nowhere to be seen. The cemetery had grown silent.

"I don't understand. I thought the tattoo only held your demon powers."

Dax turned back to her. He looked defeated, as if he'd reached the end of his strength. He spoke in a monotone. "I'm a demon, Eddy. My demon powers are who and what I am. If the tattoo succeeds in gaining sentience and crawling off my body, it will take my powers with it. Those powers are all that keep this body alive. I'll be just another demon, a black smudge of sulfuric stink. Something for Alton's sword to destroy."

Eddy shook her head. "No, you won't. I'm not leaving your side. If I could hold the snake back tonight, as powerful as it was after the demon cursed you again, I can control it for as long as I have to." She grabbed his hands and held on. "You're mine for three and a half more days, Dax. Don't forget that."

She heard the crunch of boots on gravel and turned around. Alton and her dad were walking toward them. Bumper bounded alongside, obviously delighted with the battle they'd just fought. From the silence and the grins on the men's faces, it appeared it was a battle they'd won.

"Dax? Are you okay?" Alton sheathed his sword as he drew near. His concern was obvious as he stepped up close to Dax.

"Good to see you standing, son." Ed wiped his hand across his forehead. "Whatever that damned thing hit you with sure knocked your pins out from under you."

"I'm fine, thanks to Eddy. . . ."

Dax turned and stared at her, and once again, Eddy wished she could read his mind.

"Did you get all of them?" She tore her gaze from Dax's face and looked beyond the two men, but it was too dark to tell if anything moved.

"We did." Alton frowned and gazed toward the cemetery. "It's gone quiet. What's happened to the demons that were gathering over there?"

"I don't know." Eddy turned toward the now silent cemetery. "I can't tell from here. We're too far away."

They walked toward the silent memorial park, following the beam from Dax's flashlight. When they reached the berm, he swung the beam across the parklike grounds.

Eddy ran to the top of the low rise. "Look! The statues are back in place!"

Angels stood guard by the mausoleum door, and cherubs rested upon headstones. Everything appeared as it should.

There was no sign of the gargoyle.

Standing on top of the berm, she planted her fists on her hips and shook her head in disbelief. "We've been here for almost an hour watching them. Every single one of those statues was animated. Could the demons still be in them, waiting?"

"There's one way to find out." Alton strode forward, far enough away that he could safely unsheathe his sword. He held it aloft and crossed over the berm. When he reached the first stone angel that stood beside a grave, he swung his sword in a shimmering arc that decapitated the angel.

The head landed on the grass and rolled to one side. Blank eyes stared blindly toward Eddy and Dax. Nothing flew forth from the hollow body. There was no scent of sulfur, no black mist.

Nothing.

Eddy clung to Dax's hand. "Where'd they go? I remember that angel. It flew overhead, and the eyes were glowing red." She turned and gazed up at Dax.

He shook his head. "No idea, but the gargoyle is gone as well. Somehow, it has to be the key. We have to kill the damned thing, but I have no idea how to defeat it." He held up his free hand and stared at his fingertips. "I gave it everything I had, tonight. It wasn't enough."

Eddy glanced at Alton. He shook his head, answering her question before she even had a chance to ask. "I don't know." He reached over his shoulder and lovingly caressed the hilt of his sword. "It's a powerful weapon, but I'm not even sure if it's killing the demons I strike, or merely sending them back to Abyss. If only it would speak . . ."

"I'm convinced they're dying, Alton." Eddy looked to Dax for confirmation. "Aren't they going back to the void? They flame out when he hits them. The smell of burned demon and sulfur is the same as when you hit them, Dax. The sword has to be destroying them."

Dax shook his head. "There's no way to prove it. Even if they're not destroyed, they're gone. Into the void, back to Abyss . . . it's not important. With the portal closed, either works. We can only do our best and hope it's good enough."

They all looked at one another, but there were no firm answers. Ed yawned, and it was obvious he'd reached the end of his strength. Willow perched on Alton's shoulder. Dax turned and began walking back toward town. Eddy grabbed his hand and walked beside him. Ed and Alton followed, while Bumper, still unleashed, bounded and bounced around them as if this was the greatest event in her life.

"Eddy, will this road take us through town, near the library building?"

"It can." Eddy glanced at Dax. The sparkle was back in his eyes.

"I want to see if the gargoyle is back in its place where we saw it today. If it returns there to rest . . ."

"You're thinking maybe you can sneak up on it?" Ed moved up beside them. "Maybe if we went after it during daylight hours . . ."

Dax nodded. "That's what I'm thinking. Alton with his sword, me nearby with whatever powers I can muster." He squeezed Eddy's hand. "I'm sorry. I'm not proving to be a very powerful DemonSlayer, am I?"

"I disagree." She squeezed back, wrapping her fingers tightly around his. She didn't say any more. As far as Eddy was concerned, there was no room to argue.

Ed was practically asleep on his feet when they finally reached the library building. "Eddy? Stay with your father, please?" Dax glanced at Ed and back to Eddy, hoping she'd understand.

She nodded. "We'll wait here." She called Bumper to her

and put the leash back on the dog. "C'mon, Dad. I'm beat. Will you sit with me?"

Ed didn't say a word, but he didn't complain when she sat down on a park bench in front of the old library and patted the spot beside her. Eddy set her crowbar on the ground by her feet. Ed leaned his iron pry bar against the seat and sat heavily on the wooden bench.

Eddy glanced over her shoulder and mouthed something to Dax. He wasn't sure what she said, but the look in her eyes gave him a fresh burst of strength. He realized she'd quickly become the most important thing in his life. The reason he fought. The reason he would continue to fight, no matter how hopeless the battle might seem.

His gaze lingered on Eddy, on the curve of her lips, the line of her jaw, the long sweep of her throat. It required a conscious act of will to turn away, but somehow he found the strength to focus on the job.

How had she become so important to him in such a short time? He shook his head. It didn't really matter how, only that she had. He realized he was smiling when he and Alton walked across the worn patch of lawn to the front steps of the library.

Dax flashed the beam from the flashlight across the corner pieces. Both platforms were empty. The gargoyle had not yet returned to its resting place. Disappointed but not entirely surprised, Dax flipped the flashlight off. The soft glow of a nearby street lamp illuminated the sidewalk well enough to see.

"What now?" He spoke quietly. There was no need to worry Eddy any further.

Alton stared toward the bench where Eddy and Ed waited. Then he turned and quirked one eyebrow at Dax. "Now I think we go back to Ed's and rest," he said. "Tomorrow we need to see where the gargoyle is hiding out when he's not where he belongs. You said he was here this morning, right?"

"He was, but in daylight the streets are busy, people are around. I couldn't very well climb up there and engage him in a fight."

Alton smiled his agreement. "True, but if I'm with you to do a little manipulation of what people see and remember . . ."

Bumper growled.

"Dax?"

Eddy? Dax turned and raced across the lawn with Alton right behind. Eddy held on to her father's arm. Both of them stared at a grotesque figure standing not twenty feet away, staring right back at them. It stood perfectly still for a moment longer. Then it seemed to straighten up on bowed legs and made a low, keening sound that raised the hairs on Dax's arms.

He'd seen the creature in flight and this morning when it was sitting in place on the corner of the library building. He'd seen it lying on the ground after he'd hit it with his freezing mist, but he'd never seen it stalking its prey on the ground.

The gargoyle turned its head and surveyed the area around them. Then it began to move slowly toward the park bench. It walked awkwardly, dragging its stone wings, using its front legs or arms or whatever they were to pull itself forward while the hind legs hopped more than walked. Its eyes glowed an unholy shade of red, and saliva dripped from a gaping mouth filled with rows of sharp teeth.

It stopped when Dax and Alton moved into position, one on either side of the bench. "Eddy? Can you and your dad slip over the back of the bench and get out of our way? Alton and I will have a better chance with just the two of us."

He heard movement, but didn't want to take his eyes off the creature staring so steadily at him. He felt the snake writhing across his chest. The pain seemed to grow with each beat of his heart. He forced it down. Buried it, for now.

Alton moved farther to his right. "I'm going to see if I can get around behind it," he said. After a few more steps that took him away from Dax, he drew his sword. It pointed toward the gargoyle, not toward Dax, and Alton breathed an audible sigh of relief.

Bumper whimpered. Dax heard Eddy whisper quietly to the dog. Willow buzzed close by and settled on his shoulder. He felt the pulse of energy as she drew all she could out of the air and sent it into his body.

And still the gargoyle sat and stared. It seemed larger on the ground than it had looked flying overhead, at least six feet tall when it stood, with wings that spanned more than twice that distance when it stretched them out to either side.

Dax wished he could search its mind, but he sensed only hatred. There was no real intelligence, as far as he could tell, but that didn't feel right. There had to be intelligence in some form directing the attacks, yet the gargoyle appeared oblivious to Dax. It ignored Alton's cautious movements as he circled around behind the thing.

Dax set the flashlight on the park bench with the light still pointing toward the gargoyle. When the beam moved, he knew Eddy had picked it up.

"Keep the light on him," he said. Slowly, Dax shifted his position to the left, almost preternaturally aware of the way the creature's eyes followed him. At least now it wasn't looking toward Eddy and her father.

"Dax?" Alton's calm voice carried softly in the stillness. "If you can freeze him, I can probably get close enough to try and decapitate the thing. That's worked with the others."

Dax nodded. Pain rippled over his thigh, across his chest. The tattoo was moving. He felt the life pulse of a separate entity, the struggle of its body as it tried to slither away from the cells that locked it, ink to skin.

Was the gargoyle calling it? Was that hideous creature hoping to steal Dax's demon powers for himself? He hadn't thought it capable of such a thing, but now, with the serpent beginning to move, almost as if the gargoyle directed it through the curse . . .

No! He couldn't allow himself to fear worries of his own creation. He had more than enough to keep him awake for the rest of the week allotted to him. Dax focused on the gargoyle. He ignored the sense of life, the power of the demon's curse as it fought to free itself in the guise of the snake. As it struggled to tear away from his body. He raised his hands, spread his fingers wide, called on his demon powers.

Nothing!

Stunned, Dax stared at his outstretched fingers. Stared even harder at the gargoyle. Was the damned thing smirking? Did it mock him?

Was it stealing his powers even now?

Dax kept his eyes on the gargoyle as he called out to the sprite. *Willow? I need more energy. All you can give me!*

She buzzed into the air and circled him, drawing energy, sending more to Dax than he'd ever needed before. The pain spiked, as if the tattoo ink turned to boiling lava searing a diagonal line of fire across his body.

He bit back a scream of agony and focused on the pain. Instead of trying to stop it, Dax called it forth, drawing the pain as power from the snake, calling it to him, owning it. He teetered on the edge of consciousness, certain that flames would burst from his body, consuming him.

He hung there, aware of the snake writhing and twisting in place, sensing Alton's concern, Eddy's love, Ed's confidence he would succeed. And then he felt it, his demon powers bursting to life—serving him, not the snake; following his direction, not the gargoyle's—and racing down his arms to the tips of his fingers.

Power. Familiar, steady . . . his.

He held it there.

Allowed it to build.

His torment grew stronger, intensified. He should have been unconscious, or at the very least, on his knees. He should have been screaming in agony, but he was using it, owning it, working the pain as if pain were a power entirely its own.

The snake trembled against his skin, and the tongue lashed his throat. Fire burned along the tattoo, and he was almost certain he smelled the acrid scent of burning flesh, but he held his hands high, spread his fingers wide, and sent a blast of fire, instead of ice, fire to engulf the gargoyle.

The creature howled and raised up on its misshapen legs. Dax followed his fire with a freezing blast that should have cracked the aging stone.

Should have, but didn't.

Screaming, eyes flashing red and filled with hatred, the gargoyle launched itself into the air just ahead of the mighty swing of Alton's sword. With the ragged screech of stone wings flapping, it disappeared over the treetops.

All that remained was a scorched circle on the asphalt.

Dax stared down at his hands. He'd never felt so much power coursing through his body, had never sent so much energy at any creature during an attack, yet the gargoyle still lived. He gazed in the direction it had flown. It might have been a little pissed off, but the creature hadn't shown any sign of injury.

Dax's body throbbed with a combination of pain and adrenaline overload. He swayed on his feet. Then Eddy was in front of him, touching the side of his face with her cool fingers, tearing his shirt open. From the look of horror on her face, Dax knew it was bad, but she slapped her hands against his burning skin and held them close over his heart.

Immediately he felt the cool strength in her, the healing power that calmed the snake and doused the fire burning him from the inside out. Thank goodness he managed to keep his legs under him this time while Eddy worked her magic. Barely.

Long minutes later, when she took her hands away, the pain was gone, as if it had never been there at all. She leaned her forehead against his chest and sighed. Her entire body trembled from her efforts, even as his own trembling eased. Dax wrapped his arms around her and held her close. Ed stepped up beside his daughter and patted her shoulder.

"I don't know how you do that, honey, but it's an amazing thing to see." He raised his head and looked at Dax. "That tattoo on your chest's alive, Dax. I saw its eyes. It's got fangs that were almost entirely free of your body. The tongue's a good two inches long, whipping out of the snake's mouth. It slid between Eddy's fingers, but she didn't flinch. Not a bit."

He kissed Eddy's cheek, but his eyes were focused on Dax. "How long do you think Eddy will be able to stop the damned thing without it turning on her?"

Dax shook his head. Speech was beyond him right now, but even if he could speak, he didn't know how to answer Ed. He had no idea how long Eddy could continue to help him until the risk to her became too great. But he had to wonder, what was risk when so many lives were at stake?

What was the safety of a town when Eddy's life was at risk?

There was no answer. They had a war to win, no matter what it took.

He had to see the positive. Something good had come of the night. He'd managed to use the pain. He'd drawn on it, worked with it. He hadn't been strong enough to defeat the gargoyle, but it hadn't gotten him. It hadn't hurt the ones he loved.

Neither had the snake.

In the overall scheme of things, he had to see this in a positive light. It was a good thing. Unfortunately, if they were going to defeat the demons, Dax was positive it wasn't good enough.

Chapter Eleven

There was no discussion of sleeping arrangements tonight. Ed paused for a moment in the kitchen and gazed about the brightly lit room with a blank expression. "Food in the fridge," he mumbled. Then he stumbled off to his room, practically asleep on his feet.

Alton fed Bumper while he stuffed down a leftover sandwich and drank one of Ed's cold cans of beer. He set the can down and turned to Dax. "I'm sorry," he said. "You had him tonight, Dax, but I missed. I wasted a good shot. There's no excuse."

Dax frowned. "The sword . . ."

"No." Alton shook his head. "I can't keep blaming the sword for my own failure." He smiled and turned his head away. "I guess I'm not much of a warrior. At least not as much as I'd like to be."

"I disagree." Dax forced Alton to look him in the eye. "You left your home, gave up your life with your own people to fight a battle that isn't really yours. You're a brave companion and a true friend. I could not do this without you, Alton. I wouldn't want to, and I'm proud to have you fighting beside me."

"Thank you." Then Alton chuckled. "I'll fight beside you, proudly. Just not too close."

Dax smiled. "At least not within striking distance. Good night, my friend."

"Good night, Dax. Eddy." He gazed at Dax a moment longer. Then he turned and went straight into the guest room with Bumper on his heels and Willow curled up on his shoulder, already asleep in a nest of his long hair.

Eddy cleaned up the few dishes left in the sink, while Dax finished off the last of the leftover sandwiches. He studied the long curve of her spine, the graceful way she moved, and felt the now-familiar rush of desire he'd learned to expect whenever he had a moment to actually sit and watch her.

She glanced over her shoulder as she wiped down the faucet and counter. Her smile seemed forced. Dax felt her concern. For him.

"You okay?"

He nodded and pushed physical arousal into the background. "I'm okay now," he said. "Other than feeling really pissed off and frustrated." He shrugged and slowly shook his head. "We need a plan. That thing's powerful."

Eddy nodded and draped the damp cloth over the edge of the sink. She turned and leaned against the counter with her arms folded across her chest. "I know." She raised her head and stilled, until, somehow, he fell into her brown-eyed gaze. She blinked, and Dax could have sworn he felt the brush of her long lashes against his lips. She took a breath, and he felt her breasts rise against his chest.

She shook her head, almost as if she had to physically break the connection between them. He heard her deep sigh clear across the room. "C'mon," she said, pushing herself away from the counter. "We're both exhausted." She glanced over her shoulder as she passed him on her way to her bedroom.

Dax silently followed her into the room they'd shared

earlier today . . . or was it yesterday? He was losing track, but he was much too aware that the night was almost gone. When a new dawn began, he could check off another day.

Three days gone. The fourth only hours away. So much had happened, but there was so much yet to do. At least now he knew who their enemy was: the gargoyle appeared to command the lesser demons. They followed it like a mindless army, intent on doing its will. If only he could figure out what the creature's weak point was—if it had any. Right now, Dax was the weakest of the bunch. Even Eddy's strength was more than his.

DemonSlayer. He'd taken pride in the title when Taron had named him, but now it felt like a bad joke. Without Eddy to control the curse, Willow to feed him energy, and even Ed and Alton there to fight, he was less than useless.

Even Bumper had accomplished more than he had tonight, herding the army of demons toward Ed and Alton. They'd destroyed all the avatars, either killed or banished hundreds of demons, but more kept coming. The portal was closed, but Taron hadn't been kidding when he said there'd been a sizable invasion.

They'd all greatly underestimated how sizable.

How the hell were they going to win over such terrible odds? What was the gargoyle's weakness, if it even had one?

Eddy closed the door behind him. Dax's focus shifted from demons and the battles to come, to the woman moving silently from door to bed. Wordlessly, she sat on the edge of the bed, untied her boots, and slipped them off. Dax did the same, taking a chair on the far side of the room where he could watch her every move.

Eddy tugged her shirt off over her head and slipped the jeans down her long, long legs. She stood up to unhook her bra as Dax reached for the belt holding his jeans. Suddenly Eddy's mouth split into a wide grin. "Look at us," she said, laughing softly. "Undressing like an old, married couple when we've only known each other for three days."

Dax's first thought was, *Has it only been three days? I feel as if I've known this woman forever.* He paused with his hands on the belt buckle. "Is this how an old, married couple acts?"

She nodded, but she didn't lose the smile. "I think so. I'm not sure. I've never been part of a married couple, old, young, or otherwise."

"Well, if it is, I think I would like to be part of an old married couple . . . or otherwise." He held her gaze for a moment longer; then he undid his belt, unbuttoned and unzipped his jeans, and slid them down over his legs. His boxers went down with the pants. When he straightened up and stepped out of them, Dax knew there'd be no doubt in Eddy's mind what was on his.

There was nothing at all subtle about his erection. It jutted out in front, aiming directly for Eddy. She stared at him, her eyes bright, lips slightly parted. He knew she was exhausted. He was as well, but there was something in the space between him that seemed to take on its own life. He felt a thrumming in his veins, a pulse that was hot and rich as liquid gold. It had his mind buzzing, his body reacting.

He tried to compare the feelings, the sense of arousal he felt now in this human body, with what he remembered from his life as a demon, but there was no comparison. Nothing similar at all beyond the anxious sense of need, the pressure that seemed to encompass his groin and belly, buttocks, and balls.

Similarity ended there. Ended, and expanded with feelings that went so far beyond the physical that he had no way to describe them, no way to fully understand the ache in his heart, the thickness in his throat, the feeling that he wanted, that he needed . . . but what did he need?

More than Eddy's body. More than her touch, her soft skin. His lips hungered for her taste, his fingers itched to roam across the hills and valleys of her body, exploring secrets he'd barely suspected . . . but it was more.

Still more, but what?

It had to be this human body. The demon only wanted to ease its need for blood or sex. This human body wanted more. Saw more. Desired only Eddy Marks.

She was everything to him. Beauty. Kindness and humor, the sound of her laughter, the salt in her tears, the sweet scent of her skin, and the taste of her lips. All these things, each separate, each a necessary part of the whole. All the parts that made the woman.

All the parts that made him ache. Made him want more than four more days. More than a night in her arms.

She stepped close and took his hand. He noticed there was a definite flush to her cheeks, a rosy tint that crossed over her breasts and spread across the soft curve of her belly. She tugged lightly on his fingers, pulling him toward the bathroom. He followed her, curious about what she intended, happy just to know that whatever it was, she wanted him with her.

She turned his fingers loose and reached for the faucet on the shower, and he studied the line of her back, the smooth sweep of her hip and thigh. When she turned the tap and checked the temperature of the water, he realized he was caught on the subtle play of lean muscles beneath her smooth skin.

Then she slid the glass door aside and stepped in. Held the door open, silently inviting him to join her. His mouth went dry. He wasn't sure what he'd expected, but he'd not really thought this far ahead. Hadn't considered the implications of Eddy, naked and wanting, her lips parted, eyes clear and filled with his reflection.

Suddenly the demon rose up in him, almost a separate entity beneath his human skin, struggling to emerge. To take. Power flowed through his body. The snake began to writhe across his chest, and heat surged through his cock. Dax paused with one foot in the shower, one on the cold tile of the bathroom floor.

He grounded himself on the cold tile. Swayed with the effort it took to force the demon down. Took a deep, controlling breath. Another. The tattoo stilled. The demon retreated, but Dax sensed it waiting. Sensed its displeasure.

He'd had no idea his demon self still existed. No idea it clung so tightly. No idea it retained such power. He needed to think about that. Be aware of his demon side. Later.

Much later.

Steam rose over the top of the door and enveloped Eddy in a misty cloud. In control now, Dax walked into a dream. He stepped into the big shower and closed the door behind him. Water beat down on both of them. Eddy held a clean cloth, and she carefully rubbed soap into the thing.

"Turn around. I'll wash your back. Then you can do mine."

He wasn't about to argue. Dax turned, leaned forward, and planted his palms against the tile wall. Eddy rubbed the soft cloth over his shoulders, down the length of his spine. The water pounded out a steady rhythm against him; the cloth left swirls of soapy sensation. He realized he was groaning softly with each sweep across his skin.

All too soon she stopped. "My turn," she said. Dax moved aside, and Eddy took his place while he soaped the cloth and carefully washed her back.

He ran the cloth across her shoulders, down her spine, and over the curve of her buttocks. Up the same path until he detoured. This time he swept the soapy cloth around to the front and swirled it across her breasts, over the taut nipples that had gone from soft, pink buds to tightly ruched points.

When he ran the nubby washcloth across the tips, Eddy arched her back and pressed her breast into his palm. He stepped closer and used the cloth to wash down the soft curve of her belly and then dragged it lightly between her legs.

The soft whimpers she made told him he must be doing something right, but he backed away and grabbed the shower nozzle out of its holder, pulled it close, and rinsed the soap from her body.

She dipped her head beneath the spray and washed her short hair. Dax hung the nozzle back in its holder and did the same. When he rinsed the soap out of his, Eddy was already through, but she grabbed the wet cloth once again and began soaping his chest.

He stood beneath the hot spray while she carefully ran the cloth over the quiescent tattoo. She washed down over his hip, along his flank, the full length of one long leg all the way to his toes. Then she did the same to the other. Anticipation made him harder than ever, and his penis bobbed obscenely in front of her nose, but Eddy didn't seem to mind at all.

She took the cloth, added more soap, and carefully washed all those human male parts, gently lifting his thick shaft and sweeping the cloth along his full length. She cradled his testicles in the palm of her hand and gently bathed him. The soft sweep of soapy cloth took him to the edge. His hips jerked when she swept the cloth between his legs, up the crease of his buttocks, and back over his flank.

He might have felt embarrassed at such human intimacy, probably should have, but it felt too good, too right for him to be concerned. He searched for the demon, but it remained quiet, satisfied with Eddy's perfect touch. When she was done and had finished washing him and then herself, she rinsed both of them off as if they'd always bathed together, had always shared such astounding familiarity.

She got out of the shower and handed him a towel. Dax carefully dried himself and followed Eddy back into the bedroom. She brushed her tousled hair back from her face and handed the hairbrush to him with a smile that couldn't be anything but seductive. This act of bathing had turned into more than flirtation. It was, instead, a serious prelude to mating, a dance of desire—Eddy's own brand of foreplay taking both of them to another level of awareness.

She turned off the bright overhead light and then leaned over and turned on a lamp beside the bed. It cast a pale glow about the room, lighting the bed, but leaving most of the bedroom in dark shadow.

Dax dragged his gaze away from Eddy's sleek body and looked down at the hairbrush in his hand. He brushed it through his wet hair and dragged it all straight back, but he realized he was once again watching Eddy through eyelashes still wet and spiky.

They were both clean now, but in spite of all her flirtatious moves, Eddy hadn't actually said she wanted him sexually. The night was late, and Dax figured she'd want to sleep, though he was oddly disappointed at the thought that this might be all that would happen between them.

His tattoo was beginning to burn. His demon stirred. He'd felt in control while they showered, but now, here in the darkened bedroom, watching Eddy pull the bed's sheets and blankets back, Dax was aware of the subtle slither and slink of the art taking on life, pulsing slowly over his skin, of the demon rising, watching Eddy through eyes dark with lust.

He touched his abdomen, where the wide body of the snake crossed just above the thick root of his erection. He ran his fingers over the design and felt the distinct pattern of scales beneath his fingertips, as if the pain itself took on form and substance. Was his demon working within the curse? Taking back the tattoo? Following the heat of the snake's body, he trailed his fingers across his belly and up his chest.

The pain was growing, burning him from thigh to belly to chest, but he worked it, touched it, tried to make it his as he'd done earlier tonight. His hand trembled when he traced the line of the snake's head. Its tongue flicked across his palm.

"Shit!" He snatched his fingers away, raised his head, and stared directly into Eddy's eyes. She stood on the far side of the bed with her fingers pressed against her lips, her eyes wide in absolute horror. The pain intensified. His demon roared a silent scream of frustration. Dax felt a tearing sensation—the snake tattoo was pulling itself away from his body.

Eddy suddenly sprang to life. She raced around the end of the bed and slammed her hands against his chest, against the three-dimensional head of the snake as it twisted away from Dax.

"No!" She raised her head and stared at him in wide-eyed horror. "No," she said, softer this time. "I won't let it do this to you. I won't."

Dax covered Eddy's hands with his. Together they pressed the snake's head back down against his chest; together they held it in place. He had no sense of the demon now, but the snake writhed and twisted, and the heat was intense. Eddy never wavered. Neither did Dax, though it killed him to think of the pain she endured . . . for him. She held her hands to the scalding heat of the snake with a look of grim determination on her face.

Slowly the three-dimensional head of the snake flattened out beneath their hands. The texture of scales and muscle faded back to mere ink over cool skin, until, after a few long minutes, it seemed the most natural thing in the world for

Dax to tilt his head, for Eddy to raise hers, for them to find a connection of hands and hearts and lips.

Dax had kissed her before, but never with the intent of taking the kiss beyond a meeting of lips and teeth and tongues. This time, with Eddy holding the snake at bay, with Dax holding Eddy and their bodies fresh from the shower, both of them still damp and warm and entirely naked, it felt right to draw close. Right to wrap an arm around Eddy's waist, right to pull her slim body tightly against his.

Right to spread his legs wide and draw her in to the cradle of his thighs, to tilt forward just so, until the heat of his erection nestled at the juncture of her thighs, pressing upward along the soft swell of her belly.

Her hands moved away from the now cooled and quiescent tattoo and slipped higher, trailing over his pectorals, across his collarbones. Her fingers tangled in the damp hair curling against his neck. One fingertip traced the edge of his ear, raising shivers along his spine.

She tilted her hips forward, pressing harder against his erection, teasing him with the soft brush of her pubic hair where it tickled the underside of his shaft. Her lips parted for him; her tongue dueled his in a sensual dance that left him breathless, wanting more.

Needing more. He cupped her firm buttocks in his palms and lifted her. She seemed to flow against him, and her long legs wrapped around his waist. He walked her to the bed and leaned forward with her still clinging tightly to his body.

When her back touched the mattress, she released him and sprawled shamelessly across the sheets. Her lips were swollen and shiny from their kisses; her nipples had tightened to dark points that called to him.

He couldn't avoid comparisons. Eddy was perfect, and there was nothing in his past to compare. Demons were neither male nor female. They'd been created out of the muck and residue of all creation, not born. Some had breasts and genitalia that included multiple penises or both male and female organs on the same body. Others had no genitalia at all. It didn't matter. When one demon conquered another it either ate the vanquished foe, or dominated it sexually. No matter if there wasn't a conventional orifice. Anything would work.

A demon's cock was as much a weapon as fangs or claws, as apt to ejaculate murderous venom as any other demonic fluid. When two demons came together, it wasn't about sex or pleasure or desire. Sex was a weapon, another method for conquering the opponent. It was all about force and pain, about taking control of a weaker foe.

He had survived untold millennia as a demon, had defeated and known defeat, but the law of survival was one that allowed no weakness. There was no emotion, no desire beyond an uncontrollable frenzy to vanquish and subdue.

Win or lose, conquer or be conquered. Fuck or get fucked. It was all about domination and power and survival.

This was different. So wonderfully different.

Dax looked down at his hands and realized his fingers trembled. They were hands with the power to throw flame and ice, yet they trembled before a woman. Standing here now, beside the bed, with Eddy sprawled in all her soft and feminine splendor, unmanned him as no more powerful foe ever had. He wanted her so much he ached.

He feared her just as badly, though not for what she could do to him. No, he feared loving her, knowing it would change him forever. And he realized, in that brief moment when all his battles, his wins, his losses, and all his timeless past flashed before him, that it was worth the risk. Worth the pain when he finally lost her. Worth whatever it cost him for this one night. This moment in time, spent in Eddy's arms.

He leaned over her, one knee planted firmly on the edge

of the bed, one big hand hovering over her breast. He had to touch her, wanted to taste her. He glanced from her inviting breasts to see an even greater invitation in her eyes.

"Make love to me, Dax." She raised her hands and brushed her fingers across his chest. Ran her fingertips over the snake, beginning at the fearsome head and trailing along its sinuous length. When she trailed one fingertip across the hard planes of his belly, he sucked in a harsh breath.

Her fingers brushed the thick root of his cock, lingered but a moment and then moved beyond, to trace the multicolored snake along the top of his thigh to the very tip of its tail. Fire followed her touch, but it wasn't the fire of the demon's curse. No, this heated his blood, made his heart beat faster. His breath escaped in tiny puffs, so quick and short he was hardly aware of drawing air inside in order for it to escape.

He'd never made love, never covered a woman before with a human body. Had no idea how to make it right for her, no knowledge beyond plunder and plunge deep, thrust hard and fast, take or be taken.

"Eddy . . . I . . ."

She brushed her fingers across his lips. "It's okay," she said. The knowledge of ages was in her eyes. "Follow my lead."

He nodded, but he moved slowly, still unsure. His body thrummed with growing pressure, with a need that filled every cell, tightened every fiber of every one of his human muscles. Eddy sort of rolled up and curled around until she was kneeling in front of him as he half knelt, half stood beside the bed. She sat back on her heels and gazed up at him with her velvety brown eyes sparkling. She ran her fingers over the tattoo once again, as if she calmed the beast within.

Then she cupped his balls in her warm hands and wrapped her fingers lightly around the hard length of his shaft. Dax groaned and thrust forward into her grasp. His demon roared to life, and he fought it back until his entire body quivered with the restraint he forced on himself. Denying the instinct to shove hard and fast, to cover Eddy with his larger body and force himself deep inside her feminine heat, had him trembling as if he suffered from a palsy.

Eddy held him a moment longer. Her gentle touch had him clenching his muscles until his buttocks and thighs, chest, and jaw were hard as rocks. Then she leaned close, curled her spine, and brushed her lips over the broad crown of his penis.

Dax sucked in a breath. His body went rigid. He held himself still, concentrated on maintaining control, on holding the beast at bay while her lips and tongue ravaged his senses. He clenched his fists at his sides and felt the nails dig in to the fleshy swell beneath his thumbs. Her lips danced along his heavily veined length, and when he thought he couldn't take it any longer, Eddy opened her mouth and wrapped her lips around the upper third of his cock.

He arched his back, but she held him in place with one fist wrapped tightly around his shaft while the other cradled the heavy sac beneath. Held him and took him to heaven and beyond with the sweep of her tongue and the warm suction of her full lips and the wet cavern of her mouth.

Time seemed to stand still as she loved him with her mouth, but when he knew he couldn't last, that he couldn't hold on another moment, she slowly released him, licking along his full length, nibbling the flared crown. She dipped the tip of her tongue into the weeping slit at the end of his cock, swirled lightly, and then sat back on her heels.

Her lips were shiny and soft, her breasts seemed somehow fuller, and when given the choice between lips and breast, Dax, leaned forward and wrapped his lips around her nipple, right over her heart. She threw her head back, thrust her chest forward, and he suckled her nipple into his mouth, tonguing the tip, nibbling, and then licking, until she held his shoulders in both her hands and pressed her breast against his mouth.

He didn't remember moving, but he was above her now, his knees between her thighs, his cock resting against her damp cleft. He suckled first one breast, and then the other, fascinated by the taste and texture, the sense that this amazing act was something his human body recognized.

Dax, who'd never nursed at a mother's breast, had never touched a woman, seen a woman . . . made love to a woman. Suddenly presented a feast, he was unsure where to begin. He trailed kisses along Eddy's ribs, dipped his tongue into her navel, kissed the crease between her groin and thigh.

So close, he was drawn by her scent, by the rich, feminine perfume between her thighs. He scooted back and lifted her legs, presenting her for his own perusal. At first she tried to close her knees together, but when he glanced up, stared solemnly at her, and shook his head, she lay back down, and the tension went out of her thighs.

He leaned close, touched his tongue to her mound, and swirled the tip through her crisp curls. Her labia glistened with tiny drops of dew, and he ran his tongue between her feminine lips, lapping slowly. He quickly realized that when he laved the small bump at the top of her cleft, her body jerked and she pressed closer to his mouth.

So he did it again, and again, slowly, lightly, teasing Eddy just as she'd teased him until she suddenly cried out. Her body jerked, and her thighs closed against his ears as she arched closer to his mouth. Acting purely on human, not demon instinct, he pressed his lips around the swollen bud and sucked lightly for a moment longer, until her convulsive movements ended and her body relaxed in his hands.

Her eyes were bright in the dim glow from the bedside lamp when he finally moved over her, settled himself between her legs, and used his hand to guide his erect penis between the damp and swollen entrance to her body. She arched into him as he thrust forward.

Her opening was hot and very slick, yet he was so large the fit was tight and his progress slow and not so steady. He buried himself deep, and deeper still until he was fully engulfed in hot rippling flesh.

He'd never felt anything remotely as wonderful, nothing that could compare to the hot clasp of Eddy's sheath around the thick length of his shaft. She filled him with life. Her muscles pulsed along his taut length; heat and moisture enfolded him. She lifted her hips and took him deeper; he recognized her rhythm and slipped into it as if they'd done this act together all their lives.

In and out, thrust and retreat, instinctive movements as old as time, but it was nothing like he'd ever experienced before. Nothing in his entire life had prepared him for this, for the overall sense of fulfillment, of pure, unadulterated ecstasy as his body became one with Eddy's, as his heart found a rhythm that matched perfectly to hers.

And he knew, somehow he understood, that this was not the way it always was for all humans. That this perfect synchronization of hearts and bodies, of minds and needs, was unique to the two of them, totally encompassing every desire he'd ever had, every dream he'd never known to dream.

This was what Eddy said when she called it making love. This was love. This was more than their bodies, more than their minds—it was every cell, every thought, every need and desire, fulfilled and made whole.

Eddy's body tensed beneath his. Electricity arched between them, dragging Dax into a new rhythm, a more powerful lead. The demon stirred, slipped beyond his defenses, and took control.

A deep, unearthly roaring filled his ears, a familiar, fearsome sound, one Dax thought was gone forever. He—both the man and the demon—thrust into her hard and fast, his hips moving in a compelling tempo racing against the beat of his heart, the rush of blood, the harsh intake of breath. Slamming into Eddy time and time again, until his balls slapped the curve of her buttocks and the sounds of wet flesh and hot suction and gasping breath all mingled and melded with Eddy's cries and Dax's hoarse roar of completion.

A final thrust, and his body hung rigid and unmoving above her. His sac drew up hard and tight between his legs. His cock jerked deep inside Eddy's clasping sheath as he emptied himself in spurt after spurt, trapped as he was by clenching, spasming muscles, the hard muscles of her thighs wrapped around his waist, her heels locked together against the small of his back.

He had no idea. Hadn't suspected, hadn't known enough to even wonder what this would be like. Rearing back on his heels, Dax wrapped his arms around her and dragged her against his chest. Slowly the demon subsided, retreated, and faded into the back of his consciousness. Dax held Eddy close with her legs wrapped around his body, his cock buried inside, still jerking with each pulsing release, filling her . . . claiming this woman as his own.

Long moments later, her body relaxed, and she slumped against him. Her cheek rested on his shoulder; her arms dropped listlessly to his sides. She panted, breathing in and out with quick bursts of air that tickled his sweaty skin.

Dax lay her down on the soft bed, loath to separate entirely. Her closed eyelids fluttered but didn't open. Perspiration beaded her chest and forehead, and a rosy flush spread over her breasts and belly.

Carefully, Dax pulled away. Regretfully he withdrew from her vagina. Her slick muscles still rippled around his shaft when he slipped free, almost as if they tried to hold him close, but he backed away and went into the bathroom to find a damp cloth. He quickly washed himself, rinsed the cloth carefully in warm water, and returned to Eddy.

He was almost afraid to think of what they'd done. What he had done. He'd felt the demon come to life, felt the power of his demon lust, the comingling of human and unworldly creature, taking Eddy, making love to Eddy.

He'd been afraid, but not enough to stop. He'd wanted her too much. Needed her too badly. Now she slept soundly just as he'd left her. One arm covered her eyes, one knee was still raised, the other sprawled limply to one side. Carefully, Dax washed between her legs, bathing his seed from her body, and then drying her with a warm towel.

When he was done, she rolled to her side with a soft sigh on her lips. He put the damp cloth and towel in the hamper, turned out the light, and crawled into bed behind her. His body fit perfectly against the curve of hers. He lay there with her warm bottom tucked against his belly and her damp hair tickling his chin.

It was a long time before he slept, not because he couldn't relax, but because he forced himself to stay awake. He didn't want to miss a single minute of the sweet experience of holding Eddy close. Of knowing that she slept so peacefully now because her body was sated from his loving.

Human and demon. Together they'd left her satisfied and smiling. He needed to think about that. Needed to understand how the two could work together.

Four more days to defeat the demons. Four more days in Eddy's bed before his life on her world ended. How could he bear to leave her?

How could he not?

At least the death of his human body would be acceptable if he knew he'd be leaving Eddy safe. Alive, unharmed, and safe, in a world free from demonkind.

There was no other option. There was no point in saving

the citizens of Evergreen if he couldn't save Eddy. No point at all.

She wasn't certain what woke her, but Eddy was suddenly wide awake and terribly aware of the man sleeping beside her. Dax must have turned off the bedside lamp before he slept, because the room was softly cocooned in total darkness. The sun hadn't begun to rise, yet she felt energized, as if she'd slept soundly for many more hours than their late night should have allowed.

Reacting purely by instinct, Eddy placed her palm over the tattoo, finding it easily even in darkness by the intense heat radiating along its length.

The moment she covered the snake's head with her palm, Dax sighed. His body relaxed, and he rolled from his back to his side, enveloping her in warmth and muscle. One heavy, hair-roughened leg slid across her thighs, and she felt the thick length of his partially tumescent erection against her hip.

They'd made love just the one time before exhaustion had claimed her, but Eddy's body still hummed with the aftereffects of the most amazing climax she'd ever experienced in her life.

When the sun rose, Dax would be starting his fourth day. More than half his time would be gone. Eddy didn't want to think about life after Dax, but she couldn't help herself. She knew she'd never know another man like him, a man as much demon as human, one who loved her even as he sometimes left her feeling just a little off balance, a bit unsure. No, she would never find anyone even remotely as close to perfect.

Wasn't this just like her usual luck? She'd never wanted a permanent relationship with any guy until now. Until Dax.

He was the first man she'd ever known who pushed all her buttons. He filled every need she'd ever had, including a few she hadn't even been aware of.

Typical. Softly, she stroked the tattoo, aware now how his skin cooled beneath her fingers. Dax sighed and snuggled close, nuzzling the sensitive skin beneath her ear. His hand drifted across her belly, slipped upward over her ribs, and settled around her left breast. His palm was rough, his fingers gentle, as they lightly plucked at her suddenly attentive nipple.

She felt him growing erect against her hip, knew he hovered on that plain between sleep and wakefulness. His lips pursed in a drowsy kiss against her throat; his hips thrust forward.

He began to take form in the thin, gray light of early dawn. The dark sweep of hair across his brow, the straight line of his nose, the curve of his jaw. With the growing visibility of his face came the full awareness that their time was growing shorter with each minute that passed.

The sun was rising.

Another day had ended. The new one began. Eddy rubbed her hand slowly across the firm muscles of his chest and cupped her palm over his shoulder. Gently, she applied pressure and pushed him over on his back. He rolled over with a grunt, but his eyes stayed closed.

Eddy raised up on one elbow to study him. His thick lashes curved in dark half moons above sharply defined cheekbones. His lips were pursed, but when Eddy leaned close to press a soft kiss to his mouth, they softened and reformed beneath hers, returning her kiss.

She smiled against his mouth. His muscles firmed beneath her hands as he awoke more fully. He returned her smile. His big hands found her in the darkness, stroking her flanks, her sides, cupping her breasts.

He lifted her, and, as if they'd done this uncountable times, Eddy slipped her leg across his body and straddled his hips. Rose up, grasped his thick erection in one hand, and guided him between her legs.

When she settled down over him, he sheathed perfectly within her, filling her completely. She wriggled her hips just enough to settle all of his length inside. He groaned. The faint light spilling through the blinds glinted off his sleepy smile.

Eddy began to move. She quickly found a rhythm that took Dax deep and then slipped him almost free of her tight channel, lifting and then lowering herself above him. Teasing him with tiny, rocking motions of her hips, she managed to make contact exactly where she wanted to on each rise and fall. She used the muscles in her thighs and calves to lift her up, to slowly lower her down, to take both of them to the very edge.

Fully awake now, Dax's eyes glinted in the growing light of dawn. His lips were tightly drawn as he grasped her around the hips with both hands, lifting her up, pulling her down. He lifted his hips to meet her, faster now, and harder until the *slap, slap, slap* of their bodies coming together seemed to echo against the harsh rasp of their breathing, the soft whimpers from Eddy, the deep groans from Dax.

She leaned forward and pressed her palms against his shoulders, anchoring herself as he drove into her, raising his hips hard and fast to meet her.

Her body hovered, nerves stretched thin on the sharp edge of orgasm. Eddy ran her tongue across her lips and gazed down—directly into the eyes of the snake.

Its forked tongue darted toward her with a malevolent and deviant sensuality anchored in pure evil. Eddy slammed both hands over the gaping mouth as the snake's scaled head slithered entirely free from Dax's chest. She felt the curve of its blunt snout, the strength of muscle beneath its hot, reptilian skin. With a harsh cry, she shoved the serpent back against Dax.

He seemed unaware of the impossible battle taking place over his heart. With eyes closed and lips stretched thin in what could have been either a grimace of pain or extreme pleasure, he slammed his hips upward, driving into her. Eddy arched her back, held the snake in place, and gave in to orgasm. Wave after wave of pleasure rippled from the point where she and Dax connected. Rippled and grew in a tide of sensation.

The snake moved beneath her hands, and Eddy channeled the sharp waves of pleasure, worked the full thrust of arousal, and cast it forward, calling on all the love she felt, the fears for this man, the need in her she knew no other man would ever satisfy—channeled all of it from her heart, through her hands, and into Dax.

Owning it, working the multiple strengths of her own pleasure and need, she sent it blasting into the snake.

A brilliant pulse of energy passed from her fingertips into the reptile. Eddy felt the thrill of completion as Dax cried out, as his body tightened beneath hers and his hips thrust upward and held.

Her muscles clenched, and still the power passed from Eddy, through the snake, into Dax. Back again to Eddy, a circle of power surrounding the snake, trapping it within a golden light that actually glowed along the sinuous edges of the tattoo.

Eddy felt it along her thigh, where she connected with the tail end of the snake, felt it against her pubes, where the thick body of the snake passed over Dax's groin. Felt it beneath her hands, where the snake's head stopped its powerful thrust and once again flattened into a seemingly harmless tattoo, a mere piece of art adorning her man's broad chest.

The last ripples of orgasm rolled through her body, in wave after wave of pleasure so powerful it verged on pain. Eddy fell forward as Dax's arms wrapped tightly around her and held her close. The tattoo was a cool presence between her breasts. She knew it lived, but for now she knew without any doubt she had subjugated whatever evil curse gave it strength.

Smiling, Eddy turned her face and rested her cheek against Dax's chest. Rested it directly over the snake's venomous fangs, feeling almost smug in her awareness that once again she'd bested evil.

Sunlight found them, drowsy yet complete. Dax was still buried deep inside her body, and his arms still encircled her waist. But the snake was quiet, and Eddy knew Dax felt none of the curse's pain right now. Whatever she'd done had stopped the creature, though probably not for long.

Even so, she couldn't help but smile. They'd conquered its strongest attack yet, and they'd done it with love. Maybe that was the secret to fighting the demon. There was power in love. They just needed to figure out how to use it, and there were very few days left to get it right.

Chapter Twelve

Wednesday morning—day four

The bedside telephone woke Dax from a troubled sleep—a night filled with dreams of searing fire, hopeless battles, and armies of demon-driven gargoyles. He was still trying to associate the persistent clamor assaulting his ears with the images in his head when, mumbling incoherently, Eddy crawled across him.

Dreams evaporated like a fireshot demon in the welcome distraction of Eddy's sleek, naked form gliding over his suddenly wakeful body. Still grumbling, she planted an elbow against his sternum and reached for the phone, but it stopped ringing before she could answer.

Groaning, Eddy flopped down, landing crosswise over his chest. Sunlight glowed around the edges of the blinds. He knew it was time to be up, but he felt no inclination to move, beyond the automatic sweep and stroke of his palm along Eddy's spine. She wriggled closer and groaned, but now her sleepy sounds held a note of pleasure.

As did Dax's. Somehow, all her warm parts had connected perfectly to his corresponding and now wide-awake parts.

"That feels so good," she mumbled. "Please don't stop."

Her lips moved against his shoulder, and he grinned at the improbability of their position. Less than a week ago he'd been a spirit lost in the void. Before that, a scaled demon fighting to survive one more day within the hell of Abyss.

Now he was lying in a comfortable bed with a beautiful, naked female sprawled over him. This, he thought, is paradise.

What could the Edenites offer that he hadn't already found here in bed with Eddy Marks? His body tightened as he imagined even more pleasure they could share. The physical side of love as his human body experienced it went beyond anything he'd ever known or even imagined throughout his long demonic life.

Though he couldn't deny his demon side either. Hadn't it added to Eddy's pleasure?

A sharp rap on the door stopped his musings. Ed's voice ended them entirely. "Eddy? You two awake in there? I need to talk to you."

Eddy groaned. "Sorry," she whispered. "Be right there, Dad." She pushed up with both arms, kissed Dax much too quickly, and crawled off him and off the bed.

He watched her bend over and grab a robe from the floor. Covering that gorgeous body seemed somewhat sacrilegious, but he understood the human need for modesty.

She ran her fingers through her short, tousled hair and reached for the door. Dax covered himself with the blanket as Ed stepped into the room. He gave Eddy a quick hug and acknowledged Dax with a brief smile.

"Sweetie, that was Harlan calling. He actually groveled, something I never expected from that horse's ass." He chuckled. "He had the nerve to say you took being fired much too literally, and he wants to know when you're going to get your story in for the afternoon paper. In his words, in light of the current 'events' in town, he doesn't understand how you could possibly let him down like this."

"Let him down?" Eddy snorted inelegantly. "He told me to get out and not come back."

Ed merely shrugged, but he couldn't seem to hide the grin on his face. "He claims it was a simple misunderstanding."

"Simple, my ass. The man's a jerk." She glanced at Dax. "I've had a few other things on my mind besides Harlan." Shrugging, she added, "Anyway, if we're not successful in the next couple days, there's not going to be a paper to write for or a town to write about."

Dax shook his head. "Don't even think that way. We'll succeed, Eddy. We have to."

She glanced his way. "Okay. But what can I write? Do you want me to actually do a story about the demon invasion? What can I say?"

Dax thought about it a moment. Things were coming to a head. Enough citizens had seen the demons' avatars in motion now to be feeling real concern about either their community or their sanity. "Can you put some kind of spin on things, make it sound like unusual but explainable behavior?"

Before Eddy had a chance to answer him, Bumper raced through the door and jumped up on the bed, wriggling all over as if she hadn't seen Dax in years. He grabbed her muzzle to avoid a thorough face washing, Bumper style. Willow buzzed by and landed on the headboard. When Dax finally got Bumper under control and glanced up, Alton stood in the doorway with both hands looped over the top of the frame.

Obviously, any private plans Dax might have had with Eddy were officially out of the question.

"Good morning." Alton grinned, obviously well aware of Dax's opinion of all the interruptions. "I heard what you said, Dax. I agree. If we can come up with a plausible explanation for things to run in the local newspaper, and if I cast a community-wide compulsion, we might be able to contain news of the invasion for a few more days, at least until we destroy the rest of the creatures."

"Eddy?" Dax grinned at her and received an even warmer smile in return. "Can you do that?"

"Sure," she said, with an exaggerated wave of her hands. "I can do anything. Just call me Lois Lane, ace reporter . . . as much as I hate doing anything for Harlan, after the way he fired me."

Dax laughed. "I have to agree, but unfortunately, it's not about Harlan, or any of us, right now."

Eddy's eyes seemed to bore into his for a long time. Then she quickly turned to her father and pressed both hands against his chest. "Go. Take Alton, Bumper, and Willow and let me get some clothes on. You guys think of an angle for the story, and I'll get it written, but go. Now."

The room seemed unusually quiet when they'd all left. Eddy closed the door behind them, and Dax threw the covers back. She turned and smiled at him. "You're not going anywhere. They can wait for a few more minutes. For that matter, so can Harlan and the rest of the universe."

He frowned, but she was coming toward him with a subtle exaggeration to the natural sway of her hips, slipping the robe over her shoulders to expose her perfect breasts.

Dax's mouth was suddenly too dry to form words. His brain seemed to have gone entirely on hold. Thank goodness his body didn't have any problem knowing how to react.

It really wasn't all that much more than a few minutes. A very pleasurable few minutes. Until now, Dax had no idea just how much pleasure two people could find in such a very short time. Or, how powerful the act of love could be between two souls who truly cared for one another.

The glow returned to his tattoo. Once again, the pain was gone.

* * *

Eddy figured she probably should feel embarrassed walking into the kitchen at the tail end of another of her dad's big breakfasts. Her cheeks were pink from Dax's beard, her lips were swollen from his kisses, and her body still hummed with the power of their lovemaking, but she'd skip a meal any day to spend the time with Dax.

Nor was she at all embarrassed that both her father and Alton obviously knew what she and Dax had been doing, especially when she knew time with him was so short. She glanced down at their clasped hands. She couldn't bring herself to meet Dax's gaze, even though they'd both discovered an added benefit to sex.

The term *afterglow* had a whole new meaning.

The moment they'd both climaxed, a soft, golden glow had once again surrounded the cursed tattoo and contained the curse, as far as they could tell. For now, at least, Dax's pain was gone.

As were half of his days on Earth. Already they were well into his fourth day, yet they were no closer to ending the demonic invasion than they'd been the day before.

Eddy was, however, way too close to being in love with him. In fact, she knew she was fooling herself not to admit she'd gone and fallen head over heels beyond lust with a man predestined to leave her much too soon.

Not something she wanted to think about when the fate of her entire community—crap, the whole world—was at stake.

Her dad stood by the sink, scraping leftovers into a bowl for Bumper. He glanced up as she and Dax stopped at the counter to pour themselves cups of coffee. "I saved pancakes, bacon, and eggs for you," he said. "Just give me a minute."

"Thanks, Dad. I'll have to go on a diet if I eat many more of your meals." She glanced away before Ed could respond and followed Dax to the kitchen table.

Alton joined them as Ed set plates in front of Eddy and Dax. "I've been watching the news out of Sacramento," he said. "No mention yet of anything here, but we're going to have to come up with something to satisfy the local population."

"I wonder if Ginny could help?" Eddy set her fork down. "She's a nine-one-one operator. I could at least check with her and see what kinds of calls she's getting. If anyone would know what's going on around here, what people are complaining about, it would be Ginny."

Alton cleared his throat and glanced away. Eddy got the strangest feeling he was hiding something, but then he turned his open gaze on her and merely shrugged. "Whatever you think. You're not going to tell her the truth, are you?"

Eddy thought about that a moment. "I wish I could, and if anyone can keep a secret, it would be Ginny Jones, but I think the fewer people who realize what's really going on, the better. I'll call her and see what she's heard. She'll tell me what she can, though obviously a lot of what she knows is private information that she can't share."

"Be sure and ask her how she is, will you?" Alton's soft question brought Eddy up short.

"Will she remember the concrete bear coming after her?"

Ed interrupted. "Alton let her think she got caught up in a street fight. You'll be able to tell by her answers how much she actually recalls."

"Right." Eddy stared at the plate she'd hardly touched. Food was the last thing on her mind. "I'll find out what I can, but you guys need to work on an angle for a story."

* * *

"If you think that will work, I'll send it to Harlan." Eddy glanced over the brief story she'd written about the current spate of vandalism taking place around the community of Evergreen. She'd blamed it on a suspected influx of gangs from the Central Valley.

Ginny was the one who had given her the idea, since it was what the local sheriff's department was attributing all the broken statues and lawn decorations to: gangs moving into the area, trying to establish their own turf. There was just enough truth behind their suspicions to make the entire story plausible, and it meant Eddy didn't have to write an outright lie. She was merely reporting what she'd been told.

There were problems, definitely, but not any that required military intervention. Dax was the one who'd explained that gangs today were inherently evil, and probably run by demons who'd made their way to Earth the old-fashioned way, by becoming human after spending time in the void. They weren't, however, part of the current invasion. More the standard, run-of-the-mill bad guys as compared to demonic invasion by the truly malevolent.

"Well," she said. "Will this work? It's not much of a story."

Dax stood up. "It sounds good to me. Alton? Ed? What do you guys think?"

"I think a little backup compulsion is all we're going to need." Alton stood beside Dax. "Why don't you come with me? We can walk into town, check out the library, and see if the gargoyle is back on his perch. It's a good, central location where I can cast a compulsion over the entire community. I'll make them suspect that gangs are behind all the demonic activities. Eddy's story will confirm their suspicions."

Ed glanced up from Eddy's computer. He'd been reading

the screen over her shoulder. "How long can you make the compulsion last?"

Alton shrugged. "Three, maybe four days." He looked at Dax. "I can make it last as long as Dax. He's only got until midnight Saturday, if we've got the days properly figured. If we haven't got the problem solved by then, we'll need a new plan."

Eddy caught Dax's steady gaze. He wavered and danced before her eyes, but that's what happened when you looked at a guy through eyes filled with tears. Damn. She wasn't ready to think of him leaving. Not yet. Blinking rapidly, she turned back to the computer, finished her brief note to Harlan, and hit SEND. "It's all done," she said. "What next?"

"Alton and Dax shouldn't be gone all that long." Ed straightened up. "Why don't you and I take a walk around the neighborhood, just see what people are saying?" He held out his hand.

Eddy took it. Dax leaned close and kissed her lips. It was obvious she was the only one he saw in the room. She couldn't control the fact her body swayed toward his, that her heart pounded at the merest touch of his mouth to hers.

"Be careful," he said. "We won't be gone long."

Alton grabbed Bumper's leash and snapped it to her collar. "Do you mind if she comes with us? Willow hates to be away from her."

Eddy laughed. The tall Lemurian with the curly pit bull watching him with pure adoration had no idea what a babe magnet Bumper was going to be. "You don't think Bumper's going to let you go without her, do you? Go, you fickle beast."

Dax opened the door, and Alton went through first. As he closed it, Dax gave Eddy one last, lingering glance. Then he shut the door behind him.

Eddy stared at the door. They'd never been separated

before. Not since she'd found him in the potting shed. This was the first time, and it felt horrible.

What was it going to be like when he was gone forever?

Her dad ruffled her hair, the way he'd done when she was little. "C'mon, sweetie. Let's go check out the neighborhood."

Nodding, Eddy finally tore her gaze away from the door.

They'd covered about three blocks without seeing anything out of order before Ed finally spoke. Eddy'd been waiting for "the talk." Her father rarely criticized her, but she knew he was worried. There was no way to hide her feelings for Dax.

No way that she wanted to. She loved him. For however long he had left, and long after he was gone, she was still going to love him. Some things couldn't be changed.

"It's not going to be easy, no matter how this battle pans out."

There was no point in pretending she didn't understand what her dad was saying. "I know. It's already hard."

"Any way that you can back off how you're feeling? Put some distance between the two of you?"

Eddy shook her head. They'd paused under a big ponderosa pine shading the sidewalk. Around them, the sounds of the neighborhood were as they'd always been: birds, the occasional barking dog, cars passing, lawn mowers going.

Eddy raised her head and stared into her father's sad eyes. It was obvious he worried about her. Just as obvious he wasn't going to try and change her mind. "Dad, if you'd known, before you and Mom got married, how young she'd be when she died, would you have called off the wedding?"

Smiling, Ed slowly shook his head. "Every day with your mother was worth the pain of losing her. Not only do I have you, I have the memories of our life together. But Eddy, we had years. You and Dax only have days. Knowing that . . ."

"Knowing that, Dad, I'd still do exactly what I'm doing now. I know it doesn't make sense, but even knowing he's not really human, I love him."

He wrapped his arms around her waist and hugged her close. She felt the kiss he planted on top of her head. "I know you do, sweetie. He's a good man. Worth loving. I just hate thinking of what it will be like for you when he's gone."

She looked up at her father and thought of all the things he could have said, but hadn't. Instead, just as always, he'd known exactly what she needed to hear. She laughed, well aware it sounded more like she'd choked off a sob. "It's gonna be really shitty, Dad, but there's not a thing I can do about it. Not a damned thing, except not waste a minute while he's here."

"As long as it works for you . . ."

She nodded, tucked her hand through his elbow, and started walking. Swallowed back the huge lump in her throat. "It's going to have to work, isn't it?"

"Yep."

Arm in arm, they continued down the street.

Dax and Alton strolled north along the main street. Bumper trotted alongside with her head high and her tail curled over her back. Willow remained in Dax's pocket, entirely out of sight.

They crossed the small park in front of the old library building. The gargoyle sat on its parapet, as innocent and innocuous as could be. The area was filled with the laughter of children—what appeared to be an entire group of preschoolers with a couple of harried-looking teachers. An elderly couple fed the pigeons, and half a dozen tourists walked by, obviously traveling together, pointing to their maps and speaking in a language Dax didn't recognize.

Reluctantly, Dax and Alton continued on in search of a quieter spot. There were too many potential witnesses here for Alton to try a compulsion.

They finally found a quiet corner behind the library.

"Will this compulsion of yours affect Ed and Eddy at all?"

Alton shook his head. "No. They're too immersed in the battle, too aware of what's going on. Just give me a moment. I need to try and cover a much larger area than I've done before."

He closed his eyes, raised his hands, and appeared as if he prayed. Almost five minutes later, he lowered his head and his hands and took a deep breath. "That should do it, at least for a few days."

Dax nodded. "I have a favor to ask of you, my friend."

Alton raised an eyebrow and looked at him.

"When I am gone, can you take any memories of me away from Eddy? I love her, and I will treasure my memories, knowing they are more than I ever deserved or expected. Eddy deserves more. I don't want her to grieve when I'm gone. It's not fair of me to leave her alone, but I have no choice." He looked into the dark green eyes of the Lemurian, hoping that somehow, some way, he could convince him. "I don't want to think of Eddy missing me."

He glanced away, wondering. Was his a totally selfish request? Was he assuming too much? Maybe Eddy didn't love him the way he loved her. Maybe she wouldn't miss him at all, but if she felt anything at all the way . . .

"Is that fair to Eddy?" Alton rested his hand on Dax's shoulder. "I think it should be up to Eddy whether she wants to remember you or not, don't you?"

His shoulders slumped. He stared at the scuffed boots he

wore, her father's boots. "I don't know, Alton. This is all so new to me. Emotions . . . love. Worrying about someone besides myself. Can I trust you to do what you think is best?"

"You honor me, Dax." Alton spoke solemnly. Then he gave Dax's shoulder a light squeeze and turned him loose. "That's something I can promise."

Dax tried not to think about the endless future without Eddy, but the days were speeding by, he hadn't ended the demon threat, and eternity in the void was looking like the only option left to him. Eternity without Eddy.

He might as well be back in Abyss.

"Let's go back by the library and check on the gargoyle. Can you use your powers to keep people from remembering me if I engage the demon in battle?"

"I can try."

Only the elderly couple remained in the small park. They sat on a stone bench under a tree at the corner farthest from the building, feeding a flock of milling pigeons. The space in front of the library was empty.

Bumper growled. Blond curls rose all along her back. Dax put his palm on her head to calm her, and looked up into the malevolent eyes of the gargoyle. It glared down at him from its perch on the parapet. The expression on its stone face was one of haughty arrogance, a confidence born of past battles, the knowledge it had bested Dax on more than one occasion.

Dax felt a shiver race along his spine, an awareness that he was being studied as closely as he studied the demon. Would it try and fly away, even under the brilliant morning sun? He glanced around. No one seemed to notice him.

"Alton? Can you hide us?"

The Lemurian nodded. "I can muffle sound and make us appear vague and unnoticeable, though we won't entirely disappear." He stepped to one side, looped Bumper's leash through his belt to hold the growling dog close, and spread his long arms wide. A transparent bubble of energy formed, enclosing the vacant library, the gargoyle, the dog, the sprite, and the two men.

All sound beyond ceased.

"I can hold this for but a few moments. No sound will escape, though determined outsiders can see through it. Work quickly, before I grow too weak to hold it."

Willow zipped out of Dax's pocket, and drew what energy she could from within the bubble. He felt the burst of strength racing from his head to his fingertips, raised his hands, and sent a blast of fireshot at the gargoyle.

The creature rose up on stubby legs, screaming its banshee wail. Wings unfolded. Its eyes glowed red, and it focused on Dax as swirling flames rolled off its stone chest.

Bumper tugged at her leash, snarling and growling and then frantically whining her frustration at the leash.

Dax drew more power, but now he threw an icy mist. Immense cold following extreme heat should crack the stone. All it seemed to do was piss off the demon. Dax focused more energy as Willow fed it to him. The creature stumbled and fell back upon the parapet. Dax hit it again, with flame this time, but his power was waning. Willow's glow dimmed. The tattoo across his chest began to writhe and twist. He felt the cold slice of a forked tongue beneath his chin.

Willow's light faded entirely. Dax's fire sputtered and died. The gargoyle rose to its stubby feet once more, and while its stone head sagged as if the creature were weary and hurting, it was still intact, still strong enough to take its position on the parapet.

It spread its wings in a brief show of defiance, then folded them across its back and once again took on its original guise of an innocent gargoyle protecting the abandoned library.

Agony raced through Dax. The tattoo moved! The subtle rhythm of the snake's body was impossible to ignore as it slowly writhed the length of his. He looked down in horror as the denim covering his thigh bulged and shifted over the squirming length of the snake.

Staring at the rise and fall of denim over his thigh, Dax reached deep inside for his demon. Nothing. Vaguely, through his own screaming desperation, Dax sensed Alton swaying beside him. He knew the instant the Lemurian fell. The surrounding bubble popped out of existence, and the sounds of the world returned. Bumper's leash tore free of Alton's belt, and she took off running. Dax pressed his hands to his chest. The snake's head rose to meet him, but he wrapped his fingers around its powerful jaws and held them shut.

Again he called on his demon. This time he sensed contact, a surge of power. The muscles in his biceps, shoulders, and chest bulged as he and his demon forced the snake's head back against human flesh. Burning agony shot along the tattoo's length.

Black spots flickered in front of Dax's eyes. He tightened his grip around the snapping jaws with both hands. The tail twitched and slithered over his thigh. The thick body undulated across his groin, over his belly.

He turned his face away from the flickering tongue and gasped. Willow lay on the freshly mowed grass, her light extinguished, her tiny wings spread wide—a tiny butterfly as still as death. Alton lay beside her, unconscious.

Dax couldn't tell if the Lemurian breathed or not.

The pain grew. His strength faded. His demon retreated. Was it cowed by the gargoyle? He'd not thought it possible, hadn't wanted to admit it could happen, but the tattoo was winning. Without Eddy's strength to hold the creature at bay, there was no way for Dax to stop its cursed attack.

Blinded by pain, he raised his head and caught the gargoyle's gaze. Weakened by the attack, the creature still clung to its resting place atop the library, glaring at Dax with undisguised malice. Dax returned its evil stare, even as his legs collapsed beneath him.

He fell to his knees, still gripping the snake's head in both hands. The gargoyle's red eyes boring into his were the last thing he saw before blackness overtook him.

Eddy and her dad walked briskly along the main street of town. They'd been through the neighborhood, and all had seemed perfectly normal. No demon activity to speak of, and no stench of sulfur. It had seemed like a perfectly normal morning, but Eddy's sense of unease grew stronger with each step she took.

"Let's go by the library. I'm worried about Dax."

Ed nodded. "Me too. We should have given them a cell phone. I don't like being out of contact like this."

Eddy forced a smile. "I'm sure they're fine. What can happen to a DemonSlayer, a Lemurian, and a will-o'-the-wisp, as long as they have Bumper?"

Ed laughed, but he picked up the pace.

Eddy recognized Bumper's frantic barking before she saw the dog streaking toward them, leash flying in the air behind her. "Ohmygod! Bumper!" She raced toward the dog and managed to grab the trailing leash. "Where's Dax?"

Bumper yipped once and tugged Eddy back up the road at a full run. Ed ran beside them. "She's taking us to the library. Hurry!"

Eddy wasn't about to waste breath talking. She unclipped Bumper's leash and gave the dog her freedom. Bumper raced on ahead, but seemed to know not to let Eddy out of her sight. The three of them rounded the corner at almost the same time.

Dax and Alton were sprawled on the freshly mowed lawn. It wasn't until Eddy fell to her knees beside Dax that she realized Willow lay on the ground as well. "Dad, check Alton and Willow."

She ripped Dax's shirt open, heedless of buttons flying everywhere. The snake reared up with glowing eyes and jaws spread wide. Without thinking, Eddy grabbed the creature by the throat and held it mere inches from her face.

The forked tongue lashed out, and she fought the power beneath the scales. Pain lanced her hands, raced up her arms as she absorbed Dax's agony.

She'd finally realized how her touch worked. She pulled the pain into herself, controlled it somehow with her touch, but the agony she felt right now was merely a fraction of what Dax must be suffering.

She was vaguely aware of Alton sitting up beside her, of Willow's wings beginning to flutter as Ed scooped the tiny will-o'-the-wisp up in his hands. Bumper had stopped barking. Now she merely paced around the small group, whimpering and growling as Eddy battled the snake.

It glared at her with a malevolence powered by pure evil, and it was all Eddy could do to hold the thing by the throat and keep it from striking at either Dax or herself. The flesh above Dax's heart, where the snake had ripped itself free of Dax's body, was a bloody open wound.

Determined not to lose, Eddy tightened both hands around the snake's throat and forced it back against Dax's chest. She hated the thought of hurting him, of pressing against his ragged and torn flesh, but there was no other way. Nothing she could do that wouldn't cause him more pain. As long as he was unconscious, she could only hope that he wasn't able to feel it.

The snake appeared to weaken. Dax's jeans no longer rippled and bulged with the sluggish movements of the partially bound reptile. Within a few moments, the fabric flattened out to cover the natural curve of Dax's muscular thighs and the flat contours of his belly and waist.

The snake seemed to lose a third dimension within Eddy's grasp. She gently flattened the image once more in its position around Dax's perfect, copper-colored nipple, pressed the snout into his flesh, positioned the gaping jaws over his heart.

Carefully, she smoothed the brilliant reds, greens, and blues of the tattoo over Dax's sweat-soaked skin. Then she sat back on her heels and took a long, shuddering breath. Dax breathed slowly, evenly. His eyelids fluttered. He blinked, opened his eyes, and gave her an unfocused stare that lasted but a moment; then he closed his eyes again. She wrapped her hand around his and held on.

She heard a siren, the sound of brakes, the loud slam of a car door. She glanced over her shoulder as one of the local sheriff's deputies walked across freshly mowed lawn and headed straight for them.

It was only then that she realized a small crowd had gathered. At least a dozen people stood to one side. How much had they seen? Frantically she looked at her father. He shrugged and shook his head, but she noticed that Willow was safely hidden in her dad's pocket. Only the tip of her blond head was visible.

The deputy frowned when he saw Dax lying on the ground with his shirt ripped open. He reached for his radio.

Alton rose to his full height, towering over the man. "There's no need," he said, holding his fingers in front of the deputy. "Our friend occasionally has these spells. He'll be fine."

Dazed, the deputy nodded. Alton turned away and waved

his hand in the direction of the curious onlookers. Slowly, shaking their heads and talking quietly among themselves, they dispersed. When Eddy glanced once more at the deputy, he was already walking back to his car.

She felt Dax's fingers tighten around hers. When she looked at him, his eyes were open, though still a bit unfocused. "You're here. How?"

She leaned over and kissed him. "Bumper came and got us." She glanced up at the gargoyle and shuddered. "She knew you needed help. Are you okay?"

Dax slowly sat up. He shook his head. "I am now. How did you stop it? The thing was sentient. I felt its hatred. It was crawling off my body."

"She grabbed it by the throat." Ed held his hand out to Dax and helped him stand. He swayed, but stayed upright. "Held on to the damned thing with its tongue whipping around her wrist. I don't know how much longer she . . ."

"Enough, Dad. I can do it as long as I have to." Eddy stood up without help and pointed at the library. At the creature perched on the parapet. "What about that?"

Bumper growled. The gargoyle stared down on all of them, but its eyes were mere stone and there was no sense of life in the thing.

Dax stared at it for a long moment. "I don't know. My powers aren't enough. I'm thinking we need to let Alton take his turn with it. Maybe that sword of yours . . ."

"It's too dangerous for you, and I can't do it alone. Not until we're able to communicate. Damn." Alton swung away and stared off toward the mountain. Shasta loomed over the town, like a benevolent guardian. "I'm sorry, Dax. I don't know what I need to do to bring it to life, but until we can communicate, I can't use it anywhere near you." He sighed. "I'm not enough of a warrior to take on the gargoyle myself and have any effect." Looking at his hands in disgust, he added, "That's probably why my sword isn't talking."

"Is there any way for you to check with Taron, find out if he's had any luck with your people?" Eddy touched Alton's wrist. He jerked his head up and caught her in his brilliant emerald gaze. She was shocked to see tears in his eyes.

"He will contact me if there's news." Sadly, he shook his head. "I am outcast, now. I can never go back, not unless my people decide that my actions were taken for the good of all."

Dax swayed on his feet. Ed quickly slipped a hand beneath his elbow. "Let's get you home," he said. "Maybe something to eat will help restore your strength."

Eddy slipped her arm around Dax's waist, surprised by how much of his weight she actually supported. He was obviously much weaker than she'd realized.

It was just as obvious that he didn't want the others to realize how much he suffered. Eddy flashed a bright smile at her father. "It amazes me how you stay so skinny," she said, "considering how you solve every problem with food."

Ed just grunted in response. Dax smiled, but there was no light in his deep brown eyes. Only the look of a man who knew he'd failed at his greatest challenge. Failed and put those he loved at risk.

Eddy gave her head a sharp, determined shake. "I know what you're thinking," she said. "And you're wrong. You're going to beat this thing. I know it." She placed a hand over his heart, over the now quiescent tattoo. "I feel it, here. This thing is not stronger than the two of us together, and that's how we're going to fight this battle. Together."

Dax stared at her for a long moment. Then he leaned close and kissed her. His lips were firm, his kiss filled with renewed confidence. "With you beside me, Eddy Marks, there's nothing we can't accomplish, is there?" He kissed her once more.

He was smiling when he backed away, but this time she saw the matching glow in his eyes.

They turned and walked back toward Ed's house, aware the malevolent stony stare of the gargoyle followed them until they turned the corner.

Chapter Thirteen

Wednesday afternoon—day four

Dax tried to listen, but Eddy's voice was barely audible. She was on the phone in another room next to the kitchen, but Dax couldn't hear her well enough to know who she spoke with. He wasn't sure where Ed had gone, but he'd stepped outside a few minutes earlier. Alton sat beside Dax. He finished his sandwich and pushed his chair back.

Dax grabbed his hand before he stood. "Once again, I owe you my life, my friend. Thank you."

Alton stared down at their joined hands and shook his head. "I did nothing. I failed. I can't draw my sword, without fear of harming you. I couldn't contain the battle within the sphere . . ."

"A battle I'd already lost." Dax glanced at their clasped hands and felt more discouraged than he had since the beginning. "Quite an army we make, eh? What can we do to beat this thing?"

If only they could destroy the gargoyle . . .

Alton tightened his grasp on Dax's hand and then released it. He sighed. "I thought, when I made the decision to leave my people, that I could help you, but so far, I've done nothing but fry a few demon spirits and muddy some memories. Not very warrior-like. Right now, I intend to get some rest. We will try again this evening." He shrugged. "What more can we do?"

Eddy walked into the kitchen and stopped behind Dax's chair. She rested her hands on his shoulders. That simple contact seemed to give him a sense of calm he'd been unable to find with her in the next room.

"I think that's a good idea, Alton." She lightly rubbed Dax's shoulders. "I just talked to Ginny. She's getting all kinds of calls at work about what she's calling 'woo woo' stuff. It sounds like there are rumors flying about everything from the water system being poisoned with hallucinogenic drugs to an alien invasion." Eddy laughed, leaned over, and kissed Dax's cheek. "No mention of demons. If they only knew."

She turned toward Alton. "She remembers you, Alton. I thought you said you'd made her forget. She asked about my dad's friend with the long blond hair. The one who kissed her." Eddy's eyes crinkled up with her big smile. "Is there something you're not telling us?"

Alton flushed a deep rose. "I had hoped it would make her forget."

"Obviously it didn't work the way you planned." Eddy's laughter bubbled over.

Dax leaned his head back against her belly and gazed up into her twinkling brown eyes. He never grew tired of watching her, of her touch, her scent. Her smiles. He swallowed back a million things he suddenly wished he could say, and concentrated on Eddy's conversation with Ginny. "I'm sure Alton was thinking only of our mission," he said, winking at the Lemurian.

Eddy grinned at Dax. "I'm sure he was."

Alton grunted and changed the subject. "Any talk of calling in the army? Help from neighboring law enforcement?"

"Not yet." Eddy shook her head. "Luckily, folks here tend to take care of their own problems. There haven't been any deaths or serious injuries, thank goodness, so I guess no one's totally freaked out yet. I'm wondering if things are going underreported simply because people don't believe what they're seeing."

"Could be." Ed walked into the room. "I just saw Mr. Puccini. We chatted about the weather and the vandalism at Eddy's house, but he didn't say a word about the turkey cornering him on the front porch. Looks like Alton's hypnosis is still working."

"Good." Alton grabbed his scabbard with the crystal sword and slung it over his shoulder. "I need sleep," he said. Bumper stood up and wagged her tail, ready to follow him. Willow buzzed across the room, did a little loop in front of him, and then zipped down the hallway. A pale scattering of blue sprinkles blinked out in her wake. Alton nodded and then followed the dog and the sprite.

Eddy grabbed Dax's hand and tugged him to his feet. He reached for his plate, but Ed already had it in his hand. "Go," he said. "Get some rest. I have a feeling we're going to have a busy night."

Eddy kissed her dad's cheek and headed down the hallway, but the wink she gave Dax left no doubt what was on her mind.

Dax turned to wish Ed a good rest. Ed's dark eyes, so much like his daughter's, held him in place. Dax closed his, unable to meet the man's direct gaze. He took a deep breath, opened his eyes, and found Ed still watching him. "You know I love her," he said. "I would do anything not to hurt . . ."

Ed rested a heavy hand on Dax's shoulder, interrupting him. "I know," he said, "Sometimes life hurts, but we do the best we can. Dax, my daughter is smart enough to know what she's gotten herself into. As much as I hate to think of her in pain, I would never try and make her choices for her."

Dax couldn't help but wonder, if he had been in Ed's shoes, how he would feel about his daughter loving a demon. One scheduled to disappear in a few short days.

"I have much to learn," he said, "and so little time to learn it all." He sighed and glanced out the window at the bright sun, the deep green of the trees around the house, the blue of the sky. All so beautiful, so foreign, and, for him, so entirely temporary. With a long sigh, Dax turned away from Ed and walked down the hallway to the room where Eddy waited.

"Take off your shirt." The shades were drawn, leaving the room in shadows. She stood beside the bed with her arms folded over her chest. "I want to see what that snake did to you."

Dax shrugged out of his shirt. The top two buttons were missing, so it only took him a few seconds. Eddy's eyes went wide, and she stepped up to him. "I can't believe it's right back where it belongs." She ran her fingertips over the tattoo, from the snake's broad snout to the point where it disappeared beneath his jeans. "What about on your leg?"

He glanced up at her and grinned. "Is that an invitation?"

She blinked. "What?"

"You're asking me to take my pants off. I merely wondered . . ."

"I hadn't really thought about it like that, but now that you mention it . . ." She reached for his shoulders and ran her hands over the curves of muscle and lumps and bumps of bone, from his collarbones to his biceps. Suddenly her smile faltered. Brown eyes glistened with tears. "I can't do this. I can't treat it like play, as if everything's okay. Dax, you scared me so badly today. When I saw you and Willow and Alton lying on the ground . . ."

"It's okay. I'm okay now. Your touch saved me." He put his arms around her and pulled her close. She leaned her cheek against his chest. Her lips rested on the snake. Her tears glistened against the brilliant colors, and he thought of how brave she was, how powerful her love was.

"We're both exhausted and we need to rest. The battle took a lot out of me . . . saving my life took a lot out of you." He kissed the top of her head, and she tilted back and raised her lips to his. When he took her mouth, she was everything he could have asked for. More—she was answers to questions he'd never known to ask. Love and kindness, humor and tears, bravery that was so much a part of her that she could stand beside him in battle despite her fears.

She could love him in spite of the fact she knew he'd be gone in mere days. She was more than he, stronger and truer, and yet he knew she loved him. Knew it though she'd never spoken the words.

She'd faced the demon's curse to save him. There was no greater testament to her love.

No greater love. He felt her smile against his mouth. "I agree," she said, kissing him. "We need to rest, but we really have to make love first."

"We do?" He nibbled her lower lip.

She nodded and kissed him again. "Of course we do. It seems to contain the demon's curse when we make love. I'm thinking of making love as taking proactive steps to prepare for tonight's battle."

"You are?"

She kissed him once again. Then she reached for his belt buckle. "I am. I need to see if the tattoo is where it belongs. Then I need to make sure it stays there."

"And you intend to do this how?" He watched her fingers move over the belt buckle. Watched as, tooth by tooth, she slipped the zippered fly on his jeans open.

She ran her fingers under the elastic band of his knit shorts, and he almost groaned from the light touch of fingertips against his flanks. Then she was shoving the fabric down over his hips, baring him entirely.

Dropping to her knees, Eddy traced the brilliant edges of the tattoo with her fingertips. "I can't believe it's back where it belongs," she said, stroking gently along the design. When she followed the sensitive areas her fingers had touched with the light brush of her lips, Dax almost collapsed. He reached back and grabbed the oak headboard to steady himself as she tugged his jeans down to his ankles, untied his boots, and slipped everything off of him.

She shoved the pile of clothing, socks, and boots to one side and ran her hands up his long legs. Then she paused, kneeling before him, her hands resting on the jut of bone at his hips. He stood there, entirely nude, his body so hard and ready for her touch he practically quivered beneath her steady perusal.

He wondered if the demon would rise to meet her, wondered what Eddy thought when she looked at this human body. Did she realize the demon still existed? Did anyone understand how much of him was human, how much demon?

How much of him was purely Dax, a combination of the two?

In spite of his demon side, Dax felt a stronger connection to the man who had died so bravely while clothed in this shell.

Stronger even than the connection to his demon self, but wasn't it better to connect to a hero than a demon interested only in self-preservation?

Dax wondered, would he be as brave as that hero when

his time came? Would he be able to walk away from Eddy, from all those he'd already grown to love, without faltering? Had that other man, the soldier who died in battle, left behind a woman? Children? People who loved him?

When Dax thought of leaving Eddy, his heart actually ached. He reached for her, touched the thick, dark hair that tumbled over her forehead, and ran his fingertips along the line of her jaw as she gazed up at him.

"I love you, Eddy." He hadn't meant to say the words, hadn't wanted to burden her with the emotions churning in him, but they spilled out, and once they were said, he couldn't stop himself. "I never knew what love was until you. I never understood how it felt, what it meant. Make love with me. Love me." He reached for her hands. She placed hers in his, and there were tears sparkling in her brown eyes.

Dax tugged lightly, and she came to her feet. "I love you too, Dax." She clung to his hands, her fingers gripping his so tightly her knuckles turned white. "I love you so much. I tried not to, but I . . ."

He leaned over and kissed away the words. She turned his hands free and wrapped her arms around his waist. The worn denim of her jeans teased the sensitive underside of his erection, and the taut peaks of her nipples pressed through her T-shirt, hard against his chest.

Dax had to be inside her, now.

He reached down and looped one arm beneath her knees, the other across her back, and lifted her.

"Dax!" She grabbed his neck and her sandals fell to the floor, but he managed to drop her on the bed and cover her body with his in one quick move.

"No more talking. You've got too many clothes on."

She giggled and twisted beneath him. He slipped the T-shirt over her head and dragged her jeans and panties past her slim hips until she was as naked as he was. She squirmed beneath him, laughing and grabbing at his hair, his shoulders, his back, pulling him close even as she pretended to push him away.

He kissed her breasts, her belly, the line between her groin and her thigh. Then he dipped his head between her legs and ran his tongue lightly along her damp slit. She arched against him with a cry of pleasure, so he did it again. Then he drove his tongue deep, licking and suckling as she squirmed and whimpered beneath him.

Her fingers twisted in his hair, and she arched her hips against his mouth when he found the tiny bundle of nerves with his lips and suckled her. He used his fingertips to separate her petaled folds and slipped first one and then another finger deep inside.

She was wet and slick and so very hot, and when she climaxed, he felt the muscles clasping his fingers, pulsing in rhythmic waves as she found her pleasure. She was still grinding her hips against him, still whimpering when he slipped his fingers free of her sheath, moved up her body, and placed the thick crown of his penis where his mouth and fingers had been.

She parted for him, welcoming him inside her liquid heat with sighs and soft sounds of pleasure. He thrust hard and fast, and at the same time he covered her mouth with his, swallowed her cries as he filled her. He felt the hard curve of her womb, the taut mouth of her cervix riding against his sensitive glans, and he dreamed an impossible dream, of someday planting his seed deep inside, of filling her with his child, one born of the two of them.

Eddy, growing round with his child. Could anything be more lovely? Only the sight of her nursing their babe. The image swelled beneath his heart until he saw a tiny fist against her breast, perfect cherry lips encircling her rosy nipple.

Demon and human? Or would a child of theirs be entirely

human? This body was human, the seed he gave her, human. . . . But it was not to be. Eddy had already said she took pills to prevent pregnancy, and he would be gone in three more days.

It was good that she prevented creation.

What kind of father created a child and then abandoned it?

That was something he wouldn't do. Ever. He couldn't allow himself to dream the impossible. Even to begin to imagine a life with Eddy—to imagine creating life with Eddy. It was not to be. His life was finite and his days poorly numbered.

That didn't mean he couldn't appreciate now, couldn't cherish each moment with Eddy as long as those moments lasted, couldn't love her, find fulfillment loving her. Eddy's channel pulsed around his thick shaft, and he plunged in and out, matching her rhythm with his own.

He kissed her again. She opened her eyes when the kiss ended, and then she pressed her fingertips against his tattoo. He felt a cooling wash of energy, as if she poured all the love in her heart through her hands, into the curse.

Into Dax.

Instead of the steady drain of power he'd felt since the demon's curse, this time he experienced something more, a new sense of strength, as if Eddy channeled his demon powers through herself and gave them back to him, cleansed of the curse.

He straightened his arms and raised up on his palms, wrapped his arms around Eddy and lifted her as he knelt back and sat on his heels. Her legs went around his waist, and she leaned into his embrace. Hips thrusting, heart singing, he held her close while her fingers danced over the angles and lines of the snake tattoo.

It glowed in the twilight of the room, a deep golden glow that made him think of a halo. There was no sense of evil about it, none of the sinister malevolence, the stench of corruption Dax associated with the curse. Eddy healed whatever evil it contained, and once again she held the curse at bay.

Dax thrust deep and steady. By himself, this time, without the demon. As he loved her, as he tied the two of them even more deeply together, he gazed into Eddy's shining eyes and felt hope rise in him once more.

She wanted to remember everything about this act of love. Everything about Dax. The way he felt, the smooth flow of powerful muscles and hard bone as he lifted her, filled her, loved her.

The way he smelled, an enticing blend of clean sweat and some other scent she couldn't identify. It wasn't soap, or shaving lotion or anything remotely familiar, yet it was intoxicating, addicting . . . and unique to Dax.

His touch, his kisses, the trace of an accent she'd never been able to identify, the power of his muscles, the sweet sound of his laughter.

She knew that for the rest of her life, every man she met would be compared to Dax—and every single one of them would come up short.

He made love to her as if she were the only woman on Earth. He treated her as an equal, deferred to her in so many things, and yet she knew he would gladly give his life to protect her.

Was giving his life to protect her. Three more days. Could she possibly save enough memories in three short days to last a lifetime?

She was going to have to. Eddy pressed her lips to the glowing tattoo and willed it to behave. She sensed no threat from the curse, at least for now. What she did sense was her own growing climax, a shiver of need and fulfillment racing through her nervous system, building a power of its own, screaming for release.

Dax reached between them and brushed his fingertips across her needy clit. She bit her lips to contain the scream that even her father might hear.

Now, wouldn't that be embarrassing?

Dax stroked his fingers over her once more, and then again.

Eddy screamed.

But no one heard. Dax's mouth covered hers. His tongue thrust in time with a final, powerful thrust of his hips. He swallowed her scream with his own silent cry of completion.

Perfect memories, she thought as her body pulsed and clenched, released, and tightened once again.

Absolutely perfect.

The loud knocking on the bedroom door brought Eddy awake much too fast. She grabbed her robe off the end of the bed and raced to open the door. Alton stood outside with his fist raised to knock once again. His hair hung in blond tangles down his back, and he looked as if he'd just been awakened as well.

"Your dad said to wake you. Ginny called. She's getting reports of statues and stuff massing at the freeway exit south of town. Almost as if they're trying to prevent people from leaving."

"Crap. We need to get down there. But why'd she think to call here?" Eddy grabbed her jeans off the floor and looked around for her T-shirt. Dax was already zipping his pants as he grabbed for the clean shirt he'd borrowed from her dad.

"I guess you told her your boss at the paper had hired you back. She figured you'd want to know for a story."

Alton turned to leave. Then he stopped and said, "Dax? Ed's packing sandwiches."

"Thank you, Alton." Laughing, Eddy shut the door behind him. She needed to get dressed, and Dax was the only audience she really wanted.

He'd found a brown plaid flannel shirt. It hung open and unbuttoned as he reached for his boots. The tattoo across his chest still glowed. He glanced up as Eddy leaned back against the closed door and said, "Even in an emergency, Dad's going to make sure no one goes hungry."

Dax paused in the midst of pulling on a boot. "I have to agree with Alton," he said, nodding seriously. "That is a very good thing."

They were both laughing as they left the bedroom, but in the back of her mind, Eddy wondered when they'd find anything to laugh about again.

They'd all piled into Ed's Jeep for the short drive to the exit south of town. Cars were lined up near the on-ramp. Lights flashed from a couple of highway patrol black-and-whites, and a group of about half a dozen sheriff's deputies and California Highway Patrolmen stood off to one side.

Ed pulled in behind one of the flashing black-and-whites. Eddy grabbed her camera and climbed out of the backseat. Local law enforcement officers were used to seeing her at the scene of any accident or disturbance, so she slung the camera over her shoulder and carried her tape recorder, notepad, and pen.

"What's up?" She stopped beside a couple of the local guys. Milton, the taller of the two, shoved his hat back and scratched his bald head.

"Hey, Eddy. Haven't seen you in a while." He pointed toward the on-ramp, where dozens of stone statues and ceramic garden gnomes sat in silent rows across the lane. "Craziest thing. Got a call that the ramp was blocked, and came out here to find this mess."

"I just don't see gangbangers lining up little animal statues." Bud, Milton's partner, laughed out loud. "Shit. This is just nuts. Who'd do something stupid like this?"

Alton, Ed, and Dax joined the group. Eddy noticed that Alton wore his sword in the scabbard across his back, but her view of it appeared to fade in and out. He must have used some sort of hypnotic compulsion or glamour to hide it. Neither Bud nor Milton took any notice, but as intent as they were on the mess blocking the road, they might not have needed hypnosis to miss Alton's sword.

"Milt, Bud," she said, snagging the deputies' attention. "I want you to meet a couple of old college friends who've been visiting." Eddy nodded toward Alton and Dax.

Alton held out his hand to Milton. "Interesting roadblock you're using." The men all chuckled. Bud scratched his head and grunted. Alton added, "Dax and I would be happy to move this mess out of the road for you."

Eddy jerked about and caught Alton's eye. He merely smiled at her. Then he winked. Before she could figure out what he was up to, Alton raised his hand and made a sweeping gesture that encompassed everyone in uniform.

Milton blinked. Bud stared blankly at the massed figurines. Then he looked toward Alton and smiled. "Why thank you. That's very kind of you. We'll let you take care of things."

He and Milton turned away, climbed into their car, and drove off. The highway patrolmen followed suit. Moments later, Eddy heard the scream of sirens. Lights flashed. Highway patrol and sheriff's cars raced back toward town.

Alton remained focused on the cars parked along the

on-ramp. He repeated the gesture, passing his hand through the air in the direction of the cars backed up along the road.

Engines roared to life, and people began backing their vehicles up, turning around, and leaving. Eddy took Bumper's leash from her father as the last car disappeared. Alton's talent definitely made things easier for them, but she wondered what was going on in town that would require a code-three response from all the law enforcement Alton had just dismissed.

Alton glanced at Dax. Dax nodded, and the two of them split up. Dax went to one side of the silent group of innocent-looking stone and ceramic pieces blocking the road. Alton moved to the other.

When he reached over his shoulder and unsheathed his sword, Eddy gasped. The blade spun in Alton's hand and pointed directly at Dax. Alton's shoulders strained, and the muscles bunched along his arms as he firmly grasped the hilt in both hands and directed the blade at the silent army of statues and gnomes.

After a brief struggle, he regained full control of the sword. "Bastard," he muttered, staring at the shimmering blade held upright in front of his face. He made a sweeping slash through the statues, beheading all of those within his long reach with a single stroke.

Without pausing, he struck again. And again, until the ground was littered with rubble. Dax held his hands at the ready while stone and ceramic heads clattered to the asphalt. Eddy clutched Bumper's leash in both hands, holding her tightly as the dog strained to go after the first moving target.

A bird chirped nearby. A truck passed by on the overpass, and the road rumbled with the rattle and clank of empty trailers. Alton destroyed the final figurine. He and Dax took a step back from the mess and silently stared at the beheaded and shattered statuary.

No demon stench escaped. There was no sign of black mist. No rows of razor-sharp teeth or glowing eyes. Alton raised his head and glanced at Dax. "Nothing here. What've you got?"

Dax shrugged. "No scent of demon at all. I don't get it."

Eddy's cell phone rang. She flipped it open and took the call while Dax and Alton shoved the rubble to the side of the road with Ed's help.

Ginny's frantic words made Eddy's blood run cold.

"Dax! Alton . . . Dad! Hurry. There's a riot in town. The statues from the cemetery are gathering near the library. People are showing up armed to the teeth to fight them. Ginny said it sounds like it's absolute chaos!"

Alton took the passenger seat beside Ed. Eddy, Dax, and Bumper piled into the small backseat. Eddy was still fastening her seat belt when Ed gunned the motor. "What do you make of that?" She nodded toward the pile of broken statues and figurines as Ed backed up and spun the Jeep around.

"A decoy?" Dax glanced at Alton. "Could the demons have enough intelligence to stage a false attack, one that would draw all of us away from town?"

Alton nodded. "One of them could."

"The gargoyle."

Dax's softly spoken statement sent chills racing along Eddy's spine. She turned to Dax and caught his serious gaze. "Working together's one thing. What's this mean, if they're using decoys, actually planning and organizing an attack?"

Dax just shook his head and grimly glanced away. He didn't need to say a word for Eddy to realize this was something altogether new. Something none of them had counted on.

Instead of being weakened in the fight with Dax this morning, the gargoyle appeared to be growing stronger. More cunning.

Already a powerful opponent, it had just taken the war to an entirely new level.

The Jeep bounced and rattled over potholes in the road as Ed gunned it along the short distance into town. Dax's fingers wrapped around Eddy's hand. When she glanced at him, his expression was bleak.

"Are you in pain?" she asked. "Is the tattoo burning?"

He shook his head and parted the top two buttons on his flannel shirt. A soft, golden glow still surrounded the quiescent tattoo. "Your love appears to have conquered it, if only for a little while. There is no pain at all, though I sense the curse, almost as if it lies in wait."

"I'm sorry." Eddy ran her fingers over the brilliant colors. "I wish I could do more." She blew out a gust of air in frustration. "There is something going on with the gargoyle. Something that doesn't make sense. It's not anything like the other demons, but I can't figure out why. How come it's so smart and they're all so stupid? It's like they're two different species of evil."

Dax nodded. "When I was a demon," he said, "I thought as a demon. I lived for the moment. Eat, fuck, kill. All that concerned me was the need to survive. Survival was my life, my only goal for eons. Life continued without change, one day after another. I didn't think of politics, of other demons. I had no friends, no real language to speak of, as there was no need to communicate. I went on that way from my beginning. Then a time came when I knew, somehow, I wanted more. I had no idea what it was, only that there had to be something more than eating, fucking, and killing."

He looked down at their clasped hands as the Jeep rattled along the bumpy road. Then he focused once more on Eddy. "With that realization, I began to change, to evolve into something other than a demon. Something no longer suitable for Abyss. That's when I was cast into the void. That's when the Edenites found me."

"What are you saying?" She was almost certain where this was leading. She wanted to be wrong, but Dax was shaking his head. Agreeing with her unspoken thoughts.

When he looked at her, his expression had grown, if anything, even more bleak. "What if someone on Earth, or even Eden, was so evil, so vile and depraved, that when he died the leaders of Abyss, whoever they might be, sought him out? What if they recognized absolute evil and did exactly what the Edenites did with me?"

Chills raced along her spine. Raised the tiny hairs on her arms. Bumper whined, as if she picked up Eddy's tension. Willow's head poked out of Dax's pocket, and Eddy focused on the tiny sprite as the reality of their situation hit her. "You're saying we're not fighting a mindless demon? That creature might be something with human intelligence, with the ability to plan and organize?"

Dax nodded. "How else could it have known the precise moment when I was to enter your dimension? It could have already been here, waiting for me. Aware I was coming, for whatever reason. Possibly all is not so perfect in Eden. What if there are factions there, at war with one another? What if there is intelligence beyond what I know at the upper levels of Abyss? I know nothing of the politics of my world, nor do I understand the realm of Eden. Someone chose me. What if someone else, someone just as powerful, chose another soul? An evil soul. The gargoyle seems to gain strength as each day passes. For all I know, it carries powers far beyond any natural demon. Far beyond mine."

"Could it be drawing on the demons whose avatars are destroyed? Somehow absorbing them into itself?" Alton turned around and leaned his arm across the back of the seat. "What if, instead of those demons without avatars returning to Abyss, they're being absorbed by the gargoyle? What if it's taking on the powers of the ones we miss? That would explain its growing strength over the past few days. I don't know for certain that my sword is killing the ones I hit. I've been wondering if I was merely sending them back home to Abyss."

"Or to the gargoyle. What if it's able to grab the souls of the ones we actually do kill? Grab them before they vanish into the void? If that's the case, even the ones we kill provide more energy for the creature." Dax squeezed Eddy's hand as Ed parked the Jeep at the tail end of a traffic jam blocking the main street in town. The cars ahead of them were all empty of people. A few vehicles sat with motors idling and doors flung open.

"Listen," he said.

Shouts and curses, a woman's scream. Dogs barked. Bumper strained anxiously at the leash. Eddy wrapped the leather strap around her wrist and tightened her fingers through the loop for good measure. She quickly got out of the vehicle. Dax and Alton took off at a full run and raced toward the commotion.

Eddy, Bumper, and Ed ran after them.

The scene that greeted them ranked really high on the impossibility scale. Eddy skidded to a stop and stared at the battle lines drawn across the intersection of Lassen Boulevard and State Street. On one side stood townspeople—both men and women, and a few older teens. Thank goodness there were no young children in sight. Many in the crowd of more than a hundred were carrying hunting rifles and shotguns; others held axes, shovels, and pitchforks. A group of collared priests and ministers from the various local churches had gathered off to one side. Some had their heads bowed in prayer, though one priest stood apart with hands raised, as if he was attempting an exorcism. An acolyte stood beside him, holding a cross.

Across from them, stretching from storefront to storefront and filling the entire road, were row after row of stone angels and other guardians of the dead from the cemetery. Eddy noticed a few small ceramic and stone dogs and cats. She frowned as she tried to place them until she remembered those had graced some of the plots. Now, instead of standing protectively over their masters' graves, they barked and growled and snarled their banshee howls while the stone angels stood impassively behind them.

In between, lined up as if they actually hoped to quell any potential violence, were the highway patrolmen and the sheriff's deputies. Milton appeared to be arguing with a large man at the head of the human group, while the others were lined up, facing the encroaching army of statues.

All of them looked more than a little confused.

Eddy caught up to Dax and grabbed his arm. "What are they waiting for?" she asked, pointing to the demon angels. Eyes glowed red or yellow in the growing darkness. The sun had already set, but there was more than enough daylight to see that this group was entirely animated, unlike the statues they'd just destroyed at the other end of town.

"I believe they're waiting for night to fall. The demons will have more power under full darkness." He shook his head and sighed. "We haven't seen any deaths or serious injuries so far, but I'm afraid that could change." Dax swept his hand toward the seething mob. "With all those weapons, someone is bound to be hurt. The gargoyle will use any death as a sacrifice. We have no idea how much power he could gain."

"Where is the gargoyle?" Eddy had been searching the skies, but there was no sign of the creature.

Alton and Ed scanned the evening sky as well. Milton's argument with the man who appeared to be leading the townsfolk grew louder. Bud was back in the patrol car, talking into his radio. One of the highway patrolman conferred with his partner. Another was on his radio, but his head moved from one side to the other, as if he didn't know which group posed the biggest threat—the citizens of Evergreen or the cemetery statues.

"Alton? Can you do anything at all here?" Dax rubbed his hand across his chest. Eddy wondered if the tattoo was coming to life. If it still glowed. Dax glanced at her and shook his head. They'd grown so close, so quickly, he probably knew what she was thinking.

"I can try," Alton said, "but when emotions are this high, it's not quite as easy." He raised his hands and narrowed his eyes in concentration.

For the briefest of moments, a mere fraction out of time, Eddy heard nothing. An unnatural silence settled over the entire area. Then an earsplitting banshee howl rolled over the small town.

Chapter Fourteen

Wednesday evening—day four

As if the demons took Alton's raised hands as a signal, they attacked. Another howl rattled windowpanes and drew shrieks of fear from the people in the street. The horrible screeching was so earsplittingly loud, Dax had to consciously fight an instinctive reaction to cover his ears.

Some of the angels took flight, leaping into the air like a flock of startled ducks, flapping their wings and passing low over the astonished group of humans, but most of the demon-fueled avatars charged directly into the crowd.

Some people scattered. Others fought back against the unholy horde. A discordant cacophony of banshee howls, frightened screams, gunshots, and enraged curses rent the air. The ring and crunch of stone shattering and statues crumbling grew and expanded as the melee took on its own terrible rhythm of destruction.

Alton reached for his sword and started forward.

"Wait." Dax held up one hand. "Watch the battle. The demons are no match for these folks! Let's see what happens, what he's planning." He turned his gaze back in the direction of the gargoyle.

It flew in low over the town, paused a moment as if surveying the area, and then dove straight toward the angry, frightened humans. It swooped low over the uniformed men in the center of the fight, moving with such speed that the wind whistled over its wings. Deputies crouched behind their squad cars and raised their weapons. One patrolman dove for cover as the gargoyle zeroed in on his position. Gunfire rang out. Sparks flew from the creature when bullets bounced harmlessly off its stone body.

It circled the crowd, shrieking. Then it glided toward the spire of a nearby church, circled it once, and landed with surprising grace on the steep, shingled side of the steeple. One taloned fist grasped the top of a golden cross, and its clawed feet rested against the shingles.

"Dax! Look at that!" Ed pointed toward a large stone angel. With measured steps and wings spread wide, it marched directly toward a powerful-looking farmer wielding an ax. The angel's mouth opened, exposing row after row of sharp teeth. Its eyes glowed crimson in the waning light.

The man didn't hesitate. He swung his ax at the angel. With both hands grasping the thick, wooden handle, he aimed at shoulder height and put his entire body into the blow.

The angel's head rolled out into the street. The red eyes dimmed, and the mouth closed. The body tottered in place for a moment, weaving slightly before it toppled to the ground.

The man stared at the head of the statue as if he couldn't quite believe what he'd just done. Dax watched the body. Black mist rose from the angel's shattered throat. It hovered a moment over the large man, pulsing as if it drew breath. Then the mist collapsed into the shape of an arrow.

It shot straight for the gargoyle.

Clinging to the cross atop the spire, the gargoyle rose up

on its hind legs, stretched out one powerful arm, and captured the streaking mist. Jaws stretched wide, it seemed to either inhale or swallow the demon. It was hard to be sure, as dark as it was so high above the street lights, but as the mist disappeared, the gargoyle seemed to grow larger. Its eyes glowed brighter. Wings flared out from its wide, bony shoulders.

Dax stared, fascinated, as it rose up straighter, unfurling its wings to their fullest. They stretched out into the night until the gargoyle took on the appearance of a monstrous vampire bat. Then it turned slowly, pivoting about until it glared directly at Dax. He felt its hatred, the remorseless sense of pure evil—a vile loathing and malevolence aimed at him and those he loved.

He glared back, caught in the unholy malice and venomous hate, as if the creature held some personal rancor for Dax and his small band of fighters. Their gazes locked. Dax tried to see into its mind, but there was nothing familiar, nothing characteristic of demonkind or human.

Nothing but hate.

Eddy stood close behind him. She wrapped her fingers around his arm. Her presence, her confident touch, gave him strength. She was most definitely not a victim. No, Eddy was a fighter, and she'd stand beside him until his end. It was almost midnight of the fourth day. His end was coming closer, and the battle was far from over.

Even now, the street fight between humans and avatars raged, but the gargoyle ignored the brawl. Instead, it watched Dax, and now that she stood beside him, Eddy as well. Dax broke away from the malevolent stare and tugged Eddy closer.

He turned his attention back to the battle, but the image of the gargoyle grabbing that demon out of the night sky wouldn't leave him.

At least the good guys were ahead. There was no doubt

the humans were winning. Shattered statuary littered the road. Windows in a few nearby shops had been broken, but most of the damage was limited to crushed and broken statues.

Of course, they weren't killing the demons inside, but maybe once all the avatars were destroyed, the demons would be forced back to Abyss. Two women systematically beat a stone cherub into pieces with shovels. The statue was quickly reduced to rubble, but the black mist escaped.

Once again, as Dax watched, the mist hovered overhead and then shot toward the gargoyle.

A ceramic angel floated down out of the sky. One of the women hit the torso with her shovel. The other knocked its head off. Again, the black mist coalesced overhead. Again, after a brief pause, it raced directly to the gargoyle and his wide-open mouth. The mist disappeared inside the gaping jaws.

The sky was filled now with streaks of darkness, demons freed from their avatars, all of them streaming toward the gargoyle.

"We have to stop them." Dax shouted at Alton. "Every avatar they destroy feeds another demon to the gargoyle. They're not his army. They're his source of energy!"

Alton shook his head. "I see that, but how can you use your powers here, with all these townsfolk around?"

"The same way you're going to use that damned mute sword of yours," Dax said. "Very carefully. C'mon."

"Look!" Eddy pointed at the gargoyle as it grabbed yet another wraith out of the sky. "Hurry. He's getting bigger!"

Dax kissed Eddy and raced toward the fight. He wasn't sure how to use his powers without creating a panic, but he had to keep as many demons away from the gargoyle as he could. Alton moved to one side, closer to the church. A dark mist flew toward him. He intercepted it with his crystal blade, and the demon disappeared in a shower of sparks.

The gargoyle howled.

Alton pumped his fist in the air. "Proof at last that I'm actually destroying the damned things. He's pissed now!"

Dax shot Alton a quick grin. Then he found a spot close to the crowd, but still far enough away not to draw too much attention. He glanced toward Eddy to make sure she was safe. She stood in the shadows, holding tightly to Bumper's leash with Ed close beside her.

The stench of sulfur filled Dax's nostrils. He glanced up and spotted the mist just over his head, already forming into a long, dark arrow.

Controlling his flame wasn't easy. He was accustomed to frying the damned things with all the fire he could throw, and finesse had never been necessary. He sent a small burst of ice, then a quick flash of flame.

The demon mist dissolved and disappeared. Willow buzzed overhead in a flash of blue sparkles. She pointed to yet another demon. Dax spun around and fired at the black mist, but it dove beneath the icy blast. Alton caught it with the tip of his crystal sword. The stink of sulfur blossomed as the demon disappeared in a flash of light.

The gargoyle howled again. His frustration echoed over the town.

Dax gave the Lemurian a thumbs-up. Alton grinned and took a swipe at yet another demon mist. Sparks exploded overhead.

Within seconds, Dax found a rhythm of ice and then fire, keeping his bursts as small as possible. Alton managed to catch most of the demons Dax missed.

The gargoyle got the rest.

Dax raised his hands and zapped yet another. "We were wrong, Alton," he said. "He's not commanding the demons at all. They're not his army. He might be encouraging them to fight, but he doesn't want them to win."

"No, he just wants them out of their avatars." Alton slashed his sword through another demon. One just behind it got away. "Those suckers are fast."

"So's the gargoyle." Dax watched as the gargoyle captured the stinking demon soul. It wrapped clawed fingers around the mist and popped it into its mouth. Then it turned and grinned at Dax, spreading thick lips wide, exposing row after row of razor-sharp teeth.

The tattoo shivered over Dax's flesh, as if the strength of the demon's glare was enough to bring the snake to life. There'd been no pain from the thing until now, no sense of the curse. He willed it down and remembered how it had felt to call its power, to own the pain.

Could he do that again? Could he once more use the evil that coursed across his chest, that crawled over his thigh and across his groin? He felt the tattoo pulse in a slow yet relentless rhythm. He concentrated on the ebb and flow of energy and attempted to link the rhythm to the beat of his heart.

Nothing. Tonight, the tattoo had its own rhythm, its own life force.

Eddy's soft touch on his shoulder startled him. "The tattoo? It's moving again, isn't it? Are you in much pain? Here, let me. . . ." She reached for the buttons on his shirt.

Dax shook his head and covered her hand with his. Black mist against a dark sky sped by, and he reached out with one hand, sent a freezing burst.

The mist escaped, circled beyond Alton, and reached the gargoyle. Once again he'd failed. He covered Eddy's hand with his. "No, Eddy. There's no time. I'm okay."

He spun away and froze another burst of black mist, but another just beyond it got away. Alton missed as well, and the gargoyle snagged yet another black soul.

Dax hit the frozen shards of black ice with his flame. It sizzled and dissipated in the night air. Eddy gazed up at him with tears in her eyes and frustration in every move she made as she persisted. "You can't fight as well when you're in pain. Let me help."

It hurt him more than the demon's curse, to see the worry in her eyes. "Later. I'll need you later." He leaned down to kiss her. A bloodcurdling banshee scream jerked him upright. Eddy grabbed his hand.

The gargoyle leapt from the church spire and glided low over the milling crowd. Its eyes glowed red with an even brighter fire than before. The wings had lost the look of stone. They beat now with long, smooth, leathery strokes as the creature passed over the scene of the brief yet messy battle.

Most of the statues lay on the ground. Dax had no idea how many of the demons the gargoyle had absorbed. He and Alton had destroyed dozens, but the gargoyle had caught just as many. Now it looked powerful. Invincible.

Alive.

It no longer appeared to be an avatar made of stone. No, the stone had come to life. The body appeared supple, as if blood rushed beneath the surface. As if the accumulated power of so many demon souls had given their enemy unimaginable strength.

The red eyes glowed with a new intelligence—an intelligence focused entirely on Dax.

He grabbed Eddy's wrist and jerked her behind him. Alton came closer, yet remained far enough away to safely use his sword. Ed held on to Bumper and dragged the snarling dog even farther away from Dax.

The gargoyle tucked its long wings and dove at Dax. It feinted at the last moment, pulling up like a fighter jet on a strafing run. Air whistled over the sleek wings. Dax curled his body around Eddy and ducked, but the sharp slash of claws left bloody ribbons across his back and shoulders.

He felt searing pain, but the rush of adrenaline gave him

strength. Alton was too far away to connect with his crystal sword, but he moved into position near Ed, ready to protect Eddy's dad on the creature's next pass.

Willow burst into the air in a flurry of blue sparkles. She drew energy from all corners, feeding it to Dax.

"You're bleeding!" Eddy reached for Dax, but he grabbed both of Eddy's arms and stared intently into her wide, brown eyes. "Eddy. I'm okay. Go to Alton. Hurry, before that thing returns." He fully expected her brief hesitation—he knew she was just dying to argue with him. He felt a burst of pride in her when she reached up, cupped his jaw in both hands, and kissed him hard. Then she broke away and ran to her father's side, where Alton stood with his sword raised.

Dax would give his life to protect hers, but she wasn't going to allow him that choice. She'd accepted the fact that if she remained, she'd put him at risk.

He knew it hadn't been an easy choice for her. Eddy was brave, and she wanted to fight, but she was smart. Too smart to take unnecessary risks—or to force Dax to take more risks than he should.

With Eddy out of harm's way, Dax focused all his attention on the demon. The pain in his back receded. He ignored the tattoo. The gargoyle circled the church steeple once again, screaming its bloodcurdling cry. Then it paused in midair, slowly flapping huge wings up and down as it hovered in place, staring directly at Dax.

He felt the evil in its glowing red eyes and braced himself for attack. He risked a quick glance at Willow. She glowed a brilliant sapphire, brimming with the roiling energy she'd absorbed, yet still she pulled in more. He opened to her, drawing the natural energy into his body.

The burst of Willow's power exploded into overwhelming pain.

He gasped. Taken by surprise, Dax barely remained

standing. Blood poured from the deep slashes across his back and shoulders, and the added charge of energy empowered the curse. As he absorbed the energy he desperately needed for the coming battle, agonizing pain rippled across his chest, over his belly.

The snake was feeding from Willow's energy!

As Dax gained strength, so did the curse. The tattoo writhed and shimmied its acid dance across his flesh. The bleeding slashes across his back burned with their own fire. It was all he could do not to scream in agony.

Willow flitted about, obviously worried. Dax didn't have time to explain. He felt the heave and thrust of the snake's body, but he concentrated on the pain, on the strength in the reptilian muscles. Desperate, he called on his demon. Called for the soldier, for whatever strength his allies could share.

Then he called for the pain, and made it his own.

He would not fail. Eddy was too close, her safety tied to his success. He might have been sent here to save the Earth from demons, but Eddy was his focus, the one who mattered most.

Dax glanced upward, sensing the gargoyle's attack. The creature stared back at him, a vision of evil incarnate with hatred glowing crimson in its eyes. Once again it screamed out a chilling banshee wail. Long wings arrowed back along its body, turning the gargoyle into a weapon of pure malice. Still screaming, it launched itself at Dax.

He raised his hands and sent an icy blast that solidified the air immediately ahead of the gargoyle. The creature hit the thick ice, shattered it, and blasted through, but the force of impact threw it off course. Screeching furiously, it circled right over Ed and Eddy. Alton stepped to one side and took a mighty swing with his crystal sword.

The tip of one leather wing hit the ground with a loud, wet *splat*. The gargoyle shrieked and streaked back to the church, trailing thick drops of whatever blood coursed through its veins. It caught its balance against the steeple, holding tightly to the cross at the peak. Thick fluid still oozed from the wing where the tip had been severed, but even as Dax watched, a new tip formed.

The gargoyle stretched its healed wing out to its full length, as if testing it. Then it launched itself once again. This time Dax hit it with flame. He felt the snake tattoo rise up from his chest, but he fought it, drawing on the pain as well as the energy Willow continued to feed him.

His demon roared to life, and he felt the soldier's strength of purpose. The gargoyle approached, flying directly into the streams of flame shooting from Dax's fingertips. Willow sparkled brightly, almost as if she were enjoying herself.

She hovered off to one side, drawing energy into her body, sharing it with Dax. The gargoyle kept coming. Dax felt as if he watched its approach in slow motion as the creature drew closer. He viewed the beast with preternatural clarity—its talons extended, jaws gaping wide, and teeth shimmering red in the light of Dax's rippling fireshot.

Without hesitation, it flew directly into the river of flames.

At the last possible moment, it veered off.

Directly at Willow.

Dax didn't have time to warn the sprite. He watched in horror as the gargoyle snapped her up in his slavering jaws and veered sharply away.

Silence descended. His flames sputtered out. Stunned, Dax stared after the gargoyle as it banked low and flew off into the darkness, bypassing its perch on the steeple and disappearing into the nighttime sky.

Willow was gone. He felt her absence, a physical amputation of an integral part of his body. She'd been so intent on helping him, she'd not had time to save herself. The gargoyle had feinted at the last moment and struck.

Dax had been terrified it would go after Eddy. He'd never

even thought to worry about Willow. Never realized she might be an even more vulnerable target. Heartsick, Dax turned to Eddy.

She raced across the street and flung herself into his arms. "Willow? Where is she? What happened to Willow?"

He couldn't speak. He wrapped his arms around Eddy and hung on, as much for himself as for her. The image of those foul jaws closing around his tiny friend sickened him. Alton walked slowly across the street. He looked as stunned as Dax felt. Ed trailed after him, tugging Bumper's leash.

The dog's curly head hung low, and her tail dragged, as if she, too, mourned the loss of her tiny friend.

"What about them?" Ed motioned blindly toward the crowd of townsfolk standing off to one side, each and every person staring wide-eyed at Dax and Eddy, Alton, and Ed.

Staring and trying to make sense of what they'd just been a part of—a most improbable battle. One that Dax could not allow to make the evening news. He nodded toward Alton. "Can you do anything at all?"

Alton raised his hands and bowed his head. A moment later, he raised his head and gazed at Dax. Tears coursed down his cheeks. "They won't want to speak of what they saw. I can't erase their memories—they're much too intense—but I've clouded them. They won't want to talk about any of this."

He sat down hard on a low fence beside the road. "I wish I could cloud mine. Poor, dear little Willow. What a horrible end to a brave soul. I never imagined the gargoyle would go after her."

Dax sat heavily beside him. He tugged Eddy into his lap. "He must have guessed how much I need her. She collects the energy I use to power my demon abilities, the fire and ice I throw. Without her, I'll have only a fraction of my strength. Without Willow, I . . ." His voice broke. He'd been on this world for such a short time, yet Willow had been with him since the beginning.

She'd been part of him. In his head, and very much in his heart. Not only had he lost the tiny engine that ensured his powers, he'd lost a dear and loyal friend.

Eddy buried her face in his shirt and cried. Ed stood beside them, softly rubbing her back, but he looked ready to burst into tears as well.

Almost as if it were an afterthought, Alton stood up and walked back across the street. He leaned down and picked something up off the ground, and then returned with a triangular piece of stone. He stared at it a moment, frowning. Then he held it out to Dax. "Look. It's stone again. This was the demon's wingtip. I wondered what would happen without the demon to power it. The thing had the texture of leather when I cut it, supple and strong. It looked as if it were really alive, but this is nothing more than stone."

He turned it over in his hands and pointed at a dark stain. "It's just a rock, now, but it bled when I cut it. I saw fluid pouring from the wound. It might have been green, but it's still blood. The demon bleeds when it's hurt. If it bleeds, we can kill it."

Alton's quiet statement carried the resolve of a blood oath. Dax stared into the darkness, thinking of Willow, of her horrible death, trapped in the gargoyle's jaws. He shuddered and absentmindedly rubbed his chest. It was good to know the gargoyle bled. The creature would die. He would see to it.

Eddy sniffed. "Are you in much pain? Those cuts on your back aren't bleeding as much, but I can't tell how deep they are. The tattoo . . ."

Dax frowned. He rolled his shoulders. His back and shoulders stung, but the pain wasn't nearly as fierce as it had been. Instead he felt a dull ache and the stickiness of drying blood. He rubbed his hand over his chest once again. The tattoo was nothing more than colored ink. There was no pain, no sense of life. The glow was gone, but so was the pain. He shook his head. "It doesn't hurt. I tried working the pain, drawing on it for power, instead of letting it control me. It appears to have worked." He sighed. Little good it would do. Without Willow, he wouldn't be able to draw enough power to fight. *Without Willow* . . .

Eddy hugged him close and pressed her cheek against his chest. Dax rested his chin on her head and stared off into the darkness.

Where he watched a small, glowing speck of blue grow and solidify before his eyes. "Willow?" He lifted Eddy off his lap and stood up. "Look! Do you see that?"

Bumper barked. They all stood and watched as Willow slowly reformed and materialized in front of their eyes. She buzzed up to Dax and hovered mere inches from his nose.

Willow?

The little sprite spun in a swirl of blue sparkles. *Sorry to worry you, but I disincorporated so quickly, I sort of misplaced some of me.*

"Where have you been? We thought the gargoyle . . ." He couldn't say it. His eyes burned, and his throat felt tight, but he didn't understand why, only that it had something to do with Willow. With the fact she was safe and alive and showering him in blue sparkles. He cleared his throat and tried again. "I've been worried sick about you! We've all been worried. We thought . . . damn it, Willow! Where were you?"

She tilted her head and grinned at him, cocky as ever. *I was in Bumper,* she said. *Where else?*

Before Dax could come up with a suitable answer, Willow buzzed over to Alton and crawled into his breast pocket. Dax glanced at Alton and almost burst out laughing at the bright grin on the big man's face. Then he smiled at Eddy and her dad and shrugged. "She was in Bumper. Where else?"

"Where else?" Eddy was still chuckling a few minutes later. She waited on the corner under a streetlight with her father while Dax and Alton checked the area for more demons. She didn't mind the wait at all. She didn't mind much of anything, now that she knew Willow was safe. She'd been so certain the little sprite had been swallowed by the demon gargoyle that the relief was unbelievable.

Bumper nudged Eddy's thigh with her nose, obviously searching for a little more attention. Eddy complied. "Bumper, if not for you, Willow might not have made it. You are such a good girl."

Bumper wriggled and danced, practically turning herself inside out for more of Eddy's attention. Talk about living for the moment. Nothing seemed to faze the dog—not a demon attack nor sharing her consciousness with a terrified sprite. Eddy ruffled Bumper's blond curls and wished she could be a little more doglike.

It had to be sort of a Zen thing . . . but it would be great not to worry about things she couldn't change. Wonderful not to always be thinking of what could happen next. She stared across the intersection and thought of all the things that could have gone wrong.

Bumper licked Eddy's fingers, and she sighed. Maybe she needed to think of the things that had gone right, instead, but it was hard. None of the avatars had survived the battle, but with so many of the crushed statues or garden gnomes, the gargoyle had gained another demon's energy. At least things here in town had settled down for now, and the gargoyle was gone. The townsfolk had already dispersed, confused, no doubt, by Alton's special brand of group hypnosis.

It wasn't as powerful as the first time he'd used it, but so far it appeared to be working, which meant the people weren't immune to it yet. She wondered how they'd have handled the community without the Lemurian's help.

Okay. That was a good thing—the fact Alton had the courage to choose exile in order to join them. She wondered if Taron was having any luck with the rest of Alton's people. Dax needed more help. So far, they'd survived everything the demon had tossed their way, but they weren't winning. Not by a long shot.

Eddy heard men's voices and glanced toward the scene of the fight. The highway patrolmen had taken off right after Alton's spell, but Milton and Bud were hanging around, checking the damage. Their voices carried on the still night air.

Eddy touched her dad's sleeve to get his attention. "I'm going to have a chat with Milt and Bud. I'm curious to see how they're explaining all this." She leaned over and patted Bumper's head again. "Be good, beast." Bumper yipped and licked Eddy's fingers. Then she sat and planted her butt on Ed's foot.

Eddy walked across the intersection to chat with the deputies.

"Hey, Eddy. I thought I saw you over there." Milton glanced up from his perusal of a shattered angel. "What do you make of all this? First the blocked on-ramp, and now this mess."

She shrugged. "I have no idea, Milt. What's your guess?"

Milt shoved his hat back and scratched his head. "I'm wondering if we've got some sort of cult we weren't aware of. Someone had to bring these things into town, but I have no idea what got into that mob. I watched 'em with my own eyes. It was mass hysteria, beating these statues into dust. Can you imagine desecrating graves like this?" He swept his hand to encompass all the broken statuary. "Every gosh-darned one of these was guarding a plot at the cemetery. I wish I knew how they got them all here. Even more, why did those people think they had to destroy every single one?"

Eddy knelt down to examine the angel. She glanced up as Bud joined them. "Do you think any of these can be repaired?"

Bud shook his head. "I don't think so. What a mess." He took a few steps and knelt down beside the shattered body of a tiny cherub. "This looks like the one from my grandma's grave . . . sick bastards. I need to go see if hers is still there."

He lurched to his feet and brushed the dust off his hands. "Ya know, it doesn't look like somethin' a gang might've pulled. I'm leaning more toward a satanic cult. Devil worshippers, maybe. Most of 'em are angels," he added softly, pointing to the broken wings scattered about.

Eddy nodded gravely. "I noticed that." She stood, slipped her digital camera out of her pocket, and got a few pictures of the mess, along with shots of the two deputies. "Should I mention that in my story? The cult angle? You never know. . . . I can see if it gets you some leads."

Bud nodded. "You do that, Eddy. Folks around here look out for each other, but this was just weird. What would make them all go so nuts that they'd destroy all these statues? They're good people . . . most of the time."

"Did the call come through Shascom?" she asked, referring to the 911 dispatch center in Redding, south of Evergreen.

Milt frowned. "I'm not sure. I can't really remember, but we got a call from someone after checking out a disturbance at the south end of town. Bud, what was the problem there?" He chuckled. "I must be getting old. I know we had something near the freeway."

"That's okay." Eddy gently touched his arm. "Don't worry about it, but if you think of anything important, let me know, will you?" She pocketed her little digital camera and went back across the street. Dax and Alton were there, talking softly with Ed. Her dad yawned and stretched his arms high overhead. He'd been up since dawn, and it was obvious he was running out of steam.

She flashed him a sympathetic smile and nodded toward the deputies. "They're talking satanic cult and devil worshippers. Nothing about the demon gargoyle or the shots they fired at it. They're going to notice they've fired their weapons, so that might confuse them, but whatever you tossed their way, Alton, it certainly took them off track."

"It's nice to know I can do something right," he grumbled, glaring over his shoulder at the sparkling hilt of his sheathed sword. "I can't believe this thing still refuses to speak. What does it want from me?"

Dax grinned. "It probably wants you to kill me, so I'm perfectly content that the two of you aren't communicating. I've grown attached to all these human body parts."

Alton grunted. "I'd laugh," he said, "but I have a feeling you might be right. We'll have to continue to fight separately." He glanced at the waning moon hanging low in the sky. "It's after midnight. I say we go by the library, see if the gargoyle is there or not. I doubt he's expecting us to hunt for him any more tonight. There's no sign of him here."

"Eddy?"

She turned toward the question in Dax's soft voice.

"Are you okay with that?"

"I am, but Dad looks beat." Bumper whined and rolled over on her back. Her tail flopped slowly against the ground. "And it looks like Bumper is, too." She laughed. "Dad, why don't you take the dog home and get some rest. We'll be there in a bit."

Ed gave her a hug. "Great idea. I'm ready to fold." He rested his hand on Dax's shoulder. "Check out the gargoyle, son, but I'd feel a lot better if you just looked. We're all exhausted, and I'd prefer to see you live to fight another day. You probably need to get those cuts on your back checked too." He took a closer look. "Maybe not. They're already closing."

Dax nodded. "Part of my demon powers—we heal quickly—but I agree. I want to see if the gargoyle returned to the library. Then we need to rest and figure out how to beat this creature in battle. He grows stronger by the day."

"It's all those demon souls he had for dinner." Ed patted Dax's shoulder, tugged Bumper's leash, and gave Eddy a quick kiss on top of her head. Then he slowly walked down the street to the Jeep, climbed in, and headed back toward the house.

Eddy watched him until he turned the corner and disappeared from sight. He was obviously exhausted, but she had to admit he looked better than he'd looked in years. As if the last few days had given him purpose. It had definitely confirmed all his wild theories and wilder beliefs. She smiled even as her heart clenched when she thought of how lonely he must have been before Dax came into their lives.

How lonely both of them were going to be when he was gone. How was she going to cope when Dax was no longer here? She knew she'd never love again, not like this. She couldn't allow herself to think about the future without him. Not now, while he was standing so strong, so alive, beside her.

As if he read her thoughts, Dax grabbed her hand and tugged. She linked her fingers in his and looked at the way they fit so perfectly together. Then she matched his steps, walking between him and Alton down the dark street toward the library.

"Eddy? What are you guys doing out here in the middle of the night?"

Eddy spun around. "Ginny! Hi . . . uhm, I was just out with Dax and his friend Alton. You just getting off work? You've met Dax, but this is . . ."

"Yeah," she said, focusing intently on Alton. "We've met. Hello, Alton." She turned her back on the Lemurian and smiled at Eddy. "My car's in the shop so I got a lift with one of the deputies. I told him to drop me off here. It was on his way, and not too far for me to walk home."

"Is that safe?" Alton asked. His deep voice seemed to startle Ginny. "Walking alone at night? Isn't that how you got hurt before?"

Ginny nodded, almost as if she were in a trance. "Yes. There was a street fight. I got knocked around, but I'm okay."

Eddy glared at Alton. "What are you doing?" she whispered.

Alton shook his head. "Nothing," he said.

"Yes, you are." Ginny glared at him. "I know, because you've done it to me before, but for some weird reason, I can't remember exactly what it is."

Alton's eyes narrowed. "I'm not really sure what you're . . ."

Eddy interrupted. "Do you think it's safe for you to be walking home alone this late at night?"

Ginny grinned at her. "C'mon, Eddy. This is Evergreen. That fight in town was a total aberration."

"But it happened," Alton said, "and you could have been badly hurt."

Now why did Alton sound like he had a bee up his butt? Eddy watched the Lemurian as he glared at Ginny.

Suddenly, Alton seemed to come to a decision. With a grim smile plastered on his face, he took Ginny's arm in his. "I'll feel better if I walk you home, Ginny. I remember where your house is. It's not far."

Ginny frowned and immediately tugged her arm out of his grasp. "That's not ne—"

"Yes. It is." Alton stared down his long nose at Ginny, and Eddy bit her lips to keep from laughing. No one gave Ginny Jones orders. Ever.

Before Ginny could explode, Eddy interrupted. "Ginny,

I'd feel a lot better if you let Alton go with you. There's been so much weird stuff going on lately, you can't say for sure it's safe. Which reminds me, thanks for the tips today. There really were statues and garden gnomes blocking the on-ramp. It was nuts. Then someone stole a bunch of statues from graves at the cemetery and left them at the intersection of State and Lassen. Some folks from town showed up and bashed them all to pieces. Really screwy stuff. The cops think it could be devil worshippers. Whatever's behind all this stuff, I'd rather you weren't alone. I know it's not far to your house, but please let Alton go with you."

Ginny laughed. "Oh, give me a break. Devil worshippers? In Evergreen?"

"Or gangs," Alton said. "Whatever is causing all the problems, they're not good. I'm going with you." He glared at Ginny.

Ginny rolled her eyes at no one in particular. "All right," she said, matching Alton's glare with one of her own. "But only so Eddy won't worry."

Once again, Alton grabbed her elbow. Ginny shook him off, but when he started walking, she went with him. Alton glanced over his shoulder at Dax and Eddy. "You guys check things out, and I'll meet you at Ed's later."

"Don't hurry on our account." Giggling, Eddy dragged Dax toward the library. "I've never, ever seen that look on Ginny's face in my life."

"What? The furious 'I'd like to kick your ass' look?" Dax laughed and kept walking.

"No, silly." Eddy gazed back at the two figures crossing the street. "There's something between those two. I'd bet on it." She sighed and turned away to follow Dax. "Okay. One look at the library. That's all you get. Then we're going back to the house."

"I think Alton likes her." Dax gazed over his shoulder at

the tall Lemurian as he escorted Ginny home. He sighed and turned away, still keeping pace with Eddy.

"What's wrong with Alton liking her?" Eddy wrapped her hands around his arm as they walked.

"He's got the opposite problem of mine." Dax sighed again. "He's immortal, and Ginny's not. If he falls in love with her, he will have to watch her grow old and die while he remains much as he is now. Forever."

"In just a couple more days, I'll have to watch you die, or at least disappear." Eddy leaned her cheek against his arm as they crossed the small park to the library. "It hasn't kept me from loving you, Dax. And I won't regret it. Not one minute of the time we've had."

He paused and turned to face her. "Are you certain?"

She shook her head. "No, but that isn't going to change a thing. I love you. I'm not sorry, either. But it's going to hurt when you're gone. It's going to hurt like hell."

He pressed his forehead to hers. "I know. It hurts already. I had no idea what it would be like, to love someone. To love you."

"Well, now we both know." She tugged his arm. "And it's stupid to waste what time we have worrying about the time we won't have. Now where's the gargoyle?"

They stepped out of the shadows and stared up at the parapet. The gargoyle sat there as it had before, perched on the stone platform. Even in darkness, it was obvious the creature had changed. Tonight, instead of looking like a carved stone statue, it appeared to live.

Leathery wings were folded across its back, and the toes of one foot twitched, as if the creature dreamed. Its chest moved slowly in and out as its lungs expanded with each deep breath it took.

Dax and Eddy stood and watched it for a long time. Neither of them spoke, but Eddy knew that Dax's worries were the same as hers. How did one fight a creature that not only continued to grow, but to evolve? One that gained strength from the death of other demons.

Each time they fought one of the avatars and won, unless they destroyed the demon inside, they provided more demon energy for the gargoyle.

It rested, almost as if it could relax now, as if it knew they were weaker.

So obviously confident it would win in battle.

More exhausted than she'd imagined possible, Eddy grabbed Dax's hand and silently turned away. They needed to sleep and plan, but they were running out of time.

She glanced at her watch. It was well after midnight, which meant Dax was into his fifth day. At midnight on the seventh, his time on Earth would end, whether or not the battle between good and evil had been resolved. Not a particularly comforting thought as they headed back to her father's house.

Chapter Fifteen

Thursday morning, well after midnight—day five

"Where are you from, Alton? I don't remember Eddy ever mentioning you before."

Ginny had quit grumbling half a block back. Now she looked at him with what had to be more than merely polite interest, and added, "I can't believe she wouldn't have said something about someone like you."

Someone like me?

What could she possibly mean by that?

Lemurian women were nothing like Ginny Jones. She was amazingly self-assured. Confident. He still wasn't certain if that weighed in Ginny's favor or not. She'd looped her arm through his at some point while they walked, and her tall, lean body was close enough that he felt her heat and scented her subtle perfume.

Walking down the street in the quiet hours after midnight with a beautiful woman on his arm was an entirely new experience.

So was lying.

He'd never felt so marvelously off balance in his life.

Or so dishonest. "I've been here and there," he said, shrugging as if it made no difference. "There's no reason Eddy would have mentioned me. We weren't really close friends. We met in college, but I've been traveling since I graduated."

"I'm jealous." Ginny flashed him a bright smile. He realized he was smiling back, as if her jealousy were the best thing in the world.

"But why?" he asked. "You live in such a beautiful place."

She gazed around the quiet neighborhood. "I guess, but it's all I've ever known. I've never lived anywhere else. I've been to Arizona a couple of times, to Sedona to see my cousins, but Evergreen has always been my home. I keep thinking there's got to be more out there than a sleepy little town full of people who've known me all my life."

Alton stopped a couple of steps beneath her when they reached her front porch, which put them at eye level. He gazed into her beautiful golden eyes and realized he could easily lose himself in their depths. "There is indeed a wonderful world," he said. "If you want to badly enough, I imagine you'll see it one day. But to be honest, I doubt you'll find anywhere else as perfect as your town."

Ginny seemed as interested in gazing at Alton as he was in studying her, but then she sort of shook herself, looked down, and dug through her purse. After a minute of pushing stuff around, she pulled a ring of keys out of the bottom of the bag.

When she glanced back at Alton, her beautiful tiger's-eyes sparkled. "You might be right, but I'll never know until I have something to compare it to. Thanks for walking me home. It really wasn't necessary, but you were better company than I expected."

Alton drew himself up to his full height. "What did you expect?"

She laughed. "I'm not really sure. My first impression was . . ." She shrugged.

"Was what?" He planted his hands on his hips and glowered at her.

Ginny's full lips pursed in an angry moue. "Exactly that. I thought you were arrogant and overbearing. I guess I was right, after all."

Even when she was insulting him, Alton couldn't take his eyes off her. He'd never seen a more beautiful woman in his life than Ginny Jones, with her smooth dark skin and thick black hair. Her eyes, though . . . her eyes were what held him in thrall.

Those amazing tiger's-eyes with every shade of brown, amber, and gold sparkling in their depths. He'd thought her beautiful the night he saved her, but seeing her like this, cocky and downright rude, hearing her low voice with the rich, honeyed tones even as she insulted him, had an effect on him unlike anything he'd ever experienced.

He wondered if she could hear his heart, thudding away in his chest as if it might pound clean through his ribs. He had to swallow twice to get his voice to work. "You might be right," he said. "I can be a bit arrogant at times. But I beg to disagree. It was more than necessary."

As if someone else controlled his hand, he reached out and touched her dark hair. She raised her chin and frowned, obviously confused by both his comment and his gesture.

"I haven't forgotten you, Ginny. When I saw you tonight, I realized just how much I needed to see you again, so yes, it was necessary that I walk you home."

He dropped his hand to his side and stepped back before he lost all control and did something even more insane. "Good night, Ginny. Sleep well. Please go inside and lock your door, or I'll be forced to stand guard." He glanced at a small wrought-iron chair on her front porch. "I doubt that would make a comfortable bed."

Ginny burst into laughter. Then, to his utter amazement, she planted her hands on his shoulders, leaned close, and kissed his cheek. "You're nuts, Alton. Absolutely nuts, but in a really crazy way. I like you. You drive me up a wall, but I still like you. I think. I hope I get to see you again." She unlocked the door and slipped inside. "Now get off my front porch. Go back to Ed's and sleep in a comfortable bed. Take your ego and go home."

She closed the door. He waited until he heard the sound of the dead bolt sliding into place. He hoped it was a good strong lock, with demons running the streets. He had to be certain Ginny would be safe. He stared at the door a moment longer. Then, before he could talk himself out of it, he raised his hands and sent a powerful compulsion toward the woman behind the door.

Sedona. You really miss your cousins in Sedona.

With the satisfaction he'd done what he could to get Ginny out of harm's way, Alton trotted lightly down the stairs and headed back to Ed's house. He wasn't quite sure why he was smiling.

Sending Ginny away until the demon threat ended was a good idea, but offering to walk her home had to be one of the stupidest moves he'd ever made in his life. He sighed. There was something about Ginny—something that wouldn't let go of him—and he had to admit, he liked the feeling.

Of course, there was no future for the two of them. None at all, not for an immortal Lemurian and a human woman. He'd be a fool to try and see her again, but as that cautionary thought entered his head, he swung around in midstep, walking backward so he could see the place where she lived.

The little duplex sat dark and quiet. She wasn't staring out the window, watching him walk away. He grimaced, going over their brief conversation. She was probably wondering what kind of idiot had just walked her to her front door.

A lacy white curtain twitched ever so slightly. Alton grinned like the idiot Ginny probably thought he was . . . but that had to be her peeking through the window. She *was* watching him.

No doubt about it. Whistling, Alton turned around and headed toward Ed's house. Definitely one of the stupidest things he'd ever done, but knowing that probably wouldn't stop him from trying to see her again.

Once she came back from Sedona.

They'd paused in front of her dad's house, and when Eddy glanced down at Dax's strong fingers wrapped around hers, she realized she needed a moment alone before she lost it altogether. First she checked the slashes that had torn through his shirt and into his skin.

They'd closed completely. Dried blood stained the shirt and his back, but he was okay. For now. She rested her palm against his chest. "Check on Dad, will you? I need to see if I can find my baseball bat. I think it's in the garage."

Dax stared at her for a moment, and she prayed he wouldn't notice how her hands trembled.

"Do you need it tonight?" He squeezed her fingers over his heart. "I know you're tired. We both are. Let's look in the morning. I'll help you find it."

She shook her head. He probably thought she was nuts, but she felt frantic, and frightened beyond belief. Time was speeding by much too fast, and he was going to be gone in just a couple of days—and she didn't know if she could handle it.

"I lost my crowbar," she said. She forced herself to take

slow, even breaths. "I didn't have it tonight, and I don't know where I left it. I felt naked without it."

"It's late, Eddy. C'mon inside. You don't need it tonight."

She shook her head again and tugged her fingers free of his grasp. "You never know. I might. I need to find my bat. Really. It'll just take me a few minutes." She raised her head and stared directly into his dark brown eyes. She knew he didn't understand. He couldn't.

But at least he tried.

She hated feeling powerless, hated the fact her world was spinning out of control. Hated knowing there was nothing she could do to change things. Nothing she could do to keep Dax.

But maybe she could find her damned baseball bat. It was good, solid ash, a Louisville Slugger her dad had given her the year she turned twelve. She'd hit more than one homerun with it. Her coach had bragged about her fantastic control, that when she connected, she didn't just hit it out of the park, she'd been able to place the hits.

Which was exactly what she needed now. Fantastic control.

She gazed up at Dax. Finally he nodded his head, leaned over, and kissed her quickly. He trailed his fingers through her messy curls, as if there was something else he wanted to say, but whatever it was went unsaid.

He sighed when he turned away, but he went into the house. Eddy watched him until the door shut behind him. Then she walked to the garage, opened the door, and slipped into the darkness. She shut the door firmly behind her and hoped like hell she could keep from crying.

Her emotions were all over the place, but she had to hold herself together. Dax needed her strong, not blubbering over things that couldn't be changed.

She couldn't hold him here past his allotted seven days,

but she could at least find the stupid bat. That much she could do. She took a deep breath, and then another. The lump in her throat was still there, but the stinging in her eyes eased.

Two more days. How was she going to make it without him when he was gone? A shudder rippled through her body, a mere prelude to the pain waiting for her. She'd meant what she'd said to her dad, though. Even knowing how short their time together would be, she'd never regret loving Dax.

What she was always going to regret, though, was losing him. A tear escaped her left eye and burned a trail over her cheek. She brushed it away, angry at herself, and, unaccountably, with Dax, which was definitely stupid and wouldn't do her a damned bit of good.

Well, damn it all, Eddy. That's just too bad.

She could argue with herself all she wanted, but it wouldn't save Dax. She flipped on the light and stared at the neat rows of shelves filled with boxes and bags. One thing about her dad—even with all the stuff he'd collected over the years, it was always organized.

"Now where is that blasted baseball bat?"

Dax stared out the window at the dark garage for a moment longer before walking from the kitchen into the front room. He'd fully expected to find Ed already in bed, but Eddy's father was sitting alone, sipping a glass of brandy, with Bumper snoring at his feet.

He acknowledged Dax with a brief nod of his head, but he appeared lost in thought.

Willow popped out of Dax's pocket, zipped across the room, and found her favorite spot on Bumper's curly back. Dax figured she must be exhausted, as she only left a smattering of blue sparkles floating in the air with her passage.

He watched her settle herself close to the sleeping dog before he sat down on the couch across from Ed's recliner.

"I thought you'd be asleep by now," he said.

Ed shook his head, but his focus was on the dark amber liquid he held in front of his eyes. "No. I couldn't sleep until I knew you two were home safe. Where's Eddy?"

Dax shrugged. He knew it would take him years to understand the way women thought, and with only a couple of days left . . . "Looking for her baseball bat. She lost her crowbar. I don't know why she had to find the bat tonight. She's exhausted."

Ed chuckled. "Be right back." He struggled to get out of the chair. It was obvious he was hurting after so much activity. He left the room for a moment and then returned with an empty glass, poured it half full of brandy, and handed it to Dax.

"She's looking for her Louisville Slugger, I'll bet." He took a sip of his brandy. Dax tasted his. It burned like fire, but tasted surprisingly good.

"Is that her bat? Why does she need it tonight?" He stared into the glass and wished things weren't quite as complicated as they'd become.

"Because it's something she can find. Something familiar that belonged to her when life was good, when her mother was alive, when demons weren't running amuck. Dax, all our lives have been turned upside down in the past week. None of us, save you, know what's going to happen next."

Dax took another sip before he asked, "What do you mean?"

Ed settled back in his chair. "You have a finite life span. In a few more days, no matter how the battle on Earth between human and demon plays out, your role in the fight will end." He sighed, and spoke very softly. "I'm gonna hate to lose you, boy. Already you feel like the son I never had, and it's going to hurt like hell when you're gone."

His voice was much firmer when he nailed Dax with a hard-edged glare and added, "But it's not going to hurt me half as much as it is my daughter, no matter how brave she tries to be. She loves you. I honestly believe you're the first man she's ever really loved, and I hate to think of what my little girl will go through when you just wink out of her life."

It took every bit of strength Dax had not to look away, but what Ed was saying was true. Painfully true. "I don't know what . . ."

"No." Ed set his glass down and leaned forward. "There's not a damned thing you can do differently. All you can do is love her for as long as you're here. She asked me if, knowing her mother would die so young, would I have still wanted to love her. I realized then that I wouldn't give up those few short years with Eddy's mom for anything. That woman was the best thing that ever happened to me. Maybe you're the best that will ever happen to Eddy. I hope not. I hope she'll find love again someday, after you're gone. After enough time has passed—but she's right. You go after love. You hold on to it with both hands and your heart, no matter how briefly it lasts, no matter how painful the end might be. It's too precious to waste a moment. I hope you and Eddy hang on to every second you've got."

He tipped his glass and emptied it. Then he stood. Stronger this time. More sure of his step. "And right now, young man, you're wasting what little time you've got with my daughter, sitting in here yammering with her old man. Go help Eddy find that bat of hers. Let her know you love her enough to help her wrestle her own demons along with yours."

Dax stood as Ed left the room. He held the glass of brandy up to catch the light. Then he glanced at Willow. She appeared half asleep, nestled snuggly in Bumper's thick coat of curls. "Rest, little one," he said. "Stay with your friend. I'll be with Eddy."

Willow flashed a tiny flicker of blue light. Dax finished off the last swallow of brandy and turned out the lights as he left the room. He met Alton at the kitchen door. "Is everything quiet?"

Alton nodded. "Ginny's home safe. I took a swing back through town on my way here. Nothing is stirring. I drew my sword, and there was no reaction, no sense of demonkind. I'm wondering if we've gotten all of the ones that crossed over, other than the gargoyle. I hesitate to go after him until we've all rested. I don't think either of us has the power to take him on our own."

Dax nodded. "I agree. Willow and Bumper are asleep in the front room. Ed's gone on to bed." He nodded toward the garage, where a pale light glowed through the window on the small side door. "I'm going to get Eddy. We'll be in shortly." He rested his palm on Alton's forearm. "Sleep well, my friend. Thank you."

"You, too, Dax." Alton nodded. "Tomorrow we go after the gargoyle. Again."

Dax watched Alton enter the house. Then he quietly opened the door to the garage. Eddy didn't appear to hear him. She sat on a wooden box near the rows of large shelves in the back. She had her back to Dax and held a large book in her lap. A smooth, wooden baseball bat lay on the floor beside her. She'd clipped a shop light to the closest shelf, and it spotlighted the place where she sat and the book she looked at so intently.

"Eddy? What is that?" Dax squatted down beside her and realized she was gazing at a book of photographs.

"It's one of my grandmother's old albums. See?"

She pointed to a picture of a little dark-eyed girl sitting in the lap of a powerful-looking elderly man. A sweet-looking woman who could have been an older version of Eddy stood beside them with her hand on the man's shoulder. Everyone was smiling, their eyes alight with what had to be love.

"That's me when I was about six," Eddy said, pointing to the little girl. "That's my grandfather holding me, and that's Gramma standing beside us. She died the year after my mom passed away." Eddy glanced up at Dax. There were tears in her eyes. "Grampa died years before when I was still a kid, and when Mom died, it was like a light went out of Gramma. She just sort of slipped away, but she was already pretty old. She and my grandfather were married for almost sixty years."

"You still miss her, don't you?" He brushed her hair back from her eyes. She nodded and smiled at him, but she was biting her lip and he knew she struggled not to cry. Always so brave, so intent on putting on a strong face for him that it made his heart ache to see her grieving now, to know she would grieve even more when he was gone. "I love you, Eddy. No matter what happens, I will never forget you."

She touched her palm to the side of his face and leaned her forehead against his. "I won't ever forget you either, Dax. I love you so much." She shook her head. A tear landed on the back of his hand. "I never imagined falling in love with anyone like this, not this hard, this fast." She took a deep breath, closed the album, and carefully put it back in a large, plastic box. Then she replaced the lid and made certain it was on tight.

Dax reached for the box and picked it up before Eddy could. She didn't say anything, but she pointed to an empty spot where it belonged. Dax slipped the heavy box back on the shelf and reached for Eddy's hand.

She slipped her fingers into his, and they left the garage together. Eddy turned out the light and locked the door. She was yawning when they reached the bedroom, but the tears in her eyes were gone. She held tightly to her baseball bat with one hand, and just as tightly to Dax with the other.

They showered together. Dax helped Eddy rinse her hair, and she carefully scrubbed the blood off his back and shoulder. He held her beneath the soothing spray while she cried for a few minutes. He had a feeling that tears didn't come easily to her, that she rarely showed any kind of weakness to anyone. The fact she felt comfortable enough to be herself with Dax told him more than mere words might ever say.

They stepped out of the shower, and he grabbed a towel off the rack to dry her silky skin. She brushed her teeth; he shaved. It all felt terribly domestic, and he was struck with the fact that less than a week ago he'd never done any of these things.

He'd never shaved, never showered, never bathed with a woman, yet his body seemed to know everything. How to use a razor, how to brush his teeth and tie his shoes and eat with a fork and knife. He knew the language, knew what things were, knew how to interpret his feelings, his fears, his needs.

And he knew how to make love to Eddy. He paused and stared at himself in the steamy mirror. White shaving cream covered his chin and throat, and his hair was slicked back from his head. It looked almost black in this light, though he knew it was really a very dark brown. There were even a couple of gray strands in it, though he knew he wasn't very old, even by human standards.

He'd wrapped a towel around his waist, and it hung low on his hips. A dark trail of hair ran from his belly button to his groin, and the snake tattoo ran through the trail. The thing had been quiet since the battle this evening, though he was always aware of its existence. The glow was gone, but it hadn't hurt since the fight with the gargoyle. The gaping jaws remained poised over his heart, and the beady eyes were fixed and lifeless, but he'd seen them sparkle with intelligence, had felt the tongue lash between his fingers. He'd seen the head pull away from his flesh and strike at his throat.

The demon's curse wasn't gone. Not by a long shot. It waited patiently, ready to strike when his defenses were down, which meant he needed to remain alert to it at all times.

He rinsed the razor in the sink and took another careful stroke along his jaw and down his throat, and then another. He actually enjoyed the ritual of shaving, the way the lather felt so cool on his skin, the slide of the razor over bristles that hadn't even existed earlier in the day.

Usually Eddy stayed in the bathroom to watch him, but she was so tired tonight, so dejected, she'd gone on to bed. He finished shaving and cleaned the razor. Then he rinsed out the sink and wiped it down with an extra towel, wondering, even as he performed the simple tasks, if the man whose body he owned had done the same things.

It was so easy to forget that he wasn't the original resident of these parts—these hands and feet, this strong back, and these wide shoulders. That his pair of legs had carried another man, these hands had probably made love to other women.

The only woman Dax wanted was Eddy. He rinsed his face once more, dried his skin, and looked at the man in the mirror. He'd grown accustomed to this face, to this body. He hardly thought of it as borrowed.

Hardly thought of himself as demon.

He didn't want to think of the fact he only had use of this body for a couple more days, but that was the truth, and he hated to waste a moment. Not when he could be lying beside Eddy. He glanced over his shoulder. The bedroom was dark, which meant she was already in bed. He draped the towel over the shower door and turned off the bathroom light.

Then he quietly crawled into bed beside Eddy. He lay

there for a moment, listening to the soft, even sound of her breathing that told him she slept. Then he rolled to his side and pulled her unresisting body into his arms.

He immediately grew hard and aroused. The merest touch was all it took when he was around her, but he ignored his body's reaction. It was enough to hold her. Enough to feel her body close to his, to hear the soft puff of her breath, the steady beat of her heart.

With Eddy's small sounds soothing him, Dax drifted off to sleep.

His dreams in the past had usually been nightmares of his life before coming to Earth. Fire and fights and the fear of death, terrible battles with hideous creatures of the night—the kinds of creatures that once were common in his life.

The kind of creature he once had been.

Tonight, though, was different. He was aware he was dreaming, though it had the quality of memory, not imagination. He was Dax, yet he wasn't. He struggled to hold his balance on a strange, flat boat in rough seas. He was surrounded by other men, all of them wearing the same uniform. Round metal helmets covered their heads; heavy, olive green uniforms gave little protection from the wet and the cold. He was holding a rifle, and he was terrified, absolutely scared to death, but it was okay, because everyone else was just as frightened. Some of the guys were seasick, and they'd been heaving their guts over the side of the boat. He wondered if they were too sick to be as scared as he was.

It was early in the morning, and he knew the date was June 6, 1944, and he was off the coast of Normandy, just one of tens of thousands of men making the landing on Omaha Beach.

He could see the beach ahead, and the heavy fortifications they'd have to go through or over. The boat lurched, the front opened up, and salty spray hit his face and soaked his uniform, but it didn't matter. Like lemmings going over a cliff, they all raced out into the icy sea, carrying their weapons, weighed down by heavy packs loaded with way too much gear and ammunition. The water was deeper than they'd been told to expect, but he was taller than most and it hit him at his chest.

Fear drove him through the pounding surf. He saw one of the smaller guys floundering beside him, held down by his heavy pack and ammo and the big rifle in his arms. Dax grabbed him by the arm and hauled him along, all the way to shore, where both of them hit the cold, hard sand to avoid the hail of bullets whizzing by their heads.

He crawled on his belly and made it as far as the first set of barricades, but when he looked around, there were more bodies than live soldiers scattered around him. The little guy he'd helped was with him, just a few feet back and doing his best to stick close.

There should have been tanks with their heavy weapons covering them, but he couldn't see if any tanks had survived the landing. The noise was indescribable. Gunfire and screams, and the horrible cries of dying men. Waves crashed with booming thunder, and the air shook with explosions as big shells fell all around. Confusion reigned supreme. It was Hell on Earth, and there was no hope.

He knew with a certainty he'd never known before that he would die today.

The enemy had the superior position, high up on the bluffs, hidden from sight. The infantry coming ashore were nothing more than ducks in a pond, and he was just one more duck.

He would die today, but not yet. He refused death, refused to even consider his end before he'd accomplished something worthwhile. He couldn't stay here, and damn it, their mission was to storm the beach, to take the bluffs and wipe out the mortars, to get rid of the machine gun nests and the artillery. If he was going to die on the beach at Normandy, he'd be damned if he'd die before his work was done.

He wasn't sure how it happened, but somehow he managed to get beyond the first barricade and then another, and another, and the next thing he knew, he was at the base of the bluffs. The smell of death made him want to vomit, and the unrelenting noise made it impossible to think.

So he acted. There was no one else near him, at least no one alive. He looked to his left, where the little guy from the beach had been, and there was a body lying in the wet sand. He thought it was the one he'd saved, but half the kid's face was blown away and it was hard to tell who he'd been.

All he knew was that, just moments ago, whoever that kid was had been as young, as alive, as he was now.

There was nothing he could do for the kid. Not now. He'd done the best he could when he pulled him from the water. Given him ten more minutes of life. He hoped the bullet that found the soldier had made for an easier death than drowning in the cold waves with a full pack on his back and a rifle in his arms.

He turned away from the body and began to scale the bluff. His fingers slipped on the cold, rough rocks, and he left a trail of blood behind wherever he'd grabbed hold. Hiding behind rocks and brush where he could, trusting to blind luck when he couldn't, he managed to slowly but steadily make his way up the rugged face.

Somewhere above him was the machine gunner sending death down on the men below. Probably the same one who had killed the kid he'd pulled out of the water. That knowledge gave him a sense of duty even more powerful than what he'd felt when he started up the cliff. If it was the last thing he did, he was going to take the nest out. He'd avenge at least one young man who'd lost his chance at life.

Voices drifted around him, and while he didn't know the language, he recognized the accent. German. There were German soldiers close enough for their voices to carry, which meant they couldn't be any more than a few feet above him.

His focus narrowed. He recognized that this was more than a dream. This was happening now, or at least in what he accepted as now. The burning streak of pain along his shoulder was the trail of a bullet that could have killed him, the rocks beneath his hands, cutting into his palms, were real, and that kid lying on the beach below had lived and breathed just as he did.

Pulling himself hand over hand, he ignored the sixty-plus pounds on his back and slowly worked his way across the face of the bluff. There was a lip of rock to one side, and he managed to get around it. Somehow he ended up just above the group of three men firing on the troops below. He grabbed his sidearm. His rifle was gone, and he had no idea where he'd lost it, but the Remington Rand forty-five felt good in his hand, and he'd kept it dry during the landing.

He aimed carefully, taking his time with the first shot, and his target dropped without a sound. Before the other two had a chance to react, he shot the second soldier, the one manning the gun. It happened so quickly he didn't have time to consider what he'd done, though he was surprised that their deaths meant so little to him. He aimed at the third man as the fellow whirled around with a pistol in his hand.

For the briefest of moments, he stared into eyes as blue as his were brown, into a face of a man even younger than he was, and he saw fear. Absolute terror that he would die today.

So be it. At least Dax knew he wouldn't die alone. He felt nothing when he pulled the trigger. He didn't see the young man die. No, he was too busy dying himself.

The slug slammed into his forehead, just below the curve of his helmet. There was no pain, no sense of loss, no feeling at all. One moment he was alive and aiming his weapon at a kid no older than he was.

The next, he was sitting upright in the big bed next to Eddy, and his heart was pounding and his breath rasping in and out of his lungs. Eddy was beside him on her knees, eyes wide, hands reaching for him.

He shook his head and tried to clear his thoughts, but his death was too immediate, the sense of loss too close merely to brush away. He took a deep breath, then another, breathing slowly, steadily. Assuring himself he still lived. That he was Dax and he slept beside Eddy Marks and, for now at least, all was well.

"Dax? Are you okay? I heard you thrashing in your sleep. You must have had a nightmare, but . . ."

He took another deep breath and reached for her. Eddy tumbled into his arms, and he sat back on his heels, holding her as close as he could.

"I dreamed my death," he said, surprised that the dream remained as clear now as when he was living it. "Not as I am now, but my death as a soldier on the beaches of Normandy. This body, the man who lived in it, was a soldier who landed at Omaha Beach. He was terrified. He knew he would die that day. Tonight, when I dreamed, I was with him when he died."

"Oh, Dax." Eddy cupped his face in her palms. "How horrible. I'm so sorry you had to . . ."

"No." He shook his head. Then he turned and kissed her palm. "No, don't be sorry. I think he's with me. Not just his body, but his soul as well. I thought the Edenites had given me an empty shell, but I feel his spirit, here." He pressed his hand to his heart and felt tears well up in his eyes, but he had to explain to Eddy, had to tell her what he'd learned.

His dream, if that's what it was, had changed him. It had changed everything. "I've sensed him before, but not as I do now. I know him. He was such a brave man, Eddy. He knew he faced death, yet he didn't quit. He saved the life of another young man, who was killed by a bullet a few minutes later. When that happened, he threw caution to the wind and climbed up a bluff near the beach, and he managed to kill three men who were manning a machine gun. They were Germans, young men like he was, following orders, but they were the ones mowing down the American soldiers. The ones who had killed the one he'd saved. The last man—a boy, really—that he shot put a bullet in his brain. He died bravely, and he died fighting. He was following orders to the very end."

Dax stared into the darkness, wrapping those feelings around his body, absorbing everything he'd experienced. "Eddy, when it happened, at the very moment of his death, he was no longer afraid."

"What is it you're trying to tell me, Dax? This isn't just about a dream, is it? I don't understand." Eddy leaned back in his embrace so that she could look into his eyes. She was sleep rumpled and warm in his arms. Her hair stuck out on one side and lay all squished flat on the other. She was the most beautiful, most precious thing he'd ever known.

And she deserved the truth. "I've been afraid of failing, Eddy. So afraid. I'm not as strong as the demon gargoyle. Maybe I'm not as crafty, either, but I've got you. I have Alton and Willow, your dad, and Bumper—even my demon self is still part of me. Together we make a formidable team, but all along I've felt as if I didn't have what it was going to take to win the fight. When I dreamed tonight, when I felt the strength of the man who first lived this body's life, I realized he was sharing his courage. He was letting me know him so that I'd understand what it meant to die bravely. He's sharing that with me."

Eddy wrapped her arms around his neck and drew him close for a kiss. When their mouths finally parted, she smiled against his lips. "I've never doubted you, Dax. You're the only one who thinks you can't win. I know better. Those Edenites wouldn't have chosen you if they'd had any doubt. Let's go back to sleep. We've still got a few hours before morning. When we go after the gargoyle tomorrow, you will win. I don't have any doubt at all."

She kissed him again, and he realized he wasn't nearly as sleepy as he'd thought. When her hands slipped around his waist and traced the bumps along his spine, it seemed perfectly natural to lay her down and stretch out beside her.

But when he made love to her, he couldn't stop thinking about the man who'd died on Omaha Beach. A man who'd gone into battle terrified, yet faced death bravely. A man who had followed orders, even as they led him to his death.

Dax needed to remember the orders he followed. His death was a given. His duty was to remove the demons from this small town, to ease the pressure of evil against good before a tipping point was reached. He was well on his way to accomplishing that mission. As much as he loved Eddy Marks, the mission was for the good of all, and he must not fail.

Failure was not an option. He was destined to die at the end of his week, no matter how the battle against the demons played out, so he'd better be damned sure that the outcome was what he wanted.

He would win, no matter what, because he had no fear of death. Just as the one who'd first inhabited this body had known his own death was imminent when he went against the enemy, Dax knew he'd be gone by the end of the week. That was the deal.

Ed Marks was right—Dax knew what to expect. There were going to be no final surprises. The only surprise, in fact, had been Eddy.

He realized then, as their bodies reached that final peak together, that it wasn't death he feared, not the failure of his mission, not pain, or the demon gargoyle and his curse.

No, he'd thought his only fear was leaving Eddy in a world that was no longer safe. It was worse. It was something he couldn't change, no matter how the battle on Earth ended.

He feared moving on to whatever might come next without her. He could face the demon and whatever it might do to him, and he could face him without fear, but eternity without Eddy scared him more than death.

Chapter Sixteen

Thursday morning—day five

Eddy sipped her second cup of coffee and stared at her laptop. She'd been working on a story for the paper since she'd gotten up this morning, writing about the vandalism of the cemetery statues. So far, nothing she'd written sounded all that convincing.

Organizing her thoughts with all that was going on wasn't easy. Writing lies made it even more difficult. Grumbling, she highlighted the paragraph she'd just written and hit DELETE.

Ed, Alton, and Dax studied a street map of town and threw out different plans to destroy the gargoyle. Eddy'd only been paying partial attention as they went back and forth with various ideas, coming up with plans and discarding them just as quickly as she'd been deleting story ideas. So far, it appeared that the only thing they agreed on was that the gargoyle would be at his weakest around noon, when the sun was high in the sky, but she tuned out the rest of their discussion while she worked on another angle for her story.

At least Harlan had quit giving her grief, and there'd

been a paycheck in yesterday's mail, so she knew she still had a job.

She wasn't certain she still wanted it.

Convincing the citizens of Evergreen that all the damage and weird situations affecting their town were the acts of nonexistent gangs or satanic cults wasn't easy. Even with her deputy buddies, Milton and Bud, agreeing with her—thanks to Alton—she could offer no proof beyond guesswork by local law enforcement.

At least they were still in line with the hypnotic suggestions Alton continued to plant. Of course, there wouldn't be any proof, since gangs weren't responsible. She almost felt sorry for the nonexistent gangbangers and satanic cultists who were taking the heat for the current mess.

As far as she knew, people weren't talking about the battle on Lassen Boulevard. She wondered if they were having nightmares instead. She hated to think they might be reliving the horrible things they'd seen. Things they'd been compelled not to discuss.

"How long do you think people will continue to buy this crap?" She waved her hand over her laptop. "I haven't got a lick of proof, no facts and nothing but made-up guesswork to explain what we all know is a demon invasion."

Alton laughed. "And you think they'd believe that before they'll believe that gangs or cultists are behind everything?"

Eddy frowned. "Good point. I just feel like such a fraud. I'm writing lies. It bothers me. It goes against everything that journalism stands for. Haven't you heard of the Journalist's Creed?"

Alton gave her a blank stare.

"Sheesh." She shut her laptop. "Well, essentially it's a promise to write only what I believe, in my heart, to be true."

Dax smiled. "Doesn't it also have something about suppressing the news for the good of the welfare of society?"

Eddy blinked. "How'd you know that?"

"I found it framed on the wall in your dad's workshop and read it. I know the stories you've been writing are bothering you, and when I saw a document titled The Journalist's Creed, I looked to it for answers."

Alton laughed. "Sounds as if you found them."

"That I did. The truth could cause a panic." Dax glanced once more at the map, and then at Eddy. "If people knew that a demon invasion was behind all this, they'd call in the military, and we'd have a full-scale war on our hands."

Alton agreed. "The minute we get a military presence, the fear and potential bloodshed would cause nothing but chaos, not to mention the kind of negative energy demonkind thrive on."

"I'm still lying." She crossed her arms over her chest. Anger and frustration had been her constant companions all morning. "So much of this is all lies." It wasn't just what she was writing. What about Dax? A demon, disguised as a human. And Alton? He wasn't even human.

"It's for the common good, Eddy."

Dax's soft voice broke through whirling thoughts. She was beginning to feel outnumbered, especially when her father added to Dax and Alton's argument. He glanced up and caught Eddy's stubborn gaze. "No one has been seriously injured or killed. We're dealing with nothing more than vandalism at this point, no matter what the cause, but I'm afraid the guys are right. If that gargoyle gains more power, if he reaches a point where he can proactively destroy life and steal the energy of human beings . . ."

Eddy swallowed back a gasp. "I hadn't even thought of that. Do you think that's all that's holding him back? That he's not strong enough to take a human life?"

Dax nodded. "Quite possibly. Not that he can't kill. Slicing my back open is proof he can do damage. He just hasn't evolved enough to harness the energy a human death could provide. I'm hoping Alton's right. If all the demons that crossed over have been destroyed, that would mean the gargoyle's energy supply's gone, at least for now. I was wondering where he got his strength. It's not like he's got his own Willow, pulling energy out of the air for him." He grinned at the little sprite. She twirled in a shower of blue sparkles at mention of her name.

Alton glared at his sword. Encased in its leather scabbard, it hung from the back of a kitchen chair, a mute reminder of its lack of voice. The jeweled hilt sparkled beneath the overhead lights. "I was worried the ones I thought I was killing with my worthless sword were merely going back to Abyss, or worse, directly to the demon. At least, last night, it seemed to be killing them, but even so, I'm ready to leave the damned thing here when we go out and fight, for all the good it's done me."

Eddy interrupted. "Alton, it's a good weapon even if it's not speaking to you. It cut through those stone statues like they were made of butter, and when you hit the demon mist, it flashed and sizzled and the gargoyle was totally pissed. That alone is proof to me that you're destroying them."

"We'll never know for sure, though, unless the thing decides to acknowledge me." He dismissed it with a wave of his hand. "The problem is, as long as I'm wielding it, I can't fight beside Dax. It's dividing our strength because I can't trust it." He stared at it, mumbling, "A man should be able to trust his own sword, shouldn't he?"

"I agree." Dax gave the crystal sword a wide berth, even when it hung innocently in its sheath. He stared at it a moment and then looked away. "As far as the gargoyle, I think we've been feeding him all along, with every avatar we've destroyed and every demon we've missed, but there's a good possibility the last of the demons are gone after yesterday's battle. If that's the case, there's nothing more for him to absorb, or inhale, or whatever it is he does to the demons who revert to mist. It should keep him from getting any more powerful than he already is." He glanced toward Alton. "I hope. He's already stronger than I am."

Alton laughed. "My money's still on you. I think you can take him."

Dax shook his head, but Eddy noticed he was smiling too. Alton and Dax had forged an amazing friendship in such a short time. In a way, it made her feel better, knowing she wasn't the only one who loved the man with the powers of a demon and the heart of a warrior.

"I'm hoping that piece of wing you sliced off has cost him," Dax said. "It takes a lot of energy to regenerate parts, and he grew that wing tip back last night. If I hadn't been in such sorry shape myself, I would have gone after him, but I didn't have anything left. I'm stronger today. Here's hoping he's still feeling weak and puny."

Chuckling, Ed stood up. "It's almost nine, and the last thing I need is to be worried about you guys feeling weak and puny. How about a big breakfast so you won't need lunch? Have you figured out yet how we're going to do whatever it is we have to do?"

Alton ran his hand over the map and jabbed his finger on the spot he'd circled in red, where the old library building stood. "I can use a compulsion to keep people away from the park at the library. Once it's cleared, Dax and Willow are going in."

"Agreed." Dax studied the map and glanced at the clock. "If we're there a little before noon, you should be able to keep folks away. If they're already there eating lunch, it might be harder to get them to leave. Eddy?"

He flashed her a smile that seemed terribly relaxed, considering what they were discussing. "I want you to hang on to Bumper and stay fairly close to me, just in case Willow needs a place to hide."

"I can do that." She glanced at her father. "What's Dad going to do?"

"You mean besides cook?" Ed laughed and waved his spatula.

"Ed, I want you watching the perimeter. Make sure there aren't any demons hanging around. Don't destroy any avatars, because we don't want the gargoyle to get them, but watch for anything that might be demonkind."

Eddy placed her hand over his. "And what do you intend to do?"

He flashed her a cocky grin. "I intend to kill the gargoyle. The demon has bonded so entirely with the stone gargoyle that it's gained a corporeal presence in this dimension, but it's got to take a lot of energy to maintain the body. It's no longer animating stone. It's breathing now, and it bleeds."

"Green blood. I saw it when Alton sliced off the tip of its wing. Yuck."

"Green, red, brown, or black. It doesn't matter," Dax said. "If it bleeds, it can die. We couldn't kill the gargoyle because it wasn't alive, and we weren't able to destroy it and get to the demon inside. It appears somehow to have attained life, which means mortality. The flesh should burn; bones can be broken. It may have better mobility and possibly cognitive reasoning, but I'm guessing it's lost its indestructible edge."

Alton laughed. "Well, it sounds good in theory."

"It does, doesn't it?" Dax stood up and pushed his chair back from the table. "Ed? How long before breakfast?"

"About fifteen minutes." Ed added more bacon to the pan. The sizzle and pop filled the air with enough good smells to make Eddy's mouth water. She stared at her closed laptop and pondered not sending anything to Harlan at all.

Dax rested a hand on her shoulder. "I want to take a quick

walk around the block and see if anything's stirring out there that shouldn't be."

Eddy grabbed his hand. "Do you want company?"

"Always," he said, smiling at her. "C'mon. We'll be back in a few minutes."

He held her hand as they stepped off the porch and started down the sidewalk. The morning was cool. Pine needles and dry leaves crackled underfoot. Birds chattered and chirped, a dog nearby barked. Eddy heard a lawn mower roar to life. She noticed the distinct lack of stone deer and ceramic garden gnomes. The neighborhood had been full of them just a week ago.

"Could the demons have run out of things to use as avatars? A lot of statues have been broken over the past few days."

Dax shook his head. "No. You'd be surprised. There's still a lot of stuff around. Look." He pointed to a front porch where a pair of metal birds hung in a wind chime. Then he showed her a weather vane designed like a rooster on top of a nearby garage. "There are all kinds of lifelike replicas made of stone or metal. If there were demons around who needed avatars, they'd still be able to find them."

They continued on around the block. Dax seemed so totally relaxed, it was hard to believe he'd had that horrible dream last night. He'd still been awake when she'd finally gone back to sleep, her body sated from his lovemaking.

She wasn't sated anymore. In fact, the familiar sizzle of arousal was once more awakened, merely by the touch of his hand, the sight of him walking beside her. She'd never seen such a beautiful man, never been as attracted to anyone before, the way she was to Dax, but when she'd rolled over this morning and reached for him, he was already gone. She'd found him out in the kitchen having coffee when she'd finally crawled out of bed.

"Did you get any sleep at all last night?" She stopped walking, wrapped her hands around his arm and held him close.

"Some," he said. "I had a lot to think about."

"Dax?" She tugged him to a stop and looked into his clear, dark brown eyes. Every time she looked at him, she wondered how many more chances she'd have. "Are you afraid?"

He frowned. "Of the demon?"

She shook her head. "No. Of it all ending. Of what will happen when your time is over. I can't imagine what that must be like, knowing exactly when you're going to die."

"Ah, Eddy. Sweetheart, I'm not going to die. I'll just be moving from this life to another. I'm hoping I'll end up in Eden if I'm successful with my mission, but even if I don't, I'll merely go back into the void. It's not a frightening place. It's just . . ." He sighed. "It's boring. Eternity with only memories of the life you've lived isn't an exciting proposition. I've lived for a very long time, but the only thing I want to remember is the time I've spent with you. I'm hoping these memories will be enough. The past few days have been amazing. I need to stretch these memories out and make them last."

She thought about that, about facing eternity with only memories. She'd always have such amazing memories of Dax. They started walking again. Within a few minutes, they'd circled the block, and her father's house was right in front of them.

"Eddy?"

She turned to him. "What?"

"I love you. I don't want to spend eternity feeling guilty about leaving you. Promise me you'll find love again. Please? I have to know you're able to accept what's coming if I'm going to be able to concentrate on my mission. Can you do that?"

She stood on her toes and kissed him. "I promise. I will be fine. Let's go eat before Dad sends out a search party for us."

He followed her into the kitchen, and she was glad he was behind her and couldn't see her face. It hadn't been all that hard to make an impossible promise, but there was no way she could keep the truth out of her eyes.

It was actually sort of odd, to think she worried so much about lying in her newspaper articles, yet she had no qualms at all about lying to the man she loved.

By the time they got inside, she had her emotions under control once again. The last thing she wanted was for Dax to spend his last days on Earth worrying about her worrying about him.

She sat down at the table, opened her laptop, and quickly finished her article. Then she attached it to an e-mail to Harlan and hit SEND. *Lies. All of it lies.*

She merely had to remind herself they were all for the common good.

The noon sun hung high overhead. Eddy clung to Dax's hand while all of them stood motionless as a bunch of statues in the sunlit park and stared at the empty parapet atop the library. Finally, Ed broke the silence.

"Where the hell'd the bastard go?"

Dax shook his head and rubbed his chest. "I have no idea. I was certain he'd be here. Alton? Any ideas where he might be?"

"No. I figured he'd still be healing."

"I think I know." Eddy turned away from the library and stared at Dax. "You said he gets his strength from the demons whose souls he takes, but we're fresh out of demons. Could he be trying to open a new portal?"

Alton jerked his head around and stared at Eddy. "Gods, I hope not. If he's in the mountain, there's no way to stop him."

"Why not?" Eddy frowned. "You closed the other portal without any trouble."

"That was before any of us had a Lemurian death sentence hanging over our heads. I can't be positive if it's actually been posted or not, but what I did when I broke you guys out of your cell is punishable by death. I went against my father's orders, and he's the head of the Council of nine. As far as you and Dax, before we left Lemuria, the council had already determined you two should die for your *transgression* of actually trying to help my people. If we go back inside the mountain, we might not make it out alive."

Dax crossed his arms over his chest. "If the demon opens a new portal, no one will make it out alive. Another gateway to Abyss could tip the balance beyond redemption." He shrugged. "If more demons gain entrance to this dimension, if the gargoyle achieves ultimate power, a death decree is a moot point."

Alton stared at Dax for a moment. Then he slowly nodded his head. "There is that," he said.

Ed shoved Bumper's leash into Eddy's outstretched hand. Then he swung around and headed down the sidewalk. "I'll get the Jeep," he said, shouting back over his shoulder. "Then I'll meet you back here in a few minutes. Keep looking."

They drove as far as they could and stopped at the same gate where Ed had picked them up just five short days ago. Dax was surprised when Ed chose to join them on the hike up the mountain. He and Eddy both tried to argue her dad out of it, but there was no way Ed was going to be left behind at this point.

Now, as they drew close to the portal that had let them into the dimension that led to Lemuria, Dax had to respect Ed's dedication to their cause. He was obviously in pain from his bad hip, but he'd managed to keep up as they made their way along the faint trail winding higher and higher up the steep slopes of Mount Shasta.

The hillside was beginning to look familiar, when Willow suddenly popped out from behind Alton's long hair and buzzed into the air in front of them. She left a comet's tail of blue sparkles behind her as she zipped toward a tumble of rocks just ahead. Bumper barked and jerked the leash out of Eddy's hand.

Dax grabbed for it and missed. The dog took off, scrambling over the loose scree littering the side of the mountain. Her leash trailed behind her.

"Bumper! Come back. Here girl!" Eddy started after the dog.

Dax grabbed her arm and held her back. "Wait. See what she's after."

"But what if the gargoyle's there?" Eddy tried to jerk her arm free, but Dax held on. She glared at him. "Let me go."

He shook his head. "Look."

The gargoyle lurched from behind the largest rock, walking awkwardly over the rough surface. Bumper yipped and made a perfect U-turn. She raced back toward Eddy as the gargoyle spread its wings and rose to its full height, twice as tall as it had been the night before.

Eddy grabbed Bumper's collar when the dog ran into her legs in her mad scramble to get away from the monster. Alton moved to one side and drew his sword. Ed grabbed Eddy's free arm and tugged her and Bumper out of the way.

Surrounded at a safe distance by his friends, Dax stood

alone on the hillside, not a dozen feet from the massive creature.

He glanced to his right. Alton was slowly working his way around the gargoyle's side. It ignored the Lemurian. Its focus was entirely on Dax.

Ed and Eddy waited off to the side as they'd planned, well out of the way should the gargoyle use any sort of weapon. Dax was unsure of its powers in this form. It was obviously alive. There was no sign of the stone creature it had once been.

Now its wings waved slowly back and forth with supple grace. The muscles in its long arms bunched and stretched, and the leathery skin over its massive chest rose and fell with each breath it took.

When it opened its mouth, razor-sharp teeth gleamed white, and its disgusting tongue was long and sinewy, colored a deep grayish green. Saliva dripped from its jaws. Eyes that had once gleamed like red fire now glowed with an inner light that was both alive and cunning.

The gargoyle raised its head and let out a roar. No longer the eerie wail of a banshee, this time it had the full-blown depth of a living, breathing creature, a sound somewhere between an enraged lion and an angry bull elephant.

Bumper dropped to the ground and shivered when it roared a second time. Willow had moved to a point behind Dax where she was protected from the creature, yet close enough to Dax that she could draw energy from their surroundings and feed it to him. He felt the warmth of Willow's energy pouring into him, strengthening his arms and legs, even as it awakened the cursed tattoo now rising over his chest.

There was no way to avoid the pain. Whenever he called on his demon powers now, he called the curse to life. They were one and the same. His only hope was that he'd be able to work it once again, to make the pain his own and withstand the agony long enough to battle his greatest foe.

He stared into the gargoyle's eyes and sensed the creature's keen intelligence. No longer a mindless demon working through the body of a stone avatar, it had become—somehow, some way—a sentient, living, breathing demon. Dax wondered what its form had been on Abyss. Had it somehow found its likeness in the stone gargoyle on the library building?

Dax had been a demon since time began, but it had only been in his later years that he'd had enough self-awareness to care about his existence, to wonder if there might be something better to life than the unending hell of Abyss. Had that happened to this demon as well? Had it finally begun to question its existence?

Had it, too, been kicked out of Abyss? If so, it certainly hadn't been for questioning evil. There was nothing good about this creature. No, it was evil incarnate, with a cunning unlike anything Dax expected.

He took a step closer to the gargoyle, drawing the creature's attention. Alton was able to move a few feet closer without being noticed. Now he stood behind, not beside, the gargoyle.

It didn't appear to see him, so intent was it on Dax. When Dax took a step, the creature moved as well. When Dax moved to one side, the creature mirrored his shift. As Dax played out his little dance, testing the gargoyle's responses, Alton slipped closer to the creature's back. He'd drawn his crystal sword and held it high overhead, but he wasn't yet close enough to strike.

Dax raised his hands and let loose with a burst of fire. The gargoyle leapt in the air, barely avoiding the flame. Alton jumped to one side and swung his blade. The crystal glimmered with power as he slashed just beneath a clawed foot.

The gargoyle flapped his wings down with a powerful stroke as Alton prepared to swing. One heavy wing caught his head and shoulders and flung the tall Lemurian to the ground. He swung the crystal sword as he fell, cutting a broad slash across the gargoyle's torso.

Thick, green, acidic blood poured from the wound, burning whatever it touched. Grass shriveled and turned black as the gargoyle tried to gain altitude. Dripping blood splashed Alton's shoulder and along his sword arm, dissolving his flannel shirt and burning through to his flesh.

Alton cried out in pain and collapsed to the hard ground, clutching his injured arm. His sword lay beside him on the burned grass.

Dax threw more flame. The air filled with the stench of burnt flesh, and the gargoyle tumbled to the ground. Blood still flowed from its wound, but it managed to turn and rise to its feet just as Dax encased it with a frozen mist. The creature broke through the ice, rising up on its stumpy legs, spreading its wings wide.

It roared, trumpeting anger, pain, and frustration in a mind-numbing bellow. Dax waited for Willow to recharge him with more energy. Maybe now he'd finally have enough to kill this thing.

Alton grabbed his sword and struggled to his feet. He held the jeweled hilt in both hands as he prepared to strike a powerful blow. Dax raised his hands to throw more flame at the wounded gargoyle.

For a moment in time, it felt as if everything stood still, yet Dax's body pulsed with the power flowing into him from the tiny sprite. Willow hovered barely within his peripheral vision, a volatile whirlwind of blue light feeding energy directly to Dax. Power coursed through his veins, charged his muscles, and fired his demon abilities.

He was invincible, a demon inhabiting the body of a

strong soldier with right on his side. He could not be defeated. Not now, with his mission so close to success. Nothing could stop him.

Nothing *would* stop him.

And then he felt it. The first stirrings of the cursed tattoo as it fed off Willow's shared energy. Waves of pain slithered over his body, across his thigh and groin, above his heart.

Eddy screamed as the tattoo came to life and raised its head away from his chest. Dax felt the cold stroke of a forked tongue beneath his chin and the burning twist and turn of the serpent's body as it moved across his torso. Quiet until now, almost as if it had been lying in wait, it came to life with more strength than ever before.

Alton stumbled, apparently from the pain of his acid burns. He lowered his sword as weakness gained the upper hand. His body visibly trembled. The gargoyle raised its wings and then lowered them in a powerful downstroke. Slowly it lifted off the ground.

Green blood still oozed from the wound across its belly, but the flow was slowing as the creature flapped its wings again and gained a few more feet of elevation. Dax tried to send fire against his enemy, but the pain from the curse sapped his strength. Somehow, the serpent had tapped into Willow's flow of energy and must have commanded it all for itself.

Dax wrapped his hand around the snake's head to keep the fangs away from his throat. He flung a short burst of flame with his free hand, but it was barely enough to singe the tip of the gargoyle's left wing.

Barking and growling, Bumper fought her leash with an unending cacophony of frustrated complaints. The gargoyle turned its eyes on Dax, and Ed set the dog free. Bumper leaped for the gargoyle and managed to catch one wing in her jaws.

She pulled the creature to the ground where it knelt, snarling. Instead of racing for safety, Eddy and her father ran directly at the gargoyle. Eddy swung her baseball bat and connected with the gargoyle's shoulder. It flinched, obviously surprised by the blow. Ed held his iron pry bar with the chiseled tip like a jousting sword. He raced directly at the beast.

Horrified, Dax tried to send another burst of flame, but there was nothing left. The tattoo had absorbed all his reserves, and it was all he could do to hold the snapping jaws and extended fangs away from his throat. Willow no longer sparkled beside him. She lay on the trampled grass, a tiny little sprite without a hint of light.

Eddy took another swing at the gargoyle, but it rose to its feet and brushed her aside with one vicious swipe of its taloned paw. She tumbled inelegantly to the rocky ground and lay still. Ed swung his bar and connected with the gargoyle's head.

It grabbed the end of the iron bar and ripped it out of Ed's hands. Then it simply bent the sturdy bar into a twisted circle and threw it. Ed stumbled back. The heavy length of iron barely missed him. He dropped to his knees and grabbed Eddy under the arms as Dax reached the two of them.

The gargoyle hesitated a moment, as if considering the easy target lying on the ground just a few feet away, or freedom. Screaming an unintelligible battle cry, Alton ran at it from behind with his sword held high, but the gargoyle flapped its huge wings once again and lifted into the air with another ear-splitting roar. Bumper took one last leap into the air, snapping at the huge, leathery wings, but she missed. She came down hard and rolled along the steep slope. Then she scrambled to her feet and stood up, barking, as the gargoyle flew down the mountain, heading directly for town.

Dax fell to his knees beside Eddy as she struggled to sit up. She didn't say a word. She just slammed her hands over his and held the writhing snake against his chest. He felt the strength go out of him as Eddy gently pushed him back to the ground. Everything faded to black.

It must have only been a few moments later that he came to in the small patch of grass, gasping for air while Eddy calmed the cursed tattoo. He wrapped his fingers around her wrist. Her head snapped up, and she stared into his eyes. He tried to tell her, without saying the words, how much he loved her. That she was much too good for him. That once again he'd failed.

If he'd spoken those last words aloud, Eddy would deny them, but he couldn't ignore the truth. The gargoyle would heal from its wounds and be ready to fight another day.

But what of them? How had his small band fared?

Dax struggled to sit up. "Eddy? Are you okay? What about your dad? Alton? Willow?"

Eddy sat back and grabbed his hands, tugging him into a sitting position. "I'm fine," she said, staring at his chest as if she dared the snake to move. "Dad's okay. He's resting over there. Alton's got Willow."

Dax looked over his shoulder and saw Alton lifting Willow from the ground. "Is she okay?"

"I think so," Alton said. "She's alive."

"What about you? Did the blood burn you?"

Alton carried Willow over and sat down beside Dax. "Damned right it burned. It's some sort of acid. Ate right through my shirt and into my arm." He held out his right arm. The burns were deep and ugly, but the demon blood had cauterized the wounds so there was no bleeding. He had a particularly nasty wound on his shoulder where the white of bone showed through.

"Is the stuff still burning you?" Dax leaned close to study Alton's injuries. "Did you wash it off? The pain must be horrible."

Alton nodded. "I'm using some self-hypnosis to control the pain. Ed washed the wounds out with some bottled water. I'm concerned about my sword arm. I think the one on my shoulder went into the muscle."

Dax shook his head. "A little more than just muscle, I'm afraid."

Willow sat up in Alton's palm, stood up, and buzzed into the air. She hovered over his injured shoulder for a moment, gathering energy in the form of blue sparkles. Then she clapped her tiny hands together and pointed at him.

The sparkles came together in a perfect arrow that went directly to the deepest part of the wound. Alton blinked. "Amazing, Willow. The pain is gone."

"So's the hole in your shoulder." Ed stood behind Alton. "Look at that."

"Willow, you're just full of surprises, aren't you?" Eddy held out her hand, and the sprite landed in her palm. "Can you heal the rest of Alton's burns? They look horrible."

Willow repeated the process over Alton's damaged arm. Within minutes, healthy, pink flesh covered what had been blackened, disfiguring injuries.

Dax stared at Willow and shook his head. "Amazing," he said. Then he glanced at the pile of rocks. "I need to go inside, see if he managed to open a new portal."

Alton slowly stood up. "Thank you, Willow." He flexed his arm, now healed and strong. "Dax, I'll go with you." He leaned over, slowly picked up his sword, and shoved it in his scabbard.

Dax frowned at him. "Your sword didn't try and behead me. What's up?"

Alton gave him a puzzled look. "I don't know. I wasn't thinking about the risk at all when I sheathed it. I'm sorry. Gods. That was stupid."

Dax shook his head. "Not really. It ignored me, yet we're close enough for you to have struck a fatal blow. I don't understand."

Alton reached back and touched the hilt. He shrugged. "Me neither." He held his hand out to Dax. "C'mon. We need to get down the mountain before dark."

Dax took Alton's hand, and the Lemurian pulled him to his feet. He leaned over and kissed Eddy. "We'll be right back. Wait here."

She nodded and then went to sit beside her father on a fallen tree. Dax gave her one last smile. Then he stepped through the portal into the vortex with Alton.

The portal Alton had closed showed signs of tampering, but it was still closed to Abyss. Whatever the demon had intended, it hadn't had time to finish. Dax and Alton stared at the melted stone for a moment. Then both men turned away.

Alton gazed toward the portal that opened into Lemuria. "I keep hoping we'll hear from Taron, receive some news from my people. It saddens me to think they would ignore such a threat as the one the demons pose."

"It saddens me that you've cut ties to your family, your home. I hope that, when this is over, you'll return to your world as a hero."

Alton chuckled. "If this sword ever decides to talk to me, I just might do that. C'mon. We need to go back. Eddy and her father will be worried."

Dax nodded and followed him through the portal. Another

day gone and only two left, yet so far the gargoyle had emerged the victor from every confrontation.

He thought of the hero who had lived and died in this body. He needed some of that man's confidence, his personal strength. Hell, he needed something, anything, to give him an edge.

Without it, Dax feared he didn't have a chance of winning.

Chapter Seventeen

Thursday night—day five

It was dark by the time they reached the Jeep. Dax and Alton linked their arms with Ed and helped him for most of the journey. He grumbled a bit about getting old, and apologized for holding them back, but it was more than obvious he was in agony after all the climbing they'd done today.

He never mentioned the pain. Never complained about hurting, though he didn't turn down the offer of help from Dax and the Lemurian.

Dax's admiration for Eddy's father grew with each step the man took. His heroism was in his quiet strength, his willingness to suffer if it was the only way to stay close to his daughter and protect her.

That was something Dax understood. He felt that same need to protect Eddy. It gave him a sense of peace, knowing she would have her father here for her when Dax's time on Earth ended.

"Dad?" Eddy held the passenger door open. "I want you to sit here. I'll drive."

Ed nodded. "Probably a good idea. I doubt I could handle

the clutch." Obviously resigned to riding shotgun, he slipped gingerly into the front seat. Dax lifted Bumper into the back and climbed in beside Alton.

Eddy glanced over her shoulder as she started the engine. "You two big bruisers going to fit back there?"

Alton laughed and threw his arm over Dax's shoulders. "We fit fine. Just a little closer than we're used to."

Bumper squeezed between the two of them and licked Alton's face. Dax laughed. He turned and caught Eddy's smile. The love in her eyes melted his heart. He shrugged and slowly shook his head. They should have been going home victorious. Instead, they were merely heading down the hill to regroup.

Eddy grinned and shook her head at his unspoken comment. "We might not have won today, but we didn't lose either. Quit looking so glum. It was a good day, Dax."

He agreed. "You're right. It was. There's always tomorrow."

Eddy's smile got bigger. "That there is. Don't you forget it."

She turned around, shifted gears, and backed the Jeep around on the narrow road until she found a wide enough spot to turn. The loud roar of the engine made conversation with Eddy and her dad impossible.

Dax turned to Alton. "How're the burns? Are you okay?"

"They're almost entirely healed. I had no idea Willow could do that."

Dax laughed. "I don't think Willow knew she could, either, though the slashes on my back healed quickly. I never thought to ask her if she'd helped. You are immortal, after all. Have you been injured before? How long did it take you to heal?"

"Just because I'm immortal doesn't mean I can't be injured. And yes, I've been hurt. I heal quickly, but it usually takes a lot longer to get better." He flexed his burned arm.

"No pain at all. Just pink, healing skin. It's amazing. Which reminds me . . . where is Willow?"

Dax reached behind Alton's back and lifted his long hair. Willow peeked out from her spot on his shoulder. "Where she usually is, when she's not in my pocket. I should be jealous."

Willow buzzed out from her hiding place and hovered in front of the two men. Then she zipped into Dax's pocket and disappeared.

Alton grinned and winked at him before turning his attention to the road they traveled. The Jeep bumped along through the ruts, and the lights of the town of Evergreen grew closer. In just a couple of hours, Dax would have only two short days left to complete his mission.

He searched for some sense of the soldier whose body he shared, a soul he'd come to regard as a sort of talisman. A gentle, now-familiar warmth spread through him. He smiled as he found a more comfortable position in the tiny backseat. Eddy was safe, his friends were all together, and the soldier had not abandoned his post.

Dax settled back for the ride home and let his thoughts drift. More and more, now, he felt as if he channeled the once-unknown entity who had first inhabited this body. Now, he saw the other as a friend, a mentor, an advisor. Not necessarily as a separate individual, but more like another side to his own existence, another aspect of himself.

Channeling the other's memories gave Dax a new perspective. Opening his mind to a different approach gave him new options, new ways of dealing with things. A new focus.

His ultimate focus must remain on the gargoyle, and how he could successfully fight and defeat his foe. Like the machine-gun nest and the enemy firing down on his fellow soldiers, he had to make the demon gargoyle the target of everything he had.

Where once he'd climbed an almost sheer wall of stone to slay his enemy, now he must somehow overpower a creature physically more powerful, more deadly, more cunning.

Eddy, Ed, Alton . . . even Bumper and Willow—they were the soldiers he had to protect. Granted, the mission was to save many lives, not merely a handful of his personal friends, but it was easier to face the whole by concentrating on the few.

The few who mattered most of all.

It was well after midnight before they practically carried Ed into the house and helped him to bed. When Alton shut the door behind him, Ed was already half asleep. Dax wrapped his arms around Eddy and kissed her soundly. "Your dad will be fine. Stop worrying. He's taken some pain medicine for his hip, and a good night's sleep should work wonders. Go to bed. I'll be there in a minute."

"Why aren't you coming with me?" She kissed his chin and rested her cheek against his chest.

"Alton and I want to make a last pass around the yard. We'll take Bumper out. She's been stuck in the backseat of that Jeep for much too long."

Eddy giggled. "So have you. I'm surprised you and Alton both fit."

"Me, Alton, and a large dog. It was tight. Good night. I'd say don't wait up, but you have to know I hope you're still awake when I come in."

Eddy covered her mouth as she yawned. "Then you'd better hurry." She kissed him quickly and walked away. Dax watched the gentle sway of her hips and almost followed. Then Alton stepped into the kitchen with Bumper's leash in his hand.

"You ready?"

Dax nodded. They'd decided not to take any chances, which meant not letting their guard down at all. He whistled softly for the dog. Bumper trotted out of the bathroom with a sloppy grin on her face and wet chin whiskers. She left a trail of drips behind her.

"I see she's been drinking at her favorite fountain." Alton leaned over and snapped the leash on her collar.

Chuckling, Dax followed them out the back door. The night was clear and cool, and stars twinkled brightly overhead. He gazed at the sky and took a deep breath, filling his lungs with clean air that was perfumed with pine and cedar.

That had been one of the nicest surprises of being human—breathing air that didn't stink of sulfur. Nights here carried the scent of the evergreens that defined the neighborhood, of flowers in bloom, of hot asphalt in the afternoons and wood smoke on cold mornings. He'd grown to love the smell of a freshly mowed lawn, or the rich scent of curry when Ed's neighbor down the street cooked dishes from her native India.

This world was filled with good things to feed the senses. Tastes and smells . . . touch. Whether it was the clean, crisp sheets on the bed or Eddy's soft hands, Bumper's cold, wet nose nuzzling his fingers or the firm grasp of another man's hand when they met, all of it was good. All a powerful reminder of what he'd be leaving in just two short days.

Yet he couldn't help but be thankful for every single experience, every touch, every taste, every smell. He wondered what new thing he would miss the most, and realized it in the very instant he asked himself the question.

Love. He would miss love most of all. Not just Eddy's, though that was by far the greatest. No, he would miss the love he felt for her father, for Alton. He'd miss Willow and Bumper, two amazing creatures who would always hold places in his heart.

Thank the gods he would always have his memories.

"Dax?"

Jerked out of his musings, Dax spun around at Alton's soft alert. Bumper growled. "What is it?"

"I'm not sure, but there are lights on all of a sudden at Mr. Puccini's. Should we go check on him?"

Dax nodded. He hadn't seen Ed's old neighbor since the ceramic turkey had attacked the man on his front porch. He and Alton walked across the street with Bumper trotting along between them.

The old man was sitting on the front porch.

Dax waved. "Hello, Mr. Puccini. How are you? Everything okay?"

"Who are you?" Mr. Puccini grabbed the railing and hauled himself to his feet. "What are you doing?"

"I'm Dax. This is Alton. Remember? We're friends of Eddy Marks. We met you the other day when you tripped and fell."

The old man stepped out into the light and glared first at Dax and then at Alton. "I remember you. And I also remember that I didn't just trip. I was attacked. That damned turkey of Muriel's somehow came to life and attacked me. And you . . ." He pointed at Alton. "You did some kind of magic and made me forget. Well I remember now, and I want to know what's going on."

Alton looked as innocent as a three-week-old puppy. He shook his head. "I have no idea, Mr. Puccini. That morning, we heard you yell, and we came over to help. You'd fallen, and you kept saying something about the turkey, but it was in pieces here on the porch. Did you ever go to the doctor?"

The old man frowned. "No. I didn't need to see the doctor for a cut on my hand. That's all that happened."

"Are you sure you didn't bump your head?" Dax leaned against the corner post. "That could have scrambled your memory of what happened."

"I remember just fine." Mr. Puccini leaned over the railing. "Now you two get out of here before I call the sheriff. I'm not sure what you boys did, but I know what happened and it's not the way you say it was. Now get!"

Dax tugged Bumper's leash. "We're going. C'mon, Alton. He's awfully ungrateful, considering the fact we came over here to see if he was all right."

"I agree. Good night, sir." Alton nodded, but he lifted his hand before he turned away and swept it slowly across the old man's line of vision. Mr. Puccini blinked, frowned, and then smiled at both Dax and Alton.

"Thanks for stopping by, boys. I'm fine, but I appreciate your checking."

Alton nodded. "You're welcome, sir." He smiled, turned, and followed Dax across the street to Ed's house. They walked Bumper around the yard once more without saying anything. Then they went inside.

"It's wearing off," Dax said, the minute the door was closed. "The compulsion you gave him . . . I thought it would last longer."

Alton leaned against the closed door. "So did I, and I don't know how long the new one will last. If it wore off on him, that means it's got to be wearing off on the townsfolk too. Or it will be, shortly."

"It's not human nature to live a lie." He should have thought of that. Eddy's difficulty with her newspaper articles was an obvious clue. Humans wanted the truth. They didn't want to be protected. Thoughtfully, Dax rubbed his chin, felt the new growth of whiskers, and realized how quickly time was passing. "I imagine they fight the compulsion instinctively. We have got to get rid of the gargoyle by tomorrow."

Alton stared at Dax. "And what if we don't?"

Dax shook his head, but he grinned as he turned out the

porch light. "Then we'd better do it the next day, because after that, you guys are on your own."

He wasn't smiling when he reached the bedroom. Standing outside the closed door, Dax thought of the woman inside. She'd gone after the gargoyle today with that stupid baseball bat as if the demon were nothing. She and her dad, both mortal humans, had stood up to a creature that was stronger, meaner, more cunning than any of them, and they'd done it for love.

They'd gone after it without any thought for their own safety because it threatened those they loved. The power of that single emotion was enough to bring him to his knees, and yet, as much as he loved her, Dax knew his time was running out. His chance to destroy the gargoyle grew slimmer every day the creature lived.

It grew stronger, and he grew weaker. As the gargoyle gained sentience and strength, so did the snake crawling over his body. The tattoo had almost gotten him today. He didn't know what would happen if it ever managed to bury those long fangs in his throat, but it couldn't be good.

Quietly, Dax opened the bedroom door and slipped inside the room. The bedside lamp was still on, but Eddy slept, curled up on the far side of the bed. He went into the bathroom and took a quick shower, though he didn't take time to shave. He was too tired, too dejected to worry about whether or not he had a dark shadow of beard on his chin.

When he crawled into bed beside Eddy, she surprised him by rolling over and wrapping her arms around him.

"I thought you were already asleep." He kissed the end of her nose.

"You told me to wait up for you." She kissed him back.

"Do you always do what you're told?" This time he nuzzled

the soft skin beneath her ear and rubbed his beard-roughened jaw along her neck.

"Never," she said, arching away from the tickle and scratch. "Unless I want to. Unless you're the one telling me."

"What if I told you to take your nightgown off?"

"I imagine I'd do as you asked." She sat up, slipped her short gown over her head, and lay back beside him.

His breath caught. She was lovely. So absolutely perfect he didn't know where to look, what to touch first. He lay beside her, propped up on one elbow for a better view, and ran the tips of his fingers along her rib cage and over the rise of her hip.

Her breasts called to him. He leaned forward and took one taut nipple between his lips. He could never grow tired of this, her sweet taste, the way the rosy peak pebbled between his tongue and the roof of his mouth. When he sucked on her, she moaned and thrust her chest forward. Her fingers fluttered over his shoulder and down his arm, leaving shivers of sensation in their wake. He rubbed against her like a cat marking its owner, dragging his face with his stubbly chin over her breasts, down her belly. He could have spent the night like this, touching and being touched, but she wouldn't have it.

Eddy rose up on her knees beside him and pushed against his big shoulders. For such a slender thing, she was much stronger than she looked. Of course, he put up absolutely no fight at all as she tumbled him to his back. He thought she was going to come astride him, but instead she slithered down between his knees and, without any warning at all, took him in her mouth.

One moment he was erect and waving in the cool night air—the next much of his length was engulfed in the liquid heat of her mouth. She took him deep, sliding her lips and tongue around him, scraping gently with her teeth, sucking hard so that her cheeks hollowed with each powerful draw.

He moaned and fought to keep from thrusting into her mouth, but the demon inside him would have none of it. His dark side roared to life, and his cock slipped forcefully past Eddy's lips.

She wrapped her hands around his thick shaft and held on, controlling Dax, controlling the demon. Dax fought the need to rut like the creature he'd once been, but the struggle tested him, had him clenching the tumbled blankets beneath his rigid body in both fists. His muscles tensed and knotted as he struggled to hang on to some semblance of whatever sanity Eddy chose to leave him.

He raised his head and looked down the length of his body, over the shimmering colors of the tattoo, directly into Eddy's deep brown eyes. Her lips stretched wide around his shaft, but she still managed to smile at him as she worked her mouth slowly up and down his length.

Again he felt the demon's frustration, but he worked it now, raising and lowering his hips to a rhythm Eddy set. Then, so slowly he almost cried out, she raised her head until her lips clasped nothing more than the broad flair of his crown. She suckled him there for a moment, ran the tip of her tongue beneath the lip, and dipped it into the tiny eye at the center of his glans.

Then she released him.

Cool air brushing over his damp skin made him shiver, but when he raised his head, the look in Eddy's eyes made him burn. Dax felt the demon growl with barely contained need as he reached for her. She crawled up over his body, kissing his belly, his ribs, the scar where the demon's fireshot had first struck and burned him with its deadly curse just five days ago.

Five short days. He'd lived a lifetime during those hours,

and yet there was still more to learn, more to experience. Eddy straddled him. She came down slowly over his erection and took him deep inside. He felt the powerful clench of feminine muscles, the strength of her thighs clasping his hips.

He fought his demon side even as he gave himself over to Eddy. She leaned over and kissed him, dragging her pointed nipples across his chest while her lips plucked at his mouth and her tongue teased his. His demon grumbled, but Dax held firm until the darkness faded into the background.

Then, without warning, as he raised his hips to thrust into her heat, the snake came to life.

Eddy's eyes went wide. She stared at his chest. Then glared at him, as if the colorful tattoo writhing painfully over his body were all his fault. "It's moving, damn it. Why, when all I really want is to make love with you, does that damned thing have to show up?"

She slapped her hands down over Dax's heart and scowled at his chest. Dax realized he was grinning as he kept up the steady rise and fall of his hips. Her irritation was actually endearing. From what he'd learned of the females of the race over the past week, most women would have been screaming and recoiling in horror.

Not Eddy Marks. She just got pissed.

She'd shown him she could handle his demon, and it was obvious she could handle the snake. She was tough, and she loved him. He didn't doubt her abilities at all.

Warmth radiated from her palms to his heart. He felt the snake twitch along its full length. The tail flicked against his inner thigh; the tongue slipped out between Eddy's fingers.

She held it down, pressing the serpent close against his body while Dax continued his thrust and retreat, lifting her up with each rise of his hips, then dropping low to do it again.

After a moment, she raised her head and grinned at him.

"I'm actually getting used to the little sucker. Are you in pain? Is it hurting you when it moves?"

He shook his head. "When he comes to life while we're making love, it's different. The pain is part of the pleasure. I feel it rippling over my thigh and across my chest, I feel the heat in my groin, but it's one more sensation, another part of the whole."

He arched into her. Eddy closed her eyes, groaned in pleasure, and ground herself against him. Her palms held the snake in place, and she tilted her head back. Dax wrapped his hands around her hips and held her close. Then he rolled with her, until she was beneath him, smiling at him as he took her higher with each powerful thrust of his hips.

Suddenly she arched her back and cried out. Her palms flattened against his chest, and he felt the heat flowing into him, felt her strength and her love. The snake thrashed along his body, rippling in time with Eddy's tight contractions. Lifting away from his flesh, then clinging once more as if it were merely a colorful tattoo without life or form.

The combination of writhing snake, shivering woman, and the knowledge that she loved him enough to fight for him, loved him enough to stay even as his days grew short, took him over the edge. He felt the rolling charge of power radiating from the base of his spine, spreading out through his balls and along his hard length.

He groaned with his final thrust as orgasm took what little control he might have thought was his, stole it away, and left him sated and sweating in Eddy's warm embrace.

Quiet now, the snake glowed between them, the soft golden glow they'd ended with before. There was no pain from the tattoo, no sense of the curse. Even his own demon lay quiet. Dax wrapped Eddy in his arms and rolled to one side. Her palms still pressed against the tattoo, and her vaginal muscles clenched in a rhythmic pulse along the full length of his shaft.

He thought of rising long enough to find a soft washcloth to bathe her. Thought of it for a good ten seconds or so. And then he thought of nothing.

Eddy woke during the night. The house was quiet, the bedroom dark. Dax must have shut the light off at some point. She'd loved making love with him with the light glowing softly beside them tonight. He was such a beautiful man, all broad shoulders and muscled chest, with more muscles defining his thighs and the most perfect butt she'd ever seen on any man.

Now though, the only light came from the softly glowing tattoo that ran from the top of his thigh to his heart. She lay beside him, propped up on her elbow, studying everything about him, saving and savoring the memories.

When she'd first seen him, he'd been so badly hurt she'd not noticed what a perfect specimen of a man he actually was. Now, though, the deep burn on his chest was mostly healed, and the four holes along his side where the garden gnome had stabbed him with a pitchfork were gone altogether. The glowing tattoo should have freaked her out, but it was part of who Dax was. Not a good part. No, nothing that hurt him was good, but it had been there as long as she'd known him.

And she alone could keep it in check. Eddy had no idea how she did it, why the mere touch of her hands to his tattoo should have the power to quiet the serpent, but as long as it worked, she'd be there for him.

As long as she could. She glanced at the bedside clock. It was almost four in the morning. They'd be getting up soon, but the sixth day had already begun. Not even two full days left, and he'd be gone.

She would not cry. She wouldn't do that to Dax. She loved

him too much, and he had no control over when his time here ended, when his borrowed body went back to wherever bodies waited for things like this.

She lay back beside him and stared at the ceiling. Who'd have thought, less than a week ago, that she, of all people, would be having this conversation with herself. She'd teased her dad for years about his acceptance of all things weird.

She grinned into the darkness. It didn't get any weirder than this—lying in bed beside a demon turned warrior, a man in a borrowed body with an impossible deadline to save her town.

She rolled her head to one side and gazed at him for a moment. Well, maybe it did get weirder. . . . He was a *glowing* demon turned warrior. She traced the golden outline of the shimmering tattoo with her finger, and realized she didn't know quite what to make of it.

The tattoo was cursed, and it kept turning on Dax, trying to kill him, but she had the power to stop it. That fascinated her, that she could stop the pain, stop the whole damned thing, something as dangerous as a demon's curse, merely with her touch.

Not only stop it. She made it glow.

Life would never be the same again. She'd always been so pragmatic and rigid in her thinking, so quick to tease her dad about his acceptance of the strange and unusual. No longer. She'd experienced things she'd never imagined existed, never in her wildest dreams would have accepted as real.

Now she believed.

She'd never been in love before either. Never expected it to find her, but it had, and it was wonderful. She refused to think of the future, of going on without Dax, but just as she'd told her dad, she honestly wouldn't have traded the past few days for anything. Dax had changed her life in so many ways.

All of them for the better.

Eddy stared once more at the ceiling, smiling into the darkness. "And I'm the one who makes him glow," she whispered. Still smiling, she closed her eyes.

Friday morning—day six

Dax awoke with Eddy's arms and legs wrapped around him and her nose buried against his chest. Her tousled hair tickled his chin, and she was naked. Vaguely he recalled waking once during the night, turning to her, making love yet again.

Or maybe it was a dream. She pursed her lips and licked his nipple, and it all came back to him. No, they'd definitely made love. He remembered that part really well, when she'd run her lips across his chest, sucked on his nipples and shocked him with how sensitive they were. He'd had no idea. . . . He ran his fingers through her dark curls. "Eddy? Wake up, Eddy," he said in a singsong voice. "It's almost seven."

"Mmph." She wriggled her hips and snuggled even closer.

He kissed the top of her head. "I forgot to tell you that Mr. Puccini remembered the turkey coming to life. Alton and I saw him last night."

She muttered against his chest, grumbling, "And you're waking me up to tell me this why?"

He laughed. "Because it changes some of our plans for today. Alton gave him another compulsion, but he doesn't know how long it will last. If Mr. Puccini's memory came back, you can bet the townsfolk are beginning to remember stuff. Alton needs to strengthen the earlier compulsion, and he has to do it today."

Eddy raised her head and glared at him. "Did you really need to tell me this before my coffee?"

"Yep. I did. Now get moving." He smiled when he said it, but there was no time to waste.

A shower helped, but Eddy still felt spacey when she finally wandered into the kitchen. Dax and Alton sat at the kitchen table, but her father was nowhere in sight.

The guys both mumbled a sleepy "good morning."

Eddy glanced around the kitchen. "Where's Dad? Is he okay?" She poured herself a cup of coffee and added two teaspoons of sugar for more energy. She had a feeling she'd need it today.

Alton nodded over his steaming cup. "He's fine. I've got him soaking in a hot bath for a bit. He's stiff and sore from all the walking yesterday, but he'll be okay."

Eddy leaned over and kissed the tall Lemurian on top of his blond head. "Thank you, Alton. Did I ever tell you what a good guy you are?"

He leaned back in his chair and grinned at her. "No, but you're welcome to whenever you like."

Dax raised his head from the map he'd been studying. "Watch it, Lemurian." At least he was grinning.

"You watch it." Eddy leaned over and kissed him full on the mouth. "You boys play nice."

"Yes, ma'am." Dax gazed at Alton. "Don't ever, ever make her mad."

Alton grinned and nodded, and went back to reading the morning paper. Eddy's father had the *Sacramento Bee* delivered daily, and so far they'd not seen any articles about the odd events in Evergreen. Alton was careful to read the paper from cover to cover each day, just in case.

He folded the last page. "So far, so good. Eddy, we need to get to some of the central points in town today so I can strengthen the compulsions I've used."

"Dax told me about Mr. Puccini." Eddy still hadn't figured out all of Alton's Lemurian abilities, but so far he'd managed the seemingly impossible on more than one occasion. "Can you cover an entire community? How do you do that?"

"I can," he said, as confident as always. "There are various points of energy around town, places I can sense when I'm near them. I already know a few, but I want to see if there are others. If I stand at those points when I broadcast a hypnotic compulsion, it has more power and affects more people. Remember, though, that it's never as strong after the first time. I'm hoping that if I renew it today, it will hold through the weekend."

Eddy nodded. Alton didn't need to say what he meant—that he hoped it would hold until Dax was gone, because it wouldn't matter after that. If they didn't defeat the demon by tomorrow night, there was no telling how long the battle would go on.

But it would go on without Dax. Keeping the invasion of demonkind a secret if they failed wouldn't change things or help at all. People were going to find out, eventually, what evil faced the world. At least while Alton and Dax worked together in secret, they had some chance of success.

A very slim chance, but still a chance.

Eddy glanced up as her father walked slowly into the kitchen. He was using his cane, something he only pulled out when he absolutely had to. "Hurting pretty bad this morning?"

Ed nodded. "I'll be better once I loosen up. Alton insisted I soak in the tub. I have to admit, the hot bath helped." He hung the cane over the back of his chair. Eddy jumped up to get his coffee.

"Sit down, Eddy. I'm sore, but I'm not a cripple."

"Sore and stubborn, it appears to me. Sit." She glared at him. He sat. She flashed a big grin at Dax. "You're right, you know. It's a bad idea to make me mad."

She poured coffee for her dad and set the cup in front of him. "Okay, guys. I'm cooking, so don't expect miracles."

A short time later, Ed pushed his empty plate away and smiled at Eddy. "I taught you well. Delicious!"

Dax glanced at Alton. "I though she didn't like to cook."

Alton nodded. "She doesn't. Doesn't mean she can't. Plus, she swings a mean baseball bat. The girl is definitely multi-talented."

Feeling inordinately proud of herself, Eddy stood up and began grabbing empty plates. "Woman. I am not a girl."

Dax patted her fanny. "Definitely all woman."

Ed laughed. "Watch it. That's my daughter you're groping."

Eddy walked away from the table with an exaggerated sway of her hips, and the men all laughed. Inside she felt close to shattering. They'd been laughing and teasing for the past hour, as if their world didn't hang in the balance of what they accomplished over the next couple of days.

They'd laughed as if Dax would still be around and Alton didn't have a death threat hanging over his head. Willow buzzed through the kitchen, and another thought hit Eddy. *Willow!* What would happen to her when Dax was gone? Would she just disappear? Would she go back to Eden?

She heard the scrape of chairs as she rinsed the dishes in the sink. Warm hands circled her hips, and she felt Dax's broad chest against her back.

"All will be okay, Eddy. I can practically hear your thoughts, but please don't worry. Let's see what today brings. Tomorrow we'll see what comes, but only when it's actually tomorrow. We don't need to ask for trouble, but we will win this fight. I have to believe it."

She carefully wiped her hands dry, turned in his warm

embrace, and placed her palms against his cheeks. "It's not the fight I'm worried about. It's you, Dax."

No. She had to stop lying—to herself and to Dax.

She leaned her head against his chest. "Oh hell, I'm totally being selfish. You'll be fine. You'll be in Eden, loving your life in Paradise." She sniffed. "I'm worried about me . . . about me missing you." She laughed, but it broke off in a sob that somehow managed to escape. "I'm even worried about Willow! What will happen to her when you're gone?"

He raised her chin with his fingertip and looked at her with so much love in his eyes it broke her heart. "I don't know," he said. "I never thought to ask. She's a creature of Eden, but for all I know, Willow didn't exist before. If she was created to be my companion and my source of energy, she might end when I do."

Eddy shook her head. "That's as wrong as you ending. Willow is a living, thinking creature. She's got a mind of her own. She's compassionate and caring. Just like you, Dax. Just *like* you. No one in Eden could ever love you like I do."

His arms tightened around her waist. "I know, Eddy. I know."

He didn't say anything else, but he held her for a long, long time. Eddy listened to the steady sound of his heart and tucked the memories of his scent, his strength, his love away in her heart.

They would have to last a long, long time.

Chapter Eighteen

Late Friday afternoon—day six

"Where could he have gone?" Alton leaned against the cold fireplace. Willow perched on his shoulder, and Bumper lay at his feet. If he hadn't been almost seven feet tall with silky blond hair falling in a straight line to his butt, he might have looked like any other rangy cowboy in town for the weekend.

"I don't know, and I don't like it. I fully expected he'd be back at the library. That's been his home base all week." Dax sprawled in her dad's recliner. He, like Alton, was wearing faded jeans and a worn flannel shirt. They'd both pulled their boots off, and both men looked frustrated and exhausted.

At least her dad was doing better this evening, though he'd chosen the couch, where he could stretch out and rest all his "old man's aches," as he referred to the hip that definitely needed replacement.

"If we don't find the gargoyle, I imagine he'll find us." Eddy shrugged, but then she smiled at Alton. "And you got the compulsion reset. Thank goodness! I'm really glad you managed to get that done." Now that had been a shock when they'd walked to town this morning. Total strangers coming up to her, getting in her face, and complaining about her newspaper articles.

All those stories about the so-called vandalism, every single one blaming the problems on gangs or, as she'd alluded to in one story, an unknown cult—except some of the townsfolk remembered things differently. Remembered, and wanted to talk about them.

One man had said it felt as if he'd had fog on the brain, but the fog had cleared. Thank goodness Alton had reset the fog!

As much as she hated writing lies, Eddy hated getting caught even more, which was a fairly selfish and dishonorable way to look at things. Discovering that lack in her own ethics hadn't been a very pleasant revelation.

She'd just have to keep reminding herself it was all for the common good, but she was glad her father had stayed home. She would hate for him to see her defending stories that weren't true. Someday, she hoped she could come clean on all this, but she couldn't do it yet. Not now.

Damn but it had been a long, frustrating day. Even more frustrating knowing that Dax only had a little over twenty-four hours left. She couldn't dwell on that, though. She just couldn't.

Willow buzzed through the room, followed by her usual trail of sparkles, but instead of her usual blue, they were dark red, almost as if she were angry.

Or frightened. Dax held his hand out, and she skidded to a halt in his palm. He stared intently at the little sprite, then practically jumped out of the recliner.

"Close the shades and turn out the lights," he said, moving swiftly toward the kitchen and the window that faced the backyard. "Check the locks on the doors. The gargoyle's outside. Willow said he's flown over Ed's workshop twice now."

Ed struggled to his feet. "How'd it find us?"

Alton turned away from the front door he'd just secured. "I'm not sure, but this changes things. We've been hunting it. Now it appears the gargoyle is hunting us."

Eddy helped her dad into the kitchen and grabbed a straight-backed chair for him. Dax had already turned out the lights and stood in the darkened window, staring toward the workshop. He glanced over his shoulder as Eddy slid the chair across the floor and set it near the window. Ed carefully sat down where he could see outside.

"Look." Dax pointed at Ed's shop.

Eddy felt her blood run cold. The gargoyle perched on the roof like a huge vulture and stared directly at the kitchen window where all of them were gathered. It leaned forward, supporting itself on its hands and feet with its leathery wings folded against its back.

Its eyes glowed with incandescent fire reflected from the nearby streetlight. It swung its head from right to left and back again, as if assessing the area in preparation for an attack.

Bumper growled low in her throat, but she seemed to know enough to keep it quiet. Dax patted her head, and she whimpered. It was obvious she knew there was something out there that she really didn't like at all. Willow stood on the windowsill with her tiny hands planted on her hips. Anger absolutely radiated from her little body.

The sun had set, and there was just enough light left to see the gargoyle's dark silhouette, but the eyes seemed to grow larger and brighter as darkness fell.

Eddy was glad they'd turned off the lights inside. The kitchen was almost entirely dark. She didn't want to think the gargoyle was watching them, though she imagined he probably had much better vision than she did. It gave her the creeps.

Alton slipped his crystal sword out of the sheath hanging

over the back of a kitchen chair. It ignored Dax. Alton stared at it a moment and then held it down at his side. "I'm going out the front door. I'll work my way around behind the shop."

Dax kept his eye on the sword as he agreed. "I'll go with you until I can find a good spot to attack, but I'll wait until you're in position before I show myself. I don't want him to see us leaving the house." He glanced at Eddy. "Is there a backyard light you can turn on from inside? I have a feeling the gargoyle can see in the dark much better than me."

She pointed to the set of switches by the wall. She realized they were all whispering, and wondered if it was necessary, but the damned thing had gone from stone to flesh in a matter of days. For all they knew, it could hear through walls.

She kept her voice low. "A couple. There're lights on both the back porch and the door to Dad's shop, but nothing that will throw a beam on the roof."

Ed moved slowly, but he got up and opened a utility closet by the back door. "I've got this." He held up a heavy flashlight shaped almost like a handgun with a halogen bulb. "It throws a pretty good beam a long way."

"Good." Dax nodded. Then he leaned over and kissed Eddy. "Stay out of the creature's sight, and hang on to Bumper. I'm taking Willow with me." He glanced down at the baseball bat she'd grabbed without even realizing it, and laughed. "It's good to know you're armed."

"You're making fun of me, but I'll get the last laugh. This is one fine baseball bat." She kissed him and stepped back. "Be careful, Dax. I love you."

"I love you too."

She wasn't sure how long they stood there staring into each other's eyes, but she didn't want to turn away. Dax was the first to break the spell that had so quickly trapped them both.

"Ed, as I recall, there's a ladder against the north side of the shop, so Alton will be using that. I want you to shine the beam directly on the gargoyle—in his eyes if you can—the minute Alton signals you. That should momentarily blind him and might give us an advantage. Can you get outside without him seeing you?"

"I'll use the sliding glass door from my bedroom. I should be able to flash this at him without leaving the house." He held up the flashlight. "It's really bright. With any luck, he won't be able to see me once the light's in his eyes."

"Eddy, don't turn the lights on until after your dad flashes the spotlight. Then we'll need both yard lights. Alton, can you just raise your sword so Ed knows you're ready? That crystal should show up just fine. If you're behind the gargoyle, hopefully he won't see it. Ed, watch out you don't get me or Alton with that beam."

Ed nodded. "I will. Be careful, boys. Both of you. And Willow? You be careful, too." He grabbed his cane and the spotlight and slowly made his way down the hallway. Dax hid Willow in his pocket, and he and Alton slipped out the front door. Eddy waited alone in the kitchen with only Bumper for company. She heard the steady *tick, tick, tick* of the clock over the kitchen sink. The sound of Bumper panting. A car passed by on the street out in front.

Darkness closed in. The gargoyle was barely visible now, though its eyes still glowed an unearthly shade of red. She had no idea where Dax or Alton were. They had to be getting into position.

Eddy sensed a change in the pressure inside the house and knew her father had opened the bedroom door. Bumper whined and stood close beside Eddy in the darkened kitchen. Her curly blond hackles rose along her spine, and her whine turned to a rather startling growl that seemed to roll out of her chest.

Eddy kept her gaze on the gargoyle, though all that really showed right now were the flashing red eyes. Then Alton's crystal sword glowed behind the creature's dark silhouette. Immediately after, the brilliant beam from Ed's spotlight caught the gargoyle directly in the eyes.

It rose up, roaring. Its loud trumpeting cry echoed throughout the neighborhood. Eddy flipped on the backyard lights as the gargoyle leapt from the roof and shot directly toward Dax with leathery wings outspread.

Alton's sword swept through the air and severed a large section of the gargoyle's right wing. The piece spun off in a shower of dark blood and landed in Ed's rose garden just outside the workshop.

Dax stood at the edge of the yard, partly hidden beneath a sycamore tree. Fire flashed from his hands and burned away more of the gargoyle's wing as the creature landed on the ground just a few yards away from him. It screamed this time, an earsplitting cry of absolute fury. Then it turned on Dax.

Flames still shot from Dax's fingertips. The heat of the fire singed the gargoyle's chest, but it continued its awkward walk directly into the flame, drawing closer with each step it took.

Dax switched from heat to cold. Icicles formed on the gargoyle's face and hung from its damaged wing as well as the good one. Still it moved forward, listing toward the injured wing. Bumper growled and clawed at the door. Alton was clambering down the ladder and racing toward the gargoyle with his sword raised.

Dax switched back to flame. Suddenly his body jerked. The flames died. Alton took another swing with his crystal sword as Dax went down with both hands pressed to his throat.

The tattoo! She'd totally forgotten the damned tattoo! Ignoring danger, Eddy swung the door wide and raced out into the yard. Snarling and barking, Bumper went directly for the gargoyle. She sank her teeth into the creature's one good wing. It spun around, reaching for the dog, but Bumper managed to hang on and stay out of reach of the long claws.

Alton raced across the yard and swung his sword, but he missed as the gargoyle leapt into the air. Bumper hung on to its wing until only her hind legs raked the ground. Then she let out a sharp yelp and dropped, rolling and frantically rubbing her face in the damp grass.

Eddy fell to her knees beside Dax. His eyes were closed, his mouth open as he gasped for air. The tattoo rippled and slithered over his skin, but he held on to the head of the snake with a white-knuckled grasp. The forked tongue whipped between his fingers. He held the viper's mouth shut with both hands.

There were two perfectly round puncture wounds in his throat, just beneath his jaw. Already the skin was beginning to swell. Alton dropped to his knees beside Eddy. "What happened?"

"The damned snake bit him." Her voice cracked with fear as she pressed her hands over Dax's and forced the serpent down. Beneath her touch, it slowly lost dimension. Within a very few seconds, it was nothing more than a tattoo, though pain radiated up Eddy's arms all the way to her spine.

She ignored it. "Dax? Can you hear me? What can I do? How can I help you?"

Ed stood over them, leaning heavily on his cane. He handed a small plastic box to Eddy. "Snake-bite kit. It's old, but the theory's the same. It might help if you can get the poison out."

She tried to open it, but her hands were shaking too badly. Alton took it from her, flipped open the catch, and removed a razor blade wrapped in a sterile covering, along with a small suction cup. Eddy grabbed the packet of disinfectant and tore it open. She splashed the alcohol over the puncture wounds, took the razor from Alton and, with surprisingly steady hands, made a quick slash in Dax's throat to connect the two holes.

She used the suction cup to draw blood and venom out of the wound and prayed the creature hadn't struck a vein or an artery. Dax's head lolled to one side as she suctioned blood and venom and emptied the cup. It was so damned slow!

She shot a quick look at Alton, but his attention was entirely on Dax. Willow stood on Alton's shoulder, but she was sending blue sparkles the length of Dax's body. Frustrated, terrified, Eddy finally leaned over and put her mouth to the seeping wound. She sucked hard, filling her mouth with his blood and something with a vile, bitter taste that burned her lips and tongue and had to be venom.

Over and over again, she sucked at the wound on his throat, turned her head and spit, and sucked again until the taste changed and she knew she drew only pure, clean blood from the bite. Finally she sat back on her heels. Ed handed her a damp cloth, and she wiped Dax's blood from her lips. Then she folded the cloth to a clean side and pressed it against the slowly seeping wound on his throat. He seemed to breathe easier, but he was still unconscious.

"Should I carry him inside?"

She blinked and gazed at Alton. "Can you lift him? He's awfully big."

Alton smiled gently. "So am I, Eddy." He stood up and handed his sword to Ed. Then he pulled Eddy to her feet. "Get the bed ready. I'll carry him into your room."

She nodded, took one last look at Dax, and raced toward the sliding door to the master bedroom. Alton followed a moment later. He carried Dax in his arms like a very large child, through Ed's room and down the hall to the room Dax shared with Eddy. There Alton carefully laid him down on the big bed. Eddy removed his boots while Alton unbuttoned his shirt. Bumper sat near the foot of the bed with her chin resting on the edge of the mattress while Alton and Eddy finished undressing Dax.

Willow took a position on the headboard. Blue sparkles still rained down over Dax, but even with Willow's energy, his skin felt hot. Sweat beaded his upper lip and glistened across his chest. The tattoo gleamed, but it was just a tattoo—for now.

Eddy glared at the thing. Then she went into the bathroom and found a clean washcloth, rinsed it out in cool water, and used it to bathe the sweat and blood from Dax's face and chest. "I feel so helpless," she said, running the cool cloth over his shoulder. "What kind of poison comes from a cursed tattoo? How do you fight it?"

"With love."

Alton's soft words brought her to a stop. "What do you mean?"

"He's breathing easier. His color is already better. Even the place where you slashed through the puncture wounds with the razor has begun to heal." He grinned and gazed up at Willow, sitting on the headboard. "Of course, some of that could be due to Willow and her marvelous blue sparkles, but Eddy, everything you do for him, you do because you love him. Evil can't fight that. It's a powerful weapon, and you wield it well."

She sat down beside Dax. He did seem to be breathing better. She touched his forehead. His skin felt cool beneath her palm. "Alton, I sure hope you're right. I didn't even think of the snake when both of you went outside. All I could think was maybe now you guys could beat the gargoyle at his own game."

She raised her head and looked at the tall Lemurian. "Purely selfish, on my part. I wanted Dax all to myself tomorrow. I don't want him fighting the gargoyle on his last day on Earth. I want him with me."

Alton swept his hand over her hair and brushed it back from her eyes. "I know. I feel the same way. I don't want to lose him. Not tonight. Not tomorrow. He's become a very dear friend in a very short time. Only Taron and I are this close. When Dax is gone, I will have lost a brother."

Dax reached up and wrapped his hand around Alton's wrist. "You haven't lost me yet, my friend."

"Dax!" Eddy covered her mouth with her hand to bite back a cry. "I've been so worried!"

"What happened? I was fighting the gargoyle and the tattoo at the same time. Something bit me, I think, but . . ."

"The snake bit you." Eddy traced her fingers over his throat. The puncture wounds were no more than tiny pinpricks now. The razor slash was a narrow pink line, connecting the dots. "I think I got the poison out, but I was so scared."

"How?" Dax planted his hands on the bed and carefully shoved himself upright. He leaned against the headboard and gazed from Eddy to Alton and back at Eddy. "What did you do?"

"She played lady vamp." Alton grinned at Eddy. "Pretty impressive, actually."

Dax frowned. Obviously he didn't get the reference. Eddy shrugged and said, "I used a razor to open up the puncture wounds and sucked the poison out."

"Well, that's gross." Dax gazed steadily at her for such a long time, Eddy blushed. "You really did that? Sucked blood and poison out of my neck?"

"Well, it's not like I could ask anyone else to do it." Eddy stood up and planted her hands on her hips. "What else did you expect?"

"Only you would do something so courageous."

He reached for her hand. She took his and squeezed. "It wasn't brave. I was terrified you might die. Your neck was swollen where it bit you, and you were having trouble breathing."

He stared at her a moment longer. Then he tugged, and she tumbled to the bed beside him. "So, what happened to the gargoyle?"

She glanced at Alton. "Alton sliced off a big chunk of its wing. It fell in the rose garden, but it didn't keep the gargoyle from flying away."

"Your fire and ice slowed it down, but it still escaped." Alton patted Bumper's curly head. "Bumper got it by one wing, but as soon as she bit through and got a mouthful of that corrosive blood, she let go."

Eddy reached down and rubbed Bumper's head. "I don't blame you, girl. I would've let go too." She tried to part Bumper's jaws without any luck. "Did she get any burns on her mouth?"

"No. She's okay. I checked. No burns." Ed eased himself into a chair next to the bed. "I found the piece of gargoyle wing. It's now a big, delta-shaped slab of stone. It smashed my Peace rose."

"It may be flesh and blood, but it still reverts to stone. It's not entirely alive." Dax looked at Alton. "Where do you think the gargoyle is now?"

"Holed up someplace where he can heal. After I sliced that piece of wing off, the bleeding stopped almost immediately, so it's definitely stronger and healing faster. Your flame burned it, but not enough to stop the damned thing."

Dax sighed. "And it knows where Ed and Eddy live." He turned his focus on Alton. "No matter what, we need to kill it, but we have to find it first. Any idea where it's gone?"

Alton shook his head. "Have you thought about sending Willow out to scout for us? She can sense the demon. She might have better luck."

Dax shook his head. "I can't risk her like that." He looked up at Willow, sitting atop the headboard. "She's too important to all of us."

Willow fluttered blue sparkles over the pillows, but she'd helped Dax heal from the serpent's bite. Eddy figured she could afford to celebrate a bit.

Ed stood up. "I've got a pot roast in the Crock-Pot that's probably cooked itself into soup by now. Dax? Are you okay to come out to the kitchen for a meal?"

"I actually feel pretty good, thanks to Eddy." He swung his legs over the side of the bed and grabbed her hand.

Alton stood up and grabbed his sword. It didn't react to Dax at all. "I wonder if I'll ever figure this thing out?" He shook his head. "Ed, save me something for dinner. I want to go out and check the area before I eat. You guys go ahead."

In the kitchen, Eddy watched Alton slip into the harness that held his scabbard. He carefully sheathed the sword. "I'll be back in a while," he said. Then he quietly walked out the door and left them to their dinner.

Alton walked swiftly through the quiet neighborhoods, alert to the sounds of the night. He made a point of going by Ginny's house, but the shades were drawn, the lights out.

With luck, she'd be in Sedona by now, well away from whatever chaos occurred here in Evergreen. He gazed about, absorbing the sense of peace in the quiet streets and darkened homes. Homes filled with families, with mothers and children and fathers, older couples enjoying the later years of their lives, expecting a peaceful old age.

What if he and Dax failed? What if the gargoyle prevailed? What would happen if demonkind took over this peaceful town? If they eventually ruled this world? If the tipping point were reached in spite of everything they did to stop the creature?

What would happen to Lemuria? He might be an outcast there, but he still loved his people, his world. He'd expected to hear from Taron by now, but his friend's continued silence didn't bode well. Of course, with the elders capable of discussing even the simplest of questions for millennia, it was probably asking far too much to expect a decision on such a weighty topic in less than a week.

He heard a sound, as if someone walked through dry grass. Drawing his sword, Alton slowly turned to face the enemy.

He looked into the dark eyes of a large doe. Her speckled fawn stood beside her. Sighing Alton turned away and headed back to Ed's house. His sword glowed brightly, showing him the way.

Glowed but did not speak. Maybe it was all a myth, nothing more than mere legend. Maybe the swords had never spoken and he expected the impossible.

Or maybe, just maybe, he'd already failed. Maybe he didn't have what it took to be a warrior, to help Dax and Eddy save Earth from demonkind.

He paused and stared into the glowing crystal, but there were no answers in its shimmering depths. With a soft curse of pure disgust, Alton sheathed his sword. Then he walked swiftly through the darkness along the quiet road to Ed's house.

Eddy awoke with the unfamiliar sense that she was alone in the bed. She'd fallen asleep wrapped tightly in Dax's arms, well aware this was their last night together. Even more aware he was still not feeling a hundred percent after the attack by that damn serpent tattoo. She wondered if they'd have a chance to make love at least one more time before he was gone.

Then she wondered how it would happen. Would he just disappear? Would the body die and Dax's spirit go on to

Eden? She hadn't even thought to ask him. Didn't really want to know.

She sat up in bed and glanced around the dark room. He wasn't in the bathroom. She got up, wrapped her robe around her light gown, and went down the hall toward the kitchen. The back door stood open to the cool night air.

Quietly, she slipped through the open door. Dax sat on top of the picnic table, staring into the darkness. His legs were folded, and his elbows rested on his knees. He wore nothing but a pair of boxer shorts against the cool air.

"Dax? Are you okay?" She slid her hands over his shoulders and leaned against his muscular back. He tilted his head back and smiled at her.

"I'm fine," he said. "Just needed a little time to think."

"About what?" She sat beside him on the edge of the table.

"You. Me. Tomorrow." He gazed off into the darkness and spoke softly. "Nothing has happened the way I expected. I didn't expect the demon to catch me unprepared. Didn't expect the spirit of the soldier who first owned this body to still be hanging around." He grinned and leaned against her shoulder. "Now that's an experience I'm still getting used to. I'm sensing him more every day. Maybe he wants his body back."

"Maybe he just wants to help?" She kissed his cheek.

"Actually, I think you're right, and I've grown to depend on his presence, and that of another as well. I didn't realize I'd still have part of my demon self to contend with, but he occasionally rears his head, especially when we make love."

He smiled into Eddy's wide-eyed look of surprise. "It's true. I've managed to keep him under control, but I don't stop him entirely." He leaned close and kissed her lips and trailed kisses along her jaw. "He's a much better lover than I am."

"I find that hard to believe." She tilted her throat to give him better access.

Dax kissed her again. "I didn't expect Alton or your dad,

or Bumper. Didn't realize how fond I would become of Willow. When the Edenites first came to me, I figured this would be a simple job. A lot more exciting than mere existence in the void. I thought I'd come in, clean out the demons, and get my ticket straight to Paradise. It hasn't worked at all the way I planned."

"You'll get him tomorrow, Dax. I know you will."

He shook his head. "Eddy, he knows where you live. When I'm gone tomorrow, I can only hope and pray that Alton will stay here to protect you. I can't imagine Paradise as anything more than hell if I'm there and you're here—especially if you're in danger. Of all the surprises, you are the biggest one of all. I love you. I never understood what love was, and now all of a sudden it's the most important emotion I never had before. It's more important than doing my job, than spending eternity in Paradise. You're more important, but you're not one of the choices they've given me."

She ran her fingers through his dark hair. "No chance to choose what's behind door number three?"

Dax frowned. "I don't understand."

"Stupid game show on television." One more thing he'd never understand because he wouldn't be here long enough. She felt the tears threatening to choke her and swallowed them back. She wasn't going to cry. He didn't deserve the burden of her tears. Not on his last night and day of life on Earth.

She held his face in her hands. "Dax, I love you too. Don't worry about us. We'll be fine. You've done the best job you can, and you've still got tomorrow. You'll find the demon, and you'll get rid of him. I know you will."

She stood up and took his hand. "Come to bed. Make love to me. Let's spend what time we can doing things that will give us good memories to last." She tugged.

He gazed down at their entwined fingers and sighed. Then

he untangled his long legs, slid off the table, and stood up. Eddy wrapped her arms around his waist and pressed her cheek to his chest, well aware it rested against the serpent.

One more day. He was going to be gone in one more day.

But we still have tonight. Eddy pulled slowly out of his embrace and, still holding his hand, led Dax to her bedroom.

Memories. It was all about making memories at this point, and she refused to think about tomorrow.

Chapter Nineteen

Saturday morning—day seven

The sun was high in the sky when Eddy awoke. Dax slept so soundly beside her that she had a moment of panic. Had they miscalculated his time left? Was his spirit already gone? She leaned over him to see if he still breathed.

His eyes popped open. She bit back a scream. "You're still here."

He frowned. "It's Saturday, isn't it? What time is it?" He sat up and leaned against the headboard, blinking himself awake.

Eddy snuggled against his side. "It's almost eight. We slept in."

He gave her a drowsy kiss. "That's because we had a busy night."

Eddy blushed. They'd definitely been busy. As proof, her body ached in places she wasn't normally all that aware of. Then reality came tumbling down, and she sighed. Would she ever awaken again with this marvelous sense of having been so well loved? She gazed at Dax, at the dark shadow covering his jaw, the sleepy smile on his face, and couldn't imagine ever loving anyone the way she loved him.

And there wasn't a damned thing she could do to change that. She kissed him hard. Then she spun around, and her feet hit the floor. "I need a shower," she said. She glanced over her shoulder. "Want to join me?"

He nodded, still smiling at her. Then he followed her into the bathroom.

Alton greeted them when they walked into the kitchen a little while later. He sat with the Sacramento newspaper and a cup of steaming coffee. Dax poured himself a cup and one for Eddy and joined them at the table. "Where's Ed?"

Alton glanced at the clock. "He's in the tub. It helped him yesterday so he's soaking again this morning." He folded the newspaper and set it aside. "Still nothing in the *Bee*." He frowned and gazed around the room. "Where's Willow?"

Dax glanced up. "Isn't she with you?"

Alton shook his head. "No. She didn't sleep in my room last night. I just figured she'd chosen to stay with you for your last night. She didn't?"

Dax shook his head and turned to Eddy.

"I haven't seen her." She whistled for Bumper. The dog trotted into the kitchen. "Bumper? Where's Willow? Have you seen Willow?"

Bumper whined. Alton turned to Dax and said, "You don't really think the dog understands her, do you?"

"She does when Willow's around to help her. Willow? Are you here?" Dax shoved his chair back. He hadn't thought of her once during the night. He'd only thought of Eddy, of how much he loved her. How much he was going to miss her. Now where the hell was Willow?

He went to the back door and opened it. There was no

way she could have gotten outside. Even with all her abilities, she still needed an open door or window to get in and out of the house.

He glanced up at one of Ed's decorative birdhouses that was nailed to the back porch. Willow's tiny blond head appeared in the round opening. She slipped out and sat on the perch in front of the house. There were no blue sparkles, and her tiny wings drooped.

"Willow!" Dax reached up and held out his hand. She crawled into his palm and curled up as if she was totally exhausted. Frowning, Dax carried her into the kitchen. "She must have gotten locked out last night, but how?" He sat down at the table with Willow cradled in his palm. "Willow? What happened."

Slowly, she roused herself and stood up. Dax heard her musical voice in his head.

I searched for the demon most of the night. I should have told you, but you probably wouldn't have let me go.

"You're right. Willow, you're exhausted!"

I'll be okay with a little rest. She held her chin up and planted her hands on her hips. A very pale blue glow outlined her tiny figure. *I found him. His wing is completely healed. He's up on the mountain, inside, working on a passageway to Abyss. He needs more demons if he's to grow stronger, but he won't be able to complete the portal until late tonight or early tomorrow. That is where you'll find him.*

"How long do you need to rest, little one? I never would have thought to hunt him there. You've done a very brave thing."

Blue pulsed brighter around her. *A few hours*, she said. Then she zipped off of his hand and found her favorite spot in a nest of blond curls on Bumper's head.

Dax turned to Eddy. "Did you hear what Willow said?"

"I did. I can't believe that little thing flew all that way alone. What are we going to do?"

With a thoughtful look on his face, Alton watched Willow settle herself. "We need a plan," he said. "One that will not fail." He gazed at Dax and then at Eddy. "This is our last chance to go after the creature with a united front. We can't afford failure."

Ed stepped into the kitchen, walking carefully but without his cane. "What's up?" He poured himself a cup of coffee.

Dax explained. Then he asked, "Do you think you can drive?"

Ed nodded. "I do. I'm sore, but nothing like I was yesterday. I doubt I can hike very far, though."

"Not necessary," Dax said. "You've got a weapon—a shotgun, I think it's called. I want you to take it with you, along with plenty of shells. Eddy, you've got your bat, and you've got Bumper. The dog has no fear of the demon. If we set her free to go after the creature as soon as we find it, it might be distracted enough for Alton and me to get closer. Alton's crystal sword might not be talking to him, but it's quit trying to kill me."

Alton laughed. "Last night it definitely wanted a taste of the gargoyle. I think it's decided you're one of the good guys. That's a good thing."

"A very good thing." Dax smiled at him, and a wave of emotion almost brought him to tears. He would miss Alton terribly. A good friend, a powerful warrior, an honorable man. The gods had been smiling on him when he'd found Alton in Lemuria. He swallowed and took a deep, steadying breath. "As soon as Willow's rested enough and can start channeling energy, we're going after the demon."

It took much longer than he'd expected. It was late afternoon before Willow finally regained her energy and they loaded into the Jeep for the ride up the mountain. It was dusk by the time Ed parked the vehicle beneath a small copse of shrubs and stunted trees, but he'd driven them as high as he could possibly go. Once the tires began slipping on the loose scree, it was time to continue on foot.

Dax climbed out of the Jeep and stopped beside Ed. "You've got the spotlight and the shotgun. Stay alert. If the thing tries to get away from us, it'll probably come this way. Hopefully it will be wounded and weak." He rested a hand on Ed's shoulder with the realization he might never see the man again.

"It's a double-barreled twelve gauge. I'll let the damned thing have it with both barrels. You can count on me, Dax. Good luck."

"Be careful, Daddy." Eddy leaned over and kissed him.

Ed kissed her back. "You haven't called me 'Daddy' in a long time. You be careful too, sweetie. Don't take any chances."

She laughed and swung her bat over her shoulder. "It's a little late for that, don't you think?"

"It was too late about the time you turned twelve and started hitting the ball out of the park. Good luck."

Dax refused to look back, but he held Ed's words close to his heart. *Good luck.* He hadn't had much good luck hunting the demon this past week. It was about time for his luck to change.

It was almost dark on the dormant volcano by the time Dax stopped and put a finger to his lips. "There," he said, pointing to the now-familiar pile of rocks. "I don't see him outside. He must be within the vortex."

Alton studied the surrounding area. "Let's hope he hasn't completed a new gateway to Abyss."

"Wouldn't there be signs of demons if he had?" Eddy

leaned on her bat. "There's no scent of sulfur at all. The air smells clear."

"You're right. Okay . . . we need to go in together." Dax glanced at Alton. "I would imagine he's trying to repair the passage you destroyed, rather than attempting to create a new one."

"I agree. That puts him just beyond the entrance. When we pass through the portal, be ready to move quickly." Alton unsheathed his sword.

Dax laughed. "I still don't trust that thing."

Alton nodded. "The important thing is, it's obviously decided to trust you."

Dax agreed with a quick jerk of his head. He took Eddy's hand in his. Willow snuggled down deep in his shirt pocket. Alton leaned over and removed Bumper's leash and stuck it in his pocket. He held on to the dog's collar with his free hand.

The three of them exchanged glances, and once again Dax felt the tide of emotion wash through him. They trusted him. In spite of his failings, they still looked to him as their leader.

He would not disappoint them. Not this time. With a deep, steadying breath and Eddy's hand held tightly in his, Dax stepped through the portal.

Ignoring the brief sense of disorientation, Eddy immediately turned loose of Dax's hand and crouched low the moment she entered the cavern. She moved to one side as they spread out, according to plan.

The gargoyle spun around. Obviously it hadn't been expecting them. Bumper didn't make a sound when Alton released her. She merely launched her curly blond body like a guided missile, straight for the gargoyle.

Willow'd been right. The creature's wing was entirely healed, but here, inside the cavern, there was no room to spread them, no way for it to do anything but turn and fight with teeth and claws.

Bumper didn't bite. She threw her solid body directly at the gargoyle's knees. One buckled, and the creature slipped as it tried to regain its balance.

Eddy stayed back to give Alton and Dax the freedom to use their weapons. Alton swung his sword. The gargoyle feinted, moving faster than a creature his size should be able to move. The blade left a shallow cut in its shoulder, but Bumper latched on to a rear leg as Dax threw a barrage of flame. The gargoyle let out a horrifying scream and dove straight for Eddy.

She stepped aside, swung her bat, and connected solidly with the creature's left arm. There was a resounding crack and another satisfying scream. Eddy ducked and rolled across the uneven ground as the gargoyle spun around and came at her with jaws gaping wide.

The quarters were too tight for Alton to swing his sword, but he resorted to short, sharp jabs that penetrated deep. Dax measured the use of his burning and freezing, using his powers to herd the creature out of the corners and into the center of the cavern, where Alton had room to swing his sword to his best advantage.

Willow buzzed about in a shower of blue sparkles, careful to avoid the green blood oozing from numerous wounds on the infuriated gargoyle. Dax hit the blood with flame, incinerating it where it fell. Bumper backed off and resorted to barking and growling. The deafening cacophony echoed off the cavern walls.

Eddy dodged a swipe of the gargoyle's talons, and then another. It had chosen her as a target, obviously hoping to draw Dax's attention, but fear lent her speed. Twisting, turning, and rolling, she stayed out of reach of its sharp claws.

Bleeding profusely, screaming in rage, the beast lunged past Eddy with Bumper at its heels and burst out of the vortex through the portal.

Dax grabbed Eddy's hand while Alton hung on to Bumper, and they followed the gargoyle out into the night. Full darkness had fallen, but red, glowing eyes glared at them. Labored breathing echoed on the still night air, and the sound of leathery wingtips dragging over the rocky ground had a hollow, almost drumlike quality.

Alton didn't pause. He materialized out of the rock, released his hold on Bumper, and charged the gargoyle. Swinging his crystal sword, he aimed for the creature's neck. The gargoyle raised one clawed arm and grabbed the sword in its powerful fist.

Two long, bony fingers tipped with razor-sharp claws dropped to the ground when Alton pulled the sword free. Trumpeting its anger, the gargoyle launched itself into the air. Its mighty wings stretched out, knocking Eddy to the ground as it coasted down the mountain, riding the wind currents.

"It's headed straight for Dad." Eddy didn't even pause. She leapt to her feet and took off running down the rubble-strewn hillside. Dax, Alton, and Bumper followed close behind, slipping and sliding in their haste to reach Ed and the Jeep.

An explosion echoed off the mountain. "Both barrels," Alton said, racing on ahead of Eddy. Dax grabbed her arm as they made the trip down in a fraction of the time it had taken them to climb the same distance.

Another loud bang, closer this time. Obviously the first shots hadn't stopped the thing. Dax let go of Eddy's hand and raced on ahead.

Pale moonlight illuminated the area where Ed had parked. The Jeep lay on its side. There was no sign of Ed. Dax thought he must be hiding behind the wreck. He hoped the man wasn't under it.

Alton followed the gargoyle. He'd landed a few minor hits, but every time he went for the kill, the creature eluded the shimmering blade. The gargoyle stalked the Jeep, bleeding now from a dozen wounds. The grass and weeds beneath his feet sizzled and smoked wherever drops of blood landed. Dax raised his hands and threw a column of fire.

The gargoyle turned around and snarled. Then it said, very clearly, "Die."

Sentience. Speech. There was no doubt the thing grew stronger by the day. More dangerous. It had to be destroyed. Now. The image of the machine-gun nest filled his mind, along with the knowledge that both he and the gargoyle would die today.

Dax pulled more energy from Willow. Power surged through him and erupted from his fingertips in wave after wave of fire, searing the creature with roiling flames that rolled off its grotesque body.

A few small trees and shrubs burst into flame, lighting the darkness. The cursed tattoo slithered to life, beginning its writhing dance across his flesh. Dax ignored it. He felt Willow's strength falter. He called on her for more. Somehow, she gave it.

Eddy arrived, gasping and out of breath, but she circled around behind Dax to get to Ed. Alton moved into position beside Dax, sword in hand, ready to strike.

Bumper growled but stayed back, out of the way of the fire. The serpent pulsed against Dax's body, and agony ripped through him as it pulled itself free. The tongue slashed beneath his chin. He had mere seconds before the snake buried its fangs in his throat.

Then he felt Eddy's hands grabbing the serpent. She stood behind him with her arms around his body, holding the snake, preventing it from attacking.

Protected now for however long she could hold it back, Dax continued throwing flame at the gargoyle. It had almost doubled in size since the day before, and like a giant living torch, it lunged toward him.

Alton leaped forward and swung his sword, but the creature knocked it aside, twisted around, and landed fully on Alton, crushing the Lemurian to the ground beneath his huge body. Then, moving almost too quickly to follow, it leapt to its feet, reached up, and snatched Willow out of the air. Huge talons impaled and crushed her tiny body. Her blue sparkles disappeared. Dax's flames died.

The gargoyle popped the sprite into his mouth, chewed obscenely, and swallowed. Eddy cried out in protest, but she still held on to the serpent as Dax backed them both away. Another loud shot rang out. Ed leaned against the side of the Jeep and fumbled with the spent casings as he struggled to reload the shotgun.

He'd obviously aimed wide to draw the creature's attention. It worked all too well. With its leathery hide smoking but no longer flaming, the gargoyle launched itself at Ed before he could reload. Dax pulled out of Eddy's grasp and raced after the gargoyle.

He had no weapons, and he sensed that his time was almost over, but he was sure he had what he needed: focus and his will to complete his mission, to save Ed Marks. To leave Eddy in a safer world. He threw himself at the gargoyle and landed on its back between the huge wings. The creature's hide was slippery with its corrosive blood, and it burned through Dax's clothing and into his skin.

Bumper rushed at the creature and sunk her teeth into its back leg, biting deep in spite of the burning blood. The gargoyle kicked hard, and Bumper went flying. Her body bounced off a stunted tree and lay still.

Flames still flickered from a few burning trees and shrubs, but in their wavering light, Dax couldn't tell if the dog lived or died. The serpent on his body came to life once more as he wrapped his arms around the gargoyle's throat. Ignoring the slithering reptile, Dax squeezed with all the strength left in him.

It wasn't enough. The gargoyle reached around and plucked him off its back as if he were nothing more than a nuisance. A very small nuisance. It held him high, staring into Dax's eyes with much more intelligence than Dax ever expected the creature to possess. The cursed tattoo chose that precise moment to sink its fangs deep into Dax's throat. Agony seared his flesh. Corrosive venom poured into the big vein in his neck.

Then the gargoyle lifted him high in its powerful talons and twisted his body, snapping bone and tearing muscle.

Dax winked out.

"No!" Eddy screamed. Dax hit the rocky ground in a twisted, bloody heap. He lay without moving. The gargoyle ignored Eddy completely and turned its attention back to her father. She looked to her right, to Alton for help. He lay still, either unconscious or dead, barely visible in the flickering light from a few burning shrubs. Bumper had stopped barking. Eddy couldn't see her anywhere. It was too dark.

But she could see the crystal sword. It lay beneath Alton's body, glowing brightly. He'd warned her not to touch it. Had told her she could be killed if she ever tried to wield it.

At this point, she didn't give a damn.

She'd lost her bat when she'd tried to quell the cursed serpent on Dax's chest. Now she reached for the crystal sword. She wrapped her fingers around the jeweled hilt, surprised by the perfect fit. She tugged, and it slipped from beneath Alton's body, lighter than she'd expected.

She spun around, held it high, and raced toward the gargoyle. The creature hovered over her father, arms spread wide and talons extended as Ed crouched down low beside the wrecked Jeep. He grasped the useless shotgun in both hands like a club.

Eddy didn't pause, didn't take time to think. She merely leapt at the gargoyle to gain the height she needed, and swung the crystal sword.

It made a clean pass through the thick neck and came out the other side. The creature's head wobbled a moment, and then toppled neatly to the ground as Eddy collapsed beside it. She didn't have either the energy or the will to go after the thick, sulfurous mist that poured out of the body and disappeared into the night.

A body that shattered into fragments of stone and toppled to the ground.

Dax blinked and saw nothing. Felt nothing. No heartbeat. No need to breathe. Darkness was absolute, silence complete.

Damn. He recognized this place. He was back in the void.

He'd failed. He searched memories and realized the last thing he recalled was the horrible pain when the serpent sunk its venomous fangs into his throat and the gargoyle mangled his human body. The body he no longer had.

If he could have, he would have sighed. When he failed, he did one hell of a job. No chance at Paradise now. No opportunity to tell Eddy again how much he loved her. At least he had his memories, but time had no meaning here, and he'd brought fear with him, too. Was Eddy okay? Had she escaped the gargoyle? And what of Alton? Was he killed when the creature crushed him?

And Willow. Poor Willow. Gone. What a horrible end to a loyal and faithful friend.

He wanted to weep, but there were no tears. Not here.

He sensed change. Darkness, and then light, swirled about him, and he was back in his borrowed body, healed now, sitting at a long table surrounded by men in white robes. Blinking, he gazed at the silent faces until he saw one that stopped him cold. It was his own face, smiling back at him.

"It's you," he said, recognizing the soldier. Sensing his familiar aura of courage. His focus.

The man nodded. "Yes," he said. "Thank you. You fought bravely and with honor. Because of you, I've gained Paradise."

"Because of me?"

"Because of you."

His image faded and was gone. And just as quickly, Dax sensed the void in himself, the space the other had occupied. It wasn't painful, and there was no sense of loss, but he knew he was alone now in this body that was suddenly all his.

But why? There was no need of a body in the void. He raised his head, and his gaze connected with the man sitting closest to him. Though he'd never seen him before, it was a face he recognized. Somehow, he knew the white-haired gentleman was one of the elders who had offered him the chance to battle demons on Earth.

Was it only a week ago?

"We have made a terrible mistake," the man said. "Because of our error, you failed. It was not your fault. It was ours." He bowed his head. Then he raised it again and once more looked at Dax. "To atone for our wrong, we offer you eternity in Eden. You are welcome in Paradise, even though you've not completed your part of the bargain. It's only fair."

A mistake? "What kind of mistake?" Dax met the eyes

of each man at the long table. Every one of them looked away. Suddenly his mind was spinning. He felt hope. Unbelievable but true.

"What if I said I had already found Paradise?" Heads turned in his direction, and he forced each man to make eye contact. "What if I were to ask you for something else to ease your troubled souls?" He put his hands on the table and smiled at all of them, well aware of the feral quality in his eyes. *Focus*, he thought. *It's all about focus.* "Gentlemen? Are you at all interested in a deal?"

Eddy sat beside Dax's body and held his cold hand in hers. Though he'd died horribly, he actually had a peaceful expression on his face. There were two deep puncture wounds in his throat, and his back had been badly twisted, but Alton had helped her straighten him out so that now he looked merely asleep.

Asleep. Not dead. She'd run her fingers through his thick hair and straightened the tangled strands. She'd used her dad's clean handkerchief dipped in some of her bottled water to wash the soot and blood off of him.

She glanced up as Alton walked out of the darkness, carrying Bumper. "Oh." Eddy's free hand went to her lips. She was not going to cry. "Is she . . . ?"

"She's alive. Still a little stunned, but she was trying to get up and walk." Alton sat down beside them and set Bumper on the grass beside Dax. She rested her chin on his chest and sighed.

Ed sat down beside Eddy. "I've looked all over and can't find a trace of Willow. I was hoping I was wrong, that I didn't really see her die, but I can't find her."

Eddy wiped her hand across her eyes. None of this seemed real. She glanced over her shoulder, just to make sure the gargoyle was really dead. The crumbled pile of stone hadn't moved. "It hasn't sunk in yet, what's happened." She ran her fingers through Dax's hair again. "I keep thinking he'll wake up and tell me there was a big mistake, that he's okay."

She laughed and sniffed back a sob. She'd promised herself she wasn't going to cry when he was gone, but damn, it was hard. "The demon's not dead, you know. I blew it. I had the sword, and I saw the mist escape, but I just couldn't get to it."

Alton wrapped his big hand under her chin and turned her face to his. "You saved all of us, Eddy. You managed to do what none of us could—you destroyed the demon's avatar and sent him back to Abyss. Yeah, he may return, but we're still alive to fight. We wouldn't be, without your bravery."

"Thank you. I just . . . I wanted to do it for Dax. I wanted him to succeed at his mission. That was all he asked for, to complete his mission with honor."

She wanted to lie down beside his still body and hold him until he was warm again. It didn't feel right, that he should be so cold and still. She touched his throat, slipped her hand beneath his shirt, and wondered if the curse had died along with Dax.

For some reason, she needed to know. She unbuttoned the top buttons on his flannel shirt. There was no sign of the snake's head. Frowning, she undid the rest of the buttons, all the way to his waistband.

"Eddy? What are you doing?" Ed gently rubbed her shoulder.

She shoved the flannel shirt open and ran her fingertips over the fresh colors across his chest. The snake was gone. In its place was a new tattoo, some sort of a bird. She wasn't sure what it was. "Alton? Dad? Do you recognize this?"

Alton nodded. "It looks like a phoenix. The symbol of rebirth. But how . . . ?"

Eddy felt the tears come. This time she didn't try to stop them. "Don't you see?" she sobbed. "It means he made it. He got into Eden. He's been reborn in Paradise." She grabbed his hand again, and she could have sworn it felt warmer. He'd made it. Thank goodness he'd gotten his dream.

Bumper whined. Alton ran his hand along her rumpled coat. "You okay, girl? You took quite a wallop when you hit that tree. I bet you're a little sore."

I'm okay, but the demon ate my body. I think I'm stuck in Bumper for good.

"Willow?" The familiar flutelike voice filled Eddy's mind. She snapped her head around and stared at Alton, who looked right back at her with a stupid grin on his face. Then she stared at Bumper. "Is that you?"

It's me. I got my consciousness free just in time to hide in Bumper, but I have no body to return to. Bumper says she'll share. She doesn't mind.

Eddy heard what could only be a sigh.

I've always liked Bumper. At least I'm still a blonde. And Eddy, Dax is back!

Stunned, Eddy looked at Dax's hand. She'd been so sure the phoenix meant he'd made it into Paradise, but . . . did his hand really feel warmer, or was that her imagination?

She stared at his throat. The puncture wounds were gone. A pulse beat, slow and steady. "Dax? Dax, wake up." She leaned over him, crawled across him, straddled his body, and held both his hands against her breasts.

"Eddy? He's not . . ."

"Yes he is, Dad. Yes. He is." She leaned down and kissed his perfect lips.

He kissed her back. She burst into tears. She felt his hands come up around her back, felt the steady beat of his heart beneath her chest, and cried even harder.

Bumper barked and licked his face. Alton sat beside them with tears streaming from his eyes, and Ed just sat back and grinned. Still sobbing, Eddy scooted down Dax's legs and helped him sit up. He folded her in his arms and rested his cheek against the top of her head.

Finally, she managed to get herself under control. "What happened? I thought you were dead. I saw the gargoyle literally break your body; the snake had his fangs in your throat. Damn you, Dax! You scared me to death!"

"I'm sorry, Eddy." He kissed her. "But you'll never guess what happened."

Alton rested his hand on Dax's shoulder. "Whatever it was, I'm glad you're back."

"Me too, son." Ed handed him a bottle of fresh water, and Dax took a long swallow. "Now tell us what the hell happened."

"They made a mistake."

Eddy burst out laughing. "I was sitting here thinking you couldn't be dead, that someone must have made a mistake."

Dax hugged her. "You were right. We haven't been fighting a typical demon. I told you I was kicked out of Abyss because I was too good to be a demon. Well, our demon was originally from Eden. He was banished because he was evil, sent into the void. The same way I was recruited by folks from Eden, he was recruited by leaders of Abyss—leaders I didn't even know existed. He lost much of his intelligence in the transition, but he gains it back the longer he's on Earth, and he does get his strength from the demons he devours. The Edenites' mistake was in sending me against him unprepared. They didn't expect the curse, and they didn't know I'd have more to fight than the usual run-of-the-mill demons. Sending me in woefully unprepared was their fault.

They're the good guys, and they're not supposed to make mistakes like that. They were willing to deal."

Eddy couldn't stop touching him. She finally contented herself with slipping her hands inside his shirt against warm, living flesh, and hugging him close. "So, what's the deal?"

Dax kissed the top of her head. "They offered me eternity in Eden, even though I failed my mission. I got my shot at Paradise."

Eddy frowned. "But you're . . ."

"I turned them down."

"What?" She reared back and gaped at him.

He smiled at her and ran his fingers down her cheek. "I told them I'd found my own paradise with you, Eddy Marks. Nothing else could compare." He kissed her lips. "They sent me back to continue the fight. I still have my demon powers, plus a few I've yet to discover, only now they're in the tattoo of the phoenix. Because this body is mine eternally, I can use them without Willow's help."

He ran his fingers through Bumper's curly coat. "I'm still going to need you, Willow. Both of you." He stroked Bumper's ears. Then he raised his head and turned his focus on Eddy, even though she knew he spoke to all of them. "It's not going to be easy, and I told them I couldn't do it without my warriors. I made a huge decision without consulting you, and I don't know if it can be undone if you don't agree, but I did the best I could. I've got immortality for you and Bumper, and for me."

He glanced at her dad. "I tried, Ed. I think you've got a new hip, but I couldn't swing the rest. I'm sorry."

Ed shook his head and grinned. "I wondered why the pain went away. Thank you. Don't worry, son. I've got a damned good life. I'll leave immortality to you kids."

Dax nodded. He ran his hand through Bumper's curly coat. "I know you're in there, Willow, and it was the best I could do once your body was gone. You're tied to my mortality and would have ended when I did. This way you're part of our team, but you're stuck in Bumper. I hope it's okay."

Bumper sat up and barked. Her tail went like a metronome set to a polka. *There's got to be a better way to communicate,* Willow said. Then she barked again.

The sun was rising before they felt rested enough and ready to head back to town. Alton and Dax eyed the Jeep. It wasn't damaged, merely tipped over. "Do you think we can right it?" Dax checked the ground beneath the downhill side. At least the gargoyle, in his fury, had pushed it uphill when he'd rolled the thing over.

"We can try." Alton took his sword out of the scabbard and set it on the ground. He and Dax each grabbed an end of the Jeep and shoved. It rocked back and forth. Then with grunts and groans and straining muscles, the two men managed to right the vehicle.

Blowing hard from the effort, Dax stepped back and grinned. "That's good. I really didn't want to walk all the way back."

Ed laughed. "I didn't want to pay the fine for leaving a vehicle up here when they're not allowed on this part of the mountain in the first place."

Eddy wrapped her fingers around Dax's. It was almost impossible to let go.

Alton leaned over to pick up his sword and very softly said, "Nine hells."

"What's the matter?" Dax spun around as Alton reached down and lifted two identical swords off the ground.

"I've heard of this, but never seen it. The sword replicated itself." He held both of them out, spinning and twisting each. "I can't tell which one is mine."

"I am, you fool."

"Holy shit." Alton stared at the sword in his right hand. "You talked."

"You've been wanting me to all along. So what's the problem?

"But you never said a word. Why now?" Alton shot a quick glance at Dax, Eddy, and her dad, and then stared wide-eyed at the sword.

"I had nothing to say. You managed to figure things out without conversation, but the least you could do is learn to recognize me. Have a little respect."

"Okay." Alton shook his head and took a deep breath. "Then explain why there are now two of you."

There was a long silence. "There are three, actually. I am HellFire. DemonFire, in your left hand, is my twin. He belongs to Dax."

Alton frowned. He handed the sword to Dax, who very gingerly wrapped his hand around the hilt. He stared at the crystal blade, studying its length and width, testing the balance. "Where's the third?" he asked.

His new sword answered formally, in a voice completely unlike Alton's sword. "It was born of the first," it said. "We are three."

"It's here." Eddy pointed to the spot on the ground where the other two had been. A third sword, identical in every way except for its smaller size, lay shining in the dirt. Like filings to a magnet, she felt drawn to it. Very carefully, Eddy reached down and picked it up.

The jeweled hilt fit perfectly into her palm. She held it up and turned it in the morning light so that the sun slanted through the crystal blade. It threw a multicolored rainbow against Bumper's curly coat.

"I am DemonSlayer."

The sword's voice was decidedly feminine. Awestruck,

Eddy raised her eyes and stared at Dax. "That was the name Taron gave to you," she said.

Dax wrapped his arm around her waist and pulled her close for a long kiss. "True. But it's the name you earned, Eddy Marks. I'm afraid it's one we'll all have to continue earning until we defeat the demon threat."

Eddy gazed at him. She not only had Dax back, she had him for all time. She wrapped her fingers in his and raised her sword. Dax raised his, and Alton held his high. The three of them touched the tips together, and a brilliant light flashed where they met.

There was no need for words, no oath they had to swear. It was there—in their hearts, in their hands, in the stone remnants that had once been a gargoyle born of demonkind, now lying in a pile of rubble on the side of Mount Shasta.

They lowered their swords and turned their backs on the remnants of the gargoyle. Then with Ed at the wheel, Alton riding shotgun, and Eddy, Bumper, and Dax in the tiny backseat, they headed down the mountain to town.

If you enjoyed DEMONFIRE,
don't miss Kate Douglas's

***HELLFIRE*.**

Read on for a special preview
of this next thrilling paranormal romance
in the DemonSlayers series.
A Zebra paperback on sale in September 2010.

Ginny Jones wrapped a clean kitchen towel around her torn fingers and glared at the screeching cat she'd finally managed to shove into the carrier.

Her cousin Markus leaned over her shoulder and sighed. "Poor Tom. I sure hope he's not rabid."

"No shit, Sherlock." She glanced at the blood-soaked towel and then at Markus. "And what do you mean, poor Tom? Did you see what that cat of yours did to my hand?"

Markus shook his head, sending his long dreads flying. "I don't understand. Tom's a sweetheart. He's never even scratched anyone, much less bitten before."

"Tell that to your neighbor. She's going to need stitches in her leg, not to mention what he did to my hand. C'mon. We need to get him to the vet so they can quarantine him before animal control shows up, or they might just take him and put him down."

Markus grabbed the keys off the hook by the back door and picked up the carrier. Tom screeched, a long, low banshee wail that sent goose bumps racing along Ginny's arms and raised the tiny hairs on the back of her neck. Tom didn't sound anything like any cat she'd ever heard. Why did that screech sound so eerily familiar?

Like it was skirting with the edges of her memory?

She stared at Tom glaring back at her through the bars of the carrier, but nothing clicked. She'd never seen a cat with eyes like his. They flashed blood red. When he snarled, she was almost certain he had extra rows of teeth.

She shivered again and wrapped her arms around herself. *Beyond weird.* Everything about the stupid cat was freaking her out. Frowning, Ginny followed Markus at a safe distance through the back door to the garage and watched while he stowed the sturdy carrier in the backseat of the Camry.

Tom howled again. Ginny shook her head. "I don't like this one bit. Shouldn't we maybe put him in the trunk?"

Markus ignored her suggestion and got into the driver's seat. "Get in. No cat of mine rides in the trunk."

Ginny stared at the red-eyed cat. Tom returned her stare.

Markus glared at her. "You scared of a cat? Cripes, Ginny. Get in."

She took a deep breath. The last thing she needed was to look like a coward in front of her baby cousin. "Well, if he gets loose from the carrier, you're putting him back in—and I'm outta here. I've bled enough for the cause." Ginny slammed the door and reached for her seat belt, wondering for the hundredth time what she was doing visiting her cousins in Sedona anyway. It wasn't like they were all that close, but for some reason she'd gotten a wild hair, packed her bags and headed to Arizona without any plans or advance notice at all.

So far, her timing sucked. She'd barely parked the rental at her aunt's house when the shit hit the fan. Old Tom, the fattest, laziest-looking cat she'd ever seen, had suddenly launched his porky butt off Aunt Betty's front porch, screaming like the devil was on his tail.

He'd practically flown over the six-foot hedge separating Aunt Betty's house from the one next door. Every hair stood on end and he looked like a flying fur ball with fangs. He'd gone straight for the poor neighbor lady who was just getting out of her car with her arms loaded with groceries.

The bags had gone one way, the woman the other, but Tom latched on to her left leg and buried his teeth deep. It had taken both Markus and Ginny to pull the cat off the poor woman, and then he'd taken off, still screaming. Aunt Betty freaked out, grabbed the two little ones, and as far as Ginny knew, she was still hiding in the bedroom with the kids.

Markus with typical teenaged thinking had gone after the cat with a big bass net like it was a four-legged fish. Ginny'd been the one who finally cornered Tom against the fence, but he'd gotten her good with claws and teeth before she managed to shove him in the carrier and latch the damned thing.

Not quite the entrance she'd imagined on the flight from Sacramento to Phoenix. If she had to go through a course of rabies shots, she was going to kill Markus, and anyone else who gave her grief.

Like Alton. Especially Alton.

Now why in the hell would she be thinking of her friend Eddy Marks's tall, drop-dead gorgeous, egotistical jackass college buddy Alton? They'd barely met, though for some reason Ginny kept associating him with her being here in Sedona, which made no sense whatsoever.

Neither did the fact he'd kissed her the first time she saw him. For some reason, her memories of that kiss were all fuzzy, but she knew they'd locked lips, if only for a moment.

And very nice lips they were, in spite of his bossy attitude. He was a spectacular kisser. She remembered that much, but little else.

Like *why*. She couldn't recall anything leading up to the

kiss, or even what happened directly after. This wasn't like her. Not at all, but confusing memories of Alton were all jumbled up with boarding a plane for Phoenix and grabbing a rental car for the drive across the desert to Sedona.

And now she was headed to the local vet with a crazy cat, her crazier kid cousin, and a hand that was bleeding through the dish towel she'd wrapped around the scratches.

If this was a vacation, she'd definitely had better.

"Is it always this busy?" Ginny rewrapped the towel around her hand while Markus drove around the block again, looking for a parking place. All the slots at the vet's clinic were taken and there wasn't a single empty spot along the road.

Markus shook his head. "Never. Especially on a Saturday morning."

He finally pulled into the parking lot in front of a grocery store a block away. "I'll carry the cat." He glanced at Ginny and seemed to notice the blood-soaked rag for the first time. "Is that still bleeding?"

"Yes, it's still bleeding. Your sweetheart of a cat nailed me good." She got out of the car and started walking toward the clinic. Markus fell into step beside her with the carrier clutched in one hand. Tom had quit screeching, but his incessant growling and snarling was almost as bad.

Markus was big for eighteen—at least six foot six with broad shoulders and legs like tree trunks. As tall as she was, Ginny had to look up at him. He might not be the sharpest tack in the box, but she figured if he couldn't protect her from a stupid cat, no one could.

Though, come to think of it, she was the one bleeding, not her cousin. She was still thinking along those lines when Markus grabbed the door to the clinic and held it open for her. Ginny stepped into total pandemonium.

The small clinic reeked of sulfur, which made no sense at all. Usually vet clinics smelled like cat pee. This one was filled with crying kids, screeching animals—most of them in cages, thank goodness—and a couple of staff members who looked as if they were ready to run and hide. Ginny turned and looked at her cousin.

Markus stared wide-eyed at a large cage holding a big blue macaw. The bird spread its beak wide and screeched. It sounded just like Tom. Markus swallowed with an audible gulp. Ginny took a closer look at the macaw. Teeth. Rows and rows of teeth.

Now, she was no expert, but she'd never heard of birds with teeth. Ginny blinked and refocused, but the macaw's mouth was still filled with way too many razor-sharp teeth. A sharp yip caught her attention and she glanced down at a scrawny little Chihuahua that was, thankfully, wearing a muzzle.

More teeth. Not just sharp doggy fangs, but rows of shiny, razor-sharp teeth filled the little mutt's mouth. A lop-eared bunny in a cat carrier just like Tom's snarled and hissed and curled its lips back. More teeth. Every single animal in the clinic looked like something out of a cheap horror film, all of them snarling and screeching and trying to take bites with mouths filled with way too many rows of sharp teeth.

And just like that, her memories crashed back into her head. The big concrete bear chasing her that night back home in Evergreen, her best friend Eddy's dad, Ed Marks, and Alton—though she hadn't known him then, that tall, good-looking friend of Eddy's from college—rushing out of the darkness and attacking the impossible creature, saving her life.

She saw it like a movie on fast-forward—Alton carrying a huge sword made of glass or crystal, jabbing it into the concrete bear like the thing was made of butter. Jumping up on the creature's back, riding it like a bucking bronco, with the bear screeching and wailing.

Screeching and wailing, just like the animals here, in the veterinarian's clinic.

Ginny sucked in a breath as images flowed into her mind. Alton lopping off the concrete bear's head with a powerful swing of his sword, the crystal blade flashing by in a slashing arc.

The bear crumbling, just turning into a pile of rocks and dust and sulfuric stink, like it had never been alive at all. And the smell. That horrible stench.

Just like this vet clinic in Sedona.

She remembered Alton and Ed walking her home. How could she have forgotten that night? That was the night Alton kissed her! A girl didn't forget a night like that. It made no sense at all.

Except she was remembering, now. Remembering it as clearly as if it had just happened. The bear, the battle . . . Alton's lips. Oh Lordy . . . his lips, warm and full and so sweet, pressed against hers, moving over her mouth in a whisper of sensation and seduction.

The noise, the screeching animals, the stinky veterinarian's clinic all faded away as Ginny pressed her fingertips against her lips and let the memories flow.

There'd been another night, too. She blinked as it came into focus. Just the two of them, walking arm in arm down the street to her house, standing on her front porch. She was thinking of inviting Alton in. He'd been just as bossy and arrogant as the first time they'd met, but she'd laughed with him, too, and even though they'd only met the night he'd saved her life, he was really very nice under all that bluster.

How could she forget that he'd offered to stay the night on her front porch? Offered to protect her. That was sweet, even though she didn't need any protection. Not in her little town of Evergreen on the slopes of Mount Shasta. Safest place in the world.

She remembered saying good night and for some reason she'd kissed his cheek when she'd really wanted nothing more than to drag him inside and take him straight to her bedroom. Her toes actually tingled, remembering. Her womb felt heavy, her breasts full, recalling now how she'd gone in alone and closed the door. Leaned against it, thinking of Alton. Hearing his voice.

Hearing his voice? How could she have forgotten his voice in her head, that sexy whisper . . . giving her orders?

Damn it all!

Telling me to come to Sedona.

Ginny clenched her hands into fists and bit back a scream that would probably have shut up every screeching animal in the room. It was Alton's fault! Somehow he'd hypnotized her. That had to be it. He'd hypnotized her and made her forget the bear and his kiss and . . .

She growled. The macaw shut its big mouth and stared at her, but all Ginny could see was Alton. That insufferable jackass had sent her here. He'd saved her from a bear made of concrete with rows of razor-sharp teeth, a bear that couldn't have been real, and he'd sent her down here to frickin' Sedona, Arizona, where the cats and bunnies and birds had the same kind of impossible teeth.

Ginny spun around and glared at her cousin.

Markus took a step back. "What'd I do?"

"Nothing. Not a damned thing." She took a deep breath and let it out. Something very weird was going on, and Alton was involved, all the way from the tips of his sexy cowboy boots to the top of his beautiful blond head. "I have to make a phone call. You sign in. I'll be right back."

* * *

There wasn't a stitch of clothing covering her perfect body. She was tall and slim and her stylishly bobbed hair swung against her jaw with each step she took on gloriously long legs. If she hadn't been trying to kill him, Alton might have found her attractive. Instead, he wrapped both hands around the jeweled hilt of his crystal sword and swung with practiced ease.

The blade sliced cleanly through the juncture between her neck and shoulder. He watched with grim satisfaction as the mannequin's head bounced off the wall and rolled across the sidewalk. The jaws gaped wide, exposing row after row of razor-sharp teeth framed by perfectly painted pouty lips.

Alton stepped back out of the way, giving Eddy Marks plenty of space to aim the point of her crystal sword. She held DemonSlayer high, slashing through the demonic mist as it flowed through the hole in the mannequin's plastic neck.

The eerie banshee cry of the escaping demon sent shivers down Alton's spine. The screech ended abruptly the moment Eddy's sword sliced into the mist and it burst into flame. All that was left was a puff of foul-smelling smoke.

"Well done, my lady."

Eddy smiled at the sword in her hand. "Thank you, Demon-Slayer." Then she sheathed her weapon and rose up on her toes to accept a kiss from her beloved Dax.

Alton couldn't help but think that Dax was one very lucky ex-demon, to find a woman like Eddy Marks, one brave enough to have gained immortality along with her own sentient sword. There weren't many women like her, not in the world he'd come from.

In fact, there were none like Eddy in the lost world of Lemuria. As far as he knew, she was just as unique to Earth.

"That was a new one," Eddy said when she finally peeled herself away from Dax. "Have you seen any more like her?"

She nodded in the direction of the mannequin lying on the sidewalk.

Alton dragged his gaze away from Eddy and Dax and stared at the mannequin. "Thankfully, no, but this isn't good. It was bad enough when demons were using ceramic and stone creatures as avatars, but plastic's a new medium for them. Can you imagine the chaos they're going to cause? There's no way to get rid of all the potential hosts for the damned things."

Dax knelt down and ran his hand over the body, as if he needed to see for himself what it was made of. "What I want to know," he said, "is where the demons are coming from. All of a sudden, there's no shortage of them, either. There shouldn't be so many. Not since Alton sealed the gateway from Abyss."

Eddy shoved her bangs out of her eyes. "Maybe they've opened a new one."

Nine hells.

The three of them stared at one another. A new portal was the last thing they needed. Alton sighed. Not two weeks ago he'd been a perfectly bored resident of the lost world of Lemuria, wondering why nothing exciting ever happened. Then he'd helped two humans, a tiny will-o'-the-wisp and a mongrel dog escape from a Lemurian prison deep within Mount Shasta, and nothing had been the same since.

Exiled from Lemuria with a price on his head, he'd joined the battle against demonkind's invasion of Earth. Not that he was complaining about all the changes in his life, but was there no end to the demon invasion?

Of course, Dax and Eddy's lives had changed just as drastically. Dax the demon had become a DemonSlayer, working for the good guys to halt the demonic invasion of Earth, and Eddy Marks was a newspaper reporter who had saved Dax's life without a clue what she was getting into. Alton figured she probably hadn't expected immortality, a demon lover or a crystal sword that talked to her.

And Bumper had been just a dog. The dog barked. Alton leaned over and scratched her curly head. Bumper looked up at him, and Willow's thoughts flowed into Alton's mind.

I think that demon was the only one. Bumper and I checked.

Thank you, Willow. And Bumper.

He couldn't imagine Willow's life now, trapped inside a mongrel like Bumper. The tiny will-o'-the-wisp had been sent as Dax's companion, able to draw energy from the air to fuel his demon powers. In that last big battle on Mount Shasta when the demon ate Willow, she'd managed to transfer her consciousness into Bumper just in time. While Dax no longer needed Willow for energy, Alton knew they all needed her as part of their team. Whether she looked like a tiny fairy or a curly blond pit bull, Willow had the soul and spirit of a warrior.

Just like his other companions.

Alton carefully sheathed his sword. HellFire, the crystal sword he'd had since reaching manhood, had finally, after so many millennia, gained sentience and begun to speak. Proof that it finally considered Alton a warrior, a man of respect.

They'd all earned that respect in the final battle with the gargoyle, which explained the crystal swords Dax and Eddy now wielded as well, replicates of his own sword.

DemonFire for Dax, DemonSlayer for Eddy.

Sentient crystal swords, perfect for fighting the demon invasion that threatened to offset the balance between good and evil. Three warriors, their sentient swords and a mongrel dog melded to the mind of a will-o'-the-wisp.

They were all that stood between a demon invasion of Earth and the unsuspecting citizens of this world.

Alton couldn't help but worry they might not be enough.

Eddy's cell phone played *Ode to Joy*. She reached for the phone and turned away to take her call.

A chill raced along Alton's spine.

Eddy stared at the phone in her hand for a long, long time. Then she slowly slipped it back into her jeans pocket. Alton and Dax were deep in conversation, and it looked like BumperWillow was right in there with them.

BumperWillow. Eddy couldn't think of one without the other. Not anymore. Thank goodness she'd been able to get things straightened out with the shelter and they'd agreed to let her adopt her foster dog, Bumper, or they'd really have been in a fix. When the gargoyle had eaten the little sprite's body and she'd slipped into the closest available host, at least she'd found one who loved and welcomed her.

The symbiosis between the brave little will-o'-the-wisp and Eddy's funky mutt couldn't have been better, though after seeing how gorgeous Willow'd been as a sprite and how silly she looked as a pit bull crossed with a blond poodle, Eddy couldn't help but wonder if Willow ever had second thoughts about her choice of borrowed body.

But that was the least of Eddy's problems. Ginny Jones's phone call had just opened up a whole new can of worms.

"Guys," Eddy said. "We've got a problem."

Alton kept his arms tightly folded across his chest. He was afraid if he didn't hold himself contained, he'd fly to pieces. Ginny was in danger, and it was his fault. All his fault, for sending her to Sedona.

He'd known there was more than one vortex in that Arizona town, but he hadn't even thought of the demons using one as a passage from Abyss to Earth's dimension. No, all he'd thought about was getting Ginny away from Mount Shasta and the demon invasion here, but this community was probably the safest one around for now, especially with the three of them keeping things under control.

He glanced at the headless mannequin lying in the alley.

Well, moderately under control.

This was not good, but the problem in Sedona sounded even worse. Family pets with glowing eyes and multiple rows of razor-sharp teeth? Loving animals suddenly going berserk and attacking their owners? It sure sounded like demon possession to Alton, and he knew the others agreed. Until today, they'd thought demons could only animate things of the earth—ceramic or stone, concrete or clay. Plastic was essentially more of the same, just a different material, but taking on living creatures as avatars took a lot more power, showed more intelligence.

Ginny could be in terrible danger.

BumperWillow whined. Alton looked at Dax and Eddy, and realized they were staring at him too. All three of them. What had he missed?

"Well?" Eddy slapped her hands down on her hips.

Alton blinked. "Well, what?"

She rolled her eyes. "Are you going? Is there a passage through the vortex that will get you to Sedona now so you can check on Ginny? My best friend's in danger because you sent her there."

He cringed. "I know. Yes, there's a passage, and yes, I'll go."

Eddy's sudden smile hinted at something more than mere concern for Ginny. "Be sure and pack some extra clothes," she said. "You might be gone for a while."

Eddy's dad, Ed Marks, gunned his old Jeep up the last steep stretch of dirt road. He'd offered to take Alton as far as he could up the rough flank of Mount Shasta, but they'd just about reached the end of the road. Alton knew he still had a good hike ahead of him to find the portal.

The way was steep, the ground slippery with loose rock and scree that often meant slipping back two steps for every step forward, so the ride this far was welcome. Plus, he enjoyed spending time with Ed.

It shouldn't have surprised him, how much he liked Eddy's dad, but their close friendship had been an unexpected bonus. Alton figured it was as much his need for a father figure who treated him with respect as the fact Ed was just a hell of a nice guy. His own father still hadn't accepted that he was an adult, a capable man able to make his own decisions. Ed saw Alton as a warrior, a brave companion to Dax and Eddy.

And he treated Alton like a man grown, which might have been silly under other circumstances. As an immortal, Alton was already centuries older than Ed Marks, something that didn't seem to bother Ed at all.

He wondered if his own father would ever see him as anything other than a disappointment. What would the ruling senator of the Council of Nine say if he knew his son's sword was now sentient, that Alton had proven himself as a warrior?

Fat chance of that ever happening. Now that he had a Lemurian death sentence hanging over his head for helping Dax and Eddy escape from their prison cell, Alton had to accept the fact that going back to his world inside the volcano probably wasn't going to happen.

Still, it was something to dream of—his father actually learning his only son had accomplished what no other Lemurian in recent history had done—he'd established communication with his crystal sword. Even though the story of Lemurians as warriors and demon fighters was a huge part of their history, no one alive now could actually remember anyone strong enough or brave enough to bring their sword to life.

Yet Alton's sword spoke to him. Respected him enough to communicate, sword to Lemurian.

In fact, he was the only Lemurian alive today who'd actually taken part in a battle with a weapon other than words. While his people took pride in being known as philosophers and statesmen, they'd lost their fighting edge—the very qualities that had kept their society safe for so long.

Just as they'd lost their strongest allies—their sentient, speaking crystal swords. The sword each young man received when he came of age had become nothing more than a fancy ornament.

Crystal swords had no reason to speak to men they didn't respect. Why talk to a warrior who didn't know how to fight and wasn't willing to risk his life for something of importance?

Alton had not only risked his life, he'd discovered an inner strength he hadn't known he possessed. He'd proved to both his sword and himself that he was a warrior, one willing to die for a cause he believed in—protecting the known worlds from the threat of demonkind. All of them—Eden, Earth, Atlantis, and Lemuria—were at risk from the encroaching evil of Abyss.

The danger of reaching a tipping point, of the ages old balance of good and evil finally slipping over to the dark side was still very real. Thank goodness the demon invasion of Earth had barely gotten under way before the Edenites recognized the threat and recruited Dax, a fallen demon, out of the void. With his borrowed human body and Willow by his side, he'd become the perfect leader in the fight against demonkind, against a demon king powerful enough and smart enough to lead the demon hordes to victory.

Gaining strength by the hour within his stone gargoyle avatar, the demon king had almost won. Dax's brave sacrifice and Eddy's strength and determination in the face of certain death had bought a temporary victory when Eddy'd courageously risked death by wielding Alton's crystal sword.

The demon king was gone, for now. But, he'd be back.

Had he resurfaced in Sedona?

Alton stared at the trees they passed and thought about Dax and Eddy and the love between them that seemed to grow stronger each day. He'd be jealous if he didn't love both of them so much. Eddy was brave and true, and Dax, a man who had begun as a demon, had shown more integrity and good than anyone Alton had ever known in Lemuria. Dax and Eddy deserved the immortal love they'd found with one another.

So why did that make him think of Ginny Jones? She was nothing like Eddy Marks. Nothing at all. Ginny was mortal, her life no more than a tiny blip on his life's screen. Plus, she was stubborn and opinionated and had no respect for a woman's place—a woman's role as the helpmate to her man. Not that Eddy was anything like the Lemurian women Alton had known, either, but she was Dax's problem.

Did that make Ginny his?

The engine revved up and the Jeep's wheels spun as forward motion ceased. Alton glanced at Ed.

The older man shrugged. "This is as far as I can go, Alton. You'll have to hoof it the rest of the way." He slipped the gears into neutral but left the engine running. The trail wound upward from here, climbing through the last of the trees before it crossed areas of slippery scree, the shattered stones that littered the sides of the dormant volcano above the tree line.

Alton climbed out of the Jeep. He checked his scabbard to make certain his sword was secure, grabbed his pack and slung it over his shoulder. "Thanks, Ed." He glanced around, orienting himself. A harmless-looking pile of rocks lay beside the road.

Harmless now, but they were the remnants of the gargoyle that had become the avatar of a powerful demon. Eddy had destroyed the avatar with her singular act of bravery, but she'd missed the demon's soul and it had escaped back to Abyss. Unfortunately, it could still return to create havoc on Earth.

Alton shook his head. "Hard to believe this is the same place where we fought the demon—and almost lost."

Ed sighed. "I'll admit, I've never been so afraid in my life. For myself, for my friends—the image of that monster twisting Dax's body and throwing him to the ground still wakes me up at night. I never thought I'd see the boy alive again." He cleared his throat, wiped a hand over his eyes. "The truth, though? Mostly, Alton, I was afraid for my daughter. Her bravery astounds me, even now."

Alton reached out and shook Ed's hand. "We don't need to worry about Eddy. She's a lot tougher than she looks."

Breaking into laughter, Ed threw the Jeep into gear. "That she is, son. Now you get. I'm worried about Ginny. She doesn't know what we went through here, so she doesn't have any idea what she's up against. You go take care of that girl." He winked, turned the Jeep and headed down the hill.

Alton watched until the Jeep disappeared into the forest. Then he started the long hike up the hill. The mountain might be the vortex, but there were only a couple of places where he could cross into the other dimensions and access the portal that would take him to Sedona.

Or the one that led to Lemuria.

No. He couldn't think about home. He'd made his choice when he helped Dax and Eddy escape from their Lemurian prison cell. He'd walked away from everyone and everything he'd known and loved his entire life, but he'd chosen for the greater good.

He wondered if his friend Taron had had any luck at all convincing the council to join the battle against demonkind. That was Alton's only hope of ever going back home. Taron could be persuasive, but were his powers of persuasion a match for the council's stubbornness?

The sun had moved to the west by the time Alton paused in front of a mass of tumbled boulders and knew he'd reached the portal. He wrinkled his nose against the stench of sulfur. There shouldn't be any sign of demons here, but their smell was all around him. That made no sense. He'd closed the portal to Abyss.

Unless they'd managed to open a new one.

Alton faced the lichen-covered rock, but before he stepped through, he removed his sword from his scabbard. As he wrapped his fingers around HellFire's jeweled hilt, he realized how much the sword's sentience had changed things. He no longer felt alone—not when he had HellFire beside him. Addressing the crystal blade, he asked, "Do you smell their stench as I do?"

The hilt vibrated in his hand. "I do," the sword answered. "I'm ready."

With a nod, Alton stepped through the portal, walking through what appeared to be solid rock. The dark cavern he entered glistened with the light from the various gateways leading to other dimensions—the green and turquoise that led to Atlantis, the gold and silver that would take him to Eden—and certain death should he attempt to pass into that hallowed land.

The portal glowing gold would take him home, to Lemuria, a land where he'd always been welcome. Now, were he to attempt to cross into Lemuria, he feared he faced death as surely as if he'd tried to enter Eden's sanctuary.

Facing Ginny Jones and a whole passel of demonkind sounded a lot safer.

Alton turned his back on the gateway to his home world. The one that had once led to Abyss was still sealed shut. Why, then, did he smell the sulfuric stench of demons? Where were they coming from?

He held his glowing sword high and used the light Hell-Fire cast to search along the stone walls. A small portal, tucked into a nook toward the back of the cavern, glowed with the colors of a setting sun.

Sedona. He recognized the multicolored hues of red rock and blue skies, but swirling within the portal's depths he sensed something else.

Demonkind.

Demons had passed this way, and not so long ago. Were they somehow making their way from Abyss to Sedona, and then north through the connected vortexes to Mount Shasta? He'd have to ask Eddy and Dax about that.

After he got to Sedona.

He touched the cell phone Eddy had tucked into his pocket and wished it worked within the portals, but Eddy'd explained to him how they needed towers to carry the signal, and there certainly weren't any deep inside the volcano.

Alton took a step toward the portal, but he caught himself, pausing in midstep as a dark mist slipped through the multicolored gateway. Silently it flowed along the wall toward the portal leading to the flank of Mount Shasta.

Demon!

His sword vibrated with power. Alton swung. The crystal blade connected with the black mist and it screeched and burst into flame. Crackling and sizzling, it disappeared in a puff of smoke, leaving only the stench behind.

Alton stared at the spot where the demon had emerged. A shiver raced along his spine. This one had come directly from Sedona. His heart gave an unfamiliar lurch. Ginny was in Sedona—and so were the demons.

Demons powerful enough to take on living creatures as their personal avatars. Creatures strong enough to kill.

Holding his sword aloft, Alton stepped through the portal.

"Who'd you have to call?"

Markus's question snapped Ginny out of her convoluted thoughts. "Eddy. I called my friend Eddy Marks."

"I hope it was important." Markus backed out of the parking place he'd taken at the supermarket. Without Tom. The vet had insisted on keeping the cat for observation, which suited Ginny perfectly. Damned cat had really chewed up her hand. She peeked under the bloody towel and wished she hadn't looked.

"You were gone so long I had to take Tom into the vet by myself."

Ginny scowled at him. Her hand still hurt like the blazes and not once had Markus thanked her for risking life and limb while catching his stupid cat. "Well, Tom is your cat, cousin of mine, and I would really like to get back to the house so I can clean up the mess your *sweetheart* of a cat made of my hand."

Markus stared straight ahead. "Aren't you gonna ask me what the vet said?"

Ginny shook her head. "I figured you'd tell me if he had any idea what happened."

Markus curled up one lip and made a snorting noise. "He says they're all possessed. I knew he was into crystals and vortexes and all that New Age stuff, but I thought it was just for show. He's dead serious."

"Possessed? By what? The ghost of Christmas past?" Ginny stared out the side window as Markus drove the few blocks home. *Possessed.* It sounded totally unbelievable, but how else do you explain a cat with four rows of teeth, glowing red eyes and a scream like a banshee on meth? A scream that sounded horribly familiar.

Since her memories of that crazy night in Evergreen had begun to resurface, Ginny'd had the sound of the bear's ear-shattering scream in her head. A scream that was nothing more than a louder version of the strange howl coming from Markus's fat old cat.

Had the bear been possessed? Had some sort of evil entity turned a concrete statue into a slavering, screaming killer? Something made it come to life. She hadn't imagined the damned thing, though she'd thought it was just a weird nightmare.

But all those animals at the vet's—the birds and bunnies, cats and dogs—every last one of them acted unnervingly similar. Screeching, trying to bite, flashing those rows of sharp teeth, and staring out of glowing eyes.

Possession didn't sound all that crazy when you took it in context with what they'd seen today.

With what had attacked her just a few days ago.

Markus drove the car into the driveway and pulled into the garage. He shut off the engine and turned in his seat to glare at her. "You're making fun of it now, Ginny Jones, but how else do you explain all those animals? They weren't normal. Birds don't have teeth. Rabbits don't hiss and snarl and screech like that little bunny we saw today. Something's making them act crazy. If they're not possessed, what's going on?"

Without waiting for an answer, Markus got out of the car and slammed the door. Ginny sat in the front seat for a few minutes, thinking of Tom and the other animals they'd seen at the veterinarian's clinic, thinking of the concrete grizzly that had attacked her.

Thinking of Eddy's friend, Alton. Why did she know he

was the reason she couldn't remember anything? Now that she was away from him, the memories were coming back. She recalled him saving her from the bear, walking with her, even laughing with her.

Most of all, she remembered his kiss.

What she couldn't remember was why he'd kissed her—or why she'd kissed him. One thing she knew for certain—he was the only reason she'd come to Sedona.

None of this made sense, and Eddy hadn't been much help, either. She'd merely said to hold tight, that she was sending someone, but she wouldn't give Ginny any details about who or why or what the hell was going on.

Muttering under her breath, Ginny rewrapped the bloody towel around her hand and followed Markus into the house.

Covering vast distances via the vortex was more disorienting than moving between dimensions, but the one thousand and thirty miles between Mount Shasta in northern California and Bell Rock in Sedona, Arizona, took less than a minute down a dark tunnel lit only by HellFire's crystal light.

The sun was beginning to set when Alton sheathed his sword, passed through the portal and stepped out on the rocky ground near the top of Bell Rock, one of many vortexes in and around Sedona. He stood for a moment, lost in the glory of a desert sunset and the brilliant red of the rugged, wind-shaped bluffs. The gentle breeze seemed to sing to him—a deep hum that resonated within his . . .

"Where the hell did he come from?"

Alton spun to his left and blinked. Row after row of men and women, most of them wearing loose robes or colorful skirts, sat cross-legged in the dirt.

Meditating?

Well crap and nine hells. He'd materialized out of solid rock, right in the middle of a yoga class.

Straightening to his full height, Alton pressed his hands together beneath his chin and bowed his head. His waist-length blond hair, unbound, flowed over his shoulders like silk; and he knew his almost seven feet of height, aided a bit by his boots, made him look pretty impressive.

With any luck, his appearance alone might help him get out of here without too much trouble, considering the audience.

"I come from within." He kept his voice unnaturally deep and bowed his head once again. Then, biting back a powerful urge to laugh, he looked straight ahead and walked past the rows of stunned yoga practitioners.

Popping out of the portal in the midst of an evening meditation class hadn't been an issue the last time he was here. Of course, it had been a while—give or take six hundred years.

Obviously, he really needed to get out more.

Alton found a well-traveled trail that took him down off the mountain and into a parking area. The light was beginning to fade and only a few cars and one old, beat-up-looking bus remained. He figured the bus must be here for the group he'd surprised up on top.

Maybe he could catch a ride into town with them . . . or not. Grinning at the thought of Lemurian royalty hitching a ride on an old bus painted with rainbows and flowers, Alton set his backpack down and pulled the cell phone Eddy had given him out of his pocket.

He carefully followed the steps Eddy'd shown him, found Ginny's number, and pushed the button to connect the call. He almost shouted when Ginny answered on the second ring, but he managed to control himself.

"Is this Virginia Jones?" he asked.

There was a long silence. Long enough that Alton wondered if he'd done something wrong.

"Who's this?"

Nope. That was Ginny. "This is Alton. Eddy Marks's friend."

"How'd you get my number?"

Definitely Ginny.

"From Eddy. Ginny, I'm in Sedona. Would you be able to come get me?"

"Sedona? How the hell did you get to Sedona so fast? I just talked to Eddy a couple of hours ago, and there's no way you could have come . . ."

"I'm here, Ginny, and I'll explain everything once I see you. I'm in the parking lot at Bell Rock. Do you know where that is?"

"I'll be there in fifteen minutes. And you'd better have some answers for me because I've definitely got questions for you."

Before he could answer, the line went dead. Alton stared at the phone for a moment before calling one more number. Eddy's voice mail came on. He left a message and wondered where she'd gone, why she hadn't answered the phone. Then he tucked it in his pocket and leaned against a rock. Folding his arms across his chest, he waited impatiently for Ginny while the night grew dark around him.